The Cello Francesca

or

Balderdash

Tom Blackburn

ISBN 978-0-9826576-3-8

Books by Tom Blackburn
Fiction
The Cello Francesca *or* Balderdash
Surviving Mozart
Thanks to Mister Merrydown
*On Honeyman Bald
*Dancing With Granny

Nonfiction
Equilibrium: a Chemistry of Solutions
Getting Science Grants

*e-books

Tom Blackburn Books
Washington DC 20017-2949
www.tomblackburnbooks.com

The Cello Francesca, *or* Balderdash

The Cello Francesca, *or* Balderdash

I: 1953

1. Baling Wire

That particular rock fit sweetly to my hand. Flat limestone, a half inch thick, cream-colored and dusty from rubbing and banging against the others in the five-ton pile on the dock. To tell the truth, I don't know what Molar Chemical wanted with them, nor was it part of my menial job to know. A small fossil showed at one edge, and maybe that's what drew my hand to it. Feeling its mass, I knew its fate would lie farther south than the rusty reactors behind me on the Mississippi shore. If ever a stone cried out to be thrown high and far it was this one, and if that would help the little fossil live another million years, all the better. I turned to the river.

A mile of thick water sucked and chuckled its way south, with a four o'clock sun blazing off it and hiding the St. Louis plant, and just about everything over on the Missouri side, in baleful blaze. You could see a few buildings, and the excursion steamer Admiral moored like a big tin lampshade against the levee, and that was about it. The Gateway Arch was a good decade in the future, no more than a smart rumor, futuristic balderdash to those who knew "urban removal" was just a way to channel tax money into a few suburban pockets. With no distinctive architecture showing, the city I faced might have been anywhere from Minneapolis to Memphis, or for that matter Indianapolis, magically flooded by world-class waters. Except, of course, St. Louis was and would always be a major-league city.

Before I invented greater follies, I once fancied myself a prospect for the majors; if not with the Cardinals, maybe the Browns, a pretty good Class AA outfit that had the bad luck to play in the same league as the Yankees and Red Sox. In 1953, teams had not started moving around like gypsies, and I figured I had the Brownies cornered in St. Louis. My principal talent was a strong arm; my old glove bore for as long as I had it a spot of blood where I split my Dad's finger with a fastball while I was still in junior high. He couldn't play the organ for a week.

The river melted in the glare, became the green interior of Sportsman's Park, where only a heroic peg from deep left-center had a chance to cut down Boston's arrogant second baseman Bobby Doerr, rounding third to score from first on a Ted Williams double. I arched back to let the throw gather, eyes closed, sun burning on my belly, and my whole body snapped the arm like a catapult. The limestone took off for home, climbing like a saint while a capacity crowd gasped, realizing that it would be close, that at least for one play of one game, the Browns and the Red Sox were contending on equal terms; the panicked and stumbling legs of Bobby Doerr against an angelic, a celestial throw from the arm of rookie outfielder Oren Dienst. Me. And the gasp became a roar, as the crowd saw now it wouldn't even be close, Doerr was out by a mile, would be humiliated, asked by reporters in the locker room, "Didn't they tell ya you'd get that kinda throw from the kid?"

At the top of its arch, a dot hung motionless in my view - and this story begins there - then sank like a rock toward the dazzle of the Mississippi. Down, down, free falling, the sun a rising blindness behind the waiting river. Far out, a tiny splash rose and fell, traveling six feet south.

I will tell the truth. No angel could have thrown any rock, no matter how willing and sweet to the hand, more than a tenth of the width of that river. But from my shore-level perspective, that small moving splash seemed to rise and fall near mid-river, and I saw my little fossil falling, side-slipping through chill and growing darkness, a mighty chorus of gravel, the crooning of snags on the bottom, to skip and clatter on the great Northward-streaming riverbed until it fetched up in the gutted innards of a '39 DeSoto along with a couple of stone jugs, a maresnest of rotting upholstery, a big channel cat, and the partial skeletons of missing lovers, baling-wired belly to belly on the bed of the Father of Waters.

"Mist' Napperson tell you, thow all that limestone in the river, son?"

"Huh. Geez, sorry, Pear. Naw, just that one piece. He said I'd know it when I saw it."

"Hyeh. Din't he say more likely fill a bucket to grind up in the martyr and passel, get it done before quittin time? I expect that was it. Better you get a move on. I breng ya the pail."

"Thanks, Pear. It's coming."

Pear Wilson turned from the sun and the rotting, country smell of the riverbank and hauled himself back to the plant to finish his duties, and report to Napperson that he had left me what I needed to finish mine.

Baling wire. Bobby Doerr. Balderdash.

Harvey Napperson looked up briefly from a slide rule and a page of figures when my shadow, tipped to one side by 20 pounds of limestone, slid across the window of his cubicle. His tie and collar were perhaps fractionally looser than they'd been at eight o'clock - the muffle furnaces and the August afternoon had the lab in the high 80's in spite of the roaring window unit - and his face bore the gleam of productive Midwestern sweat.

"You're gonna get those rocks ground and mixed before you go, eh, Oren," Napperson didn't ask. "Stuff's been setting down there since Tuesday and we're supposed to give'm numbers on it this week, yet. You took samples from all parts of the pile?"

"Yessir," I agreed.

"Down in the middle too?"

"Yeah. Yes, I did."

"Mm. And the null hypothesis?"

"Sir?"

"Do you know what a null hypothesis is, Dienst?"

"I guess not, sir."

"Safe guess. It's what any experiment's gotta have. What is it we're looking to disprove here?"

"Disprove?"

"Why did you take samples from all over that pile of limestone, Dienst?"

Because you told me to, Harve. "Uh, to show it's all the same?"

"Wrong. You couldn't prove that in a month of Sundays. You're setting out to accept or reject the null hypothesis, which is that rocks from one end of that pile and rocks from the other end can't be told apart by our methods."

Very interesting. "You want me to weigh out the powders and put 'em in acid overnight?"

"Ye - no, no, forget it. I'll do it tomorrow."

I knew he'd insist on doing all the picky stuff himself, so it was safe to offer that at four o'clock, with - oh, at least an hour's work yet to go, grinding and sifting the pounds of rock down to a few grams for analysis. Harvey Napperson would trust a kid tech like me with the grunt work, provided he'd personally supervised the tech's training. Nobody but Harvey Napperson MS, Director of Analytical Services, would do the crucial steps like weighing out samples.

The null hypothesis here, of course, was that the Director couldn't be told apart from a higher-level grunt, using the method of career consciousness. I looked at Harvey Napperson; I saw, and I learned. Dead-ended in a hot little lab in East St. Louis for the rest of his days.

After half a year at Washington U. it was clear to me who had the good life. Profs pedaled home on quiet streets, joking each to each after a couple of hours in the classroom, briefcases of reports and proposals strapped behind them, kids and lacy hot-eyed wives, pipes and liquor ahead. Supper, a contemplative hour or two with red ball-point in hand and Vivaldi on the hi-fi, wet kisses from scrubbed moppets, invitations, ecstasy, sleep. Harvey Napperson looked short on ecstasy. I had briefly sniffed the earnest sexuality of married friends, and - when I found the willing girl - the future smelled to me of afternoons and Ortho Gynol.

I found the lab's two-gallon cast-iron mortar and matching pestle mouldering quietly under a bench at the back of the equipment shed, and hauled it out. The thing was crusty and full of cobwebs, and how any chemistry that started with it could come up with anything but 80% rust was beyond me. I wiped it out and hauled it into the lab next to the bucket of rocks, doubtfully dumped five or six of them into it, and tried grinding at them with the massive pestle.

I achieved a slight grating noise, a couple of streaks of white across the bottom of the mortar, and rust-marked chunks of limestone that were probably holding their sides with hilarity, in geological time. I looked around, conscious that I had no idea how this particular operation was supposed to be done. I mean, hell, I was no quarryman. I was supposed to be an engineer, or a center fielder. Or even a musician.

There's nothing more humiliating than having to be shown how to do some simple thing; I took all the rocks but one out and bashed down on it with the pestle with all ferocity. Bingo; after only three such hits, it split in two, and with four or five more bashes I had it reduced to a grindable rubble. I ground, emptied the mortar, put in another rock, and considered whether the scales and exercises I had so loathed when I really was a musician could have been so bad.

Not that music was an option any more. I put in two years as a cello major at Indiana over the objections of my father, who had parlayed his own musical talent into a sodden death as a church organist and high school choir director, dragging rambunctious thugs through "Oklahoma!" and Christmas chorales. During games of catch, he earnestly advised me to follow another path: any path but a musical one.

"Look, Oren, you're good at math and science. Be a scientist of some kind, play your cello for a hobby, believe me. One percent of performance students make a decent living at it. The rest end up sitting third chair in a second-rate symphony and giving lessons. Is that what you want? Or wind up like me? God gave you talent, yes, but more than one. You can earn a good living in science and play music on the side, or you can earn a lousy living as a musician and do no science at all. And I'm not sure we've got a major-league fastball here at all, either."

But, see, I knew that lots of great musicians had overcome objections from their fathers, and I was only gratified to see this vital element in place for my own career. As a soloist preferably, or in a world-class string quartet if need be. And when the scholarship letter came from Indiana, that clinched it. Music at Indiana would be a lot cheaper than science anywhere.

Off I went, and spent something over a year watching myself being sorted into one of the middle quartiles of a bunch of cello majors. Others who have followed this path will cringe like me at the names of Klengel and Popper, as pianists learn to loathe Czerny. But it wasn't the drudgery of études and exercises that finally undid me. No, one day I played a particular piece (and not a trivial one either, it was Bach, the Prelude from the D Major Suite) as well as I could play it. In fact, I played it almost as well as I could imagine anyone playing it. And nothing happened.

Nothing remotely as tangible, at least, as the gritty limestone powder I found I had now produced in the bottom of the mortar. I dumped, reloaded, and decided I had better time this next one, to get a bead on how long this was going to take. Pow. Pow! *Crunch*! Rubble to reduce to powder in three licks again. I stripped off my shirt and wiped my face with it.

Somehow that performance, and a lot of other Bach, promised more than I could deliver, and more than I could imagine anybody delivering. The progression of it as a piece of music lived up in every way to the rolling power of the opening. But all the way through, I kept having a feeling that something completely new should be happening; something that would engulf Indiana, St. Louis, me, and everyone I knew into a different existence, some kind of world where the moon and stars were visible by day, where mountains would smile.

At the end, it was only over.

I tried new phrasings, new conceptions of the whole piece, that were either worse, or no better. I took my frustration to my teacher, who corrected one or two technical matters and recommended that I try to see it not as a Great Work, but only a sort of warming up to a set of dances: in other words, to deflate what he called "this confounded mysticism about Bach Almighty."

I looked at my watch, slipping around on my sweaty wrist. Three minutes on that one, about 200 rocks to go. Don't do the math. Pick up another one. *Pow. Crack.* Hey, only two licks that time, and look here: it split into neat halves, and on the face of one of them, a truly elegant little fossil again, maybe the wife or close friend of the one that was mooching along out there on the bottom of the Mississippi. It was some kind of a little bug looking thing, and it was resting on a bed of maybe ferns. A keeper, and one half of a rock that I wouldn't have to grind to a powder. I slipped it into my pants pocket and proceeded to pound and grind the other half to dust.

I began to understand that I had really felt the same about all kinds of music, but before this had always assumed - without really getting this idea clear - that a better performance, or a more profound piece of music, would finally release what I could hear lying coiled just behind the sound. The great Beethoven A major sonata fairly shouted that Beethoven knew all about the mystery, that his writing was saturated with awareness of what it is, finally, that I was looking for.

The next rock took two minutes and fifteen seconds, and I could not imagine doing one any faster. I allowed myself a peek into the bucket - no evidence of progress whatever - and the future: I would be here at four am, still pounding, if Napperson would even countenance overtime of that magnitude; and I had other stuff to do tonight, including musical stuff. OK, how about three at once?

Pow. Very interesting; one skated up the side of the mortar, hit me under the chin, and fell back. Of the two that escaped, the first didn't actually break the window it alarmingly banged into, and the other disappeared over the partition into Pear Wilson's domain.

"Ow! Tarnation! Who thew that rock?" Pear Wilson came around the partition - not exactly steaming, since Pear never actually got that hot - but considerably warmer than his resting state, and rubbing the back of his head. "What the Sam Hell you doin here, boy? Cramanently, that how you tryin a bust them rocks? C'mere. Sweet Jesus, you gonna have this place in a dump, you keep it up. Lemme show ya how. Brang the bucket."

He led me through the receiving room, picking up a massive hammer on the way, and out onto the loading dock, where he dumped out the rest of the limestone.

"Git that poke off'na trash box."

I brought him a jute bag that was reclining over the dumpster, and he put about a third of the rocks into it, put it on the broiling concrete and whaled at it with the hammer. A series of satisfactory sounds emerged, and a whiff of pale dust.

"See? Cain't nothin get away, hit hard's ya like. Anything stickin up, swat er good. Get it down ta gravel, at's when ta use the mortal an' passer. Now get er finished up, quittin time comin right along."

"Thanks, Pear. Sorry about the one that got away. You didn't get hurt, did you?"

He grinned and rubbed his head. "Din hit nothin vital."

I brought the mortar and reduced his leavings to powder, and reloaded the bag with half the remaining rocks. Pow. Biff. This was a lot easier. See one sticking up above the rubble, give it the hammer. Crunch. Take that, you smart little peckers.

Beethoven's A Major Cello Sonata has three rather long moderate-to-fast movements with a tiny slow interlude, only 18 bars, between the last two. The allegros are noble, funny, inspired middle Beethoven at his peak. But it is during the slow movement that the miracle occurs. Over a pretty, petty, Mozarty piano aria, the cello enters softly and, for my money, without vibrato on an f sharp an ascetic fifth above the piano figure. The chilly half-dissonance of it, the obliviousness to the piano's invitation, told me as clear as words that at that altitude moons and stars unknown to daylight vision can be seen in stately dance. The aria below sings warmly of humanity and love; stubbornly, the cello remains on its tower for almost seven slow measures, nearly to the midpoint of the brief movement, before descending - it must be reluctantly - to the heart of things, taking up the handsome aria.

But relaxation into the close neighborhood of the tonic short-circuits the mystery. After a simple and almost undeveloped restatement of the piano's song - as if to say, *yes, there is this, but*... there is a lingering return to the astringent f sharp of the beginning; but whatever vision held it there before is gone. All that is left is empty scaffolding, by which the cello descends to ordinary life and does a chromatic lead into a bravura finale in which cosmic meaning is no longer to be found in individual notes. So there was for Beethoven, I was sure, a dissonant and ascetic reality above and behind the ground floor of everyday life; merely to play this passage was to refer to it, but to play it *perfectly* would be to use the hidden key and climb to that place oneself; maybe for only as long as the music lasted; maybe never to return.

The trouble was, so what? Having laid out this interpretation (of only eighteen bars of a single work), I was at a loss to convince anyone - certainly not my teachers and contemporaries at Indiana nor, in the end, myself - that the higher reality I read in a few bars of middle Beethoven was to be found, and smoked out, in all music. Not, at least, by me. Professors, visiting artists, my roommate, record jackets, spoke of the great ineffable as if they enjoyed it at least weekly, with numerous partners. And if that were so, what was it with me? Incapable of seducing the divine when it sat in my lap? Or maybe I was just barking up a phantom tree, and maybe all I thought I heard Beethoven hinting at was nothing but a hoity-toity version of the gut thrill offered by a Sousa march. The Moon and Stars Forever.

It became suddenly obvious to me that my imagination outreached my talent. If there was something more to be experienced than I had suspected in a set of Bach dances and a fleeting tease by Beethoven, someone else - maybe my insufferable roommate, a tenor from Terre Haute who wound up permanent executive director of an ASCAP office in Maryland - would have to savor it. I had followed my star up a blind alley.

I put away the mortar and pestle with a weary clang and went to clean up myself and my space against Napperson's doom-certain inspection. The whole struggle condensed to a final line in a notebook: "Lot 5308-112, limestone from Oolitic, Indiana. 10 kg. ground to powder for assay." Since that about finished out the notebook, I completed the date sticker on the cover (August 5-25, 1953), signed and stamped it, and left it on Pear's desk, Pear himself having long since creaked off home. I was soaked with sweat, and gently trembling with fatigue. Anyone, I thought, who harbored illusions of science as a practice of balletic glides from notebook to slide rule to spectrograph by steely guys in precise lab coats had never slaughtered twenty pounds of limestone in a cast-iron mortar.

I didn't discuss Beethoven or the ineffable f-sharp with my parents when I got back to St. Louis that summer. It was not the sort of thing, in the first place. In the second, mother was no music theorist but an amateur soprano and home ec. major whom Dad met in college at Cape Girardeau. And my musical father chose that May afternoon to throw himself off the Chain of Rocks Bridge while my homeward train chuffed across Illinois. When I swung myself and my cello onto the platform in St. Louis, it was into an unsmiling company of cops and a minister who wanted me to go to the morgue at Deaconess right then so I could be with mother when she identified his body.

We did that; no one, certainly not the guest of honor, adequately feeling the pain. We were allowed to see, but not to have until it had been photographed and filed, a letter, folded into 16ths and crammed in a pocket, from the Board of Education of the City of St. Louis. Dad's resignation as choir director and teacher of choral music at DeBaliviere High School was accepted in the interests of everyone involved, and assurance was conveyed that the parents would in light of his resignation seek no further redress.

I turned to mother, standing crushed under the weight of a plastic raincoat and staring through a little window at the draped form beyond. The sheet, too short for his lanky frame, was wet where it covered his hair; insufferable, a bathetic post-mortem gesture from a cowardly flop who might have been dead right about the wages of music, as much for me as for himself, but had blown out his candle and walked offstage in the middle of the scherzo.

I waved the wadded letter at him. "What ...?"

Mother put her hand on my arm. "I don't know, Oren. I never did and I don't want to. Let's go home."

Nor did I ever know. Before I reached the age to insist, I acquired mother's wisdom, and chose not to. Driving home with her, I discovered just under my heart a pound of mud that made breathing harder for a year while it gullied and dwindled, and in the end left something no bigger than a sandflake: light, transparent, with geometric edges. As far as I was concerned, that grain was all that was immortal of my father.

Mother, like many women of her generation, had never learned to drive and never held a paying job. She got busy grieving and scrambling for a way to live, finding out that Dad's death benefit consisted of two more days' possession of a set of keys before they remembered to send a guy out to collect them. My sturm und drang about Beethoven popped as quietly and meaningfully as suds. I went to work as an office boy at Riverman's Fidelity Mortgage at fifty cents an hour, and tried not to think how many hours added up to a semester's tuition at Washington University, where Dad would have had me all along. I don't suppose $335 sounds like much to pay for a semester's good education these days, but after taxes and helping mother out, I was socking it away at about $1.84 a day.

Well, you can figure it out. By Christmas of 1952, with the help of a $10 bonus, I had accumulated $200, and I went and opened negotiations at Washington. It turned out I could pass some stuff by examination and finesse the arts requirement, and go into the fall semester of 1953 not much more than a year behind schedule. I was pleased to the extent appropriate to one accepting the vile bossing of Fate, and I could see that mother was too. Which made me only a little less cheerful.

I expanded my world, then, by cutting back a little on the mortgage gopher job and sitting in an Analytical Geometry lecture. It was weird, tough stuff that I hadn't thought about, or even thought <u>like</u>, for almost three years. And yet there was a non-negotiability to it, a right-or-wrongness that cleared my head - which was full of grief, mortgages, and restlessness - to get on with my life.

And after a couple of weeks something else happened while I was pondering *Section 4.2.1, the Complex Plane*: I could not detect its beginning, which must have been feathery, riding through the math like short-wave messages from hidden guerillas; but eventually I could not ignore the Bach D major Prelude rolling and twining in my brain, full of arguments and hints and promises.

When I caught myself half-whistling it under my breath, I gave it a sarcastic grin, and it faded for a time. But the old itch was back, starting with a simple grass-roots wish of muscle, nerves, and bone to shape music again. The soft, chilly Beethoven that had promised so much; the sensuous joy of a flashing turn under my fingers; the humming spot under my breastbone where the cello rested, and the embrace that held it there - these were the physical stuff of playing, from which I found I could not remain apart. In another week I had unpacked my cello for the first time since I left Indiana. I found it still nearly in tune.

So I sat down one evening after work and played away the theorems and defaulting debtors with a solid two hours of Popper and Hindemith and finally Bach. My fingers had gone soft and weak, and they were plenty sore when I stopped. I gave it a rest for a couple of days while I shuffled paper and resolved vectors into real and imaginary parts and scouted around for girls and wondered why, if I couldn't live a life saturated with music, I could not be quit of it either. In the end I went down to the Orpheum Theater, looming out of the rubble of urban demolition at the corner of 11th and Lucas, and auditioned for a seat in the St. Louis Civic Orchestra.

Now with the dust and fatigue of my struggle with mortar and limestone washed away and tuna-noodle casserole slowly succumbing in my belly, I sat with Mollie Biedermeyer in her '48 Buick at the corner of Lindell and Skinker, waiting for the light to change. Mollie was, and looked, forty and unmarried. She was tall and gangly, and braids wrapped her head in a Third Reich style that must have been chic when she was my age. She was a fine flutist ("I am simply a flutist. Other orchestras may have 'flautists', but not the Civic.") with no hope of cracking the male ranks of the professional St. Louis Symphony's wind section. She eked out her stipend as the Civic's principal with a packed schedule of students, school bands, and the wedding-and-funeral circuit.

I sounded her out on the question of music promising more to her, too, than it delivered, or was it just me. She professed, after a pause, bland tolerance for the dissonance between what could be imagined and the best one could do about it, that I judged typical of the middle-aged. If there was more behind her words or in the eyes lifted to the rear-view mirror, I was in no position to see it.

"You play well, Oren," she said, though that wasn't what I'd asked. "You have - well, a flair. I don't know that anyone is ever really satisfied with a performance. Happy with it, yes, after you get over worrying about the little mistakes. But not satisfied. There is a sort of pain ... would you be at all interested in another little job?"

"I don't know. Sure, I guess," I sighed. Mollie was often kind to me, regularly bringing me in on little jobs like weddings and funerals where, as she put it, I "added a pleasant richness to the continuo line." I could have made more money mowing lawns, but playing continuo was a lot less tiresome, and the idea of adding a little richness to my education fund was not unpleasant. I looked out at be-boppers serenading Market Street. "What's the gig?" I asked - trying out a piece of hip vocabulary.

She smiled. "The 'gig'. The Concordia Choir is performing the Stravinsky <u>Symphony of Psalms</u> this fall, and they need cellists."

"What's it like?"

Mollie smiled and checked the ramparts of her fortress of braid as we glided to the curb outside the Orpheum. "I expect to enjoy it very much. Do you think Jacob is on strike, or has he forgotten us tonight?"

St. Louis folks, who were as closely aware of race as a tout is of bloodlines, did not have racial categories in which to fit a Lumbee Indian like our caretaker and equipment manager Jacob Oxendine, with his cafè-au-lait skin, taffy curls, and blue-grey eyes. Damnedest thing, is what they mostly said. Jacob occupied rooms in a scenery loft thirty feet above the Orpheum stage, where Mollie and I could see his window gleaming. The window frame, by a sign-painter's whimsy, formed the O in a faded and chipped whiskey ad on the bricks: WELLER'S AND WATER: IT'S WONDERFUL; and sometimes when we came out after a hard rehearsal on rainy nights with a wind snaking off the levee, and Jacob's lofty window hit the downbeat in WONDERFUL, we were easily sold.

But tonight was warm and soft, and I could see Jacob now sitting behind his screen staring southeast, following the last sunshine out over main plant of Molar Chemical, across the river and past Harvey Napperson's analytical lab to the flat, flat Illinois side, and over the curve of the earth to where his kin sat on brick porches in the dark outside Red Springs, North Carolina, slapping gnats and talking about cotton and chainsaws. Farmers, lumbermen, and craftsmen, he said. Landowners, familiars of pine and cypress, of black silent rivers and alder swamps; descendants of Cherokees and the Lost Colony, victors over the Klan in a famous skirmish, and neither slaves nor reservation-dwellers. But he never spoke of going back.

Jacob often stood beside the open stage door and watched while Orchestra personnel made their way from cars to the door, having warned us that the Orpheum stood in a tough neighborhood, when the streets were close-crowded by tenements and locals getting a breath on hot nights while food smells, snatches of crying, color, and ulterior decor burst from jagged fanlights. Now the tenements had danced to their ruin at the wrecker's ball, and the land around the Orpheum lay flat, naked and undone. As Mollie and I walked to the stage door, we could easily hear and see skinny kids hollering around a backboard three twilight blocks away. On the side of the Orpheum, ghost houses had left their outlines in roofing tar, sloping lines passing just under the lighted window of Jacob's little loft apartment.

I think Jacob liked his guardianship on high of the earnest fiddling that filled our part of the Orpheum. He was sure-footed on the narrow ladderway that was access to his domain, and on the catwalks that threaded among ropes and lighting far above. The Orpheum was a huge place, as full of shadows as a church, and the auditorium and stage where we played took up less than half of it. What, if anything, went on in the other half was anyone's guess. It had been built as an opera house in the 1880's; it had a skylit dome with *trompe-l'oeil* paintings of saints and scholars swirling overhead through formal gardens and toppled masonry. Watching Jacob against that background was like seeing one of them in miraculous animation. He had a trick of shinnying down the ropes backstage among abandoned scenery without burning his hands, so that you might see him one moment - as now - at his window and yet find him opening the stage door by the time we had walked the thirty yards from the curb.

"Good evening, Miss Biedermeyer; evening, Mr. Dienst. I believe we are due for a high-pressure front later tonight that should give us some rain and yet also relieve this mugginess. I look forward to a pleasant day tomorrow. I wonder if you have seen the review of your recent concert in the Star-Times?" And he not so much took Mollie's elbow as made a gesture that might have resulted in that, had he touched her at all, and thereby escorted us to a bulletin board on which was neatly pinned the three-paragraph review I had in fact bolted along with the tuna and noodles.

It was balanced, which was to say, the reviewer had noticed some things we did well, and had not failed to blast the unsynchronized bowing of the second violins, who could not have been made to bow together with steel manacles. It also had a handsome compliment for Mollie's flute work in the Dance of the Blessed Spirits, with which we had opened and which, in fact, had been good enough to make the hair on my neck stand up; reason enough in thirty seconds for a month of rehearsal. Jacob had circled this part in red pencil.

Others were gathered around the review, and I heard Carl Holzhauser grumping that nothing had been said about his harpsichord work in the same piece. Players are never happy with anything short of mindless raves (which they then criticize for being mindless), but good reviews, even from the Star-Times, were the lifeblood of the Civic.

Our conductor Hans Brocklin was a relentless stalker of obscure East European composers, whose names only he among us could pronounce and whose music, fittingly enough for those times, tended toward the jagged and ominous. The seven years of Brocklin's reign were sprinkled with St. Louis and world premières of works that would never see a deuxième, cunningly salted among the reliable Beethovens and Tchaikowskies. We were in rehearsal throes now of the latest of those, the

"*Bohemian Nocturnes*" of one Jirzy Przybilchek, and I wandered to my seat to have another bash at it.

A row or two behind me, Maureen Witz was doing the same from her second-flute chair and, with Mollie occupied, I thought to strike up a conversation. Maureen was a flute major at Washington U, suffering about the same as I had at Indiana. We'd exhausted our commonality there in a couple of commiserating chats, but she was pretty, which we both appreciated, and I was interested in seeing what else we might have in common. Like a blistering urge to get laid, if it were up to me.

She was willowy and delicate, a flower child well ahead of her time, meaning that her ears were pierced, and she wore her hair in a cascade of tight little curls that gave her a nilotic look: shadowed eyes in a striking face pasted to the very front of an opaque pyramid. She had appeared at 14 on a brochure for a music camp, fluting leggily on a ledge in the Smokies, and she was well aware of her looks. The curl of lip required of flutists (flautists even more) sat easily on her face.

"I have," I lied, swivelling in my chair to address her, "a couple of tickets to the Symphony this weekend. Want to go?" She kept playing, an admittedly tough line from the Nocturnes. I waited for her to get to the end before pressing the question again, but she got her embouchure tangled up with her flageolet, or something, and screwed it up.

"Shit," she whispered, stamping her foot, and started it over. It was awkward sitting there watching her, but I was on record with an invitation, and it would have looked ill-humored of me to ask her out and then turn my back on a reply. I defocused and looked in the direction her flute was pointing while she labored along, got to the troublesome passage and surmounted it, did it three more times slowly and twice fast, and finally played the whole thing through fast. She put her flute down and said, a little peevishly, "What?"

"Symphony. This weekend. Want to go?"

"Well. I was going to wash my hair. What's the program?"

"Uh. Vaughan Williams, something. The Brahms Third. Pierre Fournier doing the Rococo Variations. I forget what else. 'Bolero', I think."

She wrinkled her nose. "Gee, I don't know. The Third? I just love the Fourth; it's so ..." She sighed. "So autumnal."

Getting a date means defending a lesser Brahms symphony against shampoo. You could interpret my gesture as exasperated. "Well, of course the Fourth is a wonderful work, don't you just love that horn call to start the second movement, and all. But they seem to have scheduled the Third this week. Still, though, Fournier? Vaughan Williams?"

"The Edward Elgar of our day."

Mollie came along for that last, which surely had a source - probably a record jacket - external to the pyramid of curls. "Who's that, Maureen?"

"Oh, nothing." Maureen was Mollie's student, and she stood, or sat, in awe of Mollie's sound; though I think she was confident that hard work and good looks would take her farther in the end even though this was well before the days when female musicians used soft-porn portraits with tousled hair and acres of creamy cleavage to set off their soulful fiddling.

I was ticked at Maureen's overlooking a world-class cellist and her insulting pickiness about which Brahms symphony was good enough to compensate enduring my company to hear it, so I stuck it to her. "Miss Witz considers Ralph Vaughan Williams the Sir Edward Elgar of our time."

Mollie smiled. "Our times are not yet over; another may yet rise to challenge him. Are you considering going to the Symphony?"

"Not exactly," (Mr. Smart Mouth). "Someone did claim to have tickets."

On that humiliating note, Brocklin's baton tapped his stand, and I had to turn to business. But at intermission, a more forthcoming Maureen Witz approached. Mollified, as it turned out.

"Mollie practically sentenced me to listen to the flute part in 'Bolero'. Do you really have tickets?"

"You can work around the shampoo?"

"Don't be a wise guy. Meet you there."

"Why don't you let me pick you up? I apologize for being wise, and for the time before that, too."

She relented, in her curly-headed way, with a little shrug. "Can you make heads or tails of this Polish stuff?"

Czech. "Not exactly, but I guess we better."

"Why's that? According to you."

"Well. Not to be embarrassed? It might be OK when we get it figured out."

"I guess. Why don't we play decent, regular stuff anybody's heard of?"

"Like the Brahms Fourth?"

"Like there was something wrong with it?"

"Gosh." I cast my eyes where marble stairs wound heavenward through Doric rubble. "It's beautiful. It's autumnal as all hell. But the Cleveland Orchestra or somebody has already done the absolute definitive performance. We'd be just the Civic, clopping along on this war horse, and everybody out there would know exactly what was coming 'cause they'd played their record of it so much the needle's coming through the other side. And God help us if we don't do it just like George Szell. With a thing like the Nocturnes - "

"I notice you don't mind playing the same Bach stuff over and over."

"Well. That's different. Somehow."

She scratched her tummy and gave me a look from the pyramid of curls. "How?"

If I don't think of something, I'll never know what's making your tummy itch. "It's... I can't fool myself, maybe. Remember when we premiered that *'Lament for Dresden'*, and the Post wrote it up, and everybody thought it was so great? I think we sort of psyched each other, and everybody got all worked up over it, because no one had ever done it before, and it was sort of pinko anyhow, you know, about American bombers and stuff, so it was daring. Now there's a record coming out, I hear."

"Mm, well . . ." Maureen remained uncaptivated regardless of what flights of invention I could throw at her, and before I was finished trying, Hans Brocklin's baton had tapped the end of intermission. She called Friday night - after I'd paid a screaming $4.00 for two balcony seats - to cancel, on the grounds that her grandmother was coming to visit for the weekend, but really, I think, because I'd alarmed her by calling the Civic a "folie á soixante." Chalk up another whiff for this center fielder. I took my mother, and made a virtue of that. The Brahms Third was fine, and plenty autumnal for one who would wind up a bachelor at 40 like Jacob Oxendine, nursing gestural crushes on spinster flutists.

At the end of the rehearsal this night as every, Jacob saw to it that he was available to hold the door for Mollie, to walk before us to her car, alert to the swarming menaces of downtown St. Louis, to open the door for her while I slid my cello into the back seat, and to bid us both, but looking at Mollie, a most pleasant evening and restful sleep.

However courtly Jacob was in his worship of Mollie - it is funny and sad to think of it in these snarling times - his comings and goings were firm in Biblical ways. The public philosophy in his home territory had been Baptist and work-oriented; it was the second that had propelled him to learn machining when the Lumbee schools ran short, and had brought him to St. Louis to machine the cylinders of pistols for the War Effort. But Jacob also moved through a world coextensive with the small arms plant and the Orpheum, furnished with concepts in place of bricks and mortar: the miry clay of sin, the rock of salvation, the listening ear and observing eye of the Lord. This surely more satisfactory world was peopled by publicans, wise and foolish virgins, and women takeable in adultery, with all of whom the St. Louis that Jacob knew was crammed. Maybe he knew better than I where to look.

We shared one other thing: as an employee of Orpheum Theater, Inc., Jacob derived his bread from the same deep source as I: Mr. Julius ("Yoolie") von Bayern, owner of the Orpheum, of the Molar Chemical Company, and of much else in the St. Louis economy. Yoolie was the chief angel of the Civic Orchestra, and by rumor a ruthless bastard whom it was better never to know, than to cross. It is depressing and insulting how the lives of ordinary good people are hostage to the fortunes of the likes of Yoolie von Bayern. When Molar Chemical, as it generally did, turned a good profit, Jacob prospered in attenuated proportion. When trouble struck Molar and Yoolie von Bayern, we shared in that as well; and when eventually Yoolie's skull was crushed in a dressing room backstage at the Orpheum, my life stopped too.

2. Psalms

At two o'clock a few Sunday afternoons later, Mollie Biedermeyer, Carl Holzhauser and I were knocking down an easy fifteen bucks (total) playing incidental music for a spiffy wedding at Ladue Chapel, a noncommittally Christian venue much loved for such occasions by the hunt crowd. We were dressed severely, and our easy-listening Baroque was meant to be smooth and familiar. But Mollie's flute gave muscular downbeats; her brows knit over pursed lips. She looked like a duchess, beating not a sneezing baby but the time, Bach's time. *Sheep May Safely Graze*, one of our standards for wedding preludes because its effect is calming. Nervous customers make noise, and that spoils the music.

Trouble was, Mollie's continuo was slipping out from under the serene tempo she was trying to establish. It was Holzhauser, hasty at the harpsichord and pulling me along with him. His back was to us, so Mollie could only fight back by counter-recruiting me to her beat. I sprawled with one foot on shore and the other on Holzhauser's departing canoe. I couldn't make it sound right no matter what I did, and I'm sure it sounded like my fault. We were approaching the crisis point, with Mollie and Holzhauser getting across bar lines almost a beat apart, I anywhere between. Bach's cool and careful progressions were sounding like Scott Joplin, and there was a tensing on both sides of the aisle. I saw salvation in the form of a double-bar, the end of the A section. We could regroup, permanently I hoped, at the downbeat to the B section. But Mollie stopped there, put down her flute, and fished in her purse. To cover the silence (a relief), I plunked strings and asked Holzhauser for an A. But before his finger could descend on it, he found a $5 bill in the way, bridged across the black keys on either side.

"Mr. Holzhauser," murmured Mollie, "You seem to be in a hurry. You will do Dienst and me a favor if you will take your share and be finished now; that evidently will suit you best as well. Thank you and goodbye. B section, Oren."

And she gave an imperious downbeat. Having no choice, I played. Mollie played. Holzhauser did not play, but sat at the keyboard looking at the fiver. Bach proceeded on his laminar course and the sheep stopped blatting, lowered their fleecy heads and munched again. The keyboard part was just a sketchily outlined continuo anyhow, and my line filled all of Mollie's harmonic needs. I was the flock, she the faithful shepherd, and it was a relief to have Holzhauser out of the meadow. We floated like silk bands across the opulent silence of Ladue Chapel. Though I was then a great believer in giving the music as written a chance to show what the composer wanted, Bach certainly meant us court musicians to ornament, so I assayed a few passing notes to fill triads, and ended on a mordant that, amazingly, fit Mollie's to a turn. She rewarded that with a wink; Bach Almighty was well pleased.

Holzhauser slipped out, leaving the bill bridging across the A, while the organ cranked up something more recognizably nuptial. During the interminable service, waiting to play a postlude that would be luckily inaudible in the din of affable departure (since Handel did not have Bach's genius to make a universe of two voices) I took my mind off the bride's flawless nubility by gazing up the short, dim tunnel the fiver made with G sharp and B flat.

My access to nubile women since returning from Indiana is pretty well summed up by the Maureen Witz episode. Not that it had been a revel in Bloomington, but there had been a few social dates, and a jolly violist who organized little chamber evenings that would end with only me left; we would experience white wine, Hindemith on her hi-fi, and severely limited necking from which I emerged, as I had my life so far, a virgin. And my own country, as we have seen, was down from that. After the wedding, with the lucky pair long fled and we about finished with Handel and more than ready to get out of there, I got a jostle and a pinch on the cheek from a woman in a picture hat, and a scoop-neck dress that made it hard to concentrate on being offended. I quit playing, though.

"Hey, m'sicians, give us 'You Balong Ta Me', will ya?" She flung out an arm and snapped her fingers pretty well on the second try. "Pete, give these fi' masicians a buck, they could play somethin to dance." The arm continued to rise, and she shot her hips into a torch stance. *"Fly the oshn in a silver plane,"* she sang, and not that badly, either. *"Be the jungle when iss ...da da da."*

The Canon, or whatever, of Ladue Chapel looked stiff, and one of a snickering bunch of youngish guys came over to corral the singer. But she grabbed him in a dancing grip and rubbed the scoop neck against his white-tuxed tummy. *"Juss remember,"* she sang, kicking his ankles to make him dance, bonking her hips into pews, *"When you're home agennnn, Yooo blong to* - shit, Pete, cmon an dance - *to meee."*

The picture hat came off backwards, revealing ashy hair; Pete slipped out of her grasp to pick it up. It was perfectly clear to me that he was a good decade younger, that he had at least once slept with her; and that this was not the first time he had rued the night. (Or afternoon; I don't want you to think I was given to clairvoyance.) Good god, though, I mean, just what you always heard about the suburbs. I looked at Mollie in alarm, and found her blushing through the last measures of Handel at a tempo that Carl Holzhauser might have found hasty. Pete took the singer in hand and pushed her toward the exit, followed by a scuffling crowd of pals expiring with glee. "Yooo blong to meeee, Pete," one of them crooned as the door slammed.

Mollie and I packed and scrammed. "Who was that lady?"

"That was no lady, Oren. I believe that was Mrs. Julius von Bayern, the current version. I have no idea who the boy was, or the crowd of Yahoos with him. I think we need discuss the whole episode no further. May we drop it?"

I was more than willing; it gave me the creeps. It was odd, though, to see Mollie emerge from her deep cover of bland good manners twice in one afternoon, and I hinted as much. She was dismissive and unrepentant about booting Holzhauser.

"No regrets, Oren. I can't stand a row, and that's what we were headed for. Carl knows me better than to rush that way. It's got to be smooth and clean, or it's nothing. I hate jerkiness and that dumb *gallante* style he was trying for anyhow. What place does that have in a chorale? Your little ornamentations were tasteful and smooth. Above all."

She placed a modest arm over her chest and kneaded her right shoulder. "I have always thought *Sheep May Safely Graze* the ideal text to bless human companionship and love, and I believe our duo version gave that ideal a fine realization. Shall we go?" And as she led the way to the parking lot, I found myself wishing that there was a chance in hell someone would ever play it for her.

We weren't done for the day; our next stop was the opening rehearsal for the Stravinsky Symphony of Psalms, that I had allowed myself to be recruited for. I mean, hell, another ten bucks.

We showed up five minutes late, still in formal dress, and found that the conductor, the regular Concordia Men's Chorus director, had decided this stuff was too hot for us to actually play at first sight. This would be, he said, a "listening rehearsal," for which we would be given our parts and would just sit and follow them ("Feel free to finger your instruments, and choir, you can sing along quietly.") while he played us a tape recording of a live performance conducted by Stravinsky himself.

"All right, people," he said, clapping loudly and slowly at the milling mob of singers. "All right." (*clap, clap*) "All right. Let's have quiet and attention, please. Before we - quiet, please - before we get acquainted with this beautiful work, let's get acquainted with each other. First, the Concordia Men's Chorus" (polite applause) - "then, as you know, Stravinsky asks for a chorus of adults and children, but permits substitution of women's voices for the children in the soprano and alto lines. We are very glad to have with us the Treble Choir of Cor Mariae Academy" (A gaggle of girls in dark blue uniforms) "who will blend their lovely voices with the Concordia men and with our orchestra of fine instrumentalists; and who will be joined by some of their alumnae from the St. Louis area."

Giggles joined by pious matrons. What had I agreed to? Plus, this director definitely looked like the kind of fairy who would conduct - *espressivissimo* - without a baton, leaving one fully aware of his feelings, if in doubt where he meant the downbeats to come. I slumped in my chair and opened the music. It included a purple ditto of the words:

I.
Exaudi orationem meam, DOMINE, it said, and a lot of other stuff that made even less sense to me. "Now, folks," the Voice continued from the front, "let's start by knowing what this music is all about. Here's a fella that's pretty blue, and he gets down on his knees and prays in Latin, which is his particular way...."

II.
Expectans expectavi DOMINUM, et intendit mihi.
Et exaudit preces meas et eduxit me de lacu miseriæ
    et de luto fæcis.
And so forth. Did it really mean faecis? Something about shit? I listened to the conductor with more attention:

"Now the good Lord hears his prayer and after a while things start to look up a bit for this fella, and of course, he's tickled about it no end ..."

III.
Alleluia.
Laudate DOMINUM in sanctis Ejus.
Laudate Eum in firmamento virtutibus Ejus.
Laudate DOMINUM.

And on and on, with a boatload more *Laudate*'s. My tenth-grade Latin wasn't up to a nuanced translation, but I got the message of this part, all right. It would be dull indeed to drag you through the music. Maybe later, when it will have more meaning. It was severe; not as atonal as I had feared but with parts that jarred badly, and some tricky rhythms, and moments of unearthly melting beauty. It didn't look tough, provided the conductor kept the lines of communication clear.

I began to let my eye rove over the assembled musicians; familiar faces from the Civic were there, including of course Mollie; and Maureen Witz, hmf, gnash, and a little Italian named Pietro Di Salvo, who made violins and played bass in the

Civic. Also present were woodwinds of all sorts. No violins, no violas: the cellos would have the rare honor of carrying the string lines all by themselves.

The men of the Concordia group were, to a fellow, crewcut, houndstooth-jacketed, crewneck-sweatered. One or two held an earnest pipe in the hand that followed the music. I skimmed the Cor Mariae ranks for good-looking girls and of course found a multitude, most of whom could hardly have been seventeen, so I didn't linger. During a long dry spell when the cellos had nothing to do but count measures, I speculated on the charm potential of one who looked more my age: a broad-shouldered redhead with freckles, humming the alto line. The freckles were subdued, but promised a whole galaxy of little beauty spots all over. She wore muted colors of a sort of light brick shade that matched her bubble hair exactly. She hummed with wide-mouthed generosity. A peach milkshake in a champagne glass would have hung its head.

But as I settled into a pattern of glancing her way when I had a reasonable chance - I tried to keep the ogling at least in context of a general appreciative watching of the whole choir - my eyes kept stumbling over and coming back to her neighbor, a slight, black-haired girl in a multi-buttoned white dress that went well with her dark eyes. Where the redhead looked hearty and loose, the sidekick looked as if her whole body resonated to Stravinsky. She had neat, exact features that reminded me somehow of the keys on an oboe. Only woodwind players will think that's much of a compliment. In human terms, they amounted to small round ears, the aforementioned dark eyes and eyebrows, quite a long straight nose, saved from beakiness only by its utter femininity and the way it harmonized with the totality of her face; and a dark red mouth that appeared to be unlipsticked and covering a slight overbite.

What, you say - sounds great, a big-nosed girl with buck teeth. But there was something so slender and firm about her, so integral and trim, that the individual features were just drawn into this single beautiful pattern. Also, and please don't think I didn't check this out as lines of sight permitted, maturely equipped in the breast department. maybe not the gravity-flouting hemispheres of a teenager, but in a way that seemed perfectly in keeping with slimness, enthusiasm, intensity.

Well, what with this old-fashioned permissible ogling and the drama of the music itself, the three movements of Stravinsky slid by. I managed not to get lost, even when I found the dark girl, or woman, at one point returning my glance with a - hm, well, curious? - eye of her own. The conductor (who finally got around to introducing himself as Pierce Replogle, what a perfect name for the guy) turned off the tape, and announced that he wanted us for another half-hour, to look at some particular spots; but a universal moan of dismay rose from the treble ranks, and the peach raised her hand and declared that she, for one, needed a pit stop (only I grinned) and promised to be back in five minutes. There was a warble of agreement from her sisters, and a general standing-up and moving-about.

A hand descending on my shoulder proved to be that of the principal cellist of the Civic and of this operation as well, Armin Balakourian, an Armenian refugee who had spent the '30's as a State-subsidized cello major and professor at the Moscow Conservatory, and the next 15 years running for his life. His Commie-coddled youth had not been held against him by Immigration, but he was too pink for the Boards of most professional orchestras, including the St. Louis Symphony; so he, like many another principal in the Civic, was scraping along on its tiny stipend and what he could earn by teaching.

"Hi, Oren," he beamed. "You bring cello to help listen, clever guy. I think this guy wants to hear real notes after girls done pissing. Guess I gotta whistle part, less you might lend me yours."

I handed it over and mooched off while he sat down and belted out a stratospheric solo part from the opening. I drifted to where the music and various belongings of sopranos and altos lay scattered along the benches. Where the peach milkshake had sat lay a choral folder labeled N. von Bayern, and next to it, under a high school Spanish I text, one bearing the name A. Rosen. My heart sank in two stages: first at the news that the redhead was one whom I knew in repute as Nancy von Bayern of the mighty von Bayern family (stepdaughter of the hat-and-neckline lady) and scourge of male psyches around Washington

University; and then at what I deduced from the dark woman's books.

First of all, possession of a Spanish I text was equivalent, in St. Louis student circles, to wearing a badge saying *"Too Dumb To Take Latin."* Second, the book was the property, said a stamped logo on the side, of University City High School; ergo the dark-haired A. Rosen, besides being none too bright, was a high school kid, probably Jewish. I had engaged in the speculative eyeballing of a socialite far beyond my reach and of a dim and underaged Jewish girl. Cringe, be my guest. In that place and time, we passed these judgments with the nonchalance of Mark Twain reading the Mississippi. I returned to my seat and watched as the singers - including, chummily, my two targets, whom I now tried to see as homely and uninteresting - straggled in.

About all that happened in the second half was that Balakourian and a few singers and other instrumentalists ran through some tricky spots like the joints between movements, which were to be, in Pierce Replogle's innovative word, "seamless." He was as emotive as I'd feared, his beat was hard to follow, but he seemed comfortably familiar with the score, and showed evidence of having thought about it. Before we broke up for the night, he plucked the tape from his chunky Wollensak recorder and dropped it into a briefcase. "That's it for the tape, folks. I wanted you to hear it once, 'cause if you were paying attention and reading along, why, that saves an awful lot of time in learning your notes. Stravinsky himself conducted it, so we can pretty well figure that it's the way he wanted it to sound, and now you have that sound in your ears. But it's up to us to give our performance. That'll be our job between now and October 24, when we perform."

Well, that sounded sensible to me. It was a good piece of music, challenging and lush, and there were times when each of the three cellos - Balakourian, me, and a kid from Webster High who would sit third - had our own melodic line, though most of the time we either all had the same part, or divided into a solo line (Balakourian) and the others, meaning me and the Webster kid, who seemed to get lost pretty easily. I headed for the parking lot.

31

And got as far as the front door before I remembered bonking my cello on the frame, and returned through the gloomy hallways to retrieve it. I found it leaning against the chair Balakourian had used, and he nowhere in sight. Brushing past me came a few Cor Mariae stragglers, giggling and putting on jackets; the peach and the intense dark girl (von Bayern and Rosen, damn) not among them. Against the stage, Pietro Di Salvo was bagging up his bass viol and mounting it on the little wheeled rig he used to save strain in carrying it around.

"Decide you might need that thing?" he called. "Balakourian says tell you give it some polish and a decent setta strings. What it's got on it now?"

I thought. I hadn't had new strings since I started playing again, meaning this set went all the way back to Indiana. "Guess it's a set I put on it a couple of years ago. I didn't play it for a while."

"Coupla years? Strings get old, play or don't play. That set's probably like dishrags by now, and way outa tune. C'mon by the shop, pick up a decent set. I give you a discount."

I said sure, but I must have looked otherwise. A decent set of cello strings, even from a downscale fiddlemaker like Di Salvo, couldn't be had for under five dollars. I could take it out of my summer pay, if I didn't eat or buy books or pay lab fees for a week. Di Salvo gave me a stern look as he trundled his bass across the floor. "Sure thing, but maybe not this week, that it?"

"Well, you know, I've got some lab fees and stuff to pay, and I've got to stretch out . ."

"And strings come last, eh? Lab fees? Cello player like you doing lab stuff?" He paused a little, and a sly expression came over his sleek Milanese face. "Maybe I can help with more than discount. Got a little proposition, my dear, eh..."

"Oren."

"My dear Oren. I got a set of real good strings, out of the wrappers, but hardly used. Tomastiks, top quality, played one rehearsal and one concert by Pierre Fournier, no less; but that's all."

"Well, great, but. . ."

"No buts to it. I need lab kinda stuff done, pronto, ready for tomorrow morning. We got a short rehearsal tonight, you got a little time on your hands, how about help me out a couple hours, I give you these strings. Make your cello sound a whole lot better."

I thought about it, but not for long. Maybe good strings would make a difference. A set of Tomastiks, last time I looked, was running about $7, which would make my pay for Di Salvo's "couple hours" about ten times minimum wage.

Well, in the end of course, the couple hours ran into a couple more, cooking up varnish for Di Salvo's newest creations. Pietro Di Salvo maintained one of the few violin shops in St. Louis, and he was preferred by some players both for repairs and for new instruments. His output was small - he had his duties with the Civic as a section principal and a few students to distract him - but he had a graceful touch with wood that produced impressive instruments, even if some thought the sound didn't quite measure up to the look. A funny thing for a bass player to be good at, you might say, but then, why not? A player need not take on the personality of his instrument.

The shop was down on Walnut, in a poky little frame house hunkered between a ten-story office building and a paint and rubber warehouse. His own exterior paint was long gone, except on a gold-and-black sign over the entrance: "P. Di Salvo Violins." It was a tough neighborhood at night, and he had heavy wire mesh over the windows. After an elaborate unlocking protocol, he walked into blackness, leaving me on the sidewalk peering into clean smells of wood and glue.

"Uh, sir?" I called into the darkness, and got a thump and some rapid-fire Italian in reply. "Come in, Oren. Damn light burned out in front. I trip over a stack of wood my damn fool apprentice leave right there after I fire the damn fool this afternoon."

Light appeared - fired his apprentice, did he? - and I found myself in a room surrounded by violins, violas, and cellos in every stage of completion or need for repair. The room was lined with cabinets and whole walls that consisted of arrays of labeled drawers: Violin E, Violin A, Viola A, Cello D. Post setters, mutes, tuners, polish, rosin, chin rests, every kind of tackle and rigging for string instruments. Naked white wood shaped like women circled at the edge of vision. Behind them I heard Di Salvo calling me into a back room where the ingredients for his varnish lay ready on a work bench.

"Gotta work clean," he said, and the words dropped cleanly from his lips in illustration. "Get dust in the varnish, fiddles look like hell. Lucky thing the damn fool apprentice clean up shop yesterday before he bump this violin I'm gluing for Piccolini: second time! I tell him strike two, you're out, signore, and he drop his wood and scram. Fine thing, now I got two jobs I gotta do at once. Lemme show you how the varnish goes."

The varnish was cooked up from scratch in solvents that had to be distilled into the pot that held the binder and drier and colors. I don't know why he thought he needed a cadet engineer for it. It was a batch operation, following directions in a crabbed Italian hand that Di Salvo had to translate for me, and he must have done it himself a hundred times. But he had a rush repair job, and he really wanted to get this varnish ready for some fiddles that had been waiting for it.

It involved a lot of heat and waiting, and a lot of fumes. In regard to human lungs and livers - not the sacred wood of his fiddles - Di Salvo's industrial hygiene left plenty of room for toxic hallucination. What else could account for his asking me, after two or three hours of exposure, and for my agreeing, to work for him two evenings a week and Saturday mornings until he could come up with a new apprentice? I hadn't exactly earned his confidence by making the first batch of varnish about three shades too dark.

For my part, maybe I thought - if thought entered into it at all - I might "learn something." That to be clinically present amid the sweat and labor of a cello's birth might give me a brother's claim to share its mystery; or else reveal a hollow box that could breathe only such life as might be lent it by its player and the laws of acoustics. The physics of music, the equations of a fugue; the empty heart of a fiddle.

*   *

I was sitting groggily in Quantitative Analysis the next morning at about 8:30, trying to care about the proper pH for a chloride titration when some functionary kid from the Department office entered, blinked twice, and interrupted the flow, such as it was, to hand Dr. Eslington a note. Eslington looked astonished that any deal short of the Black Death could be big enough to come between us and chemistry, but he gave the note a glance and his chalky finger pointed at me, then swept economically through the messenger to the door.

In the Department office, a phone was sitting off its hook, and on the other end of it was Harvey Napperson. "Oren. Something's come up here, and I need your notebook from August 5 through August 25. It's not in the stack with the others. Do you have it?"

What a question. My last day at Molar had been weeks ago. "No, sir, I don't. Anyhow, I don't think so. I was supposed to give it to Pear ."

"Damn it, son, don't tell me what you were supposed to do. I made that rule. What I want to know is, <u>did</u> you give it to Pear or not? And if you did, where is it? There's one in the stack for August 26 through 28, which I guess is when you quit. And there's a bunch of them covering up to August 5th. So where's the one for the rest of August?"

I tried not to get flustered and defensive, but it wasn't automatic. Harvey Napperson had never shown any mood softer than a kind of steely bonhomie, first thing Monday mornings. I stalled. "Mr. Napperson, to the best of my knowledge, I always gave full notebooks to Pear. What does he say?"

"He says if it isn't in the stack, you never gave it to him."

That piece of ass-covering - when I had more than once in fact covered for Pear's naps and hangovers - impressed me. "Well, sir, I am quite sure that I did. What's the..."

"You better get down here. Now. Pronto."

I looked at my watch. There was still time to get back to class for the lab quiz. "I'll be there as soon as - "

"Now."

" - I can."

On the way downtown and over the bridge, I tried to remember giving Pear the notebook to be date-stamped, witnessed, and filed with the others in Napperson's strong room. The trouble was, I could remember three or four such occasions. My work there had been so menial and routine that Napperson had given me the tag ends of old notebooks, twenty or thirty pages left after some dead-end or failed project, with the used pages cut out; so I had probably filled half a dozen in the course of the summer. Could I specifically remember drawing a "neat diagonal line through the unused portion of the last page and affixing my signature and date at the bottom" as required by Napperson's lab protocols on August 25th? I worked out that the 25th had been a Tuesday, which was no help at all. Stupid bloody Tuesday, as four preadolescent Brits were waiting to sing; the dumbest day of any week, always a blank a week later.

Also in the no-help category, I remembered running across a passage Harvey Napperson had written up about himself in his own notebook (leather-bound, Roman numeraled, sewn-in, numbered pages) while I was looking for data one day, and was so taken by that I stayed late that night and copied it out. I still have it:

"This notebook is the property of Mr. Harvey Napperson." (Then, continuing in a slightly different color of ink.) *"Who is responsible for the good order and the good name of the Division of Analyses of Molar Chemical Company of East St.Louis, Illinois. Mr. Napperson feels keenly the fact that consumer dissatisfaction (even legal liability), properly the problem of those consumers and then of the client retailers, could run like a burning fuse back to Molar, and to the doorway of his lab on the east bank of the Mississippi River."*

And in the original color of ink, *"Mr. Harvey Napperson takes note. He leaves notes and takes names. Mr. Napperson takes no chances and gets no credit."*

An orator trapped in the life of a semi-grunt chemist. Probably he listened to his father about career choices. There were no cross-outs or changes in it; he must have thought the whole thing out in his head on day after day of lab prowling until he had to write it down to get rid of it.

But I had taken memory no further by the time I drove across the weedy gravel behind the Molar analytical lab on the Illinois riverbank and walked in ominous sunshine to the door. I entered to find a crowd where I had been used to a purposeful quiet handful. My eyes slid over a bunch of guys in suits without catching on anything familiar, to the lab staff grouped around, though not too close to, a stubborn-looking Pear Wilson perched on a lab stool, to Harvey Napperson seated in his cubicle with his tie completely undone, ignoring the claims and questions pouring over his shoulders from a pair whose status as Molar higher-up and reporter, respectively, could hardly have been more clearly stamped in their manner and dress. Pear broke the silence that came when they noticed me.

"Any book you give me, I put on 'at pile, right?" he said. "What business I got with them books? Ain't my - "

"OK, Wilson," interjected the executive type. He was a little fat man with a fringe of hair and a bulkily knotted regimental silk tie, and a handkerchief in the exact color of the crimson diagonals thereon. "We've already been over all that, and you've made your position clear."

The patient smile he directed at Pear did not involve much of his facial furniture, which was carefully groomed and a bit piggy. He pushed his glasses up his sweating nose - it must have been 85 in that lab, even this late in the year - and turned to me.

"Mr. Dienst, I must tell you that an - mm, an incident has occurred that may have wider repercussions on the relationships between Molar Chemical and its customers and the social community in which it is set, and in which it has always played the role of a good corporate neighbor. There has been a minor rail accident in which a Molar Chemical tank car, entirely through the negligence of the Missouri Pacific Railroad, overturned and rolled or slid some distance down Rock Hill Road, a steeply sloping residential street in the Negro section of Webster Groves, coming to rest on Kirkham Avenue and discharging some of its contents into the roadside ditches in the process. To the best of the knowledge and belief of the management of Molar Chemical . . ."

I was deeply impressed. The guy was speaking extemporaneously as if he were reading from a court brief. Which, it emerged, might soon be the case. A Molar tank car had derailed and tumbled down a hill in a rundown area of Webster

Groves, and spilled a lot of - something, and the question was, what - over the roadside, and some people's houses, and then into a little ratty creek that ran along the base of the hill. It was pretty lucky, seemed to me, the tumbling tanker had stayed in the street and not gone through somebody's house. Anyhow, according to the car's shipping manifest and Molar's records, the stuff that spewed out was glacial acetic acid; essentially hyper-concentrated vinegar, a common chemical used in making aspirin, pungent but pretty harmless once it was flushed away with lots of water. A few rats and raccoons might get teary-eyed, or even killed if a slug of the straight stuff went in a storm drain, and the street would smell of vinegar until a few hard rains had come and gone.

But here was this reporter and a bunch of sober-looking Molarites, including Harvey Napperson, whose connection to all this I couldn't figure. I was not long in the dark. The journalistic-looking guy, who was actually wearing a dark-brown fedora to match his grey suit, came over and handed me a business card, ("The St. Louis Star-Times /Fred Bonney, staff writer") on the back of which was written "That's Leon Davies, from Corporate Relations. Call me if you know anything you don't want to say in front of him." He turned to the group behind him while Davies glared at me and at the card in my hand. I broke eye contact when the reporter spoke again.

"I know what acetic acid smells like - hell, I spilled a bunch of it in college, and you don't forget that stench. And that stuff in that ditch ain't it. I don't know what it is, but folks that own those houses would like to know, I bet."

"And that's where you come in, Oren." Harvey Napperson hardly moved his mouth. "The final authority on the identity and purity of anything that leaves Molar Chemical is the analytical record of this laboratory. The lot identified on the tank car actually shows up in our records as vinyl chloride, which would be a serious matter if that's what sprayed over that neighborhood. We would have assayed and certified it around the time that's covered by your notebook that's missing. Can't you remember what you did with it?"

"Mr. Napperson, I thought about it all the way down here. Every time I finished a notebook, I crossed off the end of the last page and gave it to Pear."

"Without signing and dating it?"

"No, of course, I signed and dated it. But that wouldn't affect its being missing, so I don't . ."

"Ef he give me the book, it's . ."

"See here, son, what you think is important or not doesn't matter . . ."

"Good grief, you guys, don't you remember glacial acetic acid when you handle it? Boy, when I spilled . . ."

I held up my hands. "Wait a minute. In the first place, I must have worked on a hundred different samples in those three weeks. Some of them were acetic acid, sure, but there was lots of other stuff. And we did at least one batch of vinyl chloride. I mean, we'll have to find the notebook, and we probably will, but can't we go out to the spill and take a sample?"

"Farmen hooshed it all down a sewer," replied Pear, with gloomy satisfaction. "Tanker caught far, an' burned up what din't spill."

"Well, so it's gone, so we'll have to find the notebook, but why shouldn't it be what the records say it is? And if it is, I don't see what's the big . . ."

"Look, fella," said the reporter. "A lot of houses out there are still drinking well and cistern water, and a lot of 'em read the Star-Times. How's 'Mystery Chemical Sprays Webster Neighborhood' strike you as a story? 'Cause that's what we're running tomorrow."

"Mystery horse shit!" stormed Davies. His smooth cheeks gleamed with righteous sweat. "First place, nobody cares what gets spilled on a bunch of darkies. You think any of your readers give a good god damn what's trickling down some jig's face?"

Bonney didn't flinch at the term. "Maybe not. But a lot of them own those houses, and if all the darkies move out and no more will move in, even fifty bucks a year in taxes is gonna add up over time."

"The shipping manifest said acetic acid, and that's what it was. You guys are gonna look pretty silly in court, and you selling pencils, Bonney, when you lose a defamation suit over some spilled vinegar."

"That stuff was no more vinegar than I am. You don't forget that smell. This was some kind of sicky-sweet, oily stuff."

"I see. An experienced chemist in the Star-Times hack pool. You passed up a scientific career for journalism, did you, Doctor?"

"It doesn't take a PhD to smell the difference between vinegar and something else. Not that it's any of your business, what I . . ."

"Ha! I guess I'm a little surprised to hear a reporter lecturing me about minding my business. Just, you might ask yourself how you're going to sound in court when our chemists - many of them, such as Napperson, here, with advanced degrees in analytical chemistry, testify about the purity of the acetic acid in that tank car and you, you with the trained nose, try to convince a judge it was some kind of 'mystery chemical.' Eh, Mr. Napperson?" Metallic camaraderie beamed at Napperson.

"Mr. Davies, as soon as we find that notebook, we'll have the information we need . . ."

"Well, it's kind of hard for me to picture what more you need than the shipping records, Napperson. I'd hate to think your lab would be out of whack with the corporate record that includes production and shipping documents and the client's order."

"With every respect, sir, if the lab and the accounting records don't agree, then it's the accounting that's out of whack. We go to very great lengths to assure the integrity of our protocols and of our data."

Bonney grinned. "Except you seem to have lost one of your notebooks. What if your tech here" (nodding at me) "got the name mixed up?"

"He'd still get data that would only be consistent with the true chemical identity of that substance. With all the corporate records, that's the only real evidence of what it was."

Everybody looked at me.

3. Taum Sauk

Mornings after Civic rehearsals were always tough: wired on music, I never slept a lot when I got home, no matter how important and boring a book I might take to bed to doze off with. More than once on rehearsal nights I would look at the clock, bored to death and wide awake, to find it 'way over on the two or three o'clock side. But of course I would eventually drift off, dream of anything but music, and be rescued from a night's sleep by the alarm. During the spring I could make up for it the next night by passing out over analytical geometry and getting in a solid 8 or 9 hours. Now I had signed on to pick up pocket money as the Outing Club manager.

In 1953, an Outing Club had nothing to do with closets. This one met on alternate Tuesdays to organize little student expeditions away from the confines of the campus. Managing it was light duty: keeping track of gear that members checked out, pursuing the occasional slackers who turned it in late, dirty, or not at all, ordering expendable supplies for group trips. In return, I got dues-free membership and three dollars a week to do with as I chose.

Holding on to this plum (to which I brought no deeper qualifications than that I had signed up first) required that I attend meetings and stay awake to answer logistical questions and note requests for supplies and plans for new outings. After a few meetings – as these things go – the initial attendance and enthusiasm had shaken itself down to the hard core of a dozen who loved hiking and/or messing around in boats and who would have done it with or without an Outing Club to provide cover. There was desultory talk about getting more members to participate, and how we'd lose our access to funding and University vans if all we had was a handful of people on trips.

"Agh, let 'em go," was the opinion of the most dedicated hiker, my lab partner Markus Gewissner. Markus was a rawboned German kid who tended to be a good distance up any trail ahead of his nearest pursuers on group hikes. There was a mild murmur of protest at his elitist stand, but not much in the way of thoughtful counter-proposals, when I, at least, snapped out of my half-doze.

Standing shyly in the doorway and looking at us in turn was the dark-eyed alto I had noticed at the Stravinsky rehearsal. Seeing her now at close range, it was clear that she was older than I had taken her for, certainly not high school age. It occurred to me to doubt it was the same one, but only until her eyes rested on me. Someone plunked a C string in my belly, and our eyes stayed together until I had to look away. I think I remembered to smile, but when I looked back her gaze had moved on. Seeing our minimal attention to the membership crisis fully distracted, the chairlady, a hearty PE major, turned to see what the interruption was.

"Oh, right, hi," she boomed. "I guess you must be, uh, Annie? Bonnie? Ellie?"

A. Rosen? I implored; and she said, "Anna Rosen."

"Right. Annie phoned me today about joining. Annie, this is Ollie, uh, Diener; and Markus Gewiss; and … "

And on she went around the circle, getting sometimes half of each name right, and we all laughed and said our names, and Anna Rosen said them after us, finding each name interesting and euphonious. Her voice was as dark as her eyes and her name ('Ahna'), came with a faint European tang. She gave Markus's name the tonsil and bronze vowels it was probably meant to have, which seemed to please the guy. When we had wobbled to adjournment, I took a grip and a breath and went over to her.

"You're singing in that Stravinsky, aren't you?" I wavered. "Anyhow, welcome to the Outing Club. Can I walk you home?"

Never mind. She was almost never without graceful counterpoint. She looked struck by the cleverness of my suggestion, even as she was saying, "Well, thank you. I am singing in the Stravinsky choir; you'll have a pretty short walk, I'm afraid. I'm parked just outside." But at my evident disappointment, she added, "Well, I don't have to be home just yet. What if we had a malt or something? That's two blocks to the Velvet Freeze and two blocks back, so you'd get your walk, and you could tell me about the Outing Club. You must be the Oren that's supposed to have the tents and paddles and stuff."

I admitted to being the only Oren in the Outing Club, and probably the whole university. "Did you want a paddle?"

She sort of blinked at that. "Oh, gee. That's what my stepfather used to say when I was bad." And she sort of laughed and looked over her shoulder while she smoothed the back of her skirt. Over a pretty nice substrate, I couldn't help noticing. It was kind of small, but nicely proportioned, and flowed into a slender waist and a very straight back. She turned and of course caught me gathering data. "How do you know about Stravinsky? Are you a tenor, maybe? - oh, I know, you're in the orchestra? What do you play?"

"Cello," I confessed. And she appeared to think that a marvelous thing.

The malt errand was over all too soon; there was a line at the Velvet Freeze, so we spent five awkwardly wordless minutes waiting to get served. I made to find us a table (*Twined straws, wire-backed chairs, penny loafers*) but she gave a little frown and looked at her watch and said she had to get back. During the brisk two-block walk back to her car, we sucked mightily on our malts while she quizzed me about what it was like to play a cello, and told me she had been trained in ballet and still loved to dance, though she had of course known early on that she had no chance at a professional career (clever, lucky girl). At Washington U. she was studying European lit. and picking up a little money on the side tutoring Spanish at U. City High. The street lights, I decided, would be too dim to reveal my blush at this news.

Yet - and this was always part of Anna's charm for me, no matter how intimately I later came to know her - though I now knew better about her age and sophistication than my first bad guesses, she still retained for me a schoolgirl flavor that resided somewhere among her slenderness, her openness, and that slight delicious overbite. One would feel that in a kiss, I found myself thinking; and I tripped over the chain at the edge of the parking lot and got malt on my chin.

Anna dabbed at it with her Velvet Freeze napkin, and pulled out a set of keys. Deciding I could hardly feel more of a fool than I already did, I decided to press what was still pretty good luck, and asked her if she was free on the weekend, and if I could call her up. She gave me a considering look, not encouraging, not haughty; not at all a look from the Maureen Witz repertoire.

"I think we'll be seeing a lot of each other at the Outing Club meetings, and the Stravinsky, when that starts," she said, and made it sound a giddy prospect. "Thank you for your, your kind escort this evening."

"My pleasure completely." Maybe to take the sting out of distancing herself, maybe because she found my stiff little bow amusing or pathetic, she smiled and gave me a light touch on the shoulder before she got in her car.

Now, please. You will not understand Anna Rosen if you don't see that mute touch as intimate, promising, speaking of much and reserving more; seeming to acknowledge a special friendship that included me and no one else, that was so bursting with possibilities that she could hardly speak them aloud, and that this - all of this, whatever it was - was still only in the first fiery nanoseconds of its creation. I tell you, I stood there looking at the receding flares of her tail lights with a little dab of malt on my chin and my loins – as we politely said in those days – jumping, feeling like I'd been knighted.

Well, whatever boon her brief touch may have conferred - maybe the Gift of Insomnia, because I sure didn't make up for Monday's lost sleep that night - it was apparently not an exclusive one. Washington University was not an intimate community, but I saw Anna Rosen twice more before the next Outing Club meeting, once with some very slick-looking guy I later came to know to my sorrow as Nancy von Bayern's fiancé Rick McIntear, and once in a cafeteria line with Markus Gewissner. In both cases they seemed to be getting along rather fine, and I later learned from Markus that he had "come to know her" at church.

"You know, from her name and her dark hair I took her at first for a little Chew, but she's a goot Catholic like me," he had the infernal nerve to say.

I smiled feebly. Revelations about German Catholics and Jews were not so far in the past that I could easily overlook this unreconstructed speech from Herr Gewissner; but then, I was uncomfortably aware of my own response to the "University City High School" covers on her books. At this point I was more concerned with the fact that Markus seemed so happy about sharing a major religion with Anna Rosen.

So it was a distinct relief when he showed up early at the next Outing Club meeting with a new girl in tow, a broad-shouldered redhead with a protrusive upper lip, a puzzled look about her eyes, remarkable breasts, a real need for a good deodorant, and long, narrow feet that emerged prodigiously from a pair of yellow pedal-pushers. Markus introduced her stiffly around the circle as his very close friend Sophie Cushing, who shared with him a love of Nature and who would like to join the Outing Club; and no one present could see any reason why she should not. There was not a rush to sit next to her, since the knit jersey that molded itself relentlessly to her chest had clearly been doing so for several days without a wash. But she and Markus solved that by coiling themselves into a canvas sling chair, from which they would interrupt rapt mutual contemplation to urge longer, harder, higher climbs. The whole spectacle nearly took my mind off the fact that Anna Rosen had not yet, at 8:10, shown up for this 8 o'clock meeting. And when she did, she awarded me a friendly smile, but passed up an open seat next to me on the couch in favor of a chair of her own.

Let me not bore you with the minutes of another meeting of the Washington University Outing Club. The next outing, according to the schedule worked out by last year's officers, was to be a night cruise down the Mississippi on the river excursion boat *Admiral*. This was the kind of thing that used to be a great treat when I was in the 6th grade, but it seemed a little pale now. Markus and Sophie hooted with scorn, and when the tactfully miffed chairman responded that couples, especially, often found the *Admiral* rather romantic at night, they made it clear that theirs was a relationship that found its truest expression on the ruggedest of trails, preferably half a mile away from anyone else.

Markus proposed on the spot substituting a "real" outing for this Sunday-school stuff, and the PE major got flustered, and said that a commitment had been made, that the officers had tried to provide a varied program that would appeal to a wide range of tastes and abilities, and - this is just the stuff I said I wouldn't bore you with. In short, we agreed that the next outing would be a double-header, and anyone who wanted to hit the trail with Markus and Sophie could do so, while the social and citified types could find adventure on the *Admiral*. Markus and Sophie, after a moment of consultation, announced that their trip would be a day hike of Mt. Taum Sauk, the highest peak in Missouri. Well, that isn't saying much, but it sounded OK to me, and I was pleased to see that Anna Rosen looked interested too. Afterward, I again joined the little knot of people that included Anna and waited them out until I could gracefully isolate her.

"I haven't had a malt for two weeks, and I'm hungry for one. Thirsty, I mean. Would you, you know, do you have … "

"Well, that sounds good, Oren. Sure."

"Think you might have time to, uh, sit down this time?"

She made a stubborn little face that didn't seem to fit the topic of conversation, such as it was. "Papa - my father might ... well ... Yes, Oren. Let's do it." She sounded as if I'd proposed running away to Mexico with a circus. Assuming she'd agree to that, of course.

Over separate malts (wire-backed chairs, no penny loafers, no twining straws) at Velvet Freeze I got a better fix on her eye color (very dark brown, very clear, like strong tea) while she explained why this half-hour detour on the way home was a big deal. She had been late to the meeting because she had slacked off on a home chore and been required to redo it. Her parents - mother and stepfather, really - were strict and careful about her because they considered her still a girl.

"I've been all over the world, Oren; I was born in Austria, I went to school in Italy, and we lived in Switzerland and then in Cuba before we came here. I'm not some dumb little convent girl. They don't know everything about me, darn it. Not at all."

I nodded suavely at this new data. "You seem pretty grown up to me. I mean, you're old enough to vote and everything?"

"Sure, if we decide this country is good enough for Papa and he lets me apply for citizenship."

"Well, if you're twenty-one you can do that for yourself."

She brightened. "Really?"

"Absolutely," I guessed, making a note to check this out before she could, and changed the subject. "I think I might go on that hike with Markus and, uh, that, uh . . ."

"Sophie?"

"Yeah, Sophie Cushions."

Anna snorted malt out of her nose, a surprising result from a dumb remark, and it was almost the only time I ever saw her lose decorum in public. She blushed light mahogany, and went through four or five of Velvet Freeze's minimal paper napkins repairing herself.

"Oren, shame on you! That wasn't nice, people can't help what they look like, what their bodies have grown into."

I looked abashed, and she relented. "Besides, you made me make a mess of myself. If Papa saw that, he'd talk about horsewhipping, or something."

"I expect she's a very nice girl, and I apologize for making you get malt in your nose. And Markus certainly seems to like her. Leave it to Markus to go for the peak." I looked anxiously at Anna having said this; did her lunch-line appearance with Markus amount to a "date", and was she feeling therefore spurned? God, I hoped so. But she seemed unconcerned.

"I'm glad Markus has found someone who shares his interests so completely."

"Other than each other, you mean. She's probably a regular girl, OK, but I think she decided to like whatever Markus likes."

"Maybe so." She looked at her watch. "Oh, boy. I've gotta go, and I don't mean in a few minutes. Papa will - well, anyhow, I'd better go. No, don't bother to walk me out, I'm parked right here. 'Bye, Oren, thanks for the malt and the talk. I'll see you next time. No, on the hike! 'Bye!"

And she was gone, again taking a half second to dub me Sir Friend with a shoulder touch. In that occasional new identity, I stood in the doorway of Velvet Freeze and watched her sprint across the street. She jumped into a very handily parked Rambler - we had, as before, walked down from the Union - and roared away.

Hm. She's so scared of Papa she runs across traffic to her car, but she doesn't park in the Union lot where there were plenty of spaces. She parked at Velvet Freeze. No chance in the world this cosmopolitan, this very girl of very girls, figured she'd wind up sucking malts with me? Too many unknowns, not enough equations.

But the hike! Oh yes, she <u>was</u> going with Markus and Sophie, so was I, and with any luck at all in view of the competing *Admiral* do, so would be very few others. And Markus and Sophie, if I knew Markus, would be way out in front of whatever group they were with, even if it killed Sophie. I began, without the least justification, to think of the coming event not as the wholesome group activity the Outing Club name might imply, or even as a "date," which it was already far from being, but as an Opportunity. To … what? Impress Anna Rosen? Win her hand? Carry her off amid the brambles and mate roughly under an oaken bower? I saw no destination, only process.

The next ten days sludged by through the muggy St. Louis September with Stravinsky rehearsals (orchestra only, with Replogle booming and piping out the choral parts) and classes, including Lit 101, Classics of World Literature, which was supposed to fill in one of the big gaps my narrow specialist training at Indiana had neglected. As far as I was concerned, this had passed its apex in the first week with the Divine Comedy. Selected hot moments from the Inferno, more truthfully labeled. We each got assigned a sinner to write a paper about, which was kind of fun. I drew Paolo Malatesta, Francesca da Rimini's boyfriend. It was tough, because he doesn't get any lines, and you only hear Francesca's version of things. I managed a wooden kind of apologia that didn't convince even me; though honestly most of them, and certainly the priggish Virgil, could have fried unsung for all most of us cared at the time.

The Cello Francesca, *or* Balderdash

Of course math and chemistry were what I was really there for, and I liked them well enough. It was a tingle in the belly to see suddenly how some homework problem or quant unknown was going to work out, and I supposed that was the motive power that would pull me down the tracks that curved out of sight into the future.

Because my misspent youth at Indiana and my shortness of funds left me without the luxury of dropping or failing any course at all if I was to get down those tracks on schedule, I was also auditing a thermodynamics course that I would need to pass at the first go - something that only a little over half of its suitors managed to pull off - next year. I could see it was going to be a bear, though I liked its appealingly fictional situations (*"A weightless, frictionless piston compresses an ideal gas adiabatically and reversibly until its temperature doubles . . ."*) even if none of them seemed quite as amazing as the Doré drawing of half-naked Francesca bleeding through the blazing air of Hell with Paolo in tow. Weightless she was, and I bet plenty frictionless on a good day.

In the week before the big hike was to happen I filled out the forms I needed to get permission to drive the Outing Club van, stating "6" as the Number Of Students To Participate, on a guess that at most one other couple would be interested in dogging Markus and Sophie up the highest peak in Missouri, and a certain knowledge that any smaller number on the form would disqualify us for this use of University assets. Markus at first confirmed that, and then modified the roster.

"Your little dark-eyed friend," he boomed one day as we were waiting for supplies at the stockroom, "has invited her buddy Nancy and her boyfriend on the Taum Sauk hike. I hope they know it's a pretty stiff climb. But Bob and Lois have dropped out, so it's still six. I know a very beautiful hiking round that it needs six voices to sing. You will like it."

Or else. Wonderful, wonderful news about Nancy von Bayern the peach milkshake and her boyfriend. Or, oh shit, did he mean Anna's boyfriend? No, false alarm. Nancy had one, who, once he enters this tale, will be impossible to get rid of, so let's put it off. As for the hiking round, the last he'd tried to teach us had been a bust, partly because no one could carry the melody and remember the German words at the same time. And of course Markus refused to translate. "English words wouldn't work. And besides, Sophie learned it just fine. You should listen carefully as I lead you through it."

Well, I couldn't get around Sophie, nor wanted to try. She not only learned Markus' hiking rounds, she knew others, I guess from Girl Scouts, and taught them to Markus. That was probably a big plus, but in any case, she and Markus were now inseparable. I began to see her often, looming outside of classrooms and labs that Markus and I shared, knitting or reading a German grammar. Markus was at first dismissive and abashed, in his Teutonic way, and in a few weeks, pretty much stunned all the time.

A curt postcard from the PE major informed me that hikers should meet at the Union at 6:30 am on Saturday, September 19th, and that it would be "in the OC spirit" for each to bring some little entertainment such as a song, a story, or a reading appropriate to the natural setting. I expect she meant this as a finger to Markus and his otherwise dominant hiking songs. As far as I was concerned, the mountain would be entertainment enough, so I didn't think about it much more, other than to browse my very short bookshelves for a story to tell.

I had my own logistics in mind for meeting, so I sent a counter-postcard to Anna telling her I'd pick her up at 6:15 at her house on the way to the Union, where presumably all the others would be gathered. This way, I figured, she would naturally sit in front with me, thus establishing a healthy inevitable togetherness right from the start and encouraging any possible rivals to seek other seatmates. Alas, a return card from her said Fine, and her friends Nancy and Rick would be there too.

The 19th arrived none the sooner for my encouragement; at 6 in the morning I wheeled the "activities" van, a brown Dodge as broad as the Mississippi, out to U. City to pick up Anna and her buddies. I found Anna alone in front of her house, wearing snugly tailored bush shorts and a dove-grey oxford cloth shirt, with a Washington U. sweatshirt over her shoulders. She had on sturdy, worn hiking boots that she'd probably bought in Kitzbühel or something, and bulky socks. The pleasant gap between the shorts and the socks was bridged by slim, muscular legs, and I suppose their very slight bow was a contributing factor to her giving up a career in dance, but it certainly didn't upset me, as the slight overbite in her smile of welcome only added tang. She looked great, and I wasn't crushed that she was alone; maybe a bit hopefully puzzled.

"Where's everybody?"

"Well, Nancy called up about midnight last night to beg off with some kind of dumb excuse. I think she and Rick had been out late the night before. It was late to call me, Papa had a fit, and by the time she was done it was way too late to call you and reschedule. So I'm game if you are. Still want to go?"

"Fine with me," I understated, and she hopped in, tossing a pack into the back.

At the Union, further good news of the same sort waited. Sophie Cushing sat in a calm ungainly pile on the steps by the parking lot, knitting in a level ray of sunshine that had managed to dodge its way through most of St. Louis on its long trip from the Illinois horizon. She looked up with a sanctified expression as I pulled up next to her.

"Markus is suffering a bad sore throat this morning," she informed us. "He says he will take me there another time when he is well, but he can't hike or sing today. He sent along these maps and song sheets" (reaching them up through the window) "and asked me to give you his best wishes for a beautiful experience. And now I must go; Markus needs me."

She rose, arched her back and sighed deeply, and - twitching an airy cloak of mercy over her broad shoulders - sloped off in the direction of Markus' dorm. After a moment I said, "What a perfectly extraordinary girl. Well, it's down to us, then. Are you <u>still</u> game?"

Anna looked at me with a little smile playing about her lips. "If you had said something unkind about Sophie, I might be thinking twice about it. Papa only let me come because he thinks it's a big group. You won't ever tell him otherwise?"

"Count on me. Goodness."

"All right, then. I'm game."

"Great. Do me a favor?"

"If I can, sure."

"Say, 'Yes, Oren. Let's do it.' like you did about the malts."

She looked a little offended, but then giggled and said it, so I aimed the van down Missouri 21 into the Ozark hill country while Anna sat and watched the suburbs drop away, and the little towns come and go. As the hills rose around us, things got scarcer and more scenic, though we never got into what you'd call real wilderness. Miners and farmers had been at it in these hills for centuries.

I suppose I responded somehow to the way this soft-contoured land fed the eye, even if it could barely feed its people. I grew a little softer and less wary about the enterprise I had - against all expectations - succeeded in bringing about. I let myself think again of my guiding vision, a fantasy of Anna and me cozy in some sunny dell or streamside, reading poetry that would do for us what Launcelot's tale did for Francesca da Rimini and Paolo Malatesta, curtailing its own telling by ripening the lips from which it sprang. (And so forth; I'd had almost two weeks to gloat and moon over it.)

We were parked at the trailhead under Taum Sauk only a half-hour later than I had hoped for. The chilly morning had warmed, and Anna climbed out and stretched in early sunshine with devastating effect. I ogled, she bridled, I blushed, and she dove into the back seat for the packs.

The trail up the north flank of Taum Sauk kept us in the shade for most of the morning, in gloom that the slanting sunlight overhead did little at first to dispel. You know how these things start off - a broad path hiked by everybody and their granny, rising and falling through the low woods, climbing a ridge only to give back the altitude won, but thinner and rockier after the rustic bench at the modest overlook, where most of the grannies stop and fan themselves and say, *You go on ahead; I believe I'll just set a spell and admire the view.*

And then it starts to get a little more serious about getting you up to the summit, with an occasional tough scramble up through cedar and laurel, and even some switchbacks. We began to puff a bit (I as quietly as possible) and when the next hogback culminated in a more comprehensive view, I was glad enough to stop. Anna had been lagging behind, not from womanly failings as such but because she kept stopping and calling me back to zoom in on a millipede on a rotting log, a tiny forest of fungus sprouting from the top of a stump, dragonflies. Two of the dragonflies hooked up as we watched, so we moved on. We were not exactly embarrassed, the whole thing was too precise and chitinous for that, but there was an unspoken agreement between us that it might be ill-mannered to keep watching - whether in regard to the dragonflies or to ourselves.

Eventually I gave up on trying to make time up the trail; after all, I was just about where I had pined for days to be, and maybe I didn't want to reach that sunny meadow and find the spirits of Paolo and Francesca out to lunch or not in the mood. To keep from having to double back at each new find of Anna's I let her lead, which had the added effect of freeing me to gaze my fill at her lithe back and firm little dancer's butt flexing as she scrambled ahead up what was now becoming a really steep and rocky trail. As the time got on for eleven or so, the morning cool gave way to muggy 80's, and a line of dark sweat appeared down the exact center of her shirt. It was almost more than I wanted to think about, but of course no other topic than her downy spinal groove came to mind.

I think I was mulling how it would taste to run my tongue up that hollow from waist to neck when she made a daring sort of a leap from a tree root toward a rock at the top of a steep, loose-graveled slope above me. The rock turned out not to be well anchored, it tipped under her, and she staggered off it and began to slide backwards down the slope, crouched over, arms waving for balance. I was only a couple of feet behind her and it would have been knavish to let her slide. I reached up and steadied her with a firm hand at her center of gravity, namely directly on her rump. It was an amazing feeling, not that I lingered over it. I just gave her a firm push so she could get her balance and got my hand off in a flash.

"Thank you," she said, more or less as if I'd offered her a stick of gum. She lost no time in finding another interesting and educational sight: more insectile copulation, this time of butterflies joined at the tail and in full flight. Merciless Nature.

The spot we eventually found for lunch and the social program was not a verdant streamside pasture. I don't know what made me think we'd find such a thing on the flanks of a wooded mountain, let alone on top. But it did have some promising qualities. Seen from the valley below us it might have looked like a streak of rock just below the summit. In fact it was a flat ledge maybe fifty feet deep sprinkled with cedars and moss, with a tumble of broken rock leading up to the trail behind it, and a sheer, right-angle drop of a good two hundred feet to the woods on the flank of Taum Sauk below. There was a fallen log close to the edge and we sat against it and let our eyes stride lordly across miles of woods and farms.

With probably three counties of noteworthy sights spread before us, Anna seemed vexed only by the impossibility of showing me everything at once. I might urbanely say that I let her run on for a while, pointing out a working windmill, a passenger train headed north toward St. Louis, a big circling hawk ("Or do you think it's an eagle?") But why give myself airs? I was dumbly grateful that she was happy, lively, outgoing, and willing to carry the ball while I got a grip on myself.

OK, so this was no lush pre-Raphaelite meadow, but I had noticed a wickedly seductive carpet of moss growing within a ring of sheltering cedars, deep and sun-dappled, about ten feet back from the edge of the cliff. All the while we were sitting there with the warm thermals drying our sweaty faces and she was showing me everything, that little grove of cedars with its mossy lining was floating in the edge of my vision and the back of my mind. The day's heat pressed from the cedars a lazy essence of Old Testament afternoons. I risked a look into the blackness of Anna's eyes and heard the Song of Solomon as she pointed to a herd of deer in a churchyard far below.

Finally, having completed a first survey of all that there was to see and remark upon in the valley before us, she ran down a bit and turned to me with a heart-stopping smile and said she was having a great time, and that she was glad she'd come, and she hoped she wasn't boring me with all her chatter. I managed to stammer back something not too stupid, and we began to poke around in the backpacks for lunch and culture.

We had each opted, as it turned out, to leave the songs and games to Markus and Sophie, and bring a favorite literary passage to read, having the idea, I guess, that noble words and corny overtones would be soaked up and neutralized by the vastness of nature. I had brought, as what I hoped would be appropriate to the fantasied streamside setting, a passage I had copied out of "The Big Two-Hearted River." Luckily I asked her to go first.

"Well, OK," she said. "I've been doing this paper on Christian mystics. Of course, the Christians considered themselves Jews, early on, and didn't start drifting away from us until a long time after Jesus. It's fun to trace the slow dying-out of Jewish attitudes forward in Christian history. Anyhow, I was reading some stuff somebody just found by a 13th-Century abbess named Ariane of Tours. I know how you feel about music (*She did?*), so anyhow I thought you might like this. It's from a collection of little essays she called her Book of Devotions."

So while I looked out over the wilderness and munched on peanut butter, she began to read, in a spookily archaic voice.

"In His cosmos the Perfect Creator placed behind the illusions of everyday life just two elements, Music and Silence. And each of these two exist only for and because of the other. Silence is the destroying element who consumes all that he touches. Music is the creating dancer who weaves daringly before the great destroyer dressed only in the thinnest of veils, teasing and worshipping, tempting and pleasing. Silence is greatly tempted to reach out and devour Music, and forever after to live and rule alone. But he dares not, for he knows that it is she who brings everything to being, and that in devouring Music he would have lost everything: all change, all tension and resolution, life, and thus all that is not silence; and finally, therefore, that in devouring Music he would have destroyed himself. Our Loving Father loveth best, because it is closest to His unity, the music that brushes closest to Silence. Its veils are thin, and behind them we hear plainly the great Devourer, while naked, teasing life itself sings the dance.

"Our Most Gracious Lady the Virgin of Tours granted me this Vision after long and mortifying vigil before her likeness;

*and when I came again to myself I bore upon my hands and body
the stigmata of the Passion."*

After she finished, I sat and stared at thickening cloud-
shadows sliding across the valley floor. Holy .... I mean, filter out
the Gracious Virgin stuff, which certainly hadn't been covered in
my Sunday School, and you still had dynamite. In the first place,
Anna Rosen had chosen a passage that she "thought I might
like," meaning that she hadn't picked it for a general audience of
Outing Clubbers or just to show off, but had been thinking about
me, Oren Dienst. Second, the effortless erudition of having found
and translated a piece of archaic French mysticism just knocked
me flat. OK, maybe it was in Latin and not medieval French;
who knew, certainly not me. But I blushed again, this time in
daylight, about the Spanish textbook.

And then, the passage itself was a complete killer.
Silence? Was <u>that</u> what was going on in the drudgery of four-
octave scales, the undisciplined chaos of Civic rehearsals, or in
the chilly heart of a Beethoven sonata? If we were the music,
who was the dancer? I let this silence grow while I tried not to
think about the hearty chunk of Hemingway I had brought. She
would be polite about it, of course, but I was a dead duck if I
read it after that stuff. She was looking at me with a little
expectant frown.

"Do you believe that, about music and silence?" I
stalled.

"Do you?"

"Well...." *I asked you first.* "I guess I do. It makes sense
out of a lot of things. I can't stop playing, even when I hate the
stress."

"Oh." She looked relieved. "I'm so glad you liked it. I
got an awful lot of that Blessed Lady stuff when I was in grade
school, so it's tough for me to see past that. The central image"
(She really said that, *'the central image'*, while we were
sweating in fitful sunlight on a rock ledge in the Ozarks) "of the
dancer, of course that means something to me. Having the dancer
so vulnerable and female - well, I don't know how I feel about
that. For me music is a place. Stravinsky is one place, and Bach
is another. You can hear the place, you can almost see it.

Sometimes you can go into it, and turn corners until you can't see the way out any more, and you just stay there until the place vanishes, and you're sitting in your chair again, not quite knowing where you are. . ." She smiled. "But no stigmata, yet. What did you bring to read?"

"I didn't bring anything," I lied. "And I expect you know all about this anyhow, but I thought I'd, uh..." (Lightning flashed behind a ridge far to the southwest, and in my scrambling brain) "...I'd tell you the true story of Francesca da Rimini and Paolo Malatesta. You've read the Divine Comedy, I suppose."

She smiled. "When I was taking Italian, in Lucerne. But it's been years, I've forgotten it all. Do go ahead."

Well, that was clearly a polite lie, but I was more grateful than embarrassed. "OK, well, uh, you know how everybody always says that Francesca's trying to kid Dante about how she's this innocent helpless victim of a wave of passion and all, and how in fact, she ... she knew she was going to commit adultery when she went into it. Well, it's not that simple, not at all. She was set up and killed by her husband Gianciotto to get rid of her ... "

And off I went on the most unlikely tale I could invent, first trying to think ahead and plan sexy, exculpating circumstances that would make Francesca's treacherous lust seem OK, or at least understandable, and then getting caught up in a tale of intrigue, jealousy, aphrodisiacs and balderdash that seemed to just tell itself, gradually shifting from Francesca to the poor stumblebum Paolo, who seemed so inarticulate and clueless in Dante's rendition. In my version, he saw what had to happen, but thought he had no choice but to stand by Francesca, who had tried in vain to please her misshapen and homosexual husband.

Gianciotto had married her only out of political necessity, had grudgingly consummated the marriage to bind Francesca's assets, but spent all his time with a certain Marco ("Sofia") Pederone, whose dress, manner, and willowy form had half of Rimini convinced that Francesca was a victim only of normal heterosexual infidelity, but the revelation of whose true colors one feverish winter night humiliated Francesca and drove her to the protective arms of her (in my version) childhood friend Paolo.

The Cello Francesca, *or* Balderdash

The sunlight faded, the air around us grew still, greenish, and charged as I wove in such bits and snatches of Dante as skidded up in time to be included at the logical point. Laggard recollection about exactly what it was that Paolo was doing in Gianciotto's court missed the bus, but you can be sure that the fatal kiss of Launcelot and Guinevere, followed by the erotic truncation of their literary picnic, was primed and ready, though I didn't dwell on it or rub it in. I dropped it into the saturated ambience as a seed that might crystallize larger and more comprehensive developments later.

Also in my telling there was a fair amount of space devoted to Paolo's pining honorably from afar over Francesca's tea-colored eyes, her wit and erudition, her love of nature and her husky dark voice. And - tricky narrative footing here - her firm little butt, which he had accidentally, innocently brushed against one day in the mercato, long before their friendship proved carnal. Much telling - and particularly this, which I looped back upon and revisited as one does in dreams, until I got it right - was given to Francesca's and Paolo's tragic foreknowledge of doom, to Francesca's embrace of this doom as preferable to the ignominy of life as her husband's second choice to a perfumed boy, and to Paolo's loyal acceptance of his share in her fate.

And when at last Gianciotto burst into Francesca's bedchamber and spitted them coupled on a single sword, you can bet Francesca knew it would happen and why it had to, that she was as ready for Gianciotto's thrust as for Paolo's; and that Paolo joined her in death out of a sacrificial wisdom that gladly achieved revenge, consummation, and immortality to end his beloved's mortal humiliation.

At that point I paused for breath. I had been facing out over the valley, following the trail of inspiration through the slow darkening and wind-tossing of trees a thousand feet below us. I was thinking of prolonging things with a sort of epilog or coda devoted to the lovers' infernal afterlife, but I risked a sidelong glance at Anna to see how she was taking it, and found her glancing sidelong at me.

Our eyes met, she started to say, "What a perfectly lovely crock . . ." but either it trailed off or my hearing faded as I began to drown in the dark tea. I barely heard her whispered

"Oh, my God," and her pulse jumped and flew in the shadows at the base of her throat, and then slowly we were leaning together and kissing, Jesus, just like Paolo and Francesca, and my heart was hammering like Gianciotto hobbling up the steps to kill them. Her teeth felt exactly like I knew they would.

She bent back over the log and my legs stretched out toward the cliff. I lurched back a little when the toe of one boot slipped off the rocky edge, and she clutched at my shoulder. We pulled apart and started to laugh.

"Going off the deep end," I gasped.

She struggled to her feet and pulled me by the hand over to the cedars. We stood kissing for a moment at the edge of the bower while the first winds from the darkened valley plucked at our sweaty clothes, and I began to laugh with sudden insight. She had noticed this place with as much interest as I; well then, she thought about sex as something to be planned for and enjoyed - and with me, at that. She had probably liked the push on her rump as much as I had, had chosen to read the passage about music in part for its erotic imagery; and all in all, she was not so impossibly different from any normal human being, and I could imagine a relationship with her other - and a lot more fun - than worship.

I suppose it sounds naive and shallow to claim that seeing that a woman had the same feelings about sex as I did transformed my map of the world into something altogether joyful. But if you think so, if you have found that sex is a rubber map and the gonads a haphazard compass, you may have forgotten what it is to have no map at all. Never mind; she had spotted the cedars and foreseen their uses, and so had I. We followed the logic of that for a time long enough to get pretty far past what wholesome Outing Club types would allow themselves in those days. She had, in an early move that almost made me faint with lust, shed her hiking boots, and she was unbuttoning and rebuttoning the top of my shirt when she gave a funny little squeak, and her body stiffened.

"Oh, look," she whispered. "It *is* an eagle!" And as I turned to follow her enchanted dark gaze into the sky behind me, the rain began.

4. White Mice

Exactly a week later, the doorbell rang as I was trying to make sense of a bunch of pretty scrappy lab data ("Total Hardness of a Natural Water Sample"). I had got the water from the father of all waters, and the numbers about it by myself. Markus Gewissner was still out of classes and labs; the official word was mononucleosis, but I'd bet the real cause was Sophie Cushing: her own amoebae, her chicken soup, the drain on Markus' vital essences. I kept it to myself, following Anna Rosen's advice to say nothing if nothing nice came to mind.

In fact it was Anna herself who mostly came to mind that week. I had seen little of her and a great deal of the flaming ring of prohibitions that surrounded her. Today at last she had wiggled out to spend an afternoon out in Ladue with Nancy von Bayern - about whom, if Papa had his wits about him, he would have worried far more than about me - and had promised to call me when she could. When I heard my mother's familiar anxious tread on the steps I allowed myself to pretend that she was coming to announce that Anna was at the door.

"There's a gentleman here to see you, Oren. He looks worried about something."

Mother had never met Harvey Napperson, so that was the best description she could give. He was always worried about something. When I came into the living room, he was perched on the outer three inches of our old sofa, looking even more tense than usual.

"Oren, I'm sorry to intrude on your afternoon, and I'll try not to take any more of your time than I can help."

"Is it still about that notebook, sir?"

"Yup. Oren, we have turned the place upside down looking for it. Amos is a nervous wreck. Are you absolutely <u>sure</u> you don't have it?"

"Absolutely, sir." I spoke with a clean conscience, for I had in fact thought about it some in the weeks since the strange little interview at Molar, and satisfied myself not only that I did not have it, but had certainly turned it over to Amos. I explained this to Napperson with sufficient detail, emphasis, and documentation that he looked reconciled about it.

"Hm. Well, do you think you could go over your work with me in enough detail that we could reconstruct what that sample - the liquid in the tank car that spilled - was?"

I glanced involuntarily at the telephone in the dining room. It was silent now, sure, but even as I watched it Anna could be dialing in Ladue. I pictured that happening, but instead of "GRavois 4132" she seemed to be spelling out Be nice, Oren. So I put on an earnest face and sat next to Napperson.

"Sir, I really doubt we can pull that one sample out of all that must be in that notebook, from memory."

"Hm. And no good in court, anyhow, if we could."

"Court?"

Napperson grimaced and shrugged. "In case..."

"Well, did you know exactly what you were looking for? Maybe we could at least figure out what it looked like. Was it the one with the missing back cover?"

"Nope. We found that one in the stack."

I racked my memory, which is a good way not to remember anything. "Well, OK, what did the one just after it look like?"

Napperson gave, for him, a genuine smile. "Good thought, Oren. Let's see. That'd be the last one you used, right? It was red, with a spiral binding. Never would have used it if we'd had a real bound one."

You had plenty, you cheapskate. "OK, then it was the last partial bound notebook. It was blue, with a picric acid stain on the last page and a big white ring where I set a 600-ml beaker of caustic down on it one time."

Napperson - grateful guy - scowled. "Bad technique to get corrosive chemicals on the outside of a beaker, son."

"Yes, sir. The beaker cracked with the heat of the caustic pellets dissolving, and that's why I had to set it down fast on something soft, and why it was leaking."

"I see. You probably let a pellet fuse itself to the glass, and localized the heat of solution at that one spot. That'll crack 'em every time. Gotta keep those pellets stirring around..."

He gave himself a little shake, and me a quick smile. "Well, your mistake is our luck this time, I'd say. I can't think where it could be that we haven't already looked, but it might help to know what it looks like. Thank you, son. I appreciate your devoting some thought to this, mm, this little problem."

He didn't smile any more before he left - twice in one interview was probably over budget - but he did look a little less tense as he went out to where he had parked in a bus zone. He was looking at his watch, figuring if he had time to get over to Molar for another look, so he didn't see the cop writing his ticket. My guess is, ticket and all, he would leave it on the curb rather than let this lead grow any colder. As I was watching him push his fedora back to listen to the cop, the phone rang behind me.

"I got it," I hollered, and slammed the door on Harvey Napperson and his mystery chemical. It was Anna this time all right, the voice that could promise bliss speaking of psalms. But now it was not just her way of talking; real bliss was waiting behind the voice, and after a dry week I was ready to get on with it.

The thunderstorm on Taum Sauk - a surprise only for those who were not keeping an eye on the weather - had pretty well washed away Francesca and Paolo and left us our shivering selves, spare clothing and supplies down in the van where we'd left them. We had plenty of time left for what new wonders Mother Nature might have had up her floppy sleeve, like the sudden chill that came with the storm, but we didn't fancy seeing them in wet clothes. I pocketed a chunk of the springy grey moss that lined our bower, and we picked up our stuff, looked for shelter and found none, and headed back down a trail that was now a minor stream, pursued by jealous lightning. We both fell several times, I headlong, and Anna the reverse on a rocky switchback.

I'm not sure what made her slip; maybe a dancer's confidence in her own balance and poise. I had just negotiated a slick and rocky place, and turned to warn Anna about it as she followed. I had only time to sense her careening, hands-off entry onto it when her foot shot straight out, and she sat down hard on edgewise jutting slates. She sat biting her lip for a moment, and rose limping and fighting tears. It was sheer out-of-breath, not common sense, that kept me from telling her not to fling herself around like that. She certainly was a flinger, though. When we got warmed up by the work of falling and getting up to fall again, and fleeing lightning, we veered into a soaked euphoria that made us even less careful than we had been, and we both took muddy slides down slopes that had been easy scrambles on the way up. By the time we reached the last overlook and the rain had given way to chilly winds, we were filthy and exhausted; but we got a reward.

Stretched before us was a low-angle look at the rolling hills east of Taum Sauk, with the storm system hanging over them and heading for Illinois. As we stopped to look at it, late sunlight broke around the flanks of the mountain, and a gigantic double rainbow, starting with a little patch at the top, grew until it filled the eastern sky.

"Oh, boy," I managed. Anna leaned against me and put her arm around my waist, and we stood there steaming until the show was over. As it began to fade, Anna heaved a sigh worthy of Sophie Cushing, and I learned something new about her eyes: in certain lights, or moods, or angles, you could see little flakes of light below the surface of the strong tea.

"I don't believe," she said carefully; "No, I'm pretty sure, that I have never been so happy as I am right now. Sore tail and all. This is the very best moment of my entire life so far, is what I guess I mean. Thank you, Oren Dienst, for bringing me, Anna Catherine Rosen, to this exact moment. And for being part of it. I think you and I are going to have a wonderful time."

And there it was, folks. The ballgame.

"That is, - That is, if *you* would be interested. I mean I kind of figured you were; I didn't mean to - "

I gave a crow of joy. "Are you kidding? Interested? Holy *shit*, Anna, I've never been so interested in my life! I'm . . I'm . ."

I grabbed her, not roughly, and we kissed long and thoughtfully while the last of the rainbow disappeared over the distant river. I grew calm, thinking of all the time we had before us.

"God gave Noah the rainbow sign," she whispered at last.

"No more water but the fire next time," I gloated. I patted her butt, not completely lasciviously, but in the spirit of a fellow athlete. "Let's get down to the van before we get cold again. If we get sore throats and can't sing, what would Markus and Sophie think of us?"

"Don't mock the messenger. Markus sent us his best wishes for a beautiful experience. And we've had one."

"Two," I said, "not to brag or anything. Which one do you think was Markus's?"

"They were both ours, I think. Markus and Sophie get credit for the concept; but I think we're going to have to give you Best Screenplay."

"I want to thank Dan Alighieri, who's just one beautiful guy. After him, it was just a bunch of balderdash I was making up as I went along. Come on, but be careful."

"Wait a minute, Oren. First of all, maybe so, but it was great balderdash, the very best balderdash, and you made it up for me. But the other thing is ..."

She ran a hand through her hair. "I need to talk to you about something that ...well, I haven't been very honest with you about. I've been putting this off up to now, because who knew how this might turn out? But if you're really interested, the same as I am ..."

"What is it?" A little electric motor of tension began to spin quietly in my belly.

"You've been so much fun, and you seem to really care about me. Had you formed any opinion at all about how old I might be?"

"Not really. You seem to change, somehow. I don't know. My age, or a maybe little older, most of the time, though I've seen you looking about seventeen, when - "

"A lot older than you, Oren." She gritted her teeth and looked out over the valley. "Four years. I'm an overaged graduate student. Does that bother you?"

Not unless you mean hot and bothered. The little motor turned out to be hooked up to a generator and a big copper wire running straight spineward.

"You're 24?" *A grown woman, my God.* "Fantastic. Let me check something else here, while we're doing this. You're Jewish? You said 'us' about Jews in that, that reading. Which was simply wonderful, by the – "

She looked at the sky. "I'm Catholic."

"Right, right, Cor Mariae, sure. But I mean, your, uh, your family ..."

"My father was a Jew and my mother is Catholic. I was raised Catholic. Jews would deny it, but by certain standards, I'm a Jew, all right. Racially mongrelized, I think they used to put it. Had we better go home now?"

"No. So if we got married and had children, they'd be - "

"A quarter Jewish. It doesn't sound as if we'd better pursue this. It's been nice - "

"Hush. If anybody'd told me I would ever wind up with a 24-year-old somewhat Jewish girl friend, I'd have thought they were crazy, because why would she mess with a runny-nosed agnosto-Methodist kid four grades behind her? Well, for one thing, she seems to be willing to in spite of everything. And in the second place, her nose is running too, I guess it's the rain and all, or falling down back there, but it is, all right. So we've got that in common, and we're both pretty good at spotting likely places to neck, that's another thing. Let's see, we're both better at climbing hills than getting down, and now we're both wet and cold. We both seem to be pretty interested in sex, and as far as I'm concerned, just your eyes have simply made rosemeat of my heart. I'm kind of running on here, because I can't bear to ask if you see me as some kind of kid, or hobby, or something."

She wiped her nose thoughtfully. "Oh, Oren, God, no. I see you as the kindest, sexiest, funniest man I've ever - This is just so ... " She lifted spread fingers toward the departing storm.

"Well. I guess I can live with that. We might be on to something new here; guys always date younger women. Is there a different set of rules for this?"

"Sure, I pay you an allowance and you light my cigarettes for me. Why don't we make up our own rules?"

"OK. Well, I've got a candidate for Rule One. No further discussion of ages. Or religions. We were born a while ago, or so, on desert islands, and raised by benevolent cormorants, and all records have been swept away by a typhoon."

She traced circles on my wet shirt with her finger. "Cormorants keep lousy records anyway, write 'em on fish, and then eat the ... the ... OK, I agree to Rule One. Don't you forget it when we're middle-aged, though."

"You want me to hang around till we're middle-aged? I'm honored."

"Oh, God. That was good and presumptuous, wasn't it? I didn't mean ..."

"It was prescient. However you pronounce that. I was getting to it, so let's make it official. You want to think about hanging around till we're middle-aged? Or more?"

She grinned like the teenager I'd seen in the Cor Mariae ranks. "Yes, Oren. Let's do it. Or anyhow, get started on it this week."

OK, so I kissed her again, or she kissed me, and this time I knew who I was kissing, and it was all the sweeter. When I pulled back, she looked pretty much my age. I touched the near-invisible lines under her eyes. She locked eyes with me for a good long time, and placed a tentative hand under my heart.

"Rosemeat?"

I shrugged. "I have to admit, Markus' roommate spent a half hour making that up in lab last week, after he finally got a date with this cheerleader he's been sighing and gritting his teeth about. It started out, "Your eyes are like flowers and they make my heart into hamburger." By the time we'd all contributed, he was pretty sure it would make her knees weak. I don't think it was meant to be used in passing, that way."

I put on an earnest face. "Look, though, Anna. If you're 24 years old, how is it you're so scared of your father? You could be out on your own, couldn't you?"

She didn't really answer, but just shivered. And since I was shivering too in the blustery little after-storm winds, I suggested reluctantly that we might as well get on down to the van. "Come on, let's get warm. Be careful, though."

"Teach your granny to suck eggs, Dienst. You think I can hobble any way but carefully?"

At the van, I stood outside while she went in first to put on the dry sweatshirt and clean shorts she'd brought. I certainly had shown no such foresight, and I was in for a damp drive home. "Oh, man," came her voice, muffled by the steel panels. "Am I gonna be black and blue. You ought to see my butt."

Eventually the door slid back, and she gimped out, dry but barefoot. The sweatshirt was big enough to cover the shorts, and the effect was remarkable. "Your turn," she chirped. When I explained that I had no resources for a turn, she shrugged. "Well, you can't wear those filthy wet things all the way home. Can you? Look, there's a blanket back there, why don't you just strip and wrap up in it, and I'll drive home?"

I looked at her for a moment, and had the sense to refuse. "Because, if you think you're going to sit next to me for two hours wearing, what, at most two total garments? And then drop me out in the middle of the Washington U. campus wearing nothing but a blanket - with a mixed audience of women and children - well - "

"Well, yourself. Suffer, then. But if you think I'm going to hover over you with chicken soup and cushions like Sophie when you catch cold, you're - "

"Sophie who?"

On the way back, while sunset came across the hills, we gloated over our future like a pair of misers who'd won a lottery. We agreed that things had gone awfully fast, and maybe another good rule would be to ease up on the hormonal side for a while and have some ordinary harmless dates: movies, studying, that kind of thing, while we got to know each other better.

"I mean," I said, not meaning it at all, "besides this raging sex thing, what have we got in common? Maybe we'll hate each other's, mm, politics or something." She laughed, I laughed, and she patted my wet thigh. I noticed for the first time how graceful her fingers were, smooth and clean even after our muddy scramble.

"Well, Oren, let's take a chance. Thing is, you know how you're always anxious about whether the other person thinks you're attractive, or wants to kiss you or not, all that? We took care of that first, that's all."

Yes, and we had come to it by a fairly honorable approach. So what was left but to pay some dues on the purely social side? To become known as a "couple," to meet each other's family and that sort of thing. And if that left a little bit to luck in terms of details, give us credit for taking a stab at it.

So now, over a chaste phone line, we were at last ready to start. "Here's the deal," she said. "When I got home I went straight to my room and changed, and then I went on over dinner about what a jolly bunch the Outing Club is, and how nice everybody had been - no lie there - and how one boy in particular had seemed very pleasant and smart, and how he'd asked me for a date, but I said he would have to come and meet my parents first, because that's what I'm supposed to say. So, brace yourself: I've lined it up for dinner with them tonight at six, if you're free."

I felt a little qualm about this. Partly, maybe, about the false pretenses involved. Partly because my one contact with Anna's parents had been when I had mistakenly tried to short-circuit protocol and call her the morning after the hike. No answer the first try because, heathen that I was, I had called at 10:30 on a Sunday morning. At 1:30, though, I got an adult male who simply picked up the phone, said, "We are at dinner," and slammed it down again.

But the main source of my hesitation was the quaver I heard in Anna's voice when she said "Brace yourself." What kind of parents sent thrills of fear down the spine of a grown woman?

The kind itching to be slain by a knight in armor. "I'll be there," I said. "What's the drill?"

*   *

"You are how old, Mr. Dienst?"

"I'll be 21 in December, sir." I could see where Anna, who stood a slim 5'5", could be terrified of Arnold Rosen. I'm tall like my father, but lanky; Arnold was huge, both tall and fat, his face set in a permanent scowl. I suppose the gritty Tirolean accent wouldn't have meant much to her, who grew up among them, but it certainly completed the picture for me.

"You are twenty. Well, I suppose that is appropriate; Anna will not be in her teens much longer."

"Sir? I understood - "

"I suppose you are not employed, are you?"

"Not full time. I work about ten hours a week for a violinmaker downtown, and I have a campus job. And, of course, I'm enrolled full time at the university. But - "

"You wouldn't be here if you weren't. I can't stand a slacker, and I won't have one hanging around Anna. What are you studying?"

"Chemical engineering. My father - "

"Hnh. Beats poetry, I guess. Or music. Anna said you're some kind of musician."

"I play cello, but it's not, uh, not professionally. About ... you said Anna - "

"Speak up. Hobby, is it?"

"I suppose you could say that."

"Hnh. Don't be offended. Brandy?"

"No, thank you, sir."

"Good thing, or you'd have been out of here. Don't drink, eh?"

I took a fresh grip on temper and tongue. I had already thought of ledges and rainbows until they were worn thin. What was keeping me going now was the memory of Anna, scared but stubborn, smoothing her skirt over a fanny that this sadistic oaf had hit so many times that she flinched at the word "paddle." And considerable curiosity about his notion of her age. I mean, he ought to know, right? Well, maybe not.

"No," I lied.

"Liar. All college boys drink. If I find out you've been drinking around Anna, or letting her drink, I'll cane you, do you hear me?"

"Sir, I believe I hear Mrs. Rosen calling us to dinner."

And a damn good thing, too.

The Cello Francesca, *or* Balderdash

Dinner was a diluted form of the same punishment, but now with Anna and Mrs. Rosen - the source, I saw, of the overbite I loved - as witnesses. Anna did her best to keep the conversation general, but I could see that she knew how far she could go in managing her stepfather, and it wasn't very far. He bullied her and he bullied and insulted his wife - why in hell had she married the guy? - and he kept up his barrage at me, asking what my father worked at, and when I explained that my father was no longer living, asking what he <u>had</u> done; and then dismissing with a sniff the news that my father had been a choirmaster. Finally, he tossed his napkin on his plate and rose to loom over us.

"Young man," he said, "I cannot express with what reluctance I may give my approval for you to see Anna socially; but I suppose I must give it. I will hold you strictly accountable for her well-being in every way. If at any time she returns to this house unhappy, or disheveled, I will seek you out and thrash you myself, wherever you may be. If you feed her liquor or lead her astray in sexual matters, I will have you horsewhipped. Anna is young and inexperienced, but she can be a bit of a slut. You will not take advantage - "

"What?!" It was only because Anna turned perfectly white that I knew I had heard him right. I had a flash of Anna and myself headed for a Mexican circus in a boxcar. Well, if she would join me, I was game. For now, she was slumped in her chair with her face in her hands, looking about fourteen years old; I could see the shine of tears through her fingers. And I could see the old bastard sitting there and daring me to go on. So I gave him what he was looking for.

"Mr. Rosen, it is only because I had hoped to know Anna's family better that I've come here to listen to your pompous drivel. You have insulted me nonstop for (I glanced at my watch) almost two hours. Very well, I didn't expect that, but no harm done. You have insulted my father, but he is not here to suffer it. Your entire character is an insult to your wife, who must long since have realized what a blunder it was to have married you. You forgot to insult my mother, but perhaps you were saving that for another time. I am glad to say that you have lost the chance, for I will not return to listen to the kind of idiot -

the kind of pathetic wretch who would stoop to insulting his own daughter. Sir, you are unfit to be Anna's parent, or anyone else's, and I challenge you to satisfy me for insulting her, right now or at a time of your choosing. Well, sir?"

Quiet ensued. I sat, quivering righteously, reviewing the script. "Drivel?" Why hadn't I made it "abuse?" On the whole, though, I guessed I had done what I could. Mrs. Rosen looked frosty and resentful, Anna remained exactly as she was, and Arnold Rosen sat scowling - oddly, not at me, but at his wife.

"What say, Rosa?"

She sat perfectly still for a moment, then gave a little grimace, and leveled her dark eyebrows at him. "Peh;" she shrugged. "I'd give 'im an eight, eight-an-a-half. Intense, you know, but short, given the provocation. Never used vulgar language, that counts. Make it a nine."

"Damn sight better than those other twerps. I'll go along with an eight." He turned to me. "Not bad. 'Idiot' was weak, you should have thought of 'pathetic wretch' first. You about got to me with the part about Mrs. Rosen; don't ever try that again. And she's right, you never called me a dirty name. But I can see you're ready to fight me, and I don't think you'd let any other pathetic wretch insult Anna either. Date her, with my blessing; evenings and weekends only, and not every evening, or every weekend. The stuff about caning still holds." He grinned at me, the ... well, the pathetic wretch.

*   *

Anna smiled and put a smooth hand on my cheek.

"Honest, Oren, I had no idea he'd pull something like that. There were no other twerps, and no scoring system. He was only serious about the slut stuff, that's what he calls me when he punishes me for acting too free and easy. But he knew he'd gone too far with that when you - oh, you should have seen yourself, Oren. You about took my ... oh, my breath away, I guess. I never thought much of people who say that, but ... Mother came up with the scoring business to rescue him. She's always having to do that; that was the signal, when he asked her what she thought."

"Jesus, Anna, I don't care if he was kidding or not. If he ever talks about you like that again, I'll - "

"Hush, you sound just like him."

I calmed down at that, and looked down at brown water careening away under us while the steamer *Admiral*'s paddle wheels and dance band cast strings of pearls across it. Anna placed a careful hand over mine to soothe its clutch on the rail. I looked out at the Illinois farms and rail yards and then at her. She looked absolutely great, of course, in a black dress and creamy, buttoned-up sweater that made a crow's-quill etching of her eyes and hair in the falling sun. We were on a parentally sanctioned Date, and as long as I returned her sober, undisheveled, and on time at the foot of the gangplank where her noncommittal mother and stepfather had delivered her - God forbid I should pick her up at home on this trial run and thus maybe carry her off to a bar or a motel - why, we were welcome to repeat the experience. There was an unspoken codicil - or was it just my hope? - that if she returned undefiled, less chaperonage might be needed in the future. I held Anna at arm's length (well, a bent arm) and looked in her eyes.

"Why did he say you're still a teenager?"

She blushed angrily. "Did he say that? He knows better - I think; he has this crazy idea, he doesn't want me to get away, so he's just been pretending I'm nineteen for years. It never bothered me."

"You never thought about moving out?"

She shrugged patiently, having already ducked this question once. "Sure. The time I tried, he came and found me and spanked me with his belt until I bled, and the cops let him do it. I'm trying to save my money to get really far away, and it's cheap living there till I finish my MA. Up to now, it hasn't mattered so much. Mama is nice when he's not around."

I opened my mouth, and then thought better of my immediate reaction. After all, I was still at home too. "The thing is, how does your mother stand him? Why does she put up with it?"

"What choice does she have? They're Catholic."

"Why did she - never mind. Bad question."

She married him because Papi - Anna's real father - wanted her to. Arnold was Anna's uncle, and it was an option among Jews at that time. Papi was born in Salzburg, and he met Anna's mother on a vacation hike in the Dolomites in 1926. She was from Bolzano, a smart girl from a tight Italian family who couldn't allow her to get interested in a Jewish editor from Austria. She had to run away herself, already pregnant with Anna, and he met her at Brixen in a Daimler touring car and drove her in triumph over the Brenner to a wedding in Innsbruck that his brother Arnold had arranged with a corrupt priest. Just before the Nazis took over in 1938, Uncle Arnold converted to Catholicism and got a job as a railroad worker on the Innsbruck - Bolzano line. On the night of Anna's eleventh birthday, troopers smashed up Papi's office and came for him at home. They beat him up while she watched, still wearing her party hat.

"I remember every time they hit Papi as if it happened last night. Before they took him away, he managed to tell Mama to go to Uncle Arnold. After we got word from the prison that Papi was dead, Uncle Arnold brought us to Italy in a baggage car, in a horrible snowstorm. I'm sure they only let us go because Mama was Catholic, and I went to school at the convent. He took us in and told me he would be my new Papi. I really don't remember much about it, but living in Italy, and then in Switzerland and Cuba, Uncle Arnold just gradually became Papa. And . . ." She ended with a tearful little shrug.

How many nightmares and rebellions and spankings lay behind that shrug, it now occurs to me to wonder. It was all in that voluminous "And." I brought to it then all the insight of a relatively untroubled 20-year-old. As far as I was concerned, the South Tirol of 1938 was in an alternate universe, and Anna's troubles best approached by murdering Arnold Rosen, good riddance, and now what? But even I could see that she needed what I would be pleased to give: happiness and love. Or so it seemed to me then.

So it seemed, so it seemed to me then. "It's very complicated and sad, isn't it? I certainly admire you for coming through it as nice and cool as you are. What if we went down and danced?"

"What if? I think we'd have a good time, Oren."

And boy, did we. I made a little ceremony of it, bowing and offering her my arm for our first dance, as I told myself I would do with every first, right through carrying her across the threshold of our - whatever. She gave me her coolest Audrey Hepburn smile and lightly draped her arm over mine. And with that out of the way, we devoted ourselves to the only dance ever done in the '50's, the Slow Shuffle, which consisted of beginning in more or less Miss Conley's Dance Cotillion position and slowly getting closer and hotter and more exactly in alignment, while performing a soft, more or less rhythmic wobble. Anna shed her sweater, revealing lithe and sleeveless upper reaches. The womanly breasts I had admired but so far only sketchily approached touching proved unafraid of firmer contact, which occurred in the neighborhood of my diaphragm or, loosely, "heart," just where a cello rests. Having already put myself in line for one horsewhipping, I was quickly in jeopardy of another, as Anna found, every 16 bars, another stretch of body to press against me. Her left hand crept around to my left shoulder and played little arabesque variations around a favored point, the shy fingers reminiscing about touching me there on our first malt date.

We danced, we took breaks on the deck to cool off and talk nonsense, and we went back to it. We pooled funds to come up with $2 to get our picture taken, with two copies. I have mine still, a little battered from being taped up and taken down and moved and stared at and thrown into drawers. In sharp focus, a young couple of indeterminate age, smiling dizzily at the camera, holding hands. Their elbows are propped on a pipe railing next to a life preserver, and there is a dusky glint of water in the background. The woman is slim, relatively collected, one foot raised to the lower rail, her body a graceful integral; the boy looks like someone just swatted him with a sledgehammer.

At some point, the Admiral reached its apogee and turned around to head back to St. Louis, without our awareness. The band was winding down, playing the Jackie Gleason stuff that makes most dancers think about getting off their feet, and I whispered, drunk on secretions, "If we don't take a break I'm going to have a, uh, an ..."

"I've already had two. Not to brag or anything."

And that, straight into my ear in her hottest alto, just about did it. "Cripes," I blushed. "Is that what that little squeak was? I thought you were going to sneeze."

"I hoped you wouldn't notice. That was the second one, which was about twice as . . ."

"Stop! Jesus, you relentless girl. I'm thinking of a cow. I'm thinking about - uh, the Browns, took three out of four from the Senators this week. Oh, gosh, don't! Oh, geez . . . Darn you."

Anna sighed and went on nibbling my ear, and gently rubbed my neck and held me close so I wouldn't be embarrassed. "I just thought - well, it's like when somebody falls in a swimming pool in their good clothes. They want to share the fun with all the dry people standing around the edge."

"Marco Polo. Thing is, I get wetter than you."

"Poor boy. Seems like that's the way it is with us, doesn't it? I bet you didn't bring dry clothes this time, either."

I pulled back and looked at her; she was a little puffy and flushed, and her neatly brushed hair was sticking in little wisps to a shiny forehead. "Why don't we wrap me in a blanket for the trip home? Papa'd never suspect anything."

She tucked herself against me and whispered slowly, "We could probably find a better use for a blanket," getting her tongue right into my ear, but I was bulletproof now.

"Hah. Do your worst, sl - sister." Shit, I barely avoided saying "slut". She figured it out, though, and she got quiet and pulled away from me. I looked into her face, and it was closed and hurt.

"Anna. I did almost say that. I'm so sorry, I was just talking at random and kidding around. You know - surely you know how I feel about you."

She didn't make it easy. She turned her head away, and bit her knuckle, and I could see tears coming down the cheek that was nearest me. When I put my hand on her shoulder, she started to pull away, and then sighed, "Give me a minute. I'll be outside, cooling off. Slut that I am."

I used her minute to slink into the Gents' and sort of clean myself up. When I joined her, the Admiral was sidling up to its pier. We had only a few more minutes, for Papa himself would be there to take Anna home, as he had brought her, in the family Lincoln. I found her at the rail on the river side, looking out over darkness. Far out, lights on a string of northbound barges hung almost stationary against the current. She had combed her hair, smoothed her dress, and put on the many-buttoned sweater. She looked exactly as she had four hours ago.

"Anna, are you . . . " She reached out and drew me close.

I breathed easier. "And here we were going to have simple, wholesome dates."

"Right, and I guess this is why. Oren, I apologize for my behavior. I started it, and it got out of hand."

"I apologize, too. We egged each other on. And it was fun, you know? To hell with it, it was fun until I got stupid on it. We're going to have to be careful, that's all."

"That sounds good, Oren. Please, please take good care of me."

I kissed the top of her head, uncomfortably aware of a cold spot on my left thigh; late adolescence defined. The Admiral bumped gently on its moorings and gave a whistle blast.

"OK, here's the plan," she said, pushing me away. "I will go down the ramp first, smiling in a sheveled manner. You will stay behind me, touching me politely on the elbow to keep me from falling and bruising my maidenly - what did Paolo say? - my firm little butt again, like last time. Your behavior toward Papa will be - "

"Cool, manly, and evasive. Leave it to me. We can't possibly go another seven days before I see you again."

She gave me a quick hug as we walked toward the gangplank side of the fat steamer. "You can count on it. I will have studying I will need to do, so I will refuse your invitation to - oh, a string quartet, I think. But I will relent, right there on the phone, for a study date."

"Tomorrow."

"So long to wait? If we must."

"It won't be evening again until tomorrow."

"Lazy sun. Addio, Paolo mio."

"Call me Marco."

Her laugh faded to a cool smile as we reached the top of the gangplank.

Driving home from the levee, I was concerned with traffic and logistics, but I knew I had a lot to think about. The handover of Anna to her parents went fine; Arnold and I as nearly as possible ignored each other, which was OK with me. He seemed mostly concerned with Anna's profile, which was ivory soap. She might have just sat through an amusing lecture on cut glass, for all the heat she radiated.

In my bedroom, I climbed gingerly out of my clothes and lay down to take stock.

"A bit of a slut," said Arnold the sudden convert to Roman religion, the railwayman of 1930's fascism. As if she were a girl that a later time would find hanging around shopping malls. I could guess that might have fit some rebellious moment years ago, but the Anna I had just left would be thirty before I reached her present age. Though she seemed willing to be any age between sixteen and thirty, to be without inhibitions where I was concerned, and to have the same effect on me. Wasn't civilization built on inhibitions? I thought I'd read that somewhere. It made trains run on time. So then I evolved another theory, lying there and listening to psalms and choirs in the roar of my window fan. That inhibited speech and behavior result from being around people who don't somehow fit, as the wrong enzyme inhibits a reaction, or the wrong key rattles fruitlessly in a lock. But with one perfect partner who fits as, for example, Anna had fit against me on the dance floor, the lock opens, inhibitions fall away, one can say, do, be anything, any age at all, and to hell with chronology. And of course, I got so bothered by the implications of that, mixed with the memories of the dance floor, that I had to read *Quantitative Analysis: A Theoretical Approach* until I cooled off. When I could take no more of that, I just lay there wide awake and weightless and watched the darkness creep and modulate and suddenly blaze with the jangle of my alarm.

I will say this about our study date: sitting side by side at a scarred table in the library annex, we neither mentioned nor, as far as I know experienced, sex for the entire three hours. Anna was marvelous, lost in her work: plowing through *Le Figaro*, red-penciling a scrawled bit of Spanish homework from a tutee, settling back with a sigh over a two-volume edition of The Magic Mountain - in German, of course. The clock on the wall clicked and progressed, the floor creaked. Anna laughed gently.

"You should read this, Oren. There are things about Hans Castorp that are you, to the life. Can I ask you a question?"

I put down my slide rule, taking care not to bump it out of position until I could finish the calculation. "Sure."

"I'm sorry. I'm just barging right in, in the middle of something you're figuring out."

"Got it all figured. That's just numbers."

"Oren, did you spend a lot of time last night, you know, thinking it over?"

"Understatement."

"Well, were you as surprised as I was?"

"At myself? Yes."

"Both of us. Have you ever heard of truth serum?"

"That stuff Russians shoot into spies?"

"Oren, I just said everything that came into my mind last night. I've never talked or acted that way in my life, even bragging around other girls."

"What, you think somebody fed us truth serum?"

"No. I think we did it to each other. I have to watch everything I say around home, and in fifteen years around Papa, I've gotten good at it. This morning I was singing Stravinsky in the bathroom, and Papa got all sarcastic about 'songs of love.' I mean, hell, it was that 'Quoniam advena' passage. So, anyhow, I keep a tight lip around those two, even Mama, which is so sad. And along you come, and everything comes pouring out."

"I was thinking of it in terms of enzymes."

"How beautifully chemical."

"Well, it is, really. But I mean like when you fit some other molecule just perfectly, there's this powerful reaction that was all wound up ready to happen, and everything changes."

She aligned her books along the edge of the table. "Everything changes. And then do the enzymes say, Jesus, I'm in love?"

What gripped me then might have been fear; it felt no different. "Is that what's going on here? Is that why we act like a pair of, of white mice when they leave us alone on a boat?"

"I'm afraid we may have to be prepared to think in those terms." She was sitting like a child, hands folded in her lap and her face lowered toward the table, flushed and bright-eyed, and she really did have a worried little frown.

"Well," I husked, "It's nothing to get upset about. This is something we can get through together if we just stay calm. We'll need exercise and wholesome food and plenty of clean, shredded newspapers. And of course, we'll have to be allowed to mate regularly."

"I'll speak to Papa."

5. The Cello Francesca

The next evening I had a Civic rehearsal, and then Stravinsky, sans choir, so by the time we worked in a movie, the three-day fast had brought us to such a pitch that Anna could not quite re-shevel to the required smooth envelope by the time - following Arnold's strict chronology - I absolutely had to have her back home. Don't ask me why we put up with Arnold; he was huge, it was 1953. She was grooming furiously as I drove down Bryn Mawr Avenue, but these things take time. I got a doleful note (delivered by Markus, via Sophie, Nancy von Bayern, and a girl who, incredibly, knew them both) the next afternoon: "*I think Papa suspects something. You delivered me way too happy last night, and we are off to Springfield for a week, but I will send word when I can. Addio.*"

OK, fine, I thought. We'll know better next time, or we'll figure a way around it. In the meantime, my slide rule was still hung up in the same place it had been when Anna interrupted its slippy business Sunday night. I could finish that and get caught up, even ahead of things before she returned; I could practice my Stravinsky part, and I would spend evenings at Di Salvo's shop making up for lost hours.

That evening, I finished a week's worth of calculus and two lab reports before I collapsed and sat staring at the little piece of moss I'd taken from the bower on Taum Sauk. I picked it up and smelled it to bring back that hot, sensuous moment we had stood outside the grove of cedars, knowing what was coming. The smell was there, but faint. I took it to the sink and wet it a bit to encourage it, and lay for probably a half hour breathing through the poor thing, and then just stared at it some more. Holy Christ, I thought. This is what they mean. I'm worshiping the ground she walked on.

Monday night was Mollie Biedermeyer's turn to drive to the Civic rehearsal, but she called about an hour ahead (setting off a false dawn when my mother took the call and told me archly that "a female" wanted me) and said she was having some arm trouble that seemed to be aggravated by maneuvering her heavy Buick, and would I mind driving?

On the way to the rehearsal I thought she looked a bit raggedy; for example, as if it was getting to be more bother than it was worth to erect the fortress of braid that always circled her head. Her hair was simply pulled back into an untidy bun, from which dull little wisps were floating. When I had to slam on the brakes to keep from hitting a kid who darted into the street, she caught herself against the dash with a little cry of pain. If I had been conscious of anything but my immediate preoccupations, I might have been a bit more concerned. As it was, she seemed OK by the time I wheeled us to the stage door.

Jacob Oxendine appeared at Mollie's door like a bell captain and opened it for her. "A very good evening, Miss Biedermeyer; evening, Mr. Dienst. Indian summer, as I think we must now call it, is with us still. For all its melancholy, it is by far the loveliest time of the year, and I hope it remains for some time. It puts me in mind of a Brahms symphony. Please let me assist you, Miss Biedermeyer, while Mr. Dienst parks his car." I drove off to a weedy concrete slab in the middle of weedy earth that served as our parking lot. By the time I got back to the Orpheum, Mollie was in her seat fitting the pieces of her flute together and breathing little warming hoots into it.

We were doing the Tchaikowsky *Romeo and Juliet* as sugar coating for the Bohemian Nocturnes, and that was another piece that badly needed attention from me. Soaring solo lines, pathos, irony, rapid arpeggios in five sharps, death. It alone would have justified all the practice time I could give it, and there was always Stravinsky lurking in another venue. I sat down and got to work, at least to stave off the humiliating attentions of Hans Brocklin for missing egregiously. Luckily, some of the scale passages were straight out of Klengel, and once I recognized them they were easier. A little tougher was to arrive at what Brocklin called the "big old sex theme" at the end of a resounding triplets passage, on time, in tune, fortissimo, and with bite and penetration in the sound.

In this respect, at least, the Tomastik strings I had earned cooking varnish were a real help. Taking off the old set and putting on anything new would have been a good move, but these were way beyond that. They were "stark" (loud) gauge for Fournier's solo performance with the Symphony, and they had a lot of sound, even on my poor old cello. I had quit bonking it on doors since they were on it. I found it highly fitting that they were giving me a boost on this hyper-romantic stuff just now; I could identify with just about every element of this tale of young lovers. Except for the star-crossed part, of course.

After the rehearsal, I looked around for Mollie, and did not find her. I was wondering whether to be really worried about her at last, when Jacob Oxendine appeared at my side. "Miss Biedermeyer asked me to fetch you, Mr. Dienst. She was taken poorly during the rehearsal, and I have shown her to a place where she could lie down and rest. If you would come with me."

OK, now I was truly worried. With Friar Lawrence's theme honking mournfully in the back of my mind, I followed Jacob backstage and up four or five steps to a green door that still bore a scruffy gold star on it. Jacob knocked, and we entered. It was a dressing room, evidently still in occasional use. The light was coming from bulbs around a makeup mirror behind a dressing table that bore assorted bottles and brushes, and a powder puff that looked almost new. Furniture consisted of a costume rack, a somewhat sprung-looking easy chair, a dressing screen straight out of "Gunsmoke," and a plush couch of the Freudian sort, on which Mollie Biedermeyer was lying, ankles modestly crossed and with a cloth over her eyes. She sat up and looked alert when we came in.

"Boy, Jacob, I don't know what was in that stuff, but it absolutely did the trick. What was it?"

Jacob was evasive, though it was hard to notice that through the fog of words. It was a remedy that he knew of from back home, it was "lightly - just lightly" fermented, and gathering the ingredients could be done only by flat-bottom boat in the back reaches of the Lumber River and a few of its tributaries in Robeson County, North Carolina.

"You mean it's some kind of swamp berries?" I asked, dumbly enough. Jacob looked offended, and then relaxed into an ironic darkie slouch.

"Be's a right many parts to her, Mist' Dienst," he chuckled. "En they all f'm right far back. Yas, suh. Hyeh."

Mollie opened her eyes wider and gave Jacob a slightly flushed, appraising look.

"Jacob," she said in a very relaxed voice, "don't ever leave us. Except maybe to go back and stock up on that lovely medicine. Are you ready to go, Oren?"

"Soon as I pack up," I said, and stepped aside to let her precede me out the door.

"Go and do so. I will be with you very shortly."

OK; off I went. Mollie wasn't exactly on my heels, though she came along, still looking a good deal zippier than, now I thought back, she had in several months. In fact, she was more than flushed, she was blushing - just lightly. On the way to drop her off, she was humming the music from the rehearsal, which she had not done for a while.

"That must be some medicine," I hazarded, and then wondered if I had sounded ironic in my turn. But she just smiled.

"For the first time in weeks, Oren, I am feeling no pain. And I mean that literally, not like what people say when you're - oh, you know … "

"Drunk?"

"Exactly." A little frosty, but it didn't last. "Jacob's people were the first on that land, Oren. They know a great deal. He said a little - well, I suppose it must have been a prayer, when he gave it to me. It sounded exactly like English, with a Southern accent; but I could not understand a word of it. He said that the gatherer and the maker, and the giver of the medicine must each have a certain, oh, frame of mind at the time they do their part, and that he was getting himself straight to give it."

"Did he tell you how to get yourself straight to take it?"

Mollie raised a hand to her hair and tucked in some of the little floating wisps. The movement was apparently not at all painful. "Yes, he did."

I dropped off Mollie, yawning creakily, at her Tower Grove apartment. I suspected she hadn't been sleeping much, but that Jacob's just lightly fermented miracle would see to that. And then I indulged a guilty pleasure.

Anna was out of town and unreachable - I didn't even know whether it was Springfield, Missouri, Illinois, or Ohio she had been spirited off to. I was without obligations and, not having the advantage of Lumbee pharmacology, I was not sleepy. In fact, I was wound up tight. Montagus and Capulets were leaping and dueling across the orchestra in my brain, and there would be very little sleep until they quieted down. I headed for Di Salvo's to put in an all-nighter, hoping to wipe out my time deficit at a single blow.

And found the man himself there, standing with a broom in his hand, in the back room. "Oren! Dio mio! Looked for you after rehearsal, you already gone off somewhere with Jacob, so I don't wait. Where you been lately?"

I considered, and decided that there was no reason to be devious with Pietro Di Salvo. "Well, there's this girl . ."

"Dio! You found a girl, you even more worthless than ever. What do we keep you around for, you gonna chase girls?"

But he was giving me a sort of man-to-man grin, so I figured he was not too serious. "Anyhow, got a little something special to show you, now you just walk in out of the blue like you know it. Got your *ragazza* tucked in, have you?"

I figured having your *ragazza* tucked in might be some kind of Italian slang for having your fly buttoned, so I gave a noncommittal grunt; "Got a little something special involving a broom, eh?" Most of his little something specials consisted of situations that needed cleaning up, lifting, or re-doing, but I had wronged him this time.

"Broom for the feet, wise guy. Can't be tracking dust." And he opened a door at the back of the workshop to reveal a set of stairs ascending into darkness. I had once asked Di Salvo what lay behind this door, and his curt response, "Steps," had somehow convinced me that it was a downward passage leading to the tedious cellar, and quenched my curiosity. But now he handed me the broom and a damp rag, said "Clean shoes" with a sweeping motion, and gestured for me to follow him up. "Don't shuffle feet, now."

He had lined the stairway and the room above with old magazine covers, overlapping to hold back plaster dust from the walls and ceiling, and had a rubber runner and mats on the steps. We tiptoed past images of children and puppies, country doctors, covered bridges, Queen Elizabeth, a bombardier with a ring of soot around one eye, and Janet Leigh with an elegant hand draped over breasts that began at midpage and showed no signs of coming to an end in the lower right corner where a price, remarkably modest for all that, was printed. I noticed that this particular cover was not overlapped by any other.

At the head of the stairs we stepped into a little room with a skylight, a galaxy of <u>Lifes</u>, <u>Looks</u>, and <u>Posts</u> and, hanging by their scrolls from a wire that crossed the room, two brand-new violins and a cello. "Varnish these guys couple weeks ago. All that rain started right after, too cool for good drying. But come Indian summer, they got good and dry now " He rapped the cello's exposed belly and got a resonant bonk. "Ready to string up and start to play now, and I need a cello player for this little guy. Whaddya think?"

"OK, sure, I'd be glad to try it out. Long as you know I'm no big virtuoso."

"Don't need that, not for now. Need a guy that can pull the bow and let me listen, adjust, fix, listen some more. Come on."

He took the cello down from the wire and told me to bring the two fiddles along. Downstairs in the shop, he hung them on another wire, and picked up a rosewood tailpiece for the cello.

"Small cello, I think we try a light string, Tomastiks like yours. Expensive and don't last too long, but we're gonna give this little one a good start, eh?"

OK. So after he had installed a bridge and soundpost ("Watch close, Oren. Soundpost is what the French call the soul, we putting her soul in right now.") he plunked thoughtfully on the strings and pulled them into rough tune, swung it up to his eyes to sight along the bridge and adjusted its angle. He lowered the tailpin to the floor, spun the cello around once and leaned it toward me with a flourish.

"OK, Signore, let's hear. Wait a second, though. Bow matters, too. Wait here."

While Di Salvo was gone, I finished tuning, and looked over the cello. It was maybe a little smaller than normal, and a little deeper in the ribs to make up for it, with a dark and graceful belly and a scroll carved with a barely visible fern pattern. The fingerboard was of rosewood, lighter than the dark varnish, inverting the usual light varnish/ dark ebony contrast like a harpsichord's keyboard. It was joyful and lithe to hold; I felt a stir of delight as I turned it to look at the flame pattern on the back. The varnish was absolutely smooth; Di Salvo had rubbed it down lightly with fine pumice to give it a silken texture like a woman's skin. Feeling just a bit prurient, I held it up to peer into the *f*-holes to read the label:

Francesca
Petrus Salvatoris me fecit
in Urbis S. Ludovic.
Anno DOMINI 1953

Francesca? A little shiver started from my belly and cast about trying to decide whether to run up my spine or settle lower. I looked in the new violins: plain labels in English, no names. Di Salvo bustled in with a straight chair and a bow. "OK, sit, play."

The little cello fit nicely in my lap; it would be easy to get around on. "OK, what should I play?"

"Don't matter, just want to hear all the registers. Play a C-scale."

"OK, here goes." Well, wait, though, I thought. This is going to be the very first notes this thing will play, and with any luck it will go on for centuries. It ought to be something special. I lightly brushed the strings to check the tuning; I didn't want those first notes to be the drone of tuning up, but the new strings were still in tune. I pinged my second finger down on middle C, and played the opening bars of the Bach C major unaccompanied suite, a descending C scale followed by rolling ascents and arpeggios. It wasn't everything I had hoped for; there was a harshness around f, and I hit some unwritten double-stops when the curvature of the bridge didn't put the strings where my bow arm expected. When I ran out of memory on the Bach, I just played a scale, climbing chromatically into the high register. "No vibrato! No vibrato! Let me hear real notes!" Di Salvo yelled.

The bass was resonant and saturated, the middle register warm, but it included a wolf, and the resonance tailed off as I climbed into the higher reaches on the A string.

"Hm. Go up from open D again, then same thing on G string." I did. The wolf was much worse on the G string, where the choice was between almost no sound at all and a warbling honk.

"Gosh, that's a heck of a wolf. That's too bad."

"Any cello with a lot of resonance gonna have a wolf. Maybe we can tame him a little, otherwise gotta put on a wolf suppressor."

He peered into the shadowy interior, reached in with a curved post-setter, and tonked it gently against the soundpost, then tapped sideways on the bridge with his blunt fingertips. I heard a faint ticking sound as the bridge scooted over the new varnish. "Try again."

I tried. The whole midrange was more resonant and easy, and the wolf, though still there, was a lot quieter. "Holy sh - excuse me, Mr. Di Salvo. My goodness. Did that ever make a big difference. How'd you know which way to tap that stuff?"

Di Salvo gave me a look similar to Jacob Oxendine's in regard to swamp berries. "Luck, I guess. Better now, huh? Try up high."

I started on the open A and scaled the heights to the end of the fingerboard. There wasn't much there beyond the first octave, and in trying to bear down and make it come I produced opaque shrillness.

"Basta! Not an air raid, boy! Never mind. Probably cut some of the highs out when we fixed the wolf. But it's gonna get much better, few years. Varnish too new, joints too tight right now. Just play me something in middle range. Whole piece - if you know one."

So I played the slow *sarabande* from the C major suite. It sounded pretty good, and when I reached the end I repeated the

B section, getting some stuff that had been harsh and out of tune on the first pass. Di Salvo had closed his eyes and leaned back, his expression blank, concentrating, I guess, on the sounds. When I finished, he sat absolutely still for a few seconds, then his eyes popped open.

"Got better as you went along, hm? Knew what to expect. Player gotta get adjusted to cello too, it's not a one-way street. Cello breaks you in to what it wants, same as you break it in."

"It's a beautiful instrument. Is this that varnish that I made too dark?"

"Sure. I'm gonna waste a whole pot a varnish 'cause a punk kid can't read directions? Goes pretty good with the fingerboard, don't it?"

"It's - well. Beautiful. Who's Francesca?"

"Best fiddles get names of girls I love once upon a time. Got a Sara, a Maria, a Rosa, . ."

"I get it. Is there an Anna?"

"Your new ragazza named Anna?" he asked, giving me a better fix on the term. "Anna's a viola, belong to a guy out in San Francisco. Lighter color than this one, but just as good looking."

"Uh-huh. Listen, d'you think I could take this ... take Francesca to Civic next week, give it a little more playing and see how it stands up in the middle of a whole section? It's fun to play, it makes me sound good."

"Helps you sound good, you mean." He looked at me for about a minute in silence. Well, less than that, probably, but it felt like a long time. "For one rehearsal, and you use a hard case, and we bring it back here right after. No way you gonna start playing that thing regular."

"Sure, fine. You want to hear it too, don't you? Out in a big hall, I mean, you can't tell anything playing it in here, right?"

"Wrong. But OK, long as you know where it stays, and what it's for, which is to get sold and pay the rent."

"Yes, sir. How about if I took her home with me sometimes after work so I can practice, and then I'll bring her back here right after?"

Di Salvo looked as if his worst suspicions had been confirmed, but he only grunted a bit. "Like new puppy," he remarked; "you play it here." And that wasn't No, so I said no more. I stayed there that night until I had outlasted Di Salvo, and made sure that I was immersed in a good-sized cleanup job when he had finished stringing up the two violins. After he left, reminding me for the hundredth time to turn off the lights and lock up when I was finished, I pounced on Francesca and played until dawn.

*   *

Luckily I had no morning classes that day, and when I stumbled into quant lab, there was Markus, grinning and strutting.

"Markus! How are you feeling?"

"Couldn't be better. I've been fine for a week, but I've had better things to do than lab, I'm afraid. Could you lend me the Chapter 5 problems?"

I was not surprised to hear this. Even before his bout with mono, he and Sophie had begun to manifest two and three-hour mutual disappearances from the usual round of dorms, classes, and meals, usually on Tuesday mornings and Thursday afternoons. And God knew what they were up to on weekends. The Coral Courts Motel, out on 66, was mentioned smirkingly by some classmates, but the general effect was not mysterious at all. Besides missing labs when we were supposed to be working together, he started begging homework from me, always with some extremely logical excuse that no one had ever resorted to in the entire history of formal education. Though Markus was no particular buddy of mine, I was appalled and fascinated by his behavior with a girl whose explicit semi-odorous presence in full frontality made me squirm. I tried to reason with him:

"Markus, look. First of all, Chapter 5 was due yesterday. And aren't you, aren't you - well, I know Sophie's a really nice girl and all, but shit, Markus, you're just like you're married or something."

Markus put on an odd look, pulling back his head and squinting at me. "Sophie and I know what is being said. It does

89

not frighten or embarrass us. We are far from acting like we are married, if what I see of my family and others, including you and your little friend, is any measure. We are researching pathways in a wilderness, Oren, and we have in these few weeks passed far beyond what married people know and do."

Well, that was familiar: Markus and Sophie out of sight down the trail. And they were old enough to take care of themselves out there. I honestly doubted that this earnest pair were pioneering behaviors that a million years of human evolution had somehow failed to penetrate, but they were ahead of me, all right.

"OK, fine, Markus. Maybe you'll publish a paper on it when you're done, so the rest of us can get educated. All I'm saying is, you're getting pretty out of touch with things around here, and people who matter - if I don't - are starting to notice. I had to do the writeup on the chloride lab, and the whole water hardness lab, by myself. I can get a new lab partner, but I can't keep the dean from getting curious when your grades go to hell."

Markus gave a little bark. "Oh, my God, the dean. And his little wifelihood with the bubble hairdo. You know what I have to wonder about when I see that bubble? Does she take it off at night, or does he cut his mouth on it? Or I guess he never puts her hair in his mouth, or maybe it's never night in a dean's house. You care what a dean thinks about love?"

Grades, I thought. Expulsion. "Not at all. Are you sure Taum Sauk is high enough for you?"

"No it's not, but it's the best we can do in this worn-out countryside. We were there, Oren, the week after you and Anna. We camped on the very summit, and at three o'clock in the morning a thunderstorm broke, and the tent blew away from over us. We made love in the rain while lightning struck two trees within a hundred meters of us."

And Sophie sang *Die Wahrheit ist Ewig*. Anyhow, she got a bath.

Well, if they were a mile down the road ahead of us, Anna and I did our best to catch up after she came back from Springfield. But it was tough, carrying Arnold and his rules on our backs. His scheme of things included uncompromising suspicion of me and everything I proposed, maybe because of my abuse of his hospitality at dinner, and probably because I kept returning Anna from dates just a little shiny. But also, providentially, he uncritically approved of Anna's friendship with her old Cor Mariae friend Nancy von Bayern, and that may have had to do with the von Bayern family's unfathomed wealth. Nancy became our double agent, fronting for Anna when she was off carousing with me (over <u>Magic Mountain</u> in the library annex or malts at Velvet Freeze), and letting us use her palace in Ladue as a rendezvous. Nancy made, for me, an uneasy ally. Well, why make you figure this out for yourself? It's all years ago now. I hated her and all she stood for. She was the 1000% bigger-than-life embodiment of a negligible jot of Anna's character, the only part I didn't much like: namely, her tendency to enjoy the empty, bubble-headed social life of her Cor Mariae friends.

Nancy von Bayern had left Cor Mariae behind (in a state of thankful oblation) when she more or less simultaneously graduated and ran out of stupid ideas for ways she could have fun in its confines. Expanding into the larger world of Washington University, she careened furiously for a year through its social possibilities, flunking six of her eight utter gut courses along the way. The two she passed were in the fall, licensing her for a spring semester of further boy-wrecking. And as that semester and administrative patience with Nancy were racing each other to exhaustion, her distinguished stepmom and daddy had the honor of announcing her betrothal to Mr. Rick McIntear, probably the only male in St. Louis would could stand up to and surpass her in the depth and callousness of his libertine folly. Each recognized in the other, I think, a toy it would take years to break.

Anyhow, it would take a good year just to plan the magnitude of wedding required to license consummation of their bond, so Nancy cheated the deans by announcing an indefinite leave of absence from her studies. Her career for the next twelve months would be to plan her wedding. And since even Nancy von Bayern couldn't make a full-time job out of that, she had plenty of time most days, between arising in late morning and bedding down for good in the small hours, to continue her real career, which was to mount imaginative and tireless attacks on the social mores of St. Louis and her father's cash reserves.

Rick McIntear played the same games, but with a masculine edge. His constant grooming was directed toward boardroom domination of partners and rivals. His studies at Washington U, he pursued with a ferocious need for passing grades that did not flinch at veiled and deniable bribes and threats toward professors, culminated in a BA in "business" which, taken literally, was a fair description of this busy fellow. After experimenting with the debauchery of easy targets among the country girls, he forsook all others when Nancy von Bayern, clad in blue body paint and a g-string, took his eye at a Sigma Nu party during the spring of his last, and her only, academic year. We need no omniscient narrator to tell you he experienced at once an erection and a vision of his business career, since he often described his twin epiphanies when he and Nancy were together in public. The simpler itch was probably satisfied that night; it took longer, a good three months, before Rick found himself in a corner office at Molar Chemical, the owner's future son-in-law and assistant vice president for public relations.

I had a taste of his work in a news story I heard on my way out to Nancy's to pick up Anna for a study date; in this case, to go and see "Wages of Fear" for her French Culture seminar, the day after she reentered my life:

" . . .*and the Cards take on the Pirates under the lights. It's a beautiful night for baseball. In local news, an ailment some are calling the "Saint Louie Flu" has more than a dozen residents of the Negro section of Webster Groves down with high fever, aching joints, nausea and vomiting. The malady was at first blamed on unhealthy eating habits in the victims, but concern mounted when white workers at a River des Peres pumping station and four Webster Groves firemen came down with identical symptoms. Health officials say that most cases are confined to residents of Rock Hill Road and Kirkham Avenue below the Missouri Pacific tracks, that if any disease-causing factor in these residents is likely to pose a larger problem it will be dealt with rapidly, and that there is no reason for the public at large to be concerned. Coal for the coming winter might be a concern, though, if John L. Lewis...*"

Kirkham, of course, was the street on which Molar Chemical had involuntarily parked one of its tank cars; I found it surprising that somehow this "factor" had not been part of the story.

Anna was waiting for me in front of the von Bayern manse along with Nancy, who had on leash a tan adolescent boxer pup, and a tan and rested-looking Rick McIntear. Since Rick and I had never actually met, we got introduced, and I congratulated him on keeping Molar out of the St. Louie Flu story. He seemed uncharmed that I mentioned it.

"You know something about that, do you?"

"Well, only a little. I was in the Analytical office when that guy from the Star-Times was there, and I guess I assayed a sample of stuff from the tank car."

"What tank car?"

"Well, the one that jumped the tracks and spilled a lot of - whatever it was - in that neighborhood."

"There was no spill."

"Excuse me? I distinctly heard Mr. Napperson say . . ."

McIntear gave me a confident grin. "Was he there? Or were you, for that matter? I got five jigs that live on that street, say there was a little leak that smelled like vinegar, and four more that say they're liars, that nothing leaked at all. And they were there."

"Well, I wasn't, but I know Napperson, and if he - "

"Let me give you a little friendly advice, Aaron."

"Oren."

The boxer pricked up his ears and looked at me diagonally.

"Right, sorry. On this - "

"Nothing to be sorry about."

"Hnh. On this St. Louie Flu business, it is Molar's position that there was no spill, that if something did leak out it was MoPac's fault, and that anyhow the stuff was acetic acid, which isn't going to hurt anybody no matter how much you dump on a bunch of niggers that probably got sick from eating too much fatback and watermelon. All that but the word *nigger* is in a brief filed with the County in Clayton, and I bet anybody who thinks he might want to keep on good terms with Molar and the von Bayerns *and* their friends wouldn't say anything to contradict any of it. Don't you agree?"

While I was thinking over whether I agreed, the pup, responding to god knows what, something in my face or a silent command from Nancy, lunged at me without warning and started licking my face and humping my knee. Nancy gave a silvery laugh and yanked his leash good and hard. "Oren! Down! Oh, gosh. I hope you don't mind we named our new puppy after you. Anna said it would be all right."

I glanced at Anna, who looked pink and discomfited, and looked back at Rick.

"How important is it that I agree?"

"Not important at all. As long as you don't disagree, see what I'm saying?"

"No. Let's go, Anna."

In the car, heading back to the Hi-Pointe for our sweaty-palmed rendezvous with Fear, Anna denied categorically being consulted about the name of the pup, and I decided I preferred to believe that. Besides, I suppose a boxer pup was preferable to a snake. Just to keep the record straight, I filled Anna in about the spill, the St. Louis Flu, and the notebook, winding up with, "And if there's a record for bullshit, it's in danger from Rick McIntear. He can't decide how many different ways to contradict himself on one story."

I'd have done better to skip the editorial and let Anna come to her own conclusions. "Rick's nice enough. Don't be too hard on him."

"Nice? Sure, he's nice, unless you feel funny about racist liars."

"Well, he's Nancy's friend, and so am I."

That still wasn't warning enough, and I pressed on. "Look, accidents happen. What I'm getting at is, it seems to me the best thing to do is tell the truth, clean it up the best you can, and get on with things."

"What's the truth about this? One guy says there was a spill, and one guy says there wasn't."

"A man I know to be truthful says the tank car tumbled sideways down the hill, spraying stuff all over the neighborhood."

"People who live there say that didn't happen."

"Rick <u>says</u> they say that. And with all due respect to Rick's eye-witnesses - who even contradict each other depending on how much they got paid - when Harvey Napperson says there was a spill, I believe that."

"Appealing to authority in the absence of experiment?"

"Oh, I see. I'm not supposed to accept authority when I can do a hands-on experiment?"

"What do you wish you were getting at now?"

"Your fundamental premises. OK, from now on I'm not accepting claims of transcendental accidents while dancing unless I personally have a hand in it."

"Oh, ha ha. Didn't I give you your come-uppance? It didn't take much, either, I must say."

"That says more by a long shot about dancing, than it does about upholding rigid standards of verification."

"It's a hard man that doesn't like dancing. Doesn't it tickle your - "

"You're all wet. I only meant dancing stands in the way of judicial rectitude."

I'll give you something to stand in the way."

Maybe that will explain why this is not going to be some Hardy Boys tale about detecting the culprits in the Molar Spill. Sure, I could have gone out to Webster myself, Anna by my side as Nancy Drew (well, Effie Perrine, at her age) and poked around looking at the scars in the blacktop on Rock Hill Road. I could have flipped back to August and seen that the missing notebook was the one I finished up with grinding twenty pounds of limestone. But I had way more on my plate with classes, two jobs, and music, not to mention the steaming mound of emotional goulash Anna had heaped there, than I could do justice to as it was. I don't know that it ever crossed the backstage of my mind to play detective in regard to Molar. But that would have been just as bad a decision as the one I did make, which was to forget it.

After the movie we walked slowly down the sidewalk, holding hands and letting our minds drift back from the jungles of Honduras to Lindell Boulevard. "Now that," Anna said, "was a spill."

"Had to be. I saw it with my own eyes."

6. The Backstage Yahoos, and a Promotion

I see now that I really believed Oren Dienst was the only player in the world who could make, or allow, the cello "Francesca" to sound as beautiful as she did when I played her. That as the accidental creator of her distinctive varnish and bystander to her birth - or at least the installation of her soul - I was thus the enzyme to her substrate, the key to the great release of sound that she began to make as I played her more. I believed all that without thinking it was true, or thinking at all; if I had let myself think it consciously, the stupidity would have been obvious right away.

It is true that a player and an instrument break each other in, as Di Salvo had put it. Any stringed instrument will only sound good within a certain range, or envelope, of bow pressure, speed of stroke, and distance from the bridge at which the bow contacts the string. Light pressure of course produces a quiet sound, but so do rapid bow speed and a contact point remote from the bridge. The timbre of softness produced by each of these factors is different: light pressure gives a relatively thin sound, a distant contact point makes for fuller but still quantitatively modest sound, and a fast bow adds a breathy quality. Reverse each, and you have three qualities of loudness: mass, shrillness, and bite, respectively.

Accommodating to an instrument means learning its limits in regard to these and other factors; which are, by the way, not independent of each other, meaning that what constitutes the proper range of bow pressures depends on bow speed and contact point, and so on for all the others. A good player uses these three variables in all combinations and along a continuum of values, to produce - and this is where genius comes in for the really great players - a sound that will be varied, fresh, and appropriate to the musical idea at each moment. Beginning players sound bad until they learn to stay within their instrument's tolerances. Mediocre players have solved that problem and they may even get all the notes just fine, but they stay within a monotonous range of timbres, and make the music sound monotonous as well. And I haven't said anything about tonal effects (in addition to accuracy and speed) that you can get with the left hand, which fingers the notes, or with bow techniques other than straight back-and-forth bowing. We're not doing *Moby-Dick* here.

A very fine instrument, besides having full and noble resonances across the whole range of pitch and loudness, has a broad tolerance for poorly adapted players, and thus may sound good, or at least OK, in many players' hands. Lesser instruments, particularly when they are new, are less forgiving, can tolerate playing only within relatively narrow limits. The thing about Francesca is that she would produce all of her range of, for example, bow-pressure loudness within a very narrow range of actual pressures. She was like a car with a touchy accelerator, and it was easy to overplay and produce harshness, or to lose the bow's bite on the string with only a little too light a pressure. And she was similarly intolerant in regard to bow speed and contact point.

Nobody can dictate to such an instrument (or any other) what the relation of player to instrument is going to be. I accommodated to Francesca by playing her often; by holding the bow with a kind of receptive, soft grip (which is not the same as a weak grip), by sternly adding pressure where that was what she wanted, letting her sing easily where she had sweet spots, and letting Francesca tell me by her sound and by the feel of the bow what she would or would not tolerate. After a week of midnight practice I could release far better sound than seemed possible in that first session with Di Salvo; and of course far better than the customers who saw her in the shop and tried her out for the first time. Francesca's contribution to our partnership, once I had learned all this, was to respond with a silken, luminous sound that was as ravishing as it is impossible to describe. Her peaks of response were narrow, but they were very high. Any decent player could have found that sweet range of response; but only I, with unlimited after-hours access to her, had a chance to. So I began to think of myself as the only player who <u>ought</u> to have that chance. The world had acquired an obligation to preserve my access to Francesca, and I, in turn, had the responsibility to play her. And from there it is only a short swoon to spookier notions about the Fate that had led me to Di Salvo's shop, to my long-suppressed destiny, to dreaming again the Big Dream of a concert career.

These were some of the unacknowledged hunches, the primitive and wordless grunts and scuffles from the silly Yahoos of my unconscious mind, horsing around backstage like the kid Pete's tormentors at the Ladue wedding, while I was reciting dutiful lines about chemical engineering to an audience of professors and mentors, most of them living, in the well-lit auditorium. I expect it was Yahoos who sent that Bach rolling through my head, back when I was trying to think only of math and mortgages. The Yahoos got louder and more unruly with each midnight session on Francesca, with each time I made my own hair stand on end by singing the old songs, the Bach suites and even the scales and exercises, but in particular the Beethoven A Major Sonata, with this new voice. No one on my public stage heard either the beauty, or the clatter behind the scenes, and they would have been powerless to suppress them if they had. What I really needed was someone who understood what the commotion was about, but could talk some sense to me about it. There was Anna, who had dreamed of a career as a dancer but had had better wisdom; but it seemed to me that our love, if that was what it was to be, was too fragile to carry a load of counseling. I would have wound up treating her, rightly, as an older and wiser head, not the best persona to mix with a love life. And besides, I knew the effect she had on my common sense and inhibitions. I was worried - still unconsciously, God what a lot of business gets transacted that way without ever being published! - that she might come up with the hard answer, namely that the backstage Yahoos were right, and that she would follow me through the ice and snow of conservatory life wherever it might take us. It may be for something like this reason that I had not yet invited her to keep me company at Di Salvo's shop. Ever since her sudden abduction to Springfield, I had more or less considered the shop a piece of my territory that I would be glad to share with her, some day but not tonight. I didn't trust her, in fact. And if I had said that to myself I would have denied it hotly.

No, I needed someone who had been down this trail, as Markus and Sophie were breaking trail in the sexual wilderness, and who knew what was there in a commitment to a musical life, to be found or feared. I needed my father, but he had taken himself out of the discussion, and I had already had his opinion long before that. I needed Mollie Biedermeyer, with whom I had become close during those weeks of driving her, watching with affection as Jacob's crush began to be reciprocated; I wound up, kid that I was, lovingly avuncular toward them both. But Mollie had disappeared.

Her disappearance took place dramatically enough, for a negative event, at a Stravinsky rehearsal. We were beginning to get the thing under good control, we had worked together and separately, and in fact had weathered a major defection: Armin Balakourian announced at the end of one rehearsal that he had been offered a well-paid "geeg" on November first, and that he would regretfully bail out of this one, unless, of course, Replogle would wish to match the offer he had had from the Symphony to help them out with a Villa-Lobos piece for eight cellos on that date. Replogle said No deal, he would take his chances with me; Balakourian walked, and I experienced a sudden promotion virtually to the position of concertmaster, as the highest-seated string player present. Of course the Yahoos went into a frenzy over this one: *Destiny!*, they crowed. *Fate!* I almost brought it up with Mollie on the way home that night, but she was looking tired again, and I let it go. And by the time of the next rehearsal, she was gone.

It began with a simple phone call to Di Salvo's shop on the evening before: "Biedermeyer call - not gonna need a ride to Concordia tomorrow."

"OK. Thanks."

"Suppose you wanta take Francesca again."

"Gosh, Mr. Di Salvo, I've been working on the first-chair part on her, and it's starting to sound OK. You ought to hear how she's opening up in the high register, for that opening line."

"Hnh. Too soon for her to change. It's you, getting broken in to her. OK. But I gotta warn you, that cello's for sale, and not for no two hours' work, neither."

"Sure, I know that, sir. She's going to have a long career, and I'm just honored to be her first player. No matter where she goes, maybe on a great concert career, that'll still be true. Whoever buys her will be getting a fine instrument, and all the better for this early playing, right?" *Hnh.* And if he ever had been on it, Di Salvo silently dropped off the list of possible mentors in regard to my returning to a career in music, since that career, as far as the Yahoos were concerned, was inseparable from Francesca. I made up my mind to have a serious talk with Mollie.

I arrived at Concordia a half-hour early the next night, and self-consciously practiced the soaring principal cello lines of the first movement. This would be almost the last orchestra-only rehearsal, and I wanted to be ravishing when Anna and the other singers joined us. The rest of the orchestra slowly filled in around me, and began huffing and plunking their own warmups. The kid from Webster Groves had been offered the chance to move up in my wake, but (wisely, in my opinion) decided to stay with the part he'd been practicing all this time. My replacement in second chair was a businesslike middle-aged guy from the phone company; a guy who, if he'd ever experienced the tensions I was working through, had firmly opted for a corporate life and corporate risks and rewards. He was a pretty good player, though. I showed him a few bowing changes Replogle had asked for, and suggested some places where I had found better fingerings than the crazy ones printed in the music. He kept a pipe in his mouth the whole time, Pablo Casals style, and his only response to most of it was a clenched grunt of acquiescence.

Replogle showed up about thirty seconds early, brushed aside some technical questions from brass players, tapped the stand, and told us to start with the melancholy woodwind fugue that begins the second movement.

"Expectans expectavi DOMINUM," they're going to be singing when you get done with this, folks, and I want to hear that in the patient, humble, firm way you play this part. What's more, I want the audience to hear it too, so they'll know something's up. Like water dropping in a desert cave for thousands of years, those first notes have got to be. OK, oboe?"

"Water... Cave... Got it, chief."

OK. The first oboe dripped eerily for a little while, and looked to be soothed by the liquid sound of a flute echoing the same line; except that this time there was silence instead, from Mollie's empty chair.

"Expectans expectavi flautam," snorted Replogle. "Anybody seen our first flute? Oren?"

I looked, dumbly enough, at the empty chair and then at the door. "No, sir. She called to tell me she wouldn't need a ride tonight, so I came on without her."

"She didn't say why?"

"I didn't speak to her. It was just a message."

"Well, shoot. OK, Miss Witz, is it, move up" (smirk, bridle) "until she gets here. From the top, oboe. No, wait."

He started punching the score with his finger. "Let's back off into the end of the first movement, one, two, . . . five bars from the end. That's a long crescendo on "before I depart from here and shall be no more," most of it in the last two bars. And listen to this: No falling off from the fortissimo. Cut off cleanly. That two beats of silence at the end of the last bar is all we get to establish the context for the oboe, and I want not a single sound or motion from any of you, got it? Strings, keep your bows up; winds, keep your horns in place during that two beats, and don't even twitch. You can very quietly relax once the fugue is started with the oboe and the flute - of whom I hope we indeed shall see more."

But I at least saw no more of Mollie Biedermeyer for many days. When I pulled up to Civic rehearsal the next night, it was to find Jacob not in evidence and the stage door locked; at least until I knocked, when Lennie Marconi, setting up his percussion stuff closest to the door, came over and let me in.

"Where's Jacob?"

"Right behind you. Hope you're gonna play good tonight, we got company."

Well, I missed the second half of that, too busy being startled to find Jacob indeed at the rear quarter of my elbow. "Jacob! My heavens."

"Good evening, Mr. Dienst." He fell into a highly out-of-character slouch and rolled his eyes. "Bettuh be rill good t'night, Mist' Dienst. De man hyeah."

"The man?"

"Ol' massuh. Man what keeps dis hyeah cah own de road."

"Huh?"

Jacob smiled grimly. "I am referring to Mr. Julius von Bayern, owner of this theater and principal financial angel of the St. Louis Civic Orchestra. But I dare not speak this way in his presence, so just let's keep this little exchange between us. Mr. von Bayern has dropped in to hear a rehearsal and to see what his dollars have wrought since this time last year. As I recall, you were not with us then, and we were the poorer for it, but it is an annual ordeal that we must undergo in order to insure fair weather, bounteous harvests, and many healthy babies."

"I get it." I eyed Jacob uneasily. He, who I knew for a fact to be as self-controlled a guy as could be found in St. Louis, seemed terrifically wired about something. The ancient mariner had nothing on him for glittering eyes, and he seemed ready to flip from courtliness to servility and back at the snap of a finger. "Play good and be good, is that it?"

"There is talk of sacrificing a virgin, be on your guard. Ha, there's one I could name were I of a mind, but he'll not nose her out."

I took a flying guess. "Jacob, have you seen Mollie Biedermeyer? She missed a rehearsal of our Stravinsky thing last night, and - "

"Miss Biedermeyer? What work of Stravinsky are you two engaged upon?"

"Well, the *Symphony of Psalms*, but she - "

"Well, that is a new one on me. A symphony of psalms, is it? And I believe Stravinsky is one of these modern composers, is he not?"

"Yes, pretty modern, but it's - "

"Well, it is good to hear that composers are once again setting to music the words of our Lord. There has been a dreadful falling-away of artistic effort from sacred texts and themes."

"Jacob, do you know where Mollie is?"

"I may say in all honesty, Mr. Dienst, I do not, exactly. She has, as you well know, allowed me to help her with a painful condition in the past."

"Well, that's why I thought you might."

"This is a large and complex building, Mr. Dienst. There are any number of places she might be as we speak; or indeed she may be elsewhere entirely."

"You mean she's back in the theater somewhere? Where?"

"Hit's a sight a comp'cated tangles to her, Mist' Dienst. Yaas suh."

"Look, Jacob, Mr. Oxendine. I don't mean to pry into stuff that isn't my business, but I like Mollie, and I'm worried about her. If you should happen to see her, could you just pass on that word from me?"

"If I should see her, I will do so. Hist! He comes! Strain every sinew to the show!"

And as I gaped after him Jacob sagged away with an amiable shuffle and grinned vacantly at the silver-haired aristocrat who was walking toward us, bapping a personnel list on his thigh like a Field Marshall. "Evenin', Mist' v'n Barn," he mewled.

"Evening Jake. How's the missus?"

"Doin right good since you so kind t'ask it. Thank you, suh."

I wondered if I too would be required to invent a wife should the great man require one for conversational purposes, but he gave me a sort of blank look, and opened his personnel sheet.

"Oren Dienst," I supplied. "I just joined the orchestra this year."

"OK, Dienst. Glad to have you on board."

He gave me an arrogant stare out of cornflower eyes, and made to pass on; nor was I in a mood to detain him. But he pivoted, and came back. "Dienst, Dienst. You the fella that's gotten friendly with Anna Rosen?"

I wondered briefly how my answer might affect the fortunes of the St. Louis Civic Orchestra, but saw no reason to equivocate. "I guess you could say that, sir. You know Anna?"

"Friend of my daughter's. So I guess that makes you some kind of friend of the family. I just think the world of that little girl."

Did he mean Anna, or the vile brat he had sired? "Anna? Yes, sir, she's pretty nice, OK."

"Well, she sure thinks the world of you, son."

Great. Anna's pouring out her heart to the Molar magnate? In that compartment of my life, I rather felt that I had created Anna, had ogled her into being at the first Stravinsky rehearsal, and held full and exclusive rights to her words and opinions. This was not a wonderful development. I beamed a lying, manly smile at von Bayern. "Pleased to meet you, then, sir."

"Yes. Love to have you out to the house one of these days."

I know the way by heart, creep.

Most of the rehearsal was dedicated to the Bohemian Nocturnes. We were beginning to get it, except for a few spots, and I could see what it was more or less about. Awkward, doctrinaire music in the top voices covers a fragmentary, fluid bass line that burbles sometimes as high as the violas and low-register woodwinds. Three- and four-note fragments of melody keep getting cut off by heavy dissonance in violins and brass just before you can see what they mean. Toward the end, there is a window where the squalling quiets and the fragments coalesce. We see now that it is the fluid signature theme from Smetana's "My Fatherland," painfully twisted into six flats - couldn't these guys write anything for the white keys? - the harmonies and rhythms also sadly injured but still beautiful, worthy of love, crippled as they were.

This instant of clarity is given to the cellos with only a deep monotone from basses and some ripply sotto-voce flute accompaniment. When Armin Balakourian played it alone to demonstrate bowings, you could see the river Moldau serene in autumn haze, a yellow leaf or two floating on the surface. When the whole section played it, it was sewage. Hans Brocklin led us through it once with a pained scowl, and then asked for a reprise.

"In tune, this time, please, cellos." We got it a little closer, but that only made Brocklin madder.

"Christ! You guys, this is the heart and soul of the whole piece, this is when we get one little breath of air. You see those fiddles and trombones counting measures, just waiting till they can come down like a ton of bricks, like storm troopers... You got twelve measures to show something beautiful, and what do you do? You fart. You deserve storm troopers. Last stand, let's hear it."

And the poor suckers on the last stand of cellos made it about half way through and fell in a ditch. "Uh, huh! Thought so. Next stand!"

And so it went, up through the ranks, getting better with the increasing skill of the players and the extra warning they had to get ready. "Balakourian! They aren't even bowing and fingering it the same! What the hell do we pay you for, if not to put fingerings and bowings in the parts?"

"We've got the fingerings, Hans. It's just a hard part to get in tune," came from the rear.

"No shit. Armin, get back there and show 'em. Next stand! Why do we have to take rehearsal time for this?"

Well, the next stand was the one behind ours, and it was pretty good.

"Better. You can portamento just a little up to that high b flat. *Da da dee-yah daa.* Try it again." They did, and Brocklin nodded.

"OK, not bad. Next stand. Oren, that's you, I guess, I know Armin can do it."

And all the backstage Yahoos came crowding around the wings, grinning and nudging each other, because they knew I had spent the hours between one and three in the morning on this very passage.

Da da dee-yah daa, I went, and Jesus, Francesca looked around and saw what she had wanted since she was born: not the lonesome walls of Di Salvo's shop but an audience of musicians all looking right at her. I kept my hands receptive and let her take it; she kept me right in the sweet part of the envelope and cut

106

loose with a sound that gave us the golden leaf with a little shaft of sunlight shining through the leaf and the mist and down into the water to gentle turbulence and dissolution. It was so damn lovely I forgot about the sixth flat, and ended in confusion. Brocklin stood there for a few seconds; then said, gently for him, "C flat, son. All right, let's finish this up so we can take a break."

When we broke, I went back to the solo line and played it again, this time as written, while overweight woodwinds scrambled around me, knocking the back of my chair trying to get to their cigarettes.

Brocklin looked down with a half-smile. "Not bad, Oren - up to a point."

"Yeah, geez, I'm sorry about the C natural. I got kind of carried away."

"I could see that. You were surprised, too. But the essence of art, my boy ... " (Oh, well, here it comes . . .) " ... the essence is to discipline your inspiration with care and planning. No surprises, or most of 'em will be nasty."

"Yes, sir."

"Yoolie, come here a second." Brocklin gestured to the remotely lounging form of Julius von Bayern. "You want to meet our new young cellist."

Yoolie walked over, exuding smells of bourbon and leather. Even his ambient air was a cliché. "Mr. Dienst and I have met. Damn fine, son. You're gonna be a good one some day." I made no effort to receive this patronage gracefully, but Yoolie didn't seem to notice. "Like to get you and your little lady friend over to the house one of these days, show you some damn nice fiddles I've got there. This one yours?"

"Mr. von Bayern's collection of string instruments is well known all over the world," said Brocklin. I looked at him sardonically, and he sent me back a minuscule scowl, all in the space of a sixteenth note.

"Is that so, sir?" I gave it just enough width of eye to make Brocklin's mouth twitch. All the same, I grieved to witness sycophancy in a guy I liked and respected. "Well, this is a new one Mr. Di Salvo just finished, he's letting me use it for a while." Meaning another hour from right now better see it on its way back to the shop.

The Cello Francesca, *or* Balderdash

Von Bayern shocked me by plucking Francesca out of my hands and spinning her around on the end pin, staring at her with a half-mocking smile. I started to reach for her, but his sudden snatch had knocked loose my grip on the bow, and I had to choose between saving it from falling at my feet, and an ill-considered grab for the cello. Who it was I would be counter-grabbing it from occurred to me none too soon, and I subsided while von Bayern swung Francesca up and peered through the *f*-holes like a whorehouse doctor giving one of the girls a quick physical. (I guess.)

He grunted. "Petrus Salvatoris, no less. Little wop thinks he's Marcus Aurelius. Who was a wop too, come to think of it. Anyhow, it's a nice piece of work. Bring him a nice piece of change. Sit down, would you, son, and just play through that little Bohunk piece for me."

To hear was to obey, plus it got Francesca back into my hands (where she belonged, grumbled the Yahoos). I played the solo line once again, blushing and fumbling a bit, but got basically the same clear, soaring sound; though with the memory of the complete harmonic structure fading, it was harder to play in tune. When I finished, von Bayern seemed to have lost interest.

"Yeah, nice. The old guy, Arnold, he's a hymie, you know that? But they're converted, and I say what the hell. C'mon out some time and have a tour of my fiddles."

"Thank you, sir, I will." Yaas suh.

I took a short break, and when I got back there was a little white envelope on my side of the stand that said "Oren" on the outside and the following on the notepaper inside:

Dear Oren:
I owe you and all our colleagues an apology
for not appearing at the Stravinsky rehearsal
last night. Perhaps I will get around
to writing to them one of these days, as and if
I begin to feel stronger. For now, I must be
careful to conserve my strength.
You must have noticed that I have not been
very well lately. It is cancer, and the doctor -

after scolding me severely, how they love to do that to their worst cases - says that radical surgery is the only hope. But when I asked him exactly how hopeful that would be, I could see that there was almost none, even though he spoke soothingly.

I have no wish to end my days a pathetic and maimed old maid, so I have chosen another course; the sort for which one finds courage only at the very end of all other possibilities. You will recall that Jacob Oxendine has been attentive to me, and that his medicine was almost miraculously helpful, at least in easing the pain of what I now know - oh, and I knew it all along - is breast cancer that has invaded the lymph nodes under my arm. I was so terribly sore after the doctor's examination that I went to Jacob and asked him for another dose of the "swamp berry" cordial. He - blessed man - could see at once that I was in a bad state, and he gave me the medicine, after his little prayer, and then stayed with me and talked to me while the pain eased, and as he talked, so did the heartsickness. I responded encouragingly enough to learn that he wishes nothing more than to remain near me as I go through what I must. He is a fine Christian man, Oren, and he cares for me. I am going to disappear now from the haunts of all others, and devote what time I may have left to one who is devoted to me. I have let my landlord and most others believe that I have gone away in search of medical assistance. I know that many, and perhaps you too, will condemn my behavior as selfish, impulsive, and perhaps wanton; but please do not be too harsh in your opinion of me. You are young, and your days are unnumbered now, but you too will

*come to such a time as mine when they are
easily countable.*

*As I write this, you have just played that
lovely passage from the Bohemian
Nocturnes. I have never heard anything so
musical, so alive with art. You <u>must</u> not let
that gift fade away. Thank you for your
companionship these last months.*

*Your friend,
Mollie Biedermeyer*

*ps - I have communicated my resignation to
Hans Brocklin. I would be very grateful if
you would do so to Pierce Replogle.
M.B.*

I looked up from the note to see Hans Brocklin watching
me. He nodded, raised an eyebrow, and jerked his head toward
the door.

"Thank you, sir. I'll see you next week."

"Good night, Oren."

I went and packed Francesca carefully into the case that
Di Salvo had provided for her perilous journeys out of the shop.
At the door, I saw Jacob, back in his normal personality, and I
understood a little of what had underlain his earlier fury.

"Mr. Oxendine, I'd ... I guess change the message a
little. If you should see Miss Biedermeyer, would you please tell
her that I am not as worried about her as I was?"

"I will. Good night, Mr. Dienst."

At the shop, I put Francesca's case carefully against the
back wall, and stood staring at the latches for a minute. Then I
turned out the light and locked up.

*   *

The lab for the week was called "Spectrophotometric
Measurement of Manganese in Steel." It was kind of cute, and so

was my new lab partner, a Cindy Something-or-Other. Markus, I guessed, when she introduced herself, had cut one too many labs and suffered the consequences. "Oh, gosh, no, didn't you know? They got kicked out of school and went off to California or something."

"They? Sophie too? Just for a fight?" I had heard that Markus had been before a Dean for getting into a fistfight in which, per the grapevine, he had bent Rick McIntear's nose pretty good for a remark Rick made about Sophie. It was the kind of rumor I was happy to believe.

"Specially Sophie, if you know what I mean. She's pregnant."

"Pregnant?"

"Ye gods. You do know what that means, don't you?"

I stared at Cindy Something frostily, said, "Yes, but, I mean, they were doing all that, uh, that - "

"Screwing, I think it's called."

"Thank you. Without condoms or anything?"

"Evidently. Do you understand this lab?"

"Uh, yeah, I guess. See, there's this little trace of manganese in - "

"Right, right. I mean, what are we supposed to do first? I got cheerleading practice at four."

"Here. Go to the stockroom and get a gram of potassium persulfate in each of these beakers. Be sure it's persulfate."

"You got it."

But I didn't get it. What the heck was happening to the world of a few weeks ago? Mollie Biedermeyer dying in the arms of Jacob Oxendine in the deep tangles of the Orpheum Theater; my mind in a food fight between common sense and Byronism and my hormones in a constant uproar over a too solid friendship with Anna. And now Markus and Sophie, to whom we could always look for an example of what not to do, had jumped off the cliff for good, and could look forward to a life of sunshine and diapers. I supposed I would get a letter from Markus too, telling me how this was the next big step he and Sophie were taking, like no one else ever had.

I was wrong, it was from Sophie, and it was delivered by her (ex) roommate as I was standing there and watching little pinkish-purple swirls blossom in the bottom of the beakers with the steel samples:

Dear Oren and Anna:

By now I suppose you will know that Markus and I are on our way to the last great Frontier in America - Markus and I and our baby, that is, for in case you didn't know this, I am going to have a baby! I do not know that we would have planned for this just at this time when we first met each other, but now we are as happy as we can be. Markus says that having a baby that was conceived on top of a mountain - for we are sure that was the time, all the others we were using Precautions - and in a lightning storm will guarantee that he will be healthy and strong and brave for whatever unexpected Blows life may deal him. I hope so.

Markus and I want to thank you for being our Friends during these weeks. You were one of the few people who didn't laugh at us behind our backs, and we appreciate that. We will think of you very often in the next months, and hope that you will have a wonderful year and wonderful Lives together.

Your Friends
Sophie and Markus
ps - We will write when we find jobs and a place to live in Alaska.

*   *

"Well," Anna said. She put down the letter and looked over at the windows of the library annex. There was nothing there but the dark reflection of the room in which we sat with about forty other undergraduates, noses buried in books. "The poor thing."

It looked like her chin was trembling, and I couldn't see why she was getting so worked up. I mean, they were begging for this.

"Would you do that, if I got pregnant, Oren?"

"What, take off for Alaska with you? Soon as I got over the horsewhipping."

"No, I mean give up everything. It wouldn't have to be Alaska."

"Guess I'd have to, wouldn't I? I've always pictured us going to Mexico, somehow. Better yet, though, let's stay out of thunderstorms from now on. If you heard Markus talk about that little incident, you'd be pretty sure Wotan himself got involved. They'll be lucky if the kid doesn't look like Reddy Kilowatt."

Anna snorted, and smacked the table with her hand. "<u>Will</u> you be serious! I don't know why you have to make a stupid callous joke out of everything that happens."

I closed *University Calculus* and turned to her, but she was still staring at the window. "I am serious, Anna. You know I would stand by you if you got pregnant. And I honestly don't see why a woman your age has to get so tense about what Papa's going to do."

She ignored the editorial. "How do I know that?"

"Because you ought to know me well enough by now to know that I would, that's all, Not that it's been exactly a biological possibility up to now."

She turned to me, and down I went into the darkness. "Yes. But you know it's just a matter of time, don't you?"

"Yes."

When I was a little kid, an older boy and I found a young sparrow crippled on a sidewalk, and when it was my turn to hold it, it was nothing but fluff and fragile bones and a hard pulse beneath my dirty fingers. So I did not feel urbane and masterly to see the pulse jumping at the base of Anna's throat; I knew mine was doing the same.

<u>Magic Mountain</u> and the Mean Value Theorem had lost their hold on us, and we packed up and started out - for a walk, our only alternative to sitting and staring at books. As we passed the newspaper racks ("UMW Threatens New Unrest"; "St. Louie Flu Claims First Victim"), I heard a little muffled squeak from Anna.

"Oh, gosh, don't tell me - not again?"

"What?" She kept her face turned away, and I had to be quiet while we passed the librarian, a dream of silence by the door.

"You're not having an, uh, an event are you?"

"No, you dirty smart alec. I'm trying not to think about Reddy Kilowatt."

*   *

"Easy, easy, my dear, eh, Oren. Just enough, always wanna have just enough. Too much, that fingerboard gonna look like a bowling alley."

I squeezed out the rag and gently wiped the excess caustic bleach off the fingerboard of my old cello. Di Salvo had promised that I could get a passable imitation of Francesca's rosewood fingerboard by lightening mine a bit. "Not real ebony anyhow," he'd shrugged dismissively. "See the crooked grain? What you got is hard maple dyed black. Little caustic tone that down to something like rosewood, hard to tell the difference. Crazy project anyhow, but maybe you learn something."

The crazy project I had in hand was to remake my own cello to look as much like Francesca as possible. I called it Operation Sow's Ear, which went right by Di Salvo, but then I think most of what I did that fall was pretty opaque to him, as well as to myself. In between classes and work and seeing as much of Anna Rosen as I could manage, I was putting in an hour or so a day, usually late at night but this time just before suppertime, in a slow and superficial makeover to as close an imitation as I could manage. And, though recarving the pegs and scroll were out of the question, it was amazing how much I accomplished by filling and revarnishing the belly with Francesca's leftover dark varnish, mounting a twin of Francesca's tailpiece and end pin (paid for painfully though a solid weekend of sorting, stacking, and inventorying Di Salvo's stock of prime spruce and maple in the suffocating attic behind the varnish room) and the present counterfeit rosewood chemistry.

"You get this thing close enough, Oren, maybe it start to play like my little Francesca, that what you think?"

Well, without putting it in so many words, yes, that was my hope; or better, I thought maybe I could trick myself that way into getting as much out of the old cello as was in it. In any case, I thought the way Francesca looked was cool, and I wanted to have something as much like her as possible when the unthinkable day should roll around that a player with the skill and money to claim Francesca should come by.

But I was spared the uncomfortable confession by the phone going off in the front of the shop. Di Salvo liked to have me answer the phone, it put an authoritative distance between him and the frazzled string teachers on the other end, nagging about repairs undone. This time he took a look at my messy hands and held up one of his own immaculate ones. "I got it," he said. "You keep after that till you got the color you want, then wipe down with vinegar - stop the bleaching."

I looked at the fingerboard. No one seeing the genuine and the fake side by side would be fooled by mine; it had neither the arrow-straight grain of ebony nor the arabesques of rosewood. But it was approaching the right color, so after a few more swipes with the bleach rag and an overall polishing rubdown I applied the vinegar to kill off the bleach.

The stench was a worthy replacement for the lethal smell of the bleach, and I had to think of a whole tank car load of this, twenty-fold concentrated, or even something worse, tumbling and spewing down the Webster Groves hillside, invading the ground, sickening and now killing the luckless bystanders. But, it came real to me now, bad as this smelled, even a tank car load of it would not cause lingering death. It might kill you right then by immediate contact, or it would be no worse than unpleasant. Whatever had tumbled down that hillside, it was not acetic acid.

I put the fingerboard down next to the dismembered cadaver of my cello. It looked pathetic, scattered over the workbench like that, and I vowed that if I were lucky enough to get it reassembled and playing, I would not do this again. I gagged my way over to the alley window and threw it open as Di Salvo came back in, nose wrinkling, to inspect the results.

"I tell your ragazza you in no shape to pick up phone," he reported. "You call her back when this mess cleaned up. And keep it short, Don Giovanni, nobody tell you you can take my shop phone for your amores."

"OK, sorry. It won't be a habit." I turned, as coolly as my twanging solar plexus allowed, to pick up the transformed fingerboard. Gleaming wet with the vinegar, it did have a certain depth of grain. "What do you think?" I asked. I was still not comfortable with "*ragazza.*" OK, it was some kind of woman, but it sounded awfully dismissive. "She's, uh, part Italian, you know."

"What I think about fingerboard, or ragazza? Fingerboard look pretty good, for fake rosewood. We give it very light treatment with linseed oil to keep grain deep, like that. Don't know if it works for girls. Italian one, might hafta try olive."

I probably chuckled all out of proportion to this rare wit from the boss. I was whizzing through a cleanup and trying to look slow and cool, heh heh, a couple of guys of the world yukking about Italian girls and olive oil. When things in the shop were restored to order and good air, and my fake-rosewood fingerboard was hanging in the varnish loft, I strolled as fast as I could to the front room and called Anna. Damn, and got Arnold; as always, it was a game of patient diplomacy to get him to put her on. But Anna herself, in her sunniest diction, had a suggestion for a breakout from our virtuous round of study dates, malts, and movies. Why didn't we go out on a double date with Nancy and Rick, and let them show us some night life? She was slated to spend the night with Nancy, and this would give us lots of scope for a good time without a minute-by-minute timetable.

"Nancy von Bayern? Rick McIntear?" was my leaden echo.

"Yes, Oren."

"Well, . . ."

I was unable to suggest anything more fun and adventurous, or more worthwhile for that matter, and when I tried she brought me to my knees effortlessly.

"Oh, well, all right, you go ahead and study, and I'll just go along by myself."

The clincher was Anna's announcement that she was overnighting with Nancy, for here was not only a pressing need to buffer her against the worst of Nancy and Rick's bad influence but, frankly, a hope for access to Anna away from the overwhelming presence of Arnold. Make what you will of the moral inconsistency of that last; it seemed clear to me at the time. So, having showered off the sweat and chemicals of my last hour's work, I brought forth the cream of my formal wear - a charcoal gabardine suit with random pink threads - and went the familiar way into the heart of St. Louis wealth country.

The von Bayern villa lay along about a hundred yards of a side street called Reignleigh Court, off Ladue Road. These days, I expect there is a guardhouse at the entrance to Reignleigh Court, but things were more casual in 1953. Only the ticking of fairway-scale lawn sprinklers and the way you could see only the tops of extensive rooflines beyond the landscaped lawns let you know what kind of money called these places home. When picking up Anna here, I had simply met her at the end of the drive; now I was more or less invited by a family member, so she would be waiting inside. I started to pull into the drive and then thought better of it and parked on the street. Walking up the drive past the sprinklers and a grinning Negro jockey statue, I found the direct path to the door blocked by a good-sized pond that was crossed by a little footbridge. The drive went unswervingly around back to, I supposed, the carriage house and slave quarters. The footbridge arched quite high over the pond. I would feel a perfect high-profile jerk walking across it, but the alternative route up the drive led past a chained, three-headed dog, who eerily bristled but did not bark.

I was shuffling reluctantly toward the bridge when around the opposite side of the house came a guy, a gardener maybe, carrying a book and a tub of little flowers. He didn't look particularly gnarled or earth-stained. He looked smooth and tough, and he didn't look any too friendly, either. After a moment of silent mutual regard, he asked if I was Oren. This seemed like a pretty good sign, so I beamed and said I was. He was unmelted, but did say, "Miz Rosen ast me look out for you. This way."

So over the bridge I went, and around the corner of the house, following him to a kind of greenhouse-looking wing that extended from the right side of the house and had a kind of subsidiary front door set into it, complete with its own street number: "*Six bis*", it said, in handsome copperplate script, where the main front door had been at pains to spell it all out: "*Number Six Reignleigh Court*"

"Yo friend here, Miz Rosen," announced my guide, and turned back to rejoin his tub of flowers. From the doorway of *Six bis* emerged the only thing in this world that could for a moment have dragged me to this god-forsaken spot: Anna Rosen in a white silk cocktail dress.

It had a square-cut, pretty darn low neck that gave a (proportionate) Janet Leigh-style vista, with negligible strips of silk over her shoulders to hold it up. As low as it was cut in the back, and as smoothly as it flared over her hips, it was far from evident whether she had anything else on at all besides the little two-ounce sandals on her feet. Her hair was drawn away from her neck by a length of white yarn, tumbling down her back in a style that made me think of some kind of virgin getting ready to race for golden apples. I boggled, and immediately got started on an erection.

"Holy sh- smokes, Anna, you look great. Good lord. You want to come with me right now, and have a movie? Or run off to Mexico? Or anything?"

"Don't be silly, Oren. Do you like this? Nancy found it for me at Stix, and it fits just fine. I hoped you might like it."

"God, I'll say."

Without laying a finger on me other than a shy arm touch and a maidenly kiss that smelled of Paco Rabanne and toothpaste, she led me toward the door and into her plan for the evening.

"Come and see this truly lovely house and meet Nancy's dad."

A truly ugly brass frog leered from the lintel above *Six bis*. A voice wailed about Lucky Old Sun from a funerary urn beside the door. Postponing all hope, I entered.

7. Fiddles and Silk

At first, being inside the von Bayern house wasn't that different from being out in the garden, or in Forest Park somewhere. The room was a conservatory, and enormous plants feathered from urns or from actual plots of soil set into the red tile floor. A cricket and two or three songbirds sounded from (separate) wire-and-bamboo cages. A little fountain tinkled away somewhere. Against the back wall, a wet bar, a drinks trolley; a bit of wicker furniture and an aquarium.

Not, please, that I was so observant as to take all this in at first glance. This first penetration into the world of the von Bayerns was just a blur of impressions: the scent and ambiance of Anna in the little guest room she showed me off the conservatory; Yoolie von Bayern's careless and marginally drunken arrogance, his daughter's bubble hairdo; Rick McIntear's smooth tan, Ivy crew cut, linen blazer, and residually swollen nose, the farewell gift of Markus Gewissner.

True to his promise of the other night, Yoolie bestirred his hospitable soul so far as to give us a tour of his "fiddles." Violins, violas, and one cello – maybe a dozen captive wretches in all – hung by their necks in glass cases in a library that opened off the greenhouse, spotlit against grey velvet that set off their warm colors tastefully. Decorative ribbons announced their maker and date. He asked if I wanted to hold a real Guarneri, which I did, but hated to sound like a gee-whizzer by admitting. Anna read my little grimace and said, "Oh, Mr. von Bayern, I'd like to. I mean, I can't play it or anything - "

"Got that right, Missy," smiled our genial host. "Nobody plays these. They're worth too much to take the chance." Nancy started looking bored and made lets-get-out-of-here noises, but Anna knew where my heart lay, and insisted on a hands-on experience. "Hush, Nancy, I'm sure this is old stuff to you, but Oren and I would just love to touch it. Gently. Wouldn't we, Oren?

119

I tried for a sophisticated shrug that would also convey responsible gentleness. "I handle instruments a lot in my job," I said. "I'm careful."

Von Bayern, by way of reply, went to a little inlaid cabinet that seemed to be set into the wall, and drew out a ring of keys. "Well, let's take one out, then. Just one, though, and a few minutes. Whaddya say, the Guarneri? Or the cello, maybe, good player like you? Carlo Testore, somewhere late 17th century Milan. Milano, the wops call it. I paid - get this - I paid ten grand for it in New York four years ago, it's already worth twice that. That's seventeen percent a year. You name me the municipal's gonna appreciate seventeen percent a year, hey. Or paintings, Jesus Christ, excuse me Anna, but I know guys think they're gonna get rich backing some lousy unknown painter and cash in when he gets famous. A little common sense a'd tell 'em not a tenth of those jerkoffs could possibly get famous, and who's to tell which tenth?"

He unlocked the cabinet that held the Testore. "Nope, give me fiddles. It takes a wop three-four months to make a fiddle, and there's not more than a couple dozen of 'em working any one time - fewer now, since the war. Buy old ones, why, you know which ones are good already. Take 'em out of circulation, you know they're just gonna get scarcer. You look at this cabinet, you're looking at under thirty thousand invested, it'll be worth a million easy by the time I'm ready for Florida. Hey, Rick, you - Rick! I'm talkin ta you. You got a business degree, they tell you anything about bonds that appreciate 17 percent?"

Rick spun alertly from where he had been inspecting the inlaid cabinet and admitted that his otherwise thorough grounding in investment principles had neglected wop luthiers. "Gotta hand it to you, pops," was how he put it.

I found a voice at last, as the elderly cello emerged from its plush gibbet. "But, well, gosh. Wouldn't it be better if they were played? Good players need instruments, and they'll just deteriorate hanging in there . ."

"Deteriorate? Says who? That cabinet is temperature and humidity controlled by a thousand bucks worth a plant I had put in there." (A hum and a soft puff of air emerged from the open cabinet). "Those fiddles'll come out exactly the same as the day they went in, or I'll have that contractor's balls. Scuse me, Missy. You see anything wrong with this Testore, son?"

I brushed aside the white pedigree ribbon hanging from the scroll and held it up to plunk the strings. Other than a certain dullness to the varnish and the fact that it was badly out of tune, the cello bore only the marks of its long life as a player's instrument - a life apparently now in suspension, if not over forever.

"And you'll make a bundle selling this to a player when you retire, is that it?"

"Some player's got the couple hundred grand it'll take by then, sure. More likely it'll be another collector would have that kinda money, and he'll sell at close to a million. Think of that, son, the wop got maybe a lira for it in 1700, and you're holding a potential million dollars in your hand. Kinda makes you think, don't it?"

I looked at the cello, and thought. No rosin on the strings or around the bridge, no smell of rosin or polish to it. It was a stuffed swordfish. I handed the thing back to von Bayern. If he wanted to think I was shaking my head in admiration at his shrewdness, let him. I strolled the length of the case, looking at the other corpses. I could hear each giving the dull, out-of-tune plunks I'd drawn from the Testore cello. Anna took my arm and pivoted brightly toward the door.

"Thanks so much, Mr. von Bayern. Those are beautiful things, and it was a real privilege to see them. I guess we need to be going now, though."

"You're welcome, honey. I'd say the same to you, but the missus'd have my - excuse me, my hide. You young fellas behave yourselves with these lovely girls, and have a good time."

"Make up your mind, daddy," sparkled Nancy; and we got out of there.

Rick drove, Anna and I gladly dove into the back seat: all the raptorial chromosomes in the front, and a couple of adaptable mammals in our plush cave lit by windows no more than a foot high. Rick and Nancy recognized the folly of asking either of us where we'd like to go, and we peeled off without discussion. Nancy flipped on Spider Burke at a volume that made us scream whatever inanities came to mind, which in Nancy's case were abundant. She had little enough to say to Rick, but addressed Anna as if they'd enjoyed sisterhood from birth, referring archly to people, places, and events that predated my existence, and to who was 'dating' whom, meaning screwing, though you mustn't think that she particularly avoided vulgarity.

I was glad to see Anna was at least discomfited by some of this stuff. But she seemed to operate on two levels: in the realm of bubbles with Nancy and nonverbally with me, finding little shifts and grips and rubs of my hand and thigh that let me know every so often that she hadn't forgotten me.

Rick and I had one piece of common ground, our connection to Molar Chemical, but our points of view were so different that after a few yuks about Harvey Napperson that made me feel smart, I ran out of words and let him speak of his options. Between Rick and Anna, as between Nancy and me, there was no connection at all; and since what I shared with Anna was a world of library tables, of rain and moss, hammering pulses and Rule One and Wages of Fear and music and balderdash and landscapes viewed from on high - well, what was there to say to anyone else about that?

I think we drank at Biggie's, and I know we ate, drank, and danced at Garavelli's and the Chase – Jesus, dancing with Anna in that silky little dress – but after a while I sort of lost track. I remember a tense encounter with a cop after Rick ran a light about midnight way up north toward the airport, and a later one somewhere across the Chain of Rocks Bridge that involved Rick in some kind of negotiation with three or four Negroes.

I don't remember crossing Chain of Rocks. It kills me still how we whizzed giggling and blithering past the spot my father chose for death. At two in the morning they were showing me how to, as Rick put it, blow dope, and then things got rubbery and hard to remember in order. I know we were listening to exhausted jazz when Rick groped and shortchanged a cigarette girl, and if there was a cigarette girl to harass we must have been somewhere fairly civilized. Too civilized for us, anyhow, because the next thing a bouncer was picking Rick up by his belt, ignoring threats on his job, and hauling him off to the street. When we paid the girl and the tab and joined him on the sidewalk, Rick had reassembled his cool.

"OK then, screw this joint. I know plenty better places where . . . th'out that kinda shit. Say we run over to Belleville? Kids game?"

I was amazed at being given an option, and I took it as fast as I could get the words out. "Uh, no. No, absolutely not. I got an 8 o'clock - " (Hoots from Nancy at anybody dork enough to sign up for an early class, let alone talk of showing up for it.)

"No, really. It's-been-great-but-not-in-the-cards. Anna-'fyou-want-to-go," I heard myself babbling *molto stringendo*, and immediately regretted it; but Anna took my arm and bumped my hip with a sleepy smile.

"Don't be silly, Oren, I'm with you."

Rick gave a superior snort. "Brownies an scouts als on time. Take a cab from here, though. Can't drive y'all way back to Ladue."

That was more than fine with me, but it did raise a problem, since being stuck with paying off the recent dive had run me down to a dollar and change. Damned if I'd say so, though.

"Good enough."

I shrugged a shoulder and watched a vertical shear run down my arm and eventuate in a finger raised at the cab that had just dropped off a whore at the hotel across the street. "C'mon Anno," I said. That wasn't quite right, and I knew it, but I couldn't think how to fix it.

We got in the cab; Anna gave the address, and immediately opened the door on her side. "Come on, Oren," she chirped. "We're there."

I didn't see how that could be, since I could still see Nancy's haunch next to my window - but no, it was the fender of my Chevy, and I was out on the pavement under the stars, and the taxi's lights were receding around the corner onto Ladue Road. I breathed dark air and looked up at winter constellations wheeling. When I was about five years old, Dad made me a little wooden whistle out of bamboo and taught me the first seven notes of Twinkle Twinkle Little Star on it. I still had it somewhere in a drawer. When you see winter constellations in the summer, either it's pushing dawn, or you've lost months out of your life. In view of the warm night and how the trip had taken no time at all, I had to go with the late-hour explanation. I focused on Orion and Sirius, and rubbed my face, feeling better by the second. Anna snapped her purse shut and beamed up at me. "Feeling better?"

"Gosh, yes. Did you pay that guy? Was I asleep, or what?"

"I always have a little mad money. You sure were asleep, OK. I thought I might have to call Danny Thomas. Take me to my door?"

We walked across the grass onto the stupid little bridge, and at the top, wanting to postpone parting, I leaned over the railing to look at the reflections of stars. A stadium full of crickets and katydids yukked and yammered in the bushes, and I felt great, though I wasn't a hundred percent sure whether I was looking down or up at the constellations; Orion was inverted, I remember that. I felt Anna kind of rub her silky dress against my arm, and her reflection merged with mine against the wavering stars.

"Are you in such a big hurry to get home?" she or the silk whispered. I certainly was not. After a few preliminaries, a murmured suggestion, and some organized cheering by the crickets we staggered down the far side of the bridge and over to *Six bis* as well as we could, trying to maintain as much full length contact as possible while we walked. It involved yards of silk and softness, breast and thigh, and really it would not have broken my heart for that walk to have lasted until dawn. But there we were, and she reached into the mouth of the ugly brass frog and drew forth a brass key that slid into the lock. As she stretched up to replace it, the silk dress slid over what was recognizably the same perfect butt I had once saved from bouncing down Mt. Taum Sauk. And I knew that whatever her status, my boyhood was about to end.

Here is what I remember now from the rest of that night: Anna leading me by the hand through the purple glow of the conservatory to her little guest room, locking the door from the library as she went by. Anna kicking off her sandals during a kiss that, with all the sweet familiar overbite, was knowing and tremulous. My hand sliding as it had known all evening it must, beneath a strap and over her breast, a gesture renewing through long seconds of yielding and extension. The whole dress whispering to the floor, Anna stepping from the avalanche naked while I stood still stuffed like stupid sausage into my charcoal and pink casing.

A knotted shoelace, sweaty socks. The immediacy of her body, the transition of imperceptible down on her belly into black curls at its base. Falling from enormous height into eyes, pillow, and darkness centered in the glow of her reading lamp. A scent of distant rain. Guidance, fumbling, grace. A flashing cry from Anna, no accident now but as startling as if she really were dying. And, as I drove thunderstruck into sunrise while smells and slickness and knowledge muttered and faded through the clouds of dope and fatigue, the final: *Now what?*

8. Space

    I stood outside Pietro Di Salvo's violin shop and counted windows and chimneys, matching them with what I knew of the interior. I had wakened from a dream this second morning since the dawn I drove home from Ladue, in which I walked upstairs through the varnish room into the wood storage room, then beyond that into a room with giant ferns and an aquarium and a bed of grey moss. Anna was there, of course, stepping out of the avalanche of silk; in the dream the dress whispered words from the middle of a sentence.

    I could see the window in the varnish room; through it were dimly visible inside-front-cover spreads for Fords and Lucky Strikes. There was a stretch of windowless siding beyond, and then a boarded-up back porch that looked like a poor bet to be the love bower of my dream. There was no such place, I stipulate that at the outset. But I was desperate to think of a place - short of the Coral Courts, to which I would not have submitted Anna even if I could have afforded it - where we could "be alone," where we could "talk." Sure, and where we could indulge in further love-making. Screwing. I vowed when I began this that I would speak the truth in plain language as nearly as I could.

    Laugh out of court the notion that either of us commanded private space in our homes. And the University knew it housed a huge population of men and women at the peak of their hormone output, and had put centuries of experience and ingenuity into providing its students only well-lighted, benignly overseen spaces. There was always the option of a blanket in Forest Park, but neither of us was taken with the idea of sex al fresco in the middle of a big city. Taum Sauk or closer wilderness was not practical. We needed - we *wanted* - a place to which we could retreat at short notice, where we could rendezvous and, as the season advanced, we would be sheltered from rain and chill. The only place to which either of us had privileged access was Di Salvo's shop, and that would pose risks. But I was willing to give it a shot, and crazy enough to think -

OK, no ferns or goldfish - the dream had been reminding me of something I might have noticed subconsciously. I was a great believer in the subconscious in those days; it was an appealing alternative to much of my conscious life. Anna had been talking to me about it from her literary standpoint, and the notion of having more than one mind certainly fit a lot of experience, and it provided some kind of respectable-sounding cover for the backstage Yahoos. So, having two days ago exited boyhood at last, I put aside boyish error and gladly embraced adult balderdash.

On the theory, then, that no harm would be done by just taking a peek, I outwaited Di Salvo, taking a bin of shavings, wood scrap, and trash out to the alley for this exterior reconnaissance while he polished off a last pleading caller and got ready to close for supper.

"I'm off, Oren," he called, and I waved my virtuous dustpan at him in farewell, waited five minutes during which I became more and more certain that there would have to be unused, unsuspected space upstairs, given the small size of the varnish and storage rooms compared to the roomy layout on the first floor. I took the key from its drawer under the counter and wiped down my feet - there was no point in ruining newly varnished fiddles just to further my sex life - and carefully unlocked the stairway door. I knew Di Salvo would have a fit if he knew I was going up there, and my mental orchestra swung into *The Sorcerer's Apprentice* as soon as I opened the door.

Queen Elizabeth did not approve, the bombardier winked from within his ring of soot, and aristocratic Janet Leigh invited me to stop and consider whether a generously endowed blonde might not be more fun than the willowy, ardent girl I had found for myself. I did stop. I examined her pallid eyebrows, her regrettable lack of overbite, the insane linearity of her breasts. Sorry, Janet.

Bouncing bassoons by Paul Dukas as I eased open the door of the varnish room. Two shiny violas hung in silence, averted, nervous at my trespass. There were windows on each side of the varnish room, which made it narrower than the shop below, and I resolved to see how that worked when I got back down; meanwhile, it ruled out anything hidden in the lateral

127

direction. I tiptoed into the gloom of the storage space behind and pulled the chain on the overhead light. Stacks of wood familiar from my recent inventory. Beyond them, what I must have noticed half (sub-) consciously while slaving in the heat: no less than three doors set into the back wall. Aha!

The door on the right was a closet about three feet square, and next to that a long-dead bathroom with cracked fixtures and a peeling mirror in which I loomed, a menacing cipher against the light from behind. The left-hand door was locked and bolted from this side, so it was a moment's work to undo them. I stepped in twilight onto a second-floor screened porch with stairs descending to the alley - which had once been a back yard, I suppose. I considered for a moment: access from outside, fair privacy. Right; and squalor, peeling paint, floorboards we would be lucky, seeing how much thump and bounce this screwing business seemed to involve, if they didn't dump us in flagrante through to the first floor; and laughably public access, through the shop or from the alley. I couldn't put Anna through it.

I turned back with regret and shut the door. It groaned sarcastically and would not latch without being slammed. Great idea, Oren. I apologized to the cringing violas, and started down the stairs in defeat when I looked overhead and it struck me that I had accounted for all the space at the back end of the second floor; but hell, what was over the showroom in front?

Why, the softly carpeted, fern-endowed front room of course, the entrance to which was obscured by the stairway door when it was open into the varnish room, but plain as day when I peeked behind it. Here it was, the room of my dreams, furnished with a couple of comfortable chairs (for talks), heavy drapes over windows that looked out on the back of Di Salvo's front signboard (discretion) and a bed (all the rest). A perfect place, private, cozy, and safe. And I had a key to it for as long as I worked for Di Salvo.

Yes, perfect. I would work for Di Salvo, take his money and his tutelage, and smart-assedly sneak Anna Rosen into his private space behind his back. I looked at the little bed, picturing Anna sitting on it smiling up at me, Anna and I screwing on it, dressing quickly afterward, avoiding each other's eyes. On the bedside table lay a cheap, clothbound, gold-stamped book: LA COMMEDIA di Dante Alighieri Fiorentino. I picked it up carefully, remembering that traitors occupied the lowest circles of hell. Doré illustrations or similar, including Francesca da Rimini, but - hmm, she wasn't artfully half-nude as in Classics of World Literature *(College Edition)* but writhing in the whirlwind naked as a jay, complete with pubic hair, and so was the amazingly endowed ghost of Paolo dangling behind her like a neglected balloon. No tastefully aligned drapery here. Either our text was sanitized or this was a pornographic variant. I found other volumes of Italian pornography; that is, magazines written in Italian and containing pictures of naked men and women. They might have been medical journals, but I don't think so. On the dresser were gadgets of leather, rubber, and ebony at whose exact use I could only guess. I was overcome by guilty amazement. I checked earnestly to be sure I had disturbed nothing, and turned to go, but I couldn't resist another peek at Francesca. Goodness. I wondered if this was the "girl I loved once upon a time," and devoutly hoped not.

I started down the stairs appalled at Di Salvo. It was indecorous, one ought to respect one's own grey hairs, not belabor the juice of adolescence into geezerhood. This piquant pain in the ass horniness should, would surely be, quenched after a seemly few decades of incandescent whole-hearted screwing, nine innings and segue to leonine contentment, grandchildren, a standing ovation, the showers. *Didn't work that way for Dad, did it?* asked Paolo from above.

My feet stopped, my body didn't, and I caught myself with a hand on Janet's abundant breast. No, it certainly didn't. Your pleasure is your punishment, you manage it or it has you stumbling onto the Chain of Rocks Bridge with a page of instructions from the Board of Education. Did he see how stupid and unfair, that the hormonal calendar should not respect what would be practical for one's time of life? What was the point of dragging it on and on, extra innings with the game already won or lost?

I had no sooner returned the key to its drawer and put myself together to get out of there - I was too rattled for a session with Francesca, and slated for more Stravinsky that night

129

anyhow - than Di Salvo popped in the front door again. "Ha!" he cried, and I almost fainted. "Glad I caught you." *Glad you didn't, sir.* "Psalms gotta be at Orpheum tonight, Concordia got some kinda conflict for their space. Need a ride?"

"No, thanks, I need to drive tonight anyhow."

Boy, did I. My only contact with Anna since the definitive contact had been a stammering phone call in which we agreed that we needed time and space in which to approach head-on the great *Now What?* We would slip off somewhere, after Stravinsky - the first joint rehearsal for choir and orchestra since the initial get-together - to talk, to think about things and, we admitted, probably to wind up as we had at dawn on Saturday, that much deeper into this. We had one advantage in logistics, and that was her parents' ignorance that we shared Stravinsky - a conversational card I was glad not to have played during the convivial family dinner. But even that was little comfort; since Saturday, I had no stomach for fool-the-grownups games.

I was not in my heroic cellist persona during the Stravinsky, in spite of an earlier hope to wow Anna with the lead part. The Yahoos of ambition were staying well offstage, staring pensively out of windows. I was happy, and to judge from her face Anna was too, to dissolve in the music before us and be small parts of something larger and more solidly constructed than our own lives for a few hours. Afterward, she came back to where I was standing at Francesca's case, getting ready to pack her away.

"Is that a new cello?"

I turned; she was dressed down in choir-practice clothes, the Washington U. sweatshirt over jeans and little tennis shoes the size of thimbles. It was my first direct experience of the charm of baggy clothes. She looked edible. We were both blushing and our pulses were jumping. "Anna, Jesus, I've missed you."

"Me too, Oren. Oh, don't, people are looking . ."

"Let them."

"Wait. I told Nancy not to wait for me, and she ... That's such a pretty cello. I don't think they got home until about noon on Saturday, but maybe her parents. I'm rambling, I guess?"

"I can't tell. I have a suggestion: there's a dressing room backstage, up some steps just to the left of the stage door. You just slip back there, and I'll be there as soon as I get Fran- when I get this packed away."

She looked around doubtfully at the thinning crowd of musicians. "Won't we get locked in?"

"Absolutely not. The doors have panic bars, so you can't. What about your folks?"

"They think rehearsals last till eleven, that's what Nancy told them when she wanted to take me bar-hopping. Not that - "

"Not that they matter as much, do they? Is this some evolutionary rite of passage, am I supposed to find a hut and bring you giraffe haunches?"

"I'll settle for the hutch. The hut."

"And cab fare from the other night. No way I'm going to let you pay for a cab I ordered. It's the guy's responsibility to pay"

"Yes, you good soldier. The Good Soldier Dienst. You were so funny in the taxi. When I told him Six Reignleigh Court, you kept saying 'six bis, six bis.' He thought you were talking about money, and he started to get mad, and then he turned around, and you were completely out. He said, 'That's some tough cookie you got there, Missy.' I hate being called Missy. I told him to just get us home."

I was mortified. "I don't remember a thing about it. One second I was trying to get up the strength to punch Rick in the nose, and the next we were out in Ladue. What do I owe you for the enchanted taxi?"

"Nothing."

"Miss Rosen. If you patronize me you will be in danger of violating Rule One."

She rolled her eyes. "Very well, Mr. Dienst. I will split it with you. I am not going to tell you how much it was, but I will reluctantly tell you - "

"I cannot begin to express with what reluctance - "

" - I will tell you how much half of it was. You may reimburse me that, but wild horses could not drag me to reveal the full amount."

I raised my hands. "You are far too clever for me, and I'm not even a wild horse. How much was half of it, then?"

"Um, a dollar and eighteen cents." She held up a finger. "Don't imagine that merely by doubling that figure you can reason your way to the correct sum. I have employed rounding."

"I already admitted defeat. I will bring you the dollar eighteen shortly. Go where I suggested and wait there."

She nodded, and the black pony tail and narrow, dear sweatshirt dissolved in the backstage gloom.

I finished packing Francesca and walked to where the last choir and orchestra members were drifting out past Jacob. "Mr. Oxendine," I said. "I have a really large favor to ask."

When I opened the dressing-room door the lights - well, some of them - were on, but Anna was not there. I pulled back into the hall, lit only by the EXIT sign over the stage door. Shadows, silence, a feeling that something terrible was waiting in them. From inside the dressing room came a soft sound, the sort one might make by tossing a pillow on the floor. Inside, there was no pillow, but a pair of jeans now draped the screen behind the couch. My heart banged painfully, and a tiny sneaker flew over the top of the screen and hit me on the shoulder. I grunted with lustful relief, and snatched the powder puff off the dressing table and hook-shot it back over the screen, aiming at the irregular soft thumping I could hear behind it.

"Ow! Tarnation!"

I peeked around the screen to find her in just her sweatshirt, hopping on one bare foot, giggling and tugging at the other sneaker. I gave a little cry of pain and scooped her off the floor, still struggling with the sneaker. She dropped it and gave me about three seconds of gaze. "Did I hurt you?"

"Something just went right through me. I think we'll find it stuck in the wall back there."

"It's funny how you have to feel these things yourself before you see they aren't only clichés."

"Will this ever become routine and boring?"

" 'This'?"

"Oh. Well, I guess I sort of - not that I want to take anything for granted or anything - "

"Silly boy. You thought I was going to try on costumes?" She looked at the door. "Are we safe here?"

"I spoke to the caretaker. We have half an hour."

She closed her eyes and raised her mouth, open and hungry. I lowered her to the Freudian couch, and she stripped off the sweatshirt in a single gesture. I never knew anyone who could undress so fast. But we never did get the other sneaker off.

"Well," I said finally, "that is an amazingly good thing, even better when I am in full possession of my faculties. You must surely be the most beautiful and loving woman on earth, I suppose?"

"Loving, I expect so. Beautiful, well. In the land of big noses and buck teeth, I could be a contender. You noticed my nose and teeth?"

"I suppose it's no good saying they're the very first things I noticed."

"Why not? Anyone would."

"No, I mean ..." I drew a thoughtful finger down the miracle of her nose to red lips still a little swollen with the kisses and the discreet cry that had occupied them. "Janet Leigh has commissioned a team of Swiss surgeons to reconstruct her nose to look exactly like yours. They will fail, tragically, because - "

"There's not enough spare nose in Christendom to do the job?"

"Because it will be exactly this wonderful nose, just stuck onto pathetic Janet Leigh with organ glue. Your whole face, your whole person, including your face - and thus your nose and teeth - are you getting this?"

"Huh?"

"Everything about you is in harmony. Your nose, your wonderful breasts, your knees, all of it. I am surely the luckiest guy around, to have met such a completely integrated, completely alive, perfectly complete girl. Geez."

She smiled and began to blink. "I was doing okay until the 'Geez.' Your silver tongue."

I kissed her tears, and we stayed close for another half-minute. Then I remembered Jacob, waiting in the dark. "We better go. Speaking of silver." I picked up my pants. "Here you go, $1.18 on the button. It's not every day I allow myself to carry that much cash. Thank you for handling the taxi when I couldn't."

"Well ... Geez. I feel a lot less cheap somehow."

"Funny coincidence. Dr. Eslington claimed the other day that's the market value of a human being. Reduced to elements, you know, a little heap of carbon and another little heap of phosphorus, ten gallons of water, and stuff."

"A chemist finally admitted water is an element? But how perfectly chemical, to reckon it all up like that. You don't suppose he might have left out a few things, do you?"

"Sure. Sulfur, nitrogen, trace - "

"I was speaking noumenally. The soul, for example."

"'*Soul*'?"

"You said that just like you kept saying "Six bis" in the taxi. Well, how about, oh, music, and dancing? Even '*chemistry*' - see, I can do that too - not the chemicals, but the ideas?"

"One dance at - what, a dollar eighteen? Eighteen million?"

"A dime a dance is all I ever heard. Tough problem. But I refuse to think of myself, to be thought of by your doofy professor, as a pile of carbon worth a dollar and eighteen cents."

I paused in the process of tucking my shirt in, and a phrase from mortgage office days came to me. "How about '$1.18 and other good and valuable considerations'?"

She picked her pants off the screen and began to wiggle into them. "Well, that's a nice flexible thing. OK, agreed. Let's even make it Rule Two: one average human being, including each of us, is worth a dollar and eighteen cents and other good and valuable considerations. And we get to mean what we like by the second part." She frowned. "But you might have overpaid on me, I'm skinnier than average."

"You forgot the nose. That's about six bits - Ow! It was taxi money, anyhow."

We walked as quietly as we could to where I'd left Francesca. The stage was empty, the house lights dim, the whole place spooky. Something glimmered on the handle of Francesca's case: a small steel key on a loop of string with a tag, "Stage Door East".

"See," I said. "We're not locked in."

Anna's eyes widened. "We never were, you said. What you mean is, we're not locked out."

"My ... " I looked into the shadows of the dome. Any real figure, any actual motion would have been lost in the faintly lit dances and mythologies that lined it. I stood with Anna in one hand and Francesca in the other and peered into illusory depths. "Thank you," I called softly.

As we turned to leave, very quiet flute sound came after us, echoing from surfaces and hollows until it was without a source, just a naked voice dancing through cavernous silence. We stopped and Anna put her arm around my waist. "Sheep May Safely Graze," she whispered.

In the car I turned to Anna. "Well, I hate to wreck the mood, but speaking of safety ... "

"I am due for my period tomorrow. I tend to be a little irregular, but if I recall the teachings of Sister Maria Immaculata rightly, we were well outside the Blessed Zone both times."

"I see, I guess. The Zone being blessed for conception?"

"The only true purpose of intercourse."

"I regret the apparent purposelessness of our, uh... And Sister Immaculata was ...?"

"And is, instructor of health and field hockey at Cor Mariae Academy."

"Well. Nuns have wide experience of sex, I understand."

"Well, in this case, yes. She was known as Traudi Krummenacher when she showed up at the gates of Magdelena Haus, which is this institute for fallen women the Oblate Sisters run in Lucerne. She didn't actually confess she was fallen herself, but she was there for several years in one capacity or another, and she certainly knows her ovaries. From Ovaltine."

"Hn. I'm more impressed than ever. Anyhow, I will buy Precautions, as Sophie called them, tomorrow. Assuming, I guess, you agree this'd be a nice thing to keep doing. I didn't mean to presume..."

"A nice thing. My dear, dear Oren. 'Nice' is how it'll feel when you win the Nobel Prize, or something. This is way past that. It feels like ... would 'sacrament' be going too far? A

Vocation, at least. Precautions, I guess so. I hate it. I liked playing Adam and Eve."

We sat for a minute in contemplation of our wealth, and I thought of something. "You're about to get your period? Why aren't you bitchy and unfathomable? Why are you being so nice?"

"I spent yesterday and today in the state you so kindly describe. Igor Stravinsky - and possibly the sound of you soldiering away down there, so blithe and manly - cured it."

"It was Stravinsky, I think. I meant to show off for you, but I felt like keeping kind of a low profile. Isn't that just beautiful stuff?"

"Frighteningly. I was glad just to sink into it and wander around."

"I did that too. Did we meet?"

"I saw you. You looked like you were busy with your - what did you almost call her? - so I decided not to bother you."

"Who?"

"Your new cello. Fran something."

"Oh. Francesca."

"...I see. Francesca."

I looked at her. "Are you - does that cello bother you? It's not mine, in the first place, it belongs to Di Salvo. And anyhow, it's a cello. Wood and wire, and stuff."

She stared out the window on her side. "I'm a dollar eighteen worth of carbon and water. And stuff."

"And other good and - "

"It's those intangibles that matter, isn't it?"

"Even I can tell the difference between your intangibles and Francesca's."

"Thank you. But your voice just then, when you said the name, was not the voice of one who speaks of wood and wire."

"Anna, for heaven's sake."

"Getting unfathomable, am I? ... I need to be getting home."

"All right."

She broke a long silence as we turned into Bryn Mawr Lane. "Stop. Don't park in front of my house, Papa will see your car. Here is what I have been thinking and rearranging in my head all the way home. I still don't have it quite right, but time is fleeting. I learned several things tonight, that I was not sure of a few hours ago. One, I mean more to you than a nice drunken screw. Two - "

"Anna! How can you think that?"

"Let me finish, please. It was thinkable. My hormones were trying to make me think it all weekend. Two, you have, though you do not own, a cello you think of as female and which you have named after your favorite literary character. I can tell by watching you play, that 'Francesca' means a great deal to you, and that I do not figure in that meaning. Three, you have a friend - who it could be I have no idea, since you have not shared him or her with me - who is willing to give us a place to meet and to bless our meeting with flute music. Four, and this is not something I just learned today, but have noticed, you have never shown me the shop where you spend so many hours, in spite of the fact that I love you and you say you love me, but you never even talk to me about what you do there. You change the subject when I mention it. And five, - I forget what five was. You get the idea, though. You have a whole life in music that doesn't include me, and I'm - as you were kind enough not to say just now - jealous. Screwing is lovely, but it isn't everything, Oren. I'm not sure I trust you to come back when you go away into a world where things mean so much to you."

I was at a loss. "Well, for Pete's sake. Don't you have things that don't include me? Your buddy Nancy, for example, and your lit courses, and ... and four years of..." I trailed off with upflung hands. I was starting to sound exasperated, because I was. Irrelevant factual matters aside, she had nailed me good, and the only difference between this and so many similar scenes I would live through was that she had been completely explicit.

"Well, as I recall," she sniffled, "I have tried to share with you some of the things that I like about literature, and to involve you in things that I do with Nancy, in spite of the contempt you so obviously feel for her. *I* thought the last occasion turned - turned out rather ni - rather ni ..."

That was as far as she could get, but it was plenty to unman me. "Nicely. And how. Oh, Anna, please don't cry. Let me hold you, at least."

She collapsed toward me and banged her head on the steering wheel, and wound up clutching the place, her nose buried in my sleeve, crying "Ow, ow, damn!" I held her and smoothed the bump until she quieted down. Her voice came muffled from my elbow.

"Bitchy enough for you? How are we to repair this before Papa sees me?"

"Repair your face, or our, my -?"

"Let's start with the face."

At eight o'clock in the morning, almost two weeks later, the phone rang in the dining room and mother picked it up.

"Well," she marvelled. "Your little friend has a new one."

In the course of those days Anna and I had, first tentatively and then wholeheartedly, gone about repairing what we referred to as "the Tiff", as if in our state we were entitled not only to all the world's love, but to a lovers' tiff as well. The repair was not easy to start, but it was pleasant work. She reported the arrival of her period, a nervous two days late; I made her a propitiatory gift of the little limestone fossil I had saved from crushing at Molar. I took her around to the shop and introduced her to Pietro Di Salvo, who oozed charm at her and said she was one fine-looking ragazza, at which she blushed and replied in graceful Italian, so I decided I knew all I needed to know about "ragazza".

We spent whole evenings in the shop while I worked on reassembling my old cello, now resplendent in its new disguise, right down to a fake label inside. For closer matching it would need a name and, thinking to compensate for trouble-making "Francesca" I suggested "Anna" before I realized the problem that presented: first of all, we were producing a feeble copy of Francesca here, a circumstance not flattering to Anna; and besides, in fact I still did not have the feeling for this cello, in spite of its years of service with me, that I did for the newcomer

Francesca. I explained these awkward considerations to Anna, and she sat quietly while I worked on something else.

"In the end," she said, "when Francesca is sold, that is the cello you will use, is that right?"

"Yes."

"All right, then. I am not going to be proud. I hope over the years you and this cello will develop as good a relationship as you now have with Francesca, and if you and I don't end up married and in the old folks' home, you will at least have this to remember me by. I would be honored to have it named Anna."

And so I put that on the label and pasted it in, and Anna looked at it for a minute with a grave expression that almost broke my heart, so I kissed her, and so forth.

Once things got onto a little jollier keel we did use the dressing room at the Orpheum several times, which reminded me to explain about Mollie and Jacob and *Sheep May Safely Graze*, which reduced Anna to tears again, more fathomably this time. After that, she always brought flowers to leave at the foot of Jacob's ladder. I made Anna her own copy of the key so we could come separately, parking in the customer lot of the Galley-Ho Restaurant a worrisome block away through the weedy circle of rubble around the Orpheum.

I suppose we met there maybe eight or ten times in that two-week stretch, not exclusively for sex - though we certainly didn't shun that - but also just to talk and luxuriate in the privacy. Often, I had my cello there, and she would invent real dances to go with the formal sarabandes, minuets, and bourées of Bach, though I will tell you it is very difficult to play in tune when your lover is doing a strip to BWV 1008. I tried out my theory of Beethoven's transcendental f sharp on her, and when I played it for her, singing the piano part as best I could, she thought it was abstract enough to mean something new each time, depending on what had happened since last time. And on that sensible note, I quit worrying about it.

By far the best of these times was the night after the Civic finally performed the *Bohemian Nocturnes*, to baffled tepid applause and critical yawns, but to Anna's complete enchantment. It reminded her, she said, of when her parents took her to Prague for Christmas in her 19th year - in other words, when she was little younger than I, but she made it a world ago, a time of gas lamps and coal fires, of smoky wine and pungent cigarettes in galleries and courtyards as dense and inflected as the language and history of the place. "And," she said, rubbing the back of my neck, "don't think I didn't hear the Good Soldier Dienst stealing my soul. I heard you so hard, I remember now having that music in my heart in Prague. I heard you with my whole body." The last was breathed directly into my ear, and I certainly heard it with *my* whole body.

The Tiff made us both aware of how fragile what we had could be. Our first lovemaking after it had an awkwardness to it that was compounded by the hideous business of using a condom. Anna demonstrated more get-down-to-it practicality about that than I did, and though that might have raised some questions in my mind, I knew better than to broach them. I had known since our first time that I had been the only virgin present. In the end, it was more or less satisfactory on the glandular level, and essential to the project of restoring trust. I resolved to shop around for, and try out ahead of time, whatever that took, a brand that would leave me some comfort and dignity.

Shopping around for condoms in those days involved a car, a good supply of quarters, and the stomach to visit every men's room on Route 66. Love alone could have driven me through it. The whole business took a lot of what Anna called Adam-and-Eve out of our affair, but I would say that we worked at replacing it with trust, affection, and the companionship of overcoming difficulties, not to mention sharing the wonders of nature along the trail blazed by Markus and Sophie.

Oh, what am I trying to pull here? "More or less satisfactory;" "wonders of nature," sure. My world revolved around Anna Rosen, her voice and her body, her hungers and responses, and how much love-making we could cram into the time she could steal from Papa's jealous eye. The more we met, the more we clung and fondled and gasped, the more besotted we became; when we were together in public, I had only to turn a hand or any other appendage toward her for it to be met by some flesh of hers. I must have made a pretty good imitation of Markus at his most stunned.

Oh, sure, we did all the talking we could fit between exhaustion and returning lust. We discussed music and dance and politics and Stravinsky, we sang and worked and saw movies and read books in the library annex as before. We laughed at everything, because everything was so wonderful and so wonderfully funny. And when Anna laughed, she became fifteen years old, the tiny lines by her eyes engulfed in webs of merriment, and the golden flakes within her eyes blazing skylight as she lifted her face to the sun. I went around humming about "*Freude schöner Götterfunken*" until it drove Cindy the lab partner crazy.

We even played ball on the lawn outside the Union after I discovered she'd been something of a softball star at Cor Mariae. Anna had no arm at all; like so many women, she looked lame and awkward throwing. But she was a whiz at pepper games and with a bat; not much strength, but a good eye for her pitch, quick wrists, and great speed on the bases. She still held, she claimed, the Cor Mariae batting record for lefties.

But now all that; all the rest of it, was about sex, as politics is about power. The hands that held the bat or Magic Mountain might as well have been bare breasts; I couldn't believe the whole campus wasn't turned on by the display. I had vivid dreams of flying, or falling, coupled to Anna, reprising the falling sensation I'd had the first time, and I figured it was just another example of the truth behind a cliché - "falling in love," get it? The few days we couldn't get together involved a lot of phone calls and intellectualizing. But we weren't suffering.

So when mother cracked wise about my little friend (Why did people keep referring to her that way? She never looked little to me.) coming up with a new one, she was referring in her motherly way to a regrettable incident in which Anna had thought to disguise her third call to me within the hour by representing herself as the registrar of Washington University, forgetting that our conversation would hardly be the kind one would have with a registrar, and that mother would not be above catching a listen at my end. When I told Anna about it later she blushed sulkily, but then started to laugh. She sent mother a tastefully worded apology in which she promised never to do it again, and mother indicated her acceptance thereof by occasionally switching from "your little friend" to "the registrar" in referring to Anna.

So I knew it would not be Anna, and was unlikely to be a real registrar either. An unfamiliar voice, British and female, informed me of Mr. Julius von Bayern's wish that I present myself at his home at seven that evening for "confidential discussions of a matter of serious import to all Molar employees."

I refrained from remarking that I was not a Molar employee, but said, "I'm sorry, but I have a rehearsal this evening. Would another time be convenient?"

"mPity. Mr. von Bayern rahther expected those involved to treat this matter as of the very highest priority, and to make such arrangements as would allow them to be free this evening. It should not take long."

"Well, may I ask what this matter is, that I may assess its priority?"

"I am not at liberty to reveal that. Mr. von Bayern was quite emphatic in his expectation that you in particular, Mr. Dienst, should wish to be present."

"I will do what I can."

"mPlease do. Thank you."

That the matter of such intense concern was the Molar chemical spill and the St. Louie Flu was beyond doubt, but what I was supposed to do about it was another matter. I was still clear that I had properly handled the notebook documenting the spilled stuff's identity and there, as far as I was concerned, the matter ended. I called Pierce Replogle to warn him I might be late, but would get there as fast as I could, and waited out his protests. I was a good deal more upset than he could be, since Anna would arrive to find me AWOL. "Sir, it is not my idea, it seems to be an emergency, and I will do my very best."

"This isn't something about my alto, is it?"

I marveled at the possessiveness of choirmasters. "'Your' alto. I don't think so."

"Yes, well, get here as soon as you can. I'll have to sing your part."

I smiled at the thought. The part reached well into the soprano range. "Good show, sir. I will be as fast as I can."

Harvey Napperson hailed me gladly from the driveway of Number Six Reignleigh Court as I drove up. "Good news, Oren. We've got the notebook, and that sample was definitely acetic acid."

"Oh. Well, that's fine, sir. Is that what this is about?"

"That's it."

"Well, I mean if you've got it, why are we all here?"

His face lengthened. "Serious business, I'm afraid. There seems to be a lawsuit of some kind involving the deaths."

"Deaths? I heard about one."

"Well, I think it's been kept pretty quiet. Six people have died, Oren, and two of them were white. The county attorney is considering indictments involving Molar. It's messy, and I don't have to tell you it's a good thing we have the notebook. The lawyers have some affidavits they want us to sign, so we'll be in the clear on it."

"OK. ...Isn't that why we signed and dated the lab notebooks every day, though?"

"It - hm - appears that the fact that you used partial notebooks in some way invalidates that as an iron-clad legal record. Thus the affidavits."

Careless me, to use those partial notebooks. "Well, let's get in there. I'm supposed to be in at Concordia at a rehearsal."

He shrugged. "Music."

"Yes. Music."

Rick McIntear handed me the notebook, which now had stapled to it a document on legal-looking paper with pink marginal lines and a signature line helpfully X'd at the bottom. It said that the attached notebook was a true and correct record of my laboratory work with Molar Chemical Company, a St. Louis corporation, for the period August 5, 1953 to August 25, 1953 and a lot of other stuff about my being a legally retained employee of the said corporation and so forth. I opened the notebook, and there were the familiar columns of titrations and weights and calibrations. "What page is it on?" I asked.

McIntear, doing his best Yoolie imitation, crossed his legs and took a sip of bourbon. "Well, Aaron, I don't know that you need to get into the details. Just, is this your notebook or not?"

Davies, the chubby little Molar executive I had first seen at Napperson's lab, broke in. "Hold it, Rick. You want this guy on the witness stand, not able to put his finger right on the stuff involved in the case? It's sample number 5308-52, son, right on this page here, with the paper clip on it."

I looked at it. Sure enough, the page was headed "Titrimetric Assay of Glacial Acetic Acid, Sample # 5308-52", and was followed by data from replicate titrations with sodium hydroxide of weighed samples. I had done it dozens of times that summer. At the bottom of the page were three values of percent purity, clustering around 99.4%, that looked familiar. OK.

I glanced at the next page, and it didn't make a whole lot of sense. It was another acetic acid assay, which was reasonable, since I did samples in groups once I was set up for a particular technique. The trouble was, the columns of figures didn't start at the beginning. It was like coming in on a movie in the middle of the second reel, in a boring way. I looked back at the page with 5308-52 on it, and a pang, something between Aha and terror, shot through me. These were my numbers, in my handwriting, but they were out of place. Very conscious of the silence of the men watching me, I paged back, looking casual, just flipping through pages, and found what I was after about ten pages back. A page headed "Titrimetric Assay of Glacial Acetic Acid, Sample # 5308-14".

Boy, somebody had gone to a lot of trouble for nothing, copying the exact numbers from one page to another, and at that - I flipped the book over and looked at the back cover. Sure enough, a bleached-out ring where a beaker of something had been set down on it. But this ring was pretty much smack in the middle of the back cover, while I remembered vividly easing the cracked and oozing beaker down so that the cracked part stuck off the edge of the notebook, hoping to keep the thing from breaking open completely to pour steaming-hot caustic over the lab bench and/or myself. The whole notebook was a fake, a forgery done by someone with access to the original but without the technical experience to understand that two apparently identical experiments always show little random, stochastic variations in their data. I'd like to say my mind raced like a well-oiled machine, sifting facts, deciding who must have been behind this forgery and why. By no such feat at all I looked straight at Rick McIntear. Guilty, no doubt of it.

I turned to Harvey Napperson, who I guess might have been somehow suborned into doing this, but if he had, would have been smart enough to invent plausible fresh numbers instead of copying them from another page. I tried, with only some success, to keep my voice from shaking as I said, "Mis - 'hhm, Mr. Napperson, where did you finally find this?"

"Well, you know, Oren, that's a funny thing. Pear came in with it this morning and said he'd found it in that drawer under where they always sat. But I swear I'd looked there more than once. Funny."

"Sir, there is something that bothers me just a little about this. I wonder if you would be willing to go over it with me tomorrow at the lab?"

"Oh, no you don't. That affidavit has to be signed tonight," said Davies.

Finally Yoolie himself spoke from the back of the room. "Gentlemen, get out of here. I need to speak to Dienst privately. Davies, you're a hack, the kid wasn't fooled for five seconds. Napperson, if you ever say a word of what you've heard here, I will have to act on your mortgage. Rick, let this be a lesson; don't fuck around with cheap crooks, get the educated guys on your side. They're cheaper and they do a better job. All of you but Dienst, get the hell out of here."

Harvey Napperson spoke at last. "But - Mr. von Bayern. That's the notebook, I know it is. It's Oren's handwriting and all..." He looked at me, and I shook my head. "It may look like my handwriting, but look at the next page. The null hypothesis is, it's a complete account of an acetic acid assay."

Napperson glanced at the page and turned as white as I must have, at the in medias beginning of the page that followed the phony data. He glared at Davies, the scientist offended by an attempt on his integrity; then he tossed the notebook on the table and walked out. The others followed, and from the look of Rick McIntear, our days as double-daters were over.

Von Bayern waited until they were gone, and said, "Well, boy, we got kind of a mess here. I see I'm going to have to appeal to you to help me out, or there's gonna be hell to pay." I said nothing - what was I supposed to say to that? - and he went on. "Course I can't force you to do that, help us out. But maybe I can persuade you. You're not exactly loaded?"

"That's right."

"Having trouble doing everything you want to with that good-looking little Anna Rosen, and paying the bills, and getting along with your education, and all?"

"Could we please leave her out, and get to the point?"

"If we possibly can do that, we certainly will. All right, son, here's one way to go. I'll pay you ten thousand dollars for your signature on that affidavit. Don't think you can hold out for more, because my next offer isn't going to be more money."

"In that case, I'm surprised you made it that much."

"Well, me too. But that's about a tenth of what it's worth to me. As I say, don't think you can use that information." (*To arrive at the correct total.* How much funnier that was when it was taxi money.)

"Well. That alone sounds like a lot of money to me, sir, and it makes me wonder why you care so much about it. Wasn't that spill MoPac's fault?"

"What spill?"

"Oh, goodness, Mr. von Bayern. Have you been taking lessons from Rick?"

He laughed at that. "Got me there, son. Have pity on an old man. How'd you like that little shit marrying your daughter?"

I relaxed a little, which was no doubt the purpose. "Seriously, wasn't it?"

"Not that you need to know, but I'll give you something for the laugh. We're liable, our car got a hotbox and seized up and caused the wreck in the first place. But it's not the fact that it spilled that has our nuts in a wringer, it's what spilled."

"Well, what was it?"

"There we get into things you don't need to know. It was acetic acid, just like that notebook says."

"I see. Well, you've made a serious offer here, and I'll try to take it seriously. Ten thousand dollars is a lot of money, and it would solve a lot of problems for me. Trouble is, I bet it'd just create a lot more."

He nodded. "You're probably right about that. I'll tell you, I've given this a lot of thought, though, and I only see one other thing that's gonna get you on our side. Come on."

I followed him into the library, wondering a little what it would have felt like to slam ten thousand dollars into my bank account. The Carlo Testore cello hung there, avoiding my gaze.

"Son, I'm reluctant" (*I cannot express . .)* "to do what I'm gonna do now, so I'm gonna give you a minute to think over that ten thousand. The offer is good until you say it isn't. What say?"

"Sorry, sir. Too much imagination." Prig that I was.

"Marry Anna, that's a lot of woman, I don't hafta tell you. Live in a nice apartment, Hi Honey, I'm home, get your Ph.D. without another thought?"

"Exactly."

He looked at that for a bit, then shrugged. "Little prick. I oughta have somebody bust your fingers, but I'm gonna show you some movies - "

"What, til I say Uncle?"

"Joke time's over. These are movies I had made last spring for a group I belong to, likes to watch things you can't see down at the Hi-Pointe, know what I mean. Some of 'em are a little crude, but not the one I'm gonna show you. I think it's got merit, and I think even you're gonna like it - up to a point."

"Couldn't you just tell me about it?"

"Wouldn't be the same."

Flickering light comes up slowly into a title, "Fire Bird." An interior shot looks something like the inside of a barn or a stable. An elaborately costumed woman walks into the scene. She is wearing a tight-fitting suit that looks like red and orange flames, vertical swirls of color that play about her body, and move with her movement. There are red and orange streamers hanging from her shoulders, hips, and knees. She is also wearing an elaborate headdress and mask that carry out the flame motif. She has to walk a little awkwardly to keep from tripping on the flimsy streamers, but this will not be a problem when she begins to dance. Hanging on a wall are streamer bracelets, and she walks over to them and puts them on, her body in repose. She turns to the camera, and music starts - not the Firebird of the title but the Venusberg music from Tannhäuser.

It is one of those stereotypical modern-dance routines, in which the dancer begins from a crouched, huddled position and slowly rises and involves more and more of her body in the dance. In this case, it is at least appropriate to the fire and phoenix ideas. She is a pretty good dancer, with a nice little body that is revealed fleetingly in its tight-fitting suit by the flamelike streamers. She knows how to pace her dance so that each new movement is more daring and free than the last, and it is like both a fire and the rising sexual tension of the music.

I am sorry to note that von Bayern is right, that I am getting aroused, which is the measure of art in this genre.

There is a sort of dying-down lull coming in the music, and the dance follows it, the movements becoming less extravagant, and the dancer ends up on a raised platform, almost in the huddled position of the beginning. However, there are production values. The platform contains a powerful fan covered by a grating, and the dancer has crouched on top of it. We hear the fan start to roar - negative production value here. The flamelike streamers rise around the huddled form of the dancer, and she twitches and buries her face in her arms. After a little stretching and a show of reluctance, she rises again, driven up by the forge-like action of the fan below her. She looks cross and sleepy, dancing unwillingly, but as if she has no choice. The streamers fly, and her arms rise as well. Slowly, she moves into a kind of reluctant bump and grind, tossing her head defiantly, twitching to the rhythms of Wagner. We see both arousal and rebellion; but she conveys helpless passion in the set of her head, the spread of her legs. Her body becomes a single flame, twisting in the blast of the fan. She is so hot (Get it?) that we see smoke rising toward the rafters. The camera draws back to show an alarm box, which bursts open spontaneously, causing a sprinkler head over the dancing woman to gush, soaking the crepe-paper streamers and running the body paint that we thought was a tight-fitting costume. Still, the woman dances in the pools of red and orange that drain into the roaring fan and return to envelope her in a spray of mist, a development that seems to please her and lends further mystery. A siren sounds, and a fireman enters the frame with a massive hose, which he of course carries between his legs. The jet of water tears off the soaked streamers and begins to wash away the last of the body paint. We see a naked breast, the line of her ribs emerges. Her movements in reaction to the stream of water become spasmodic and feeble, and she is hurled to the platform, where she lies inert, a knee raised strategically to hide her groin. The camera closes toward her, gloating over the gleaming lines of her body, the rise and fall of her breasts as she pants. The masked face fills the screen. The gloved hand of the fireman removes the mask as the music swells. It is no surprise by now that the face is that of Anna Rosen. It is flushed in a way that is also familiar.

9. Arnold

"Sit down, son, and let's think about the meaning of what we've seen here."

"Why don't you just explain how you think you can blackmail me with this piece of sorry crap?"

"That's what I meant, no need to act hardass with me. So don't try. There's a couple ways this could go. Three, I guess. One, you could be so shocked at the whole thing you could tell me to stick it, she's nothing to you any more after this, and I guess we're back to the five thousand dollars."

"Ten."

"If you insist. Do we have a deal?"

"No."

"Two, you could tell me right now, Show me that affidavit and I'll sign it and give me the negatives and prints, and we're square. Three, you do nothing, and that movie goes out to stag clubs all over the country, which is bad enough seems to me, but it eventually gets back around to Arnold Rosen and he has apoplexy and beats the hell out of Anna and sticks her in a convent. And she'd let him, too but he'd have to hurry before the vice cops get there first and stick her in jail. Or, come to think of it, I could short-cut that step and show it to Arnold myself tomorrow. I have to admit that this isn't air-tight from my point of view, you could wash your hands of the girl and the money, and go right to the County Attorney, and to stop you from doing that I'd have to get rough. Which I will. I'm kind of counting on you being a decent fella that thinks the world of that little girl, as I do myself, and I'd love to be in your position, know what I mean."

"There's a law against pornography. What is it, the Surrogate Court or something that regulates that?"

"Isn't that what we're talking about here? Time she was out of jail, she'd be <u>way</u> too old for you, know what I mean, no matter how easy they went on her or what you did in the meantime."

"I mean, you made that movie. Aren't you cutting your own throat?"

"I doubt it. You see any sign of my name on that film? I bought it from a distributor in Belleville and I got a bill of sale to prove it. I thought I was getting a story about Stravinsky. I tell you, I was shocked when I saw that face. Also, I didn't see much reluctance there, did you? Beginning of that movie, she looked like a little girl ready to go to work."

"How about if you quit calling her a little girl?"

"OK, she looked like a woman ready to go to work. More so at the end, wouldn't you say? Man to man here?"

"Fuck you, Mr. von Bayern."

"Listen. You get to say that once, which you just used. You get loose like that again, I'll have some of the staff loosen some other stuff, got it?"

"I'll be seeing you."

"Not so fast. What about the affidavit?"

"I guess you'll just have to sit on it while I think this over. And if it falls in, which wouldn't surprise me, fish it out with your finger." I have to admit I didn't say the last part until I was out of reach and on my way to the door. But then I had another thought, and I stuck my head back in. "I'll call you, you don't call me. I need some time to think about this. I'll be writing a letter to the County Attorney, and if I hear you've done anything about the notebook or that stupid flick before tomorrow night, it goes in the mail. Got that?"

"Watch your back, Sunny Jim."

It was not to decide on a course of action that I needed time, but to think through the consequences of the only possible course: to sign the affidavit on the forged notebook in return for Yoolie's destroying the movie. And I must say, though I ran a lot of scripts (including guilty reminiscences of Fire Bird) about Anna, harebrained naughty bubblehead Anna, nothing really helpful came in the time I had between slamming the door in Ladue and pulling in to the Concordia parking lot. The consequences were predictable, and I was pretty much incapable of thought anyhow.

"Remitte mihi, remitte, remitte mihi," pleaded the altos, Anna among them, and I soldiered along, as I always now thought of it, the ominous march of a stranger; left, right, little eighth-note grunts of effort to lug the hollering sopranos up to the end of the first movement, where they sang about passing from this scene of woe and being no more. I looked up at Anna, her face as always charged with the meaning of what she was singing, with Nancy von Bayern next to her giving it a loose shot. All joy and all trouble in small space. We got through it somehow, and another rehearsal had gone by without cello heroics from me. Nor had I ever felt less like providing them.

It almost killed me the way Anna came up to me afterwards: relaxed, affectionate, the Tiff a funny memory and a rendezvous at the Orpheum on her mind, Hi Honey, where were you, I was starting to think we weren't going to get to blah blah. Even as the same supercharged blood started pumping through my lucky old crotch, anger that had been circulating freely through it all the way in from Ladue fell out in a hard little sludge just under my heart, burying the edgy crystal Dad had left there, and I began to tear at all that we had loved, or screwed, into being.

"Anna, I wish we didn't, but we have a very serious problem that we are going to have to deal with *now* ." (The hellish satisfaction of seeing her face constrict, of knowing what Papa knew about how to make her fear.)

"What is it?"

The sludge began right then to decay to sorrow. It would be a slow, heavy process. "I don't think we can talk about it here. Come on out to the car."

"All right." (Yes, Papa.)

I put Francesca away and carried the case to the car, taking pleasure in making Anna hurry to keep up. I got behind the wheel and let Anna get herself into the passenger seat. She stared out the windshield, nursing the minor hurt of not having the door held for her. The sludge was only about three quarters anger now, but it was a lot bigger.

"All right, Oren, what is it? Why were you late?"

"I was out having a chat with precious Nancy's gangster father. I'm going to begin my career as a scientist by signing a document swearing a fake lab notebook isn't fake."

"Well, why are you going to do that?"

"I don't have any choice."

She turned to face me. "Honey, I don't see how I can help, if you - "

"Thanks, *'Honey,'* you've been plenty of help already"

"Is this something about my being a friend of Nancy's? I don't understand why you're being so - hard and mean."

"I expect your lovely buddy was mixed up in it somewhere. Now that you mention it."

"May I please know what we're talking about?"

"Absolutely, you bet. Your little porno movie. 'Fire Bird'. "

She was shocked, I could see that from the paleness. She drew a breath and let it out, and then shrugged. "Were you shocked?"

"Nauseated, more like it."

"Well, it wasn't intended for you, and I don't see what it has to do with us." She put her hand on my knee. It was so beautiful I almost fainted. "We made it in Nancy's barn, just for a lark."

"Your lark is how Yoolie's going to get me to sign his affidavit."

"Is this about that spill out in Webster?"

"Yes."

"What's that to do with you?"

"I told you about - I 'shared' that with you."

The hand left my knee and tucked into her armpit. "The missing notebook."

"Good. Except it's not missing any more. It's reappeared in a forged version that I'm supposed to certify to keep Yoolie from getting his nuts sued off, I think is how he put it."

"And why does 'Fire Bird' have anything to do with it?"

Heavy patience. "If I sign, he'll destroy it. If not, he'll show it to Arnold, and Arnold will come steaming home and beat the crap out of you or slam you in a convent. Or jail. Or all three."

"Oh, my God...." She turned on the seat to face me. "Well, don't sign. I can deal with Papa."

"Sure, I've seen you dealing with Papa. You're scared silly of him except when you're out air-heading around with - "

"Please don't think you can talk to me that way. I'll think of something, but I certainly don't need a sermon from you."

The sludge doubled in size, and most of the new batch was fury. "Oh, right! Excuse me, Miss Fire Bird, I forgot I was addressing one of my elders. Thing is, gee, the damn movie cut off too soon. Is the rape scene in the second reel, or what?"

"Shut up!" She slapped me so fast I could barely start to react, a solid southpaw whack that landed on my right ear and cheek and would have knocked me silly if she'd been more than a singles hitter.

I sat there digesting that, and - damn it - she began to cry, and about half the sludge turned to sorrow in two seconds; but it wasn't any the less sludge.

"Aw, shit, Anna. I'm sorry I said that."

"Well, maybe that's true, but you thought it. You've been thinking it all evening, sitting over there playing your damn cello like it was your worst enemy, not looking at me." She gulped a breath and started fishing in her purse for a hanky. "Well, listen. I'm sorry I slapped you. But don't do me any favors, OK? Don't compromise your budding career just to save my butt. I didn't make that movie to get you into a mess, and if you get into one over it on my account, that's your own bad idea. I can take whatever I have to from Papa, and I will." She tried once more. "It was just for fun, Oren, we did it way last summer before I even knew you. Nancy made one, too."

"Oh, boy, I can't wait to see that. Does Rick play Sluggo?"

She slapped her brow. "Oh, good one. Hardy har."

"I guess I'm not in form tonight."

"You certainly are not. I guess this conversation, this whole conversation, has come to a natural ending point. Do not sign. Butt out. If I run, I can catch Nancy, and I intend to run. Goodbye, Oren."

She got out and slammed the door hard enough to rock the Chevy on its springs, hard enough that it didn't latch but bounced halfway open, leaving me sitting in the glow of the dome light, listening to the little catch in her voice as she said Goodbye, Oren, and the receding patter of her tiny sneakers. When the sludge reached 95% sorrow and a total mass of a hundred pounds, the dome light burned out. That was an improvement.

At the shop, Di Salvo was pacing up and down, waiting for me with more news. "Where the hell you been, Oren, you take off with the ragazza before I can turn around, you gone. Gotta have Francesca, tonight. Been sold."

"Of course."

"Got anything of yours in that case? Your bow, si; music? Rosin, stuff? Get 'em out. Guy wants Francesca tonight, he lives the hell and gone out in the county."

I took what was mine out of the case, and Di Salvo got a cloth and wiped off the rosin dust and the marks of my hands, any sign at all that Francesca had been profaned.

"Good thing you got yours finished. I see you give her a name, after the ragazza. Good idea, help you play her good. Looks good, almost good as the real one. 'Bye."

Which real one? " 'Bye."

When Di Salvo was gone, I sat in the middle of the shop floor and cried harder than I had since I was ten years old. It was hard to do, it took effort to let myself do it. And when I could not do it any longer I stopped, and felt exactly the same as before, but dumber. I got the canvas case from where it had been stashed in the work room and wrapped the old cello in it. It would take a long time and a lot of work before I could think of it by its label-name, "Anna." And it would be a long time before I would take any joy in playing music in this shop. I left.

I sat on the Freudian couch at the Orpheum and worked for an hour, writing out a truthful account of the forged notebook, ending with the admission that I had signed the affidavit knowing that the notebook to which it referred was a fake. I didn't see any reason to spare myself in this. I folded the pages to fit into the envelope I had not thought to bring, and stuck it in the pocket of the cello case. It would be ready for the County Attorney when I needed it.

As if I were peeling back a bandage, I slowly unzipped the case and brought out the cello. In the dim makeup lights it didn't look half bad. I sat on the end of the couch and tried a scale. It sounded like crap, and I didn't give a crap. I knew I was maladapted to "Anna", and it would take a long time to get back where I had been before Francesca. I played some Bach, and I suppose if Bach had gone to hell and taught one of the demons to sing, it might have sounded like that. I took one note, d above middle c on the A string, a good resonant note on any cello, and tried to make my bow arm soft and receptive and play just that one note, full vibrato, letting the open D resonate, trying for a good sound on just one note. Mud and snakes spread around my feet.

I stood up in a rage and lashed down with the bow toward the back of the rotten, half-assed, cheap cello. I suppose the moment I opened my eyes, and found I had actually stopped the blow an inch from where it would have broken the bow and scarred the cello was the first good thing since the phone rang this afternoon; and the last for a long time to come.

*   *

I walked out through the gravestones in Lakewood Park Cemetery to dad's grave in the corner nearest the River des Peres. No one else was around, which was natural enough for a Tuesday morning. But some one had been there, for I saw with sorrow there had been fresh digging, and then - and I knew as soon as I saw it - they were moving his grave again. Geez, why couldn't they let him rest in peace? Even in death, he was a stranger and a wanderer. Apparently the digging had broken off just as they reached the coffin, and I steeled myself to look down. And I saw why they quit, for the grave was full of muddy water and the coffin only a brown canvas bag with a zipper on the side. It was lying open, and I could see the dismembered cello inside half submerged, strings in a graceless tangle, the fingerboard lying across the open belly, pegs scattered like bones.

"You have neglected your Technische Studien. You spend all your time with the other one, you have none for me."

"That's not true. Listen, I can -"

"Don't do me any favors, Oren. I can take care of myself. Go on home."

"What?

"I believe it's time for you to get on home, Mr. Dienst. It's almost six o'clock. You don't want to make your mother worry about you like this."

I sat up. "Thank you, Jacob. I apologize for abusing your hospitality."

"No such thing, Mr. Dienst."

"Well, anyhow, there'll be a lot less of it in the future. I don't think Anna and I will be coming here again."

"I am sorry to hear that. She seems a very pleasant young lady, and Mollie has been touched by the flowers."

I rubbed my face and forced a breath past the lump of sludge on my diaphragm. "Please give my love to Mollie, and keep some for yourself, Mr. Oxendine. I know you don't approve of unmarried people keeping company unsupervised."

"That is true. Mollie persuaded me that your intentions in regard to the young lady were honorable, and that until you were in a position to act upon them, her music would be a sufficient token of sacrament. I must say that I was not fully convinced, but our own situation is - though entirely innocent - after all quite irregular. And I do not find it easy to oppose her."

"Isn't that the way of it, though."

"Yes, by God's grace, it is. May I suggest that you and the young lady not renounce your access to this room precipitously. You are welcome here any time."

And I was welcome as all get-out when I knocked at *Number Six* that afternoon. "Get your ass in here. I can't think how many punks I got out looking for you."

"It's a good thing you got so much money, Mr. von Bayern. You sure as hell throw it away."

"You watch your mouth. You here to sign, or what?"

"Yes."

"Yes, what?"

"Yes, I'm here to sign. Where is it?"

"In there where it was last night. Come on."

"Not so fast. Where's the movie?"

"Right here, and the negative too."

"Burn them."

"You can burn 'em yourself, kid, after you sign. I'm not gonna be suckered."

"Well, speaking of that, how do I know that's the only print of the movie?"

"You don't."

"What's my motivation to sign, then?"

"The fact I have already called Arnold Rosen to come out and look at movies tonight. But that's up to you. I will tell you this is the only print, but you don't have to believe it."

"How could I not believe an honorable guy like you?"

"I'm not the one that's about to commit perjury."

"Bring me the print you're holding back, and we'll figure that's the lot."

He laughed, and reached into the bookcase and brought out another reel.

"I'm only doing this because I like you, kid. Shit, I could have twenty copies, you'd never know 'til you saw Rosen walking around in a habit."

"We are leaving Anna out of this."

"The chance to do that went by at ten thousand miles an hour last night."

"Is that offer still good, or the five?"

"No."

"Good. You haven't explained how I know you don't still have another print."

"I could have a dozen. I also told you this is absolutely it. I don't have all day to dick around like this."

"I do."

A voice, the tipsy singer of "You Belong to Me" offered a mangled phrase from "Don't Get Around Much Any More" from the back of the house. Yoolie closed his eyes and roared, "Maxine! Shut up! Kid, you sign that thing now, or the next window's gonna close, and it'll be movies <u>and</u> a couple broken fingers."

"You can have the fingers. I came out to sign because of the movie."

"Then sign."

I did.

Yoolie took the paper and folded it into a pocket. "You tell me I throw money around for nothing. I wanna show you something you're not gonna think that about."

"I believe we have finished our business. If I don't get out of here, I will vomit on your carpet."

"Go outside, vomit, come back. Believe me, you will not want to miss this. I have bought a new cello."

"If you took delivery last night from a contemporary St. Louis maker, I do want to miss it."

"You misunderstand. I <u>want</u> you to see it."

"Mr. von Bayern, I told you last night I got too much imagination. I can see Francesca hanging next to that Testore corpse you showed me once, as clearly as if I was standing there. I bitterly regret that you should have taken a fancy to her, and I regret very much that she will die a lingering death like it and the others already did. My only comfort is the thought of the look on your face when some appraiser comes out here, you're all packed for Florida with your golf hat and your white shoes and white belt and little bolo tie, and your false teeth and your little pot belly, and you're still horny but you can't get it up any more, and that appraiser tells you, *Gosh*, sir, these instruments should have been played, you've ruined them, locking 'em away like that, they're worth damn all, and that'll be a thousand dollars for the appraisal, please." I inhaled, with effort.

"You know something, kid? You're fucking crazy."

See? Even a crook will tell you the truth if you let him talk long enough.

I didn't hear from Anna and she didn't hear from me. I spent a lot of time down at the river remembering, nursing, doing anything but thinking. I dropped Yoolie's movies off the middle of the Eads Bridge, from a little niche I found behind a brick pier. Sometimes I took calculus homework or lab reports out there with me, stuff I could have done at home if it weren't for hearing Anna's voice in my window fan, or at the library annex if it weren't for the fear she might be there. And sometimes I would work at it, but most of the time I just stared down at the water, and usually it didn't bother to stare back. My hiding place was on the track level, and sometimes freights would come along and shake brick dust down on me, and I would wonder hopefully if the whole thing was about to crumble into the sliding mud of the Mississippi. At dark I would leave, because the mud started offering me a lift toward Memphis or New Orleans. I went to the Orpheum then sometimes, and worked at getting back into adaptation with *Anna* the cello. There was not a peep from Molar or from the County Attorney to tell me that signing the affidavit had any effect on anything.

The first time a Stravinsky rehearsal rolled around Anna (herself) was not there, which was a bitter relief. The second time, she was missing again, which was worrisome to Pierce Replogle because that was the dress rehearsal on the morning of October 24. Good old Nancy was there, of course, and I did not look away fast enough to prevent her seeing me look for Anna.

That night I came early for the performance and sat down to run some passages I would just as soon not occasion public humiliation over. Parts that had sung themselves when played on Francesca were agonizing hard work on "Anna." I worked at them as if at a vigil. We were performing in a big old chapel, with sections of the orchestra spread all over the altar rail area, squeezing to avoid the baptismal font and the stairs to the pulpit. The choir, of course, was in the choir lofts, and when they marched in looking dedicated in their robes, there was Anna with them. She was thin and subdued, and she did not look my way.

There was a long pause, then I remembered that as virtual concertmaster, it was up to me to signal for the A. So I stood up and pointed at the oboe, and sat down again. We played the tuning lament and fell silent. Pierce Replogle walked in, followed by a spot, so people figured they better clap, though they were pretty restrained about it, being on sacred ground.

Mercifully, he did not bow or welcome the audience or grin in any way. He turned to us, raised his hands, got eye contact with everyone, and Plink! we were off, with the woodwinds and then the basses and celli noodling and growling.

Early on, the first cello part has a high solo line that leads the altos in with the text "Hear my prayer, Lord", ending on the e above the alto entrance. I coaxed the sound upward, praying against the brittle shrieks I had made a lot of lately. *Francesca* would have hauled me up there like the real one towing Paolo through the airspace of hell. When the altos entered, they stepped off the last echoes of my line, down an octave. Anna looked, as always, as if she meant every word.

With the heroics over for a bit, I let my sound dissolve in the ensemble, and it stayed dissolved. I wandered through the desolate place Stravinsky had made, looking for Anna and not finding her. After they sang "I am a stranger among you, and a wanderer as were all my fathers," Maureen Witz provided a dim replica of Mollie's patient waiting upon the Lord, and at last I glimpsed Anna, far away through mist as dirty as the sludge in my belly. I played to her, I coaxed a voice from "Anna" and sent it through air thick with voices, to lead her from the lake of misery. And at last, angels hovered, and grace drawn by the wretchedness of my too earthly voice. From far away I saw her lifted from the swamp and her feet placed, trim and grave, upon the rock. Alleluia.

The last movement, the 150th psalm (in the vulgate) is a long hymn of praise. Starting out peremptory, muscular, staccato, toward the end it contains a melting phrase in which the choir in four parts, the winds, and the celli resolve the slight tension of repeated slow turns in a chromatic shift as unpredictable, and as perfect, as a rainbow. Anna and I called it the Taum Sauk section, and we had sung it together in the dressing room at the Orpheum, just one dancing alto and one cello, and even in that pared-down version it was ravishing.

Now on the first iteration *(Praise the Lord in the sound of the cymbal),* our eyes met for the first time since she followed me out to my car to be dressed down about "Fire Bird". She sang, I played; but I did not feel any lightening of my sludge of sorrow. When the phrase was over, even at my great distance from her I could see the bright track of a tear. And on the repetition *(Let all that breathes praise the Lord),* she sang it once, not looking at me, and when I looked back her place was empty.

Three days later she appeared at the Orpheum, grave and aloof, as I sat grimly playing exercises, punishing myself with arpeggiated drudgery. She was dressed in her hiking shorts and the Washington sweatshirt, her hair pulled back with a piece of black yarn.

"Anna! Hello . . ."

"Shh. Play." She sat on the floor in the edge of the circle of light, and pulled the sweatshirt over her knees, resting her head on them to make a self-sufficient grey-and-black egg.

I switched to the Allemande from the Bach D Minor Unaccompanied Suite, one of the saddest dances I knew, and one of those pieces that had been most guilty of overpromising, back in the days when I had expected more from music than I could find in it. When I finished she said, without raising her head, "Yes. But it's more than I can bear now. Isn't there some perfectly harmless stuff?"

No, I thought, but I played the Prelude and the Allemande from the G Major Suite, and then started groping through some half-remembered lines of Max Reger. Her face rose into the lamplight, smiling, stopping my heart. "Perfect. No, keep at it, that groping after something - after what won't hurt us." In a couple of minutes she rose and came around behind me, and after a little rustling time the black yarn arced through the air and landed across my bow arm, and I said "Ow, tarnation," and kept playing.

I kept playing for as long as I could, but in the end it had never been so sweet, not ever. She shuddered and clung to me, her legs wrapped my waist, and our bodies arched together with thirst that we had no hope of controlling. In the end, her cry of completion led without pause into hard sobbing, and she buried her face in my neck and howled. I could feel her tears mixing with my sweat and smearing across my chest as she pushed her head against me, her skin hot with woe. She struggled and rolled us a bit onto our sides to win space to sob more deeply, and I held her as gently as I could. I stayed within her, stroking her back, feeling the delicate ribs shuddering beneath my hand.

"I'm sorry, Oren. I'm so terribly, horribly sorry, I ruined it before it ever got started. It was so … " New sobs.

"Anna. Anna, don't. It's all over with now, it's all done. I can't ... I was such a prick. I'm sorry too."

But she was sorrier, I guess. I had never seen such sorrow. She ended at last with what could have been a little hiccup, and a sigh. She drew back a few inches and looked at me, both of us exactly the same age, somewhere around fifty. "I thought I never wanted to see you again, and I found out I couldn't live and be so wretched. I don't know if we can ever ..."

"Well. Me either. We can't ever go back to where we were, but … " I wiped my nose. "There's this thermodynamics thing, stochastic processes, where what happens next doesn't depend on what came before. Rule Three: Love is stochastic, how's that?"

A weak smile. "Of great comfort to a chemist, sounds like. Does it mean we have to forget all the good things too?"

"Love is partly stochastic."

"Who decides which part?"

"We do."

"One vote each? We'll tie all the time."

"You want two votes? What is this, the United Mine Workers?"

"Yes." She snaked a leg around my butt, pinning me up against her belly. "We're united, and you're mine; and I guess that's how it works. I agree to Rule Three with the proviso that I get to make up Rule Four."

"If I agree to that, it counts as Rule Four."

"OK - aiee! Rat. I'm not asking you to agree to Rule Five, then. It will be imposed without appeal when you least expect it."

"Anna, Jesus. You can rewrite the Ten Commandments. Just don't ever go away again like that. I almost died."

She tightened the leg around my thigh and somehow got her heel in where it could rest against some very sensitive territory. "Don't die, Oren. Don't ever say that. You're so goddamn precious, I'd die too. Make me a story - no, no, please, stay close, stay inside me, and make up some of your balderdash. Something dull and nice."

With that distraction I came up with nothing better than a flat little tale about a family of field mice who lived up on that ledge on Taum Sauk and saw us up there kissing, back in September. She listened quietly for a long time, keeping me pinned against herself with her heel, and it got hard to keep thinking about mice. She asked me what field mouse families used for umbrellas when it rained so hard, and I said they didn't mind getting wet, they were like Markus and Sophie procreating away in the elements.

"But smaller," she said, and herself became small against me.

"Smaller," I agreed, "and harder to notice."

"Can't smell 'em."

"Well, not unless you get right down next to them."

"Then what do they smell like?"

I rubbed her spine and her flanks, and felt them soften against my hand. "Like the place on your neck," I whispered, "where this nice bump comes up at the top of your backbone . . ."

"I smell like mice?"

"And sunshine. And baby powder and Cape Cod."

"Fishy?" The heel began to nestle and rub. "You dare tell me I smell - "

"S - Jesus. Salty."

She began to breathe with me, and I could feel myself swelling within her, a kind of sweet wet soreness. Already transfixed, she raised her mouth to mine. It was salty indeed, and hot; I gave a little grunt of desire, and closed my eyes, and her leg slid along mine.

Heavy shoes on the stairs outside; the door of the dressing room slamming open, and a huge form loomed over us. I felt a heavy blow across my ribs. Anna screamed with fear and pain, and I saw a welt across her ribs too. I rolled on top of her to protect her, and took a couple of agonizing whacks, and all of a sudden it hurt a lot to take a breath.

I heard her yell, "Papa, no!" and then something crashed into my head and I rolled off the couch in a gray fog and lay on the floor. It was like watching a movie - one of Yoolie's, I guess

- in that there was not a damn thing I could do to stop Arnold from whaling me except finally to roll under the couch, where he started kicking and prodding at me with his cane while he held Anna. He finally tossed the couch off as if it were made of balsa, and brought the cane down on my back with both hands. This time I heard the rib break before I felt the pain.

"Anna," I yelled, or tried to, with suddenly no lung power. "He's killing me, stop him!" But she just stood there paralyzed, hunched over and sobbing with two fistfuls of black hair over her face, I guess so she wouldn't have to see me die. I began having a hard time remembering Rule Three, or in any other way recapturing the magic. Thank God, Jacob Oxendine appeared and grabbed Arnold in a subduing sort of bear hug.

"Sir! Sir!" Jacob was yelling. "Sir, stop hitting that boy!" Which Arnold of course obeyed, since his arms were firmly pinned to his sides. When I found I could move I slid out of range, trying to keep as much weight off my ribs as I could.

"See? See him crawl like the snake he is? You little slut, do you see him crawl? Take your nigger hands off me, whoever you are, and let me at him."

I stood up about halfway and reached for my shirt. I know I was in shock from all that had happened in a few days: seeing Francesca in the hands of the one owner in the world who absolutely must not have her; selling my signature to save Anna from what happened anyhow; wrenching from happiness to sorrow to bliss to dismay with the same Anna who now stood with one wrist passively in Arnold's grasp like a naughty toddler, doing absolutely nothing to save me, or even cleave to me, forsaking all stepfathers; and what turned out to be two broken ribs.

Even so I do not report this next with any pride, and if I have sometimes given myself the benefit of doubtful memory in reporting my words and actions, I make up for it now. This is exactly what I said then, raising my voice as firmly as I could over Anna's sobbing with two or three knives sticking into my lungs, with my head buzzing, and with Anna's tears and the moisture of our love drying on me:

"Jesus Christ almighty. I absolutely give up. Goodbye, Anna. You're wonderful, but you're way too much for...me to

manage alone. Come and find me if you...decide to grow up and leave this...maniac."

There was no alteration in the rhythm of her crying to show she understood any of it, and it certainly hurt too much to think of saying it again, or anything more. I handed my shirt to Arnold to drape over her, and went to find my pants.

10. The Wall

Sunday, November 8
Dear Oren:

I am writing to thank you for playing so beautifully last Sunday. From the very first, where you heroically led us in to the "Exaudi" section, I knew you were playing specially to me, because as we were singing I felt the awful load of sorrow lift from my shoulders. And when I entered Stravinsky's world I felt you reaching out with your beautiful music and lifting me out of the swamp, exactly as I was singing that part. It was that which gave me courage to come to you at the Orpheum.

And even though I will never forget our love-making, I accept what you said to me after Papa came in. I cannot explain why I could not help you when he was beating you. He has some kind of ability to make me into a helpless child, and as long as he is around, that's what I am. Maybe this is Rule Five, that I must break free of him, and I will. (If so, you still owe me one.) I was a convent girl when we met, and by loving me you have set me free. I can be my own woman and I can plan what to do with my life; you have given me a life to plan. Thank you, Oren. These words cannot express a tenth of what I feel for you, (so do not imagine...) but I had to try. I will never forget you.

I am rambling because I cannot bear the thought of beginning these last words. I do not know what they can be. It is vain to say what is true, that I want nothing more than to feel your arms around me, because I know that can not be. But I see I have already said it. I will not ever forget you. I expect that is Rule Five.

-Anna

Besides that and, surprisingly, a vase of flowers - daisies, but still, it was the thought - from my new lab partner Cindy Something, the cheerleader, other mail that lay on my bedside table while I tossed and sweated through a stay at St. Luke's Hospital under observation, sedation, and a heavy layer of rib tape included a letter from Sophie, reporting that she and Markus were working in a salmon cannery in Homer, Alaska. (*"Markus goes out on the trawler Nitro Kid every morning at 4:30, and I start on the cleaning line at 6. It is a little hard right now, since I cannot abide the smell of Fish Guts at that hour, and I almost always lose my breakfast. The Dr says the Nausea will go away after a few months. I hope so. We are making good money and the people here are really very nice, I cannot tell you how many women when they hear my story say, Well, Honey, the same thing happened to me but worse, and your lucky your man is staying by you and working. We have gotten Married."*)

And a note from my advisor:

Dear Mr/Miss _Deinst_ :

Your instructor in _Chemistry 211_ **reports several consecutive absences in that class. Please make an early appointment for a personal discussion with me. We wish to help you in any way we can with your success in college.**

Sincerely, _Alfred Saxon , Ph.D._
Department of Chemical Engineering

But I had other goals than success in college as I lay there working on breathing. Planning for success in just one small endeavor seemed to be a good way to keep from thinking about anything else.

It was not that I was unwilling to think about Chemistry 211, or Markus and Sophie canning salmon in Homer, or music; or Anna. But when I tried to work my way down that list my mind got more and more clumsy, like a seal caught in some kind of laboratory trap, and at the last step I bumped into the Wall. It was like a slab of heavy black glass in the front of my brain, in which I could see a big dark reflection of myself superimposed on a glimpse of black hair. I was unable to push it farther than that, and when I tried I got a bad headache and had problems breathing. I quit trying. The wall of blackness stayed with me for years.

I turned instead to figuring out how to steal Francesca from Yoolie von Bayern and take her to someplace far away - Chicago seemed about right - and donate her to a deserving cello student, preferably one who seemed well on the way to a concert career. Ordinarily I would have considered actually pulling off such a stunt unthinkable, but compared to any other topic for thought, it was easy.

I was not so stupid as the imagine that Yoolie, on discovering the theft, would not know right away who had done it and send "staff" after me to get it back. But I did hope that by substituting my own cello I could delay detection - maybe all the way to that appraiser's visit on retirement day - until it was too late, and Francesca was irrevocably gone. In the first place, I doubted strongly that Yoolie von Bayern had a detailed familiarity with anything but the purchase price of each of his captive fiddles, so one cello would look a lot like any other to him; and I had put a lot of effort into making "Anna" look as much like Francesca as possible. Of course, if I got caught I would be in very deep water both legally and personally; and even if I pulled it off I would be without a cello. Neither of those seemed to mean much to me no matter how real I tried to make them.

After they sent me on my way with a bottle of pain pills and another of sulfathiazole, I gave myself a few days to get my nerve up. And on a Friday night - Saturday morning, really, about two o'clock - I eased my Chevy out of the drive and set sail for Ladue. I stayed on Ladue Road past Reignleigh Court, and hung a right into a dark area of the next street parallel to it.

We have forgotten how dark the night used to be, and how completely things closed down after ten o'clock or so. There was no other traffic, and when I shut off my own motor, the silence was broken only by a few sleepy crickets. Deep night's damp stiffened the chill of November, and I began to shiver with cold and nerves.

People out here hadn't learned to worry about criminals like me, and what lights they had were low and dim. I pulled the cello out and kept the door noise to a minimum click, not bothering whether it latched; the dome light was still burned out anyhow.

Even so, a fool dog started barking about a block away, and a porch light went on a few houses back along Ladue Road. I tucked the cello under my arm and headed away from the light and the dog, figuring that I could afford the time to walk around the block for the sake of anonymity. The road stretched away into the darkness, with black woodlands on the left and two or three shallow pools of light ahead.

There was of course no sidewalk and no curb; even in 1953 nobody walked in Ladue. I walked where the Lincolns and Caddies of the well-off were meant to run. The old cello bumped against my hip. I thought of the hours and years I had spent with it, of the easy triumphs at all-state orchestras, of the time that had been spent on this friend who - if I was lucky - would not play another note until some unguessable time in the future when Yoolie caught on to what had been done. I hoped he would not smash it in his fury. If *Francesca* was a living thing, so that to lock her away behind glass was criminal, then how was it not criminal to do the same to the wood and wire under my arm? And if the criminality of von Bayern's intentions lay in robbing *Francesca* of the playing that would slowly breathe a heart into her, hadn't the decades of music my old cello had known, at many hands before mine came into possession of it, given it that much greater heart to be broken by confinement?

A fine time to think of that, mocked the alien woods. These were not, in any case, questions I could answer even if I had known who was asking. *Francesca* demanded release, she was too beautiful to deny, nor was I the one to deny her. Looking back, I would have to say that von Bayern was right, I was not only crazy but criminally so, as I trudged down that road with a little night wind cooling my left cheek.

Of course I had not reconnoitered the broad and generous layout of this suburb when I set off to walk around the block to Yoolie's house. I had no guarantee that such things as blocks even existed out there, and it dawned on me after a while that I could be on a trek down a country road parallel to Reignleigh Court but not otherwise connected to it. I had left behind the last pool of light, and soon after that the last house. The woods on the left gave way to open fields, and the houses on the right, which should have backed up to those on Reignleigh Court, to woods.

It was not, of course, blind dark. Vague illumination, probably the nightglow from St. Louis, made the road visible; but would I see a street connecting to Reignleigh Court when it came along? I turned and looked back; the last streetlight winked a hundred yards back, wanly beckoning. I was out around the orbit of Neptune looking back at the fires of Earth. My lungs started to retch for air, frost grew around my mouth, I said farewell to the green hills ... Headlights bobbed down the road toward me.

I didn't wait to greet this late driver; whoever it was could live without seeing a figure in black sneaking a cello down a back road in the dead of night. I hugged the cello with both arms and ran into the woods to the right of the road, praying against ditches and barb wire. The sudden sprint twisted my broken ribs ominously. Headlights plucked at my right sleeve as I ducked behind a cedar, thankful of its dense needles and ignoring their prickle on my face. The headlights approached, blasted by in a blare of cheesy R&B, and disappeared over a little rise in the road. I picked my way back to the pavement and looked after them sweating, light-headed, ribs on fire. I certainly would have given up the around-the-block plan if the last sweep of the headlights had not picked up what looked at last like a street sign another fifty yards down the dark direction. I set out with some hope and there, where I'd have missed it if I hadn't known it was there, was a steel post with a street sign, and gravelly hints of a side road disappearing into blackness. I squinted at the sign and finally reached up and traced out the letters, the thickness of a coat of paint, with my fingertips: *Rainly St.* This took a few seconds to settle into place. OK, it must be the blue-collar, pre-settlement name of Reignleigh Court. But the road I had walked had certainly not swerved, so Reignleigh Court must have, spilling a load of silent letters, to intersect my road here.

The Cello Francesca, *or* Balderdash

A new logistic began to crystallize, and I stashed the cello behind a tree and walked back, feeling dumb, to retrieve my car from its pool of darkness. I drove back down the road to the back entrance to Rainly (or Reignleigh) Street or Court. I reclaimed the cello, and in a fit of shrewdness, crept without lights down Reignleigh toward von Bayern's until I could just see light breaking through the woods on my right. I turned around, and parked in blackness around the curve from the last house. I felt almost in control again, though getting on for an hour behind my timeline, which involved catching an early train to Chicago.

As I crept onto the von Bayern grounds the crickets and kaydids in his bushes fell quiet, and I watched in agony to see what effect that would have within or with the dogs. None, that I could see. The only lights remained a faint fanlight above the door and what I recognized, skimming up to that wall of black glass here, as the purple fluorescents of the conservatory. I had forgotten those; I would have to go in through there, and it would be prickly in their soft glare for any passerby or sleepwalker to spot. On the other hand, I would not be bumping things in the dark. Silence - against the name of which I was submerged in this folly - would protect me better at this hour than darkness.

I stood absolutely still under a magnolia until - hesitantly, and then with what-the-hell unanimity - the night bugs again took up their chuckling and jeering. Under their cover I mooched tensely over the bridge and around to the door of *Six bis*. The key was still in the mouth of the ghastly frog, and I stood looking at it for a moment in the glow of the fluorescents inside. Up to now I had made no commitment, committed no crime (beyond perjury). The whole project, driven by a fool theory about the lives of lifeless things, had now to come into real life, or shut up and sit down forever. I did not have to do this, but I knew I would, if only to avoid wasting the effort of getting this far with it. I slipped the key into the lock, turned it, and entered the moist warmth of the conservatory.

The wicker and black foliage watched as I did my best to glide past the first layer of shrubbery - a job that would have been easier without the resonant load I carried with me. Ahead lay the shadowed doorway into the library; to my left the short hallway that led to the guest room where Anna had changed my life forever. Standing absolutely still, I thought I could hear light half-snoring over the pounding of my heart. Oh, Jesus, no.

Anna and I had never actually slept together, so I had no idea if this rosy little sound might be of her making, or of somebody's Aunt Louise, but I was completely incapable of ignoring it. I leaned the cello against the library door and stole down the little hall. There was light enough from the conservatory to see that the sleeper was dark-haired, hunched defensively, the quilt on which Anna and I had undone each other pulled around her ears. It could be no one else. She had obviously fled here, the one place she could now turn, when she'd had enough abuse from Arnold. I could right now steal to her, drop to one knee, plant a kiss, flee with her, waking ever after in the deep water of night to that gentle sound.

Sure.

I turned to the library, and almost gave myself a coronary by bumping into my cello before I was ready to grab it, starting it slithering down the wall next to the door. The lock Anna had turned for us, and now for herself alone, opened silently. In the library it was a matter of seconds to open the case of my cello - I had run the zipper outside, the first tiny phase of my criminal act while I was yet innocent - and to lay the cello on the deep rug. I slipped back into the conservatory for the cabinet key, and soundlessly opened the cabinet.

There hung Francesca, and I could feel in my gut her imperative to be freed. I took her down and transferred the maker's ribbon and a velvet player's pad (rich irony there) from Francesca to my cello and hung it in the cabinet where Francesca had been. In the dim light from the conservatory, there was no difference. I draped the case over Francesca (and saw Anna hunched in my shirt in the Orpheum dressing room while Arnold cursed and berated her) and replaced the cabinet key. Each successful step in this felony theft made the next seem easier and more inevitable, while it made the shivering in my gut grow. At the conservatory door, cursing myself, I listened for Anna's sleeping sounds one last time. They were not to be heard. I turned and faced Anna herself, standing like a ghost in a flannel nightie behind one of the giant ferns.

"Anna! Holy sh - You scared the hell out of me."

She said nothing at first, just stood there with her chin trembling and looking at the cello. She drew a long breath and ran a hand over her eyes. "That's Francesca."

"Yes."

"You're switching Anna for Francesca."

I had not let myself think of it in terms of names. "Well, yes, but - "

"I see. Good idea."

"Not the way you think. I'm taking Francesca to Chicago to give her to a real player. I had to leave something so Yoolie wouldn't notice until too late."

"Too late." She seemed disoriented by more than waking in the middle of the night.

"Yes, to catch up with me and take her back."

"Chicago?"

"Well... It doesn't have to be Chicago, though." And - why do we do these things? I dropped to my knees in front of her and grabbed the flannel nightie. "Anna, come with me. Right now. I didn't mean any of that stuff, I was half knocked out. Anna, I really do love - "

"No! ...I can't. You were right, knocked out or not. I'd fail you again, it wouldn't be fair."

"What, fair? Why too late? If Markus can stay by Sophie and work on a salmon trawler I can certainly - "

She patted my shoulder in the old knighting spot, and pulled the flannel out of my hand, shaking her head as if in fond reminiscence. "Sophie, well. I meant everything I said in that letter. I didn't mean I would run off to Mexico with you."

"Not Mexico. Chicago. Or I don't care, away from Arnold and this bunch of - "

"No, Oren. Do what you have to about cellos, but no. I can't be any plainer than that."

"But why? Why not?"

"Shh. You're going to get caught if you don't get out of here. Now please go. Please, Oren, I'm begging you, don't ask me again, I forbid you to ask me again. Go away!"

"Is that Rule Five?"

She looked down at me: remote, elder. "If that helps, yes. That's it. Go on, get out of here before - before you get caught."

My head hurt too much to think, every breath was a victory over the pain in my ribs. I rose and went out the conservatory door, and she locked it firmly behind me. The sludge flared up, I turned and accused the glimpse of black hair behind the glass: "I thought you ..."

I had just time to see the wetness on her cheeks in a stab of light from behind before I whirled and a car shrieked to a stop in the driveway.

"Hey! Who the hell's that?" came the voice of Nancy von Bayern. I pocketed the brass key. There was no escape but back over the triply damned little footbridge. I made a dash for it, but the car screeched again, roared across the lawn, and came to a stop across the far end of the bridge, cutting me off just as I got there.

"Oh, well hi there, Ornsie. How ya been? We haven't been favored with your snotty presence for days, seems like. Got tired of Anna, that it?"

I looked into the car, doing my best to breathe without panting, and was relieved to see she was alone. "Not that it's any of your business, but if you're half the buddy of Anna's you're supposed to be, you know why I haven't been around. Where's your crooked friend?"

She laughed, actually rather pleasantly. "Well, you know... One thing I gotta say, Oren, I hate polite chit-chat. Not much danger of that between us, is there?"

"Not in the least, because I've got to go. If you'd be good enough to back up a few feet. So I can get off this silly goddamn bridge ..."

Nancy pulled out a pack of cigarettes and punched in the lighter. "Not so fast. Are you taking one of Daddy's cellos there?"

I looked her straight in the eye. "No, it's mine. I was out here trying a serenade on Anna. But it didn't work."

"Liar. I can always tell when people look straight at me like that."

"OK, it did work, and now I'm real sleepy. So if - "

"I meant about whose cello it is." She leaned back on the seat and lit her cigarette. "And you know what? I actually don't give a shit, any more than you do about who I was out with tonight, do you?"

"I can't think of anything I care less about."

"See? That's something else we have in common. And actually that doesn't exhaust the list. If you were half the guy Anna thinks you are, it's her you'd be getting out of here, not some goddamn cello. And don't tell me that's not my business."

"OK, but it's pretty rich, coming from you. I tried to get her to come with me, but she won't. I don't know what's the matter with her. Why don't you see if you can get her another movie contract?"

"She wouldn't? I'm serious, Oren. Daddy's talking about movies again. I think maybe he's sorry he let you have that one."

"Well, I guess that's the attraction. I thought those movies were just a lark."

"Not to Daddy."

"Evidently not to Anna, either. She thinks it wouldn't be fair if I took her away from here. And that is absolutely all the time I have for social notes. Your folks are going to be out here any second to see why you're parked on the lawn, and here I'll be, and I don't think there's even one thing Daddy and I have in common except hate. Hold this." I handed her the neck of the cello and crept over the bridge rail to dry ground, and reached back to take it. "Thanks. You'd be doing me a favor, and boy is it the last one I'll ever ask you, if you'd turn off your headlights for a bit."

Amazingly, she did.

*   *

The Banner Blue pulled out of Union Station at 6:35 that morning, twenty minutes late at the start of the run through about twenty little towns up the zipper of US 66 to Chicago. Francesca sat next to me on the window side as insurance against the lurch of drunks and unwary travelers. I had not played her, nor opened her case, and had the sense not to.

OK, I thought. Here's where I get some of the sleep that I didn't last night. But it didn't work that way. I was more wired than I had ever been after a Civic rehearsal, my brain re-running selections from the the past eight hours in no order, with a shifting cast of characters. Once it was Anna, thirtyish and tough, sitting in Nancy's car and lighting cigarettes, and Yoolie von Bayern behind the glass door as her headlights swept across his tearful face. And time wouldn't lie straight either; I was sure we had gone through Blue Mound, Illinois twice already when we pulled into it, and at Decatur a bunch of students, noisy and beery, got on heading for Chicago for the weekend. Then we made some kind of huge loop through the corn fields, because when we hit Decatur again, they all got off, and half of them were carrying shopping bags from St. Louis.

The air in the train was so superheated that my eyes dried out and I couldn't blink; I sat staring helplessly at the plush before them, too tired to turn my head or look at my watch. When we stopped at Carbondale (God, not even the same direction as Chicago), a family of gypsies got on, brushing snow from their golden fringes and guitars, bringing a blessed cloud of cold, fresh air down the line of prisoners. In Moline, we pulled in to the station and sat, with my window exactly opposite the station sign. "Moline," it said, and slid backwards, as the train started to glide forward; but no, that was my head slumping forward, and the "Moline" sign stopped and straightened itself with a jerk that left me dizzy. Then I did sleep for hours, deeply, and with detailed and satisfying dreams; and when I woke, we were sitting in the station at Moline.

*   *

"Whaddya got there, boy, a big git-tar?"

I'd had this stupid question from the street, from little kids and newsboys - many of them thrice my age - hawking Chicago <u>Tribunes</u> and <u>Sun-Times</u>, with their alien and unfunny comics Alley Oop and Tillie the Toiler. This time it was a real toiler, a weatherbeaten lady scrubbing out the stalls in a Trailways station where I had gone to take a leak, the train coffee having had that effect if no other on the bag of uncoordinated cells I was pushing through Chicago neighborhoods in search of the University and its music students.

"No, ma'am, it's a cello."

She lost interest. "So it ain't no git-tar. I'd tell you turn around and get right back to Decatur, Bean Blossom, ever where you're from. Got too dang many gittar players in Ch'caga, and my old man's one of 'em."

"Nope. Am I getting near the university?"

"Depends which way yer headin. Walkin south, you missed it." She cackled gently at the thought of my heading for the music school by way of Nashville and the south pole with Francesca on my hip. Actually, I was pretty sure I had been heading west, but I'd been following left-and-right directions since I left the station an hour ago, and I was still lost. "Anyways, you just step along out the veranda there, and go right for a couple blocks. And you can get in line with the rest of 'em."

"Yes, ma'am, thank you. Um, they buy instruments there?"

She gave me a funny look. "Friend, they ain't but one kinda place as buys ennathing without a bill a sale, ya know. And that wouldn't be no college, ya follow me."

I left. Bill of sale. Boy, that was dumb. I could have done up a bill of sale any night I was alone in Di Salvo's shop. And made up any price, come to think of it. No, wait; who said anything about getting money for Francesca? That wasn't it, that would make it really stealing. What I was doing was putting Francesca in the hands of a player, and it had not occurred to me that there would be paperwork and codifications. To tell the truth, having pulled off this caper, I had rather pictured myself in genteel conversation with a dean of some kind, maybe discussing the merits of deserving students, future Pierre Fourniers who would look back in thankful remembrance on this my act of sacrifice.

Bills of sale, legitimate ownership. The dean presses a buzzer, *"Miss Epworth, send Mr. Rozeboom in, would you?"* and this gigantic enforcer lumbers in glaring out of lashless eyes and holds out a beefy fist for the bill of sale.

The Cello Francesca, *or* Balderdash

What if I say it was my father's, he had it for years, I never saw any bill of sale, and I don't play, so I thought . . . Yes, and who but a criminal fool, having inherited something of value, does not sell it to a legitimate dealer, with courts and attorneys, wills and other "instruments" to back it up?

"Well, yes, I could have done that, but I wanted to actually meet the new owner, not a dealer, so I'd know who was playing it." Not too bizarre, only a bit sentimental, but nothing a dealer couldn't manage. *"Fine, Mr. Dienst, you go along with Mr. Rozeboom and take care of the paperwork, just so we know we're not receiving, ha ha, stolen goods, you know."*

At this point I overloaded at last, and needed somewhere, really, to sit down and think it over. I eased my ribs onto a broken-slatted bench in a little half-block park in late sunlight with buses roaring past every five minutes. The skin next to my nose itched, my clothes (didn't bring a change, of course) stank of train upholstery and sweat. My right arm, relieved of the weight of Francesca, twitched limply. It felt remarkably good to sit down, and I thought I would just sit for a while and work out something.

I watched the storm of traffic, people, buses, and buildings so much bigger than anything in St. Louis. Real mountains you could get lost among. Now I thought of it, I was not confident I could get back to the train station without a lot more wandering around. Well, later. *Right now it was important to get ready, all the others were on stage already, and only my chair - broad as a park bench to hold me and my music and my lab reports - is empty, waiting for me. I can't see a thing for the strong stage lighting in my eyes, it's just impossible to read the music, but by squinting hard I can make out a twenty-bar rest. Good deal. The baton comes down and I start counting, and have a look at the notes I will have to play. It is the opening Prelude from the G major unaccompanied suite. Funny thing to be playing here with a big orchestra and choir all around me, but the mystery clears up. As I get to twenty and start to play it is not Bach's quiet arpeggios but a complex song.*

It would be difficult at best to describe the song. It is not just that the music is full of apocalypse and fulfillment, real music about real gods, though it is; or that the cello in my lap sings with a human voice. The hair-raising part is that the song is entirely silent.

So is the orchestral and choral accompaniment to it, probably a hundred musicians all around me joining in this silence that is so entirely and perfectly music that I am afraid. It is the silence that lies behind all music, the perfect performance at last, so perfect that the terrifying god is revealed who should never be seen by players, only brushed past in the tiny silences as a bow reverses or a singer breathes.

We are desperate, and it is my fault. I must find a covering, we must hear the music so we cannot hear the silence that the music is about. The audience is afraid too, and they begin to move restlessly in their seats. I play frantically until a faint gloss of sound, like a reflection in a dark window, begins to appear. Ah. Alleluia, it comes so faintly in the hush of maple, the moan of spruce. One voice from the choir, then another. Jacob Oxendine watches from his lofty perch.

One by one the singers are heard, and the orchestra, still singing the song that is about the silence that lies behind music. In the end only Yoolie von Bayern, standing erect with the organ pipes like a carven idol, remains without a voice. And in my lap it is Anna herself, singing and laughing and trying to turn to face me, perhaps to make love, though she looks far too young. The music becomes hilarious, I am convulsed.

Strange, though, that Anna no longer wants to sit in my lap, but pulls away from me. In a panic I hold her, not able to grip hard because wherever I can touch her is indecorous here in front of a full choir of strangers waiting for the bus on a busy street.

Seeing I was awake, the sly kid who had been trying to work Francesca out of my grip gave me a paralyzing kick on the ankle and darted away through heavy traffic. The people at the bus stop turned away, still smirking.

Thank god, the bus came that they all seemed to have been waiting for, and they filed in. On the side of the bus a placard said "F u cn rd ths u cn gt a gd jb n rn mo pa", followed by the logo of the Loop Institute of Technology, a lamp circled by the words "LIT For You." A vandal had slightly altered the first part of the coded message. In the window above it three downtown kids were grinning derisorily, and the one who had been tugging on Francesca gave me the finger as the bus blasted away, leaving a fresh coat of smoke on the surroundings.

Everything about Chicago then seemed to me so dirty, powerful, and dangerous that I would have wept without the residue of cheer from my dream. Even so, I suddenly saw it as the last kind of place that might harbor anyone who would understand about setting free a captive cello. Just the sight of a storefront across the street ("Novelties, Jokes, Gags") eroded my purpose.

I rose and leaned forward, letting inertia rather than any clear plan direct my steps; and found that I had leaned wisely, since the university was in clear sight a block ahead. I came up on some towering buildings. A small wooden sign marked them *University of Chicago/Married Student Housing/No Loitering or Soliciting/Police Take Notice.* At the foot of twenty stories of identical small balconies full of barbecue grills, hanging plants and diapers there was an aluminum foyer. Two youngish women in slacks and jean jackets emerged, pushing strollers. They had circles under their eyes, and the better-looking one had developed heavy flesh below her waist. She pulled a face:

"You know she keeps getting pregnant because she's got a crush on Dr. Nyquist."

Her friend looked solemn at this theory. I, who wanted all women to be beautiful and blithe, decided not to ask directions just yet. I would have to soon, because I wanted to catch the last train back to St. Louis. I certainly couldn't afford to spend the night, even in the Y, even if I could find it. It was getting time to do something. But what?

OK, no deans, no deals. I stood irresolute, half-leaning on Francesca, and tried to think. All I could manage was a decentralized trance that was closer to the doze at the bus stop than to thought. And as I hung there swaying over Francesca, I heard the solution whispering down from above me: a violinist practicing a chamber music part, which I recognized as one of the Opus 18 string quartets of Beethoven. "Please give me a good home," I muttered, and stepped back to get a bead on the approximate location of the player.

Whoever it was played chamber music, and was not good enough to be a conservatory student. Ergo, he must have an acquaintance who was likewise an earnest amateur, and a cellist. Well, fine. Probably the guy didn't have a very good instrument, and would be pleased to have, and to play, Francesca. Right? Sure.

It was flimsy, but I was incapable of better. I waited for another batch of moms to leave the building, and caught the door before it latched again. Having come so far, I compounded the misdemeanor by heading for the stairs, intent neither on loitering nor soliciting, but on early Beethoven. Inside the building it was no trick at all to locate the player; the sound easily penetrated the flimsy architecture, and when I had climbed to the proper floor it was only a matter of stopping by the door where the sound was loudest. I unzipped Francesca's case for a last look and pulled the Tomastiks into perfect fifths. "We want to be at our best, now, don't we?" I breathed.

I held her out at arm's length; she looked sleek and excited, though not grateful. That would be going too far. I wondered whose hands would wear the varnish into the asymmetric baldness that cellos get from the constant brush of left sleeves against the upper ribs. I re-clothed her, did up the zipper, and laid her carefully on the mat ("Holiday Greetings") outside the musical door; I rang the doorbell and ran back to the stairs as if Yoolie and all his staff were after me.

I was down a half-flight before I heard the apartment door open, and a flight and a half before a clearly audible "Hello?" echoed after me. I swung around the iron newel at the bottom of the next half-flight, and careened straight into the chubby mamas I had seen outside. I had just time to register a look of shock as I tried to vault the bannister, found a sheet of white pain from my ribs in the way, caught a foot in one of the strollers, bounced once on the stairs, tumbled sideways across the landing, and slammed my left arm into the stone windowsill with a crack that was probably noticed on the top floor. A blaze of pain came roaring out of it, somebody yelled *Oh, shit!* and I honestly don't remember hitting the floor.

11. Keys

The cop in the chair by the window was nice enough, but he certainly didn't let up on me just because of any discomfort – as when some doctor tells you, Now this may give you a little discomfort, and then gouges out your eye – that my fractured elbow and dislocated shoulder might have added to the familiar list.

"Look, Mr. Dienst, we know who you are, that's obvious from the stuff in your wallet. We'd like to know what you were doing running down the stairs in the married student housing. What did ya steal?"

"Did anyone report anything missing?"

"I'm asking the questions. Describe the contents of your pockets, and account for each item."

"Some change, I don't remember how much, but less than a dollar. Half a Wabash ticket from St. Louis. A set of keys. A - "

"Keys to what?"

"A '48 Chevy Master DeLuxe, dark blue, that's sitting in the parking lot of Union Station in St. Louis. A Yale key - "

"License number on the car?"

"Missouri 137-596. Registered to me. A Yale key to my house on Lansdowne Avenue, and one for the, uh, the stage door of - "

"What's the grey stuff in the pill bottle? Some kind of drugs?"

"It's moss. Sort of a good luck charm."

"Works good, don't it?"

At this point a doctor came in and grunted briefly over the job the technician had done on the cast, and asked me if I realized I had a couple of broken ribs that still weren't healed, and I told him they only hurt when I laughed about the elbow.

"Boy," he said. "Never heard that one before. You could be chuckling the rest of your life. I guess we can let you go tomorrow morning."

"Well, I'm glad to hear you say you will. How do I pay for this?"

"University pays, you were in their building."

"Oh. And this gentleman - "

"University cop. Not much I can do about him, eh?"

"'Fraid not, Doug. Son, I don't know that I have a whole lot of questions either, but there is just one more thing, 'cause it means a sight of trouble to me."

"Yes?"

"Can you give me any hint why the St. Louis cops are so curious about your whereabouts? They like to jump down the phone when I called them with your ID to see if I had me a famous sneak thief. I'm gonna let them take it from here, 'cause I don't know the difference between murder and manslaughter in Missouri."

*   *

There didn't seem to be much mystery about what caused Yoolie von Bayern's death. As the Star-Times put it, "The millionaire victim was discovered early Monday morning in a dressing room of the Orpheum Theater, of which he was the owner, by a plumber engaged in repair work there. Police sources indicate he had suffered massive head trauma and had been dead for perhaps twelve hours. The same sources indicate that injuries to the tycoon industrialist were inconsistent with accidental death, and that significant clues implicating one or more assailants have been discovered at the scene. An arrest is said to be imminent."

The University of Chicago police could supply an airtight alibi for me for hours on either side of Yoolie's death - I was muttering and grinding my teeth in a hospital bed that Sunday night while they waited for the anaesthetic to wear off - so they let me make the return trip to St. Louis without handcuffs. In fact, given the elaborate cast in which my left arm was cantilevered 90 degrees out from my body, handcuffs would have been a challenge. But the St. Louis cops were very interested in talking to me, and Chicago insisted on sending a guy down with me on the southbound Banner Blue. My keeper kept trying to get me to play gin rummy with him; I guess he figured he had an opponent who wouldn't play things close to the vest.

But I just sat enjoying the linear, orderly way the train went through its series of stops without skips or repetitions, letting my mind wander and savoring the unbelievable fact that I had done exactly what I set out to do. Francesca was off on her life as a player's instrument, barring the bad luck of being acquired by another collector; and that seemed unlikely, since Yoolie only bought her to punish me for having a smart mouth. She would be out there making music for centuries. I felt myself, for the first time in my life, a part of the history of the world.

The bare fact of Yoolie's death, not its venue or its manner, was revealed to me by the cop in the hospital, probably to see if I reacted guiltily. I didn't know what to make of it. Any death is a bit sobering, but I certainly wasn't consumed by mourning for that tycoon industrialist. If Nancy had reported my presence there on Saturday night, I might have some kind of a problem about that. But in fact, it occurred to me almost right away (see how well-oiled my neural machinery was getting?) that there was now no reason to be shy about the forgery of my lab notebook, since it was only Yoolie who had ever had any power to stop me by threatening Anna. And even that was moot; I doubted Arnold Rosen's fury could get any worse than what I had witnessed in a simple matter of fornication. Of course there was the perjurous affidavit I had signed, but I could finesse that with a barefaced statement that, Gee, something had been bothering me about that notebook, and maybe if I could see it again I could figure out what it was. I would send a letter to the County Attorney - Holy shit.

A shock went through me, so profound I could not believe it had not made an audible clank. No heads turned; I looked at the card-playing deputy and found him occupied with solitaire. Miles of soybeans went by while the metallic taste slowly faded. My fully written-out and signed statement to the County Attorney about the forgery was still in the music pocket of Francesca's case, which had been "Anna's" case when I wrote it. About the first thing anyone finding an apparently orphaned cello would do would be to look through the case pockets in search of a clue to the owner's identity. They would find the statement, and there I would be. If they were at all honest they would get in touch, say by putting an ad in the paper where Yoolie, or I guess his estate, and Di Salvo would see it, and Francesca's and my anonymity would be blown to hell. How could I be so goddamn careless? And I couldn't even dance up and down and tear my hair about it. I had to sit on that damn train and look calm while my alleged mind darted around the situation like a mouse in a birdcage. Jesus. I had signed and dated the thing.

Well, now. Was there anything in it to locate me absolutely? I sat patiently - how else? - and reconstructed it. No. And though I had signed with all three names, the whole thing was handwritten. It wouldn't be all that straightforward even to figure out my right name, given hand fatigue by the time I'd finished it. If they did see "Oren Walker Dienst" and not "Olen Walter Diengl" or something, who was this guy? Where did he live? I wasn't in the St. Louis phone book except as an invisible adjunct of W. R. Dienst, my father, even if they had any idea of looking in the St. Louis directory and not Chicago or Milwaukee or any of a thousand other possibilities. I began to breathe easier. In their place, I'd have tried the Chicago city books, and the University records, and drawing a blank there, figure I'd given it a good try and either chuck the thing or file it away on a deep shelf, pending developments.

Molar. Had I mentioned Molar Chemical? Of course. Would it be in the Chicago papers that the president of Molar Chemical Company of St. Louis had just died? Probably, at least among the obituaries. (Actually, it was front-page stuff in the Trib, given sensational aspects of which I was not then aware). I tried to stretch and found it too painful, so I belched and sighed. If they read Francesca's label they would find the name and city of the maker, thinly Latinized. I was not in the clear at all, the thing was a grenade that could go off any time. But it was out of my hands. What a thought: out of my hands. I leaned back and went to sleep.

At Union Station, my traveling cop handed me over to a St. Louis cop with a wink and a "Watch 'im, he's a tricky one," and went off to see if he could get laid before the next train back to Chicago. My new guardian was a dark-haired police corporal, unremarkable and uncommunicative. His badge said A. Garcia, and that was more information than he had really planned to share. I asked him how Yoolie had died, he said, "We was wondering the same thing, fella. Why don't you refresh your memory on the way over," so I shut up and did that. The trouble of course was not memory but invention. I had in fact burgled Yoolie's house on the weekend he had died, and I might have left tracks - such as the two extended conversations with members of his household that had punctuated the stealthy intervals. With no more information than I had, it was hard to know in which direction to look for danger.

My interview with Captain Enos Foster, SLPD, was long and filled with cross-purposes, mostly arising from my misapprehension that Yoolie had died at home and Foster's stubborn unwillingness to tell me otherwise. He said they'd found things of mine at what he called the locus, without telling me where that was, and I suppose he was waiting for me to reveal guilty knowledge or an ability to kill at a distance, when a sweating corporal entered and handed him a slip of paper, at the sight of which he smiled and relaxed.

"Well, I guess there's just one more thing, for now. You say you tore up your arm falling down stairs in that rabbit hutch at the University. And there's a couple momma rabbits that back that up. What was your hurry?"

"I was late for the train back here, and I was running to catch the bus down to the station."

"I see." He looked at me and I looked right back at him, which I should have known by then is a dead giveaway. "Fella," he said, "It's plain as day that you didn't have anything to do with killing Yoolie. You were 300 miles away when it happened, you don't look like the kind of guy who'd have any employees, and you don't even know where it was he got it. On the other hand, I never saw anybody so innocent in my life, so whatever it is you're holdin' out on, you better hope it don't come to my attention, like if you were screwing his wife or something. No, that ain't it either, is it? What's so funny?"

"I was never even introduced to his wife, if that's what you're asking me. I don't think she gets around much any more."

"No, that ain't what I'm asking you, but never mind. I think we got our guy, so we're gonna let you go. Thank you for your apparent cooperation. Sorry about your arm."

I rose, and my arm rose with me. "Thank you, sir. Do you suppose you could have somebody run me back to the station to pick up my car?"

"Sure. Halvorsen, take this petrified man over to Union Station. How you planning to drive with that thing?"

"Honest to God, sir? I don't know. I'm all set for turn signals, long as I turn right every time."

"Halvorsen."

So Corporal Halvorsen, who hadn't been in on me from the beginning and only knew I was being sent home with the Captain's thanks, took me back to the parking lot, where he radioed to be picked up at my house and drove me home in my car. While we were accomplishing this he cheerfully let me know about the location and condition of Yoolie's corpse. "Looked like Joe Louis worked him over, and then just kept workin' after the bell, you know?".

The fact that Yoolie had been sprawled across the doorway to the Orpheum dressing room certainly accounted for the police interest in me; I must have left evidence all over that room, and I said as much to Halvorsen. He gave me a funny look and said, "Oh, are you that guy? Yeah, the captain got pretty interested in you when we saw all your books and stuff. What the hell were you up to in there, anyhow?"

"Jacob Oxendine, the janitor, was kind enough to let me use that room as a place to practice and study. It saved me a lot of driving around with my cello. You know Jacob?"

"Geez, I guess so. Looks like you're gonna need a new practice room, though. Mr. Oxendine was also kind enough to step up and confess it was him that killed Yoolie. Saves us a lot of driving around, too."

That was Tuesday, the 17th of November. On Friday I got the cantilevered rig off my arm in favor of a regular sling cast, but the guy who did the remodeling was not cheerful about it.

"Don't think of this so much as progress as an admission of defeat. Your shoulder's OK, but you're going to have a tough time bending that elbow for the rest of your life, there's so many cracks and chips in it. OK, take yourself down to central casting and get your concrete on. You got any itchy places, scratch 'em now."

I decided that I would deal later with the implications of having a broken elbow - and they would have been depressing to think of if I were not already bottomed out; but at least I could get out of my house and drive my own car. After Jacob's confession, the legal heat went off the Orpheum, and I had urgent business there. I had fretted for days over Mollie, picturing her walking about and wringing her hands over Jacob, probably unable to leave. The newspaper coverage had made no mention of her. As far as the Post was concerned, the "courtly Lumbee" lived as a bachelor Quasimodo in the spooky old place and, courtly or not, had been driven to criminal insanity by it and by his curious genetics.

Jacob had given as reasons for his act anger over a racial slur ("Oxendine's features are to some extent those of a Negro," explained the Globe) and robbery, since he knew von Bayern to be wealthy. I didn't believe a word of it, but I couldn't imagine what possessed him to confess such a thing either. I thought Mollie, besides needing help, could explain.

I entered the east stage door at four that afternoon, looking straight ahead as I walked past the darkened stairs to the dressing room. Out under the dome I called softly, "Mollie?" and heard nothing. The whole place had the dead sound of abandonment. I walked over to the foot of the ladderway. The table where Anna had always left her flowers was gone, or invisible in the shadows. I stepped back and tried to see a light or any sign of occupation from the direction of Jacob's apartment. It was dark as hell up there. The cherubim and philosophers flickered and swirled in the half-light, and then one of them really was moving, leaning on the railing. "Mollie?"

"Oren? Is it you? Oh, thank . . ."

"Mollie? Are you OK?"

"Could you come up, please?"

"Uh, I think so. It'll take me a minute, though. Do you need anything from down here?"

"Only you. I do need you, Oren."

"I'm on my way."

It was a very steep ladderway, but not a real ladder, so with a good deal of heaving and puffing and hooking my cast over the rungs, I got up it. I had never been up here, and I turned around at the top to look at myself and Anna, hand in hand on the stage thanking Jacob for our key. We looked like children.

"Come in, Oren. I'm here."

She was lying on a day bed in what I guessed must be Jacob's kitchen and sitting room. She looked terrible. I don't see how she could have weighed 80 pounds, and her skin and hair looked dry and dusty. I suppose I didn't manage to hide the shock, because she smiled sadly.

"You see how nicely I have advanced since you last saw me, Oren. But I am not in pain. Even without Jacob's blessing it, his medicine keeps me free of pain and fear."

"Mollie - Jesus, Mollie, what a horrible damn mess this is. Why did he - "

"It is going to be all right, Oren. Jacob and I discussed contingencies before he came forward. The only error we made was in how long it would take you to come here, but now I see the reason for that. Is it very painful?"

"What contingencies?"

"It is quite simple, Oren. I have no more than a month left, and in that time I am going to see to it that a great injustice is set right."

"You mean Jacob?"

She rolled to one elbow to look at me. "I do. He will not be retained when I come forward and confess to the killing of Julius von Bayern."

"What? Oh, Molly, for heaven's sake. They won't believe that for a minute."

"And why not?"

I walked over to the window and looked at Jacob's view. It was already night over the river. "Well, look at you. You couldn't assassinate a cockroach."

190

"I am much debilitated since Jacob's arrest."

"Even so . . ."

"Consider, Oren. Mr. von Bayern was killed by repeated blows to the head, no single one of which was heavy enough to be fatal, though perhaps to stun him temporarily and leave him helpless to guard against further blows. Do you see Jacob Oxendine killing anyone that way?"

"I don't see him killing anyone any way. But - "

"Exactly. But if he did, it would be with a single, righteous blow that would be fatal immediately."

"The thing is, who's going to believe you killed him? I mean why?"

"He was forcing his attentions on me, and I acted in desperation."

"On you? Excuse me, Mollie, but Yoolie had a beautiful wife, and - "

"A promiscuous alcoholic. And what man of his sort cleaves to his wife?"

"Right, in fact he had his pick of a number of very good-looking women." How to put this?

"He was a deeply perverted and concupiscent man, Oren. I do not wish to speak ill of the dead, but yes. He was perfectly capable of raping a dying woman, just to add that piquancy to his store of experiences."

Well, that rang true enough. "Still, they've got a confession, and if I know them they'll have zero interest in another one. Especially from someone who is, excuse me again, but very involved with Jacob."

"Do they know of my involvement from you?"

"No. Absolutely not."

"Nor from anyone, I am sure. I have been away, seeking a cure for my illness, and so informed you and Maestro Brocklin and a number of others at the time of my departure. Only you and - 'hm, Miss Rosen knew I was here. As for the interests of the police, we shall just have to tweak their interests, won't we? And there is where I need your help, Oren. Do you know anyone from the press? A reporter? Second, can you arrange a private discussion with Nancy von Bayern for me? And third, do you think you can possibly get me to a hospital? Part of the reason that I have become so emaciated is that we reckoned without your injury, and I have been out of food for over a day, now."

Sitting up here, thinking, *Where's Oren, why doesn't he come?* Lying down in defeat. It almost killed me. "Mollie, I am so terribly sorry. No stupid arm is any excuse. I'll do whatever I can to help."

"We were sure you would, Oren."

"The hard part will be getting you down that ladder. I don't see that you can manage it, and I sure can't carry you down."

"That was never the plan. There is another route. Have I satisfied you that we will succeed?"

No. At what? "I suppose."

"I knew we would. Please help me stand up."

I helped her up, and she crept with me out to the balcony that runs around the interior of the dome. At the points of the compass, it had been painted with *trompe-l'oeil* exits which, seen from below, appeared for all the world to lead to hallways, illusory escapes that, had they been real, would have protruded like spokes into empty air around three sides of the dome. Now I saw that one of them was real indeed, a kind of reverse *trompe* by which, seen from below, we would have appeared to shuffle into the painting and vanish.

"This leads us straight down into the other half of the building," Mollie panted. "Jacob calls it the Road-Runner door." It felt strange to laugh. We passed a couple of pleasantly furnished rooms, one of them with a hospital bed, where Mollie stopped to point out an overnight case; and at the end of the hall a set of stairs led down into darkness.

"Down here?" She nodded tiredly. "I better carry you, then, if you don't mind."

"So we had planned."

So with her arms around my neck and my good arm taking most of the weight - which amounted to almost nothing - we made it down. Mollie sighed with relief at the bottom.

"I did not expect to make that descent in this life."

Mollie's discussion with Nancy von Bayern was so private that I was not included, except as go-between. But I can testify that it was a very shaken Nancy, enclosed in a black dress that must have set Yoolie's estate back two hundred dollars, who left Mollie's room in the Barnes Hospital cancer wing.

But I was more than a bystander when Mollie held what she referred to as her press conference on Tuesday. At her request - in spite of rest and intravenous feeding over the weekend it was difficult and trying for her to talk by now - I read her statement from beginning to end without stopping, to an assemblage of three reporters (Bonney of the Star-Times and a couple of rookies that the Post and Globe had sent over), and Corporal Halvorsen of the St. Louis police:

"I wish to confess to the killing of Julius von Bayern, which took place at 8:45 pm on the evening of Sunday, November 15, 1953. I do not do so lightly or with any other motivation than to see that a great injustice is averted before I must answer to this crime before my Maker.

"The following were the circumstances of this event: As many can testify who know me, I have been suffering from cancer for the past several months. About a month ago this illness forced me to abandon my musical career. I journeyed to Mexico to undergo an experimental cure not yet available in the United States. When I became convinced that this would be unavailing, I returned to St. Louis on Saturday, November 14 to see to closing out my personal affairs. Part of that required that I return to the Orpheum Theater, where I had left some personal belongings, including musical manuscripts and books. I did so on the next day, November 15th. I met Mr. Jacob Oxendine, custodian of the Orpheum, as he was leaving the theater, according to him, on an errand for Mr. von Bayern, who was inside the theater inspecting the progress of repairs. When I explained my mission, he opened the stage door for me and left on his errand, which he said would be likely to take some time.

"Upon entering the theater, I immediately saw Mr. von Bayern standing on the stairway that leads to the dressing room backstage. Some of the materials I had come to fetch were in that room, so I greeted him and made to walk past him on the stairs. They were difficult for me to climb. Mr. von Bayern offered to assist me, and I assented. He took my arm in a very

*familiar fashion, saying 'Let me give you little hand here, Missy.'
and walked me to the door of the dressing room.*

"When I had retrieved my things, I found Mr. von
Bayern blocking the door. He would not permit me to exit. He
began to speak in a very lewd manner, and to touch my body. I
protested and struggled, but my illness has left me quite weak. It
was not until he was so vile as to fondle and squeeze my body in
a very sore and tender place that the shock of pain gave me a
despairing strength. I tore away from him and ran onto the
raised passageway outside the dressing room, but he caught at
my dress. I seized a heavy board that was standing against the
railing and - driven by fear and pain - I turned and struck him in
the face as hard as I could with it. I was lucky or, as I prefer to
believe, the God of Justice and Mercy came to my aid. The blow
stunned Mr. von Bayern. I could have escaped then, and I cannot
tell you why I did not. I was in a very emotional state. While my
assailant was staggering against the dressing room door frame, I
struck him again on the head, and when he fell across the
threshold of the door, I saw what he had been holding in his
hand. The sight so unnerved me that I struck him again,
repeatedly, until I came to myself and I could see that he was
dead. My strength left me entirely, and I fell unconscious upon
the couch in the dressing room.*

When I recovered, nothing had changed. I threw the
board with which I had killed Mr. von Bayern behind some
scenery and fled to my home. I do not know whether the police
have found it, but if so there has been no public description of it.
It is a rough-cut two by four about three feet long. One end is
now stained with blood and other matter. I do not know if
fingerprints can be recovered from the rough wood, but if so you
will find mine on the other end. At the time of this statement,
splinters from the board are still embedded in the skin of my
hands.*

I have no great wish to face the public scrutiny that
will follow this confession, nor to suffer at the hands of the law.
But I could not remain silent while another - who as far as I
know is an innocent Christian man - stands accused of the crime
I have committed. I will answer a very few questions, but I warn
you that I do not have much stamina."*

The only movement from anyone during this was a sudden coming-alert of Corporal Halvorsen on hearing the description of the two-by-four, and a rueful display by Mollie to illustrate the part about splinters in her palms. Bonney was the first to break the silence. "OK, Miss Biedermeyer. But if you say you did it, and Oxendine was nowhere around when it happened, why did he confess?"

I looked at Mollie, and she nodded faintly. I cleared my throat, and turned to the next page of the statement. *"One of your first questions will surely be, why an innocent man should confess to a murder he did not commit. Mr. Oxendine - in a thoroughly gentlemanly and Christian manner - has long entertained an admiration for me. I believe that he is being gallant in a misguided effort to spare me the ordeal of a police examination. Yet I believe you will find that he does not even know what it was that Mr. von Bayern held in his hand at the time I killed him. I do."*

The reporter from the Post was the first to ask, but Halvorsen held up his hand. "Nope. All that's privileged information. I suppose you've got that written out, too. Hand it over."

So Mollie gave him the last sheet of paper, on which I had helped her write,

"A hunting knife about ten inches long with a staghorn handle carved into the shape of a naked woman. The thread caught on the blade is from the dress I was wearing, which is still in my possession."

Halvorsen read through it, looked at Mollie, looked at the reporters, and puffed out his cheeks.

*   *

The newspapers were unanimous in suppressing Mollie's identity and what she had said about her reasons for killing Yoolie. You'd think there wouldn't be much story left after that, and you'd be right. The Globe's fifth-page notice was typical:

195

The Cello Francesca, *or* Balderdash

A deathbed confession by a St. Louis woman has apparently saved Jacob Oxendine, 43, of 1101 Lucas St. from indictment in connection with the death of St. Louis businessman Julius von Bayern. Oxendine, caretaker of the Orpheum Theater downtown, had been held without bail since shortly after the incident. The unidentified woman was interviewed by police in her private room at a local hospital, where she is said to be near death from causes unrelated to her involvement with von Bayern.

A spokesman for the victim's family read the following brief statement to reporters outside their residence in an exclusive Ladue neighborhood yesterday:

"The family are satisfied that with this confession, any mystery surrounding Mr. von Bayern's unfortunate death has been resolved, and that the person responsible will soon be required to answer for her deed before a Higher Court. The family do not see that any material or judicial end would be served by further investigation of this tragedy."

Of course, a cynic would have seen right away that the circumstances of Yoolie's death had been at least exotic: there was first of all his demotion from "tycoon industrialist" to "St. Louis businessman," which would cover a multitude of sinners; followed by reference to him by last name only. And then, when folks as powerful as the von Bayerns called for silence rather than vengeance, you could bet there was a good reason.

As for the cops, they must have had to swallow hard to believe that frail Mollie had done Yoolie to death, but they couldn't get around her detailed circumstantial knowledge of the crime, the splinters that matched the fatal 2x4, the thread caught on the knife, and Jacob's clear ignorance, verified by lie detector, of things that he should have known if he had even been present during the struggle. His original story, when the whole thing first broke, was that Yoolie had abruptly sent him on a distant errand connected with the repair work, that on returning after midnight Sunday, he had entered the Orpheum by a door remote from the dressing room and gone straight to his apartment, and that he had been roused on Monday morning by the shouts of the plumber who found Yoolie. Not only did that story mesh with Mollie's but it looked as if it had to be true in spite of his later repudiation of it.

All of which, of course, was as Mollie wished it. "I am satisfied," she whispered when I read her the <u>Globe</u> story on Thursday. "I regret even the anonymous notoriety, but I gladly accept it for what it has achieved. Isn't that so, dear?"

Jacob, sitting beside her in his new suit, just shook his head, but if in disagreement or in resignation was not clear. "If it makes you easier, Mollie, then I am satisfied too. The wretch not only deserved to die but, in my opinion, was looking to die. Long before we reach his age we come to know in our hearts that the wages of sin is death." (Here a stern glance in my direction.) "Well, he has reached his goal, but at a great cost."

"Hush. That is enough of that, Jacob. I am as happy as a new bride, and I will not have you darken this wonderful day for any of us."

New bride indeed. The ceremony, not an hour past, had jammed into her hospital room the pastor of Mollie's Faithful Shepherd Lutheran Church, a crowd of wet-eyed students and Civic personnel, with Hans Brocklin giving her away and myself as best man, which was an extreme stretch. Maureen Witz played *Sheep May Safely Graze*, tossing her curls with emotion but on the whole honoring Mollie's teaching.

It was pretty hard to keep the lump in my throat from bursting forth then, or during Mollie's whispered "Until death do us part." But she made us all so damn happy that we just couldn't wreck things with outright sobbing. Afterwards, she rallied sufficiently on the strength of felicity to speak in a normal voice in response to the inundation of tearful good wishes.

"This is by far the happiest day of my life. That it comes so close to the end does not matter a bit, and in fact makes it all the sweeter. If I leave you and my beloved Jacob soon, I know that we will be reunited eternally soon after that, in the twinkling of an eye. And who knows what tonic effect such unconditioned happiness as I feel may have on the disease that now seems so sure of its early triumph? In any case, the length of time I have left will be sufficient whatever its duration, for it will contain the whole of my bliss." We cheered, she acquired a rosy flush of happiness that did look a bit like returning health. Then, since their honeymoon consisted of our departure, we left, soaked in exaltation; and she died in her sleep that night.

Almost nothing about my smashed elbow, for as long as it defined my exile from music, hurt worse than being unable to play at Mollie's funeral. Early on, soon after her letter to me and long before the Stravinsky performance, I had found another little envelope on my stand when I came in for a Civic rehearsal. On a 3x5 card inside it said, "Funeral music: Bach, C minor Suite for unaccompanied cello, Sarabande and Gigue; Cage, 4'33"; Bach, 'Jesu, Joy of Man's Desiring'." The Bach selections progressed from resignation through defiant joy to tranquility; and putting the Cage piece in the middle was a nice nose-thumbing at the terrible gods of silence. I could have performed that, come to think of it; but I sat and listened to the Faithful Shepherd organist desecrating the lot. Well, let's be fair: the chorale was OK and he used a flute stop that was close enough to Mollie's real sound to cloud me up again. The Cage was perfect. But the cello dances were travesties.

At the cemetery, the same Lakewood that housed my father, we laid her in the earth beneath a temporary marker that said exactly what the granite one would when I moved it to North Carolina, years later:

Mollie Elizabeth Biedermeyer Oxendine
May 11, 1913 - November 26, 1953
"Behold, I tell you a mystery:
We shall be raised incorruptible
In a moment; In the twinkling of an eye."

It didn't dawn on me until I saw it that her wedding and death had taken place on Thanksgiving.

*   *

Well, after a *grave* slow movement in a minor key, we ought to expect a rollicking *presto*, right? Give people a chance

198

to shuffle feet and cough, fishing for lemon drops in their purses. Boy, would I love to provide it. I suppose we could get a few bassoon chuckles out of my session with Alfred Saxon, Ph.D., who wished to help in any way he could with my success in college.

Part of that success, for example, consisted in managing to get an appointment with him after four phone calls to his secretary, and to get another one, which he kept this time, after only two more. He sat there leafing through a manila folder marked "Diehl Kermit/Dienst Oren", and tossing half the pages - which I could only hope referred to my foldermate Diehl Kermit - in the wastebasket. At the end of my twenty-minute slot, we agreed that I could probably salvage the two "hard" courses, Calculus and Quantitative Analysis, by dropping all the rest, and it would probably set me back a term but would preserve my good standing as a Chem. E. major, "In view particularly of your, er, apparent injury. Intramurals, I suppose?"

I admitted it had been, a particularly vicious tackle on the lawn of the Kappa Sig house, and he sighed. "It always is. Very well, Dienst. I think you're bright enough to pull it out, but only under condition that you avoid further mishap. Got me?"

I got him. I got out. I was more than willing to avoid mishap, in case any further were waiting out there. I had given this some thought and had concluded that all the large and small disasters of the past six weeks spelled out as plainly as in a new constellation (or disconstellation) a clear message across the winter sky: **Don't get your hopes up. Stay on the tracks.**

Such mishaps as the successive losses of Anna, of my cello, of the ability to play any cello probably ever again, of Mollie, and of my job with Di Salvo (He took one look at my cast, said "Where the hell you been now, Don Giovanni? I don't see you for a month, you show up broke. Come back when you got arms to work.") had that single cause, over-commitment to my own doubtful prowess. The richest man in St. Louis says it shall be X? Make it Y, and steal his cello. Washed out of conservatory? Dream of a concert career, but take care to wreck your arm as soon as possible. Fallen in love with the daughter of a crazed Nazi? Seduce her under his nose, and see if he doesn't calm down.

Good work. I must be the hottest cellist, the hottest lover, and the shrewdest operator around. The gods that manage these things - not those of silence and music and the universe but humble technician gods with sweaty arms and one eye on quitting time, had seen me sticking up above the rubble and given me a good swat. So, maybe there's a sort of a *scherzo, molto pesante*, in that. But anything I undertook from then on was just for lack of anything better. There was no heart in it.

As for things involving my own heart: The news of Mollie's death, conveyed by a gruff phone call from Jacob not a day after their wedding, broke the spell Arnold Rosen had cast with his magic cane. The anger I'd felt toward Anna, what I'd said to her while we cowered naked before him I barely remembered, except as a spell-struck idiot or a hypnotist's subject might have the uneasy dim memory that he'd done something ludicrous and grotesque. When Jacob spoke his few formal words of love that for all its restraint and civility was probably no less passionate - probably in some thermodynamic way, because of its restraint, more so - than what Anna and I had achieved, I realized that I wanted nothing more than to go to her, to swallow or brush aside whatever doubts, refusals, or evasions and devote myself to making her even a tenth as happy as Jacob had made Mollie. I reinvented courtly love.

I called, it was always answered by a von Bayern who said Anna was out, and then the number was changed and unlisted. I wrote, trying for Jacobean dignity, and this is what survived the crossed-out, crumpled drafts:

Dear Anna:

Perhaps you will have heard of Mollie's wedding and death. I am distressed to think that you can have turned your back on all that we have meant to each other. At the least, please communicate and let me comfort myself that you are safe and well. It is very lonely without you; but most important is your happiness, which means more than everything else to your loving friend

Oren

It was only dumb luck it didn't occur to me to write "*distresséd*". When that brought no response, I wrote again, and similar eloquence survived my savage editing. That one was returned unopened, with "No longer at 6 Reignleigh Court" scrawled across the envelope. I drove out one afternoon and was politely but firmly kissed off by the gardener.

"She ain't here, pal, and nobody that is wants to see you. My orders is, tell you that, and if you come back again, do whatever I have to. In other words, improvise freely. That cast and all, you don't look to me like you'd stand up to that real well, particularly when it'd be for nothing anyway."

"Can I ask who gave those orders?"

"The family, and that includes Mr. McIntear. So buzz off, now, and see if you can't stay out of trouble for five minutes."

I couldn't. I came back after midnight in my black clothes and tried the back route through the woods hoping, if that's the word for it, to creep up to the back of *Six bis*, use the key I'd pocketed, and find Anna, or any evidence bearing on her presence or absence; and if presence, to bring to bear passion, eloquence, wit, stupidity, any tool that came to hand.

After a far from silent scramble through briary woods I actually came within sight of the target. It was closed off from this direction by a cyclone fence, behind which Oren the adolescent boxer stood quivering wide awake, drooling around a tennis ball and longingly sniffing my knee. I crept down the fence, Oren mirroring my every move. There was no gate that I could see, but the fence wasn't all that high, and I thought maybe, cast and all, I could get over it. The second I put my sneaker into one of the wire diamonds to try it, Oren dropped his ball and went off like a noise bomb, barking and yowking and jumping against the fence. A light went on, a door slammed, and I retreated into the darkness.

Rick McIntear's voice came from behind a very penetrating flashlight: "Dienst, you jackass, if that's you out there, Rosen isn't here, and I don't know where she is. She told me she never wanted to see you again, so for god's sake forget her." It was all I could do to keep from yelling back, *Thanks, I'd almost lost hope until you said that.* But as I thought it, I stepped

201

in a hole and fell sideways onto the cast. It made a muffled sound as of things being ground in a mortar, and I had to bite down hard on a twig - which turned out to be poison oak - to keep from bellowing with fury and pain. When I dragged back to the car, mouth already tingling from incipient blisters, Nancy was there, alone, not looking exactly friendly but not her old vapid self either. She seemed close to tears.

"Honest to God, Oren, can't you mind? Anna isn't living with us any more. When she has something to tell you, maybe she'll get in touch. But it's out of your hands, so *please* leave us alone."

Ah. Something else that was out of my hands.

But I did get something off my chest, and that was the business about the notebook. It involved a lot of bouncing from one county office to another, finding out that people who cared much about what chemicals spilled in low-rent neighborhoods in Webster Groves were in a minority in the County Seat of Clayton, Missouri. If the stuff was actually burning, that was the local fire department's problem. If it was a threat to the health of taxpayers, maybe the Health Office would know something, but they didn't. Deaths? Try the coroner's office. Everybody was unanimous that the County Attorney would have nothing to do with it under any circumstances, so that's where I wound up.

And once I was there, it was smooth as glass. An evidence clerk in the outer office said, Oh, you mean that blue lab notebook with the affidavit stapled to it, and I went into my Geez, there's just something that's been bothering me about it, and she dimpled and went into a safe and pulled it right out. After she gave me a perfunctory ID check, I paged through it and, with very flat affect, reprised my discovery of the fakery. I then was presented with a Form 47B, Revision of Testimony, which I filled out and swore to the clerk.

The whole thing was obviously so commonplace as to be a matter of routine with them. (*Yeah, that guy Dienst came in and did a Type Three double-take on the notebook, so I gave him a 47B.*) What the consequences might be, whether to bring the Molar Chemical empire crashing to its knees or to bounce off its ramparts like a soggy tennis ball, was impossible to read from the way the clerk chewed her gum. It would be years, I was sure, before I heard anything further. Decades, as it turned out.

But Anna's cheery letter came on Christmas Eve in a heavy envelope of half-glossy foreign paper, postmarked Lucerne and slathered with exquisitely etched stamps:

Dear Oren:

I apologize for not responding to your sweet letter. I am truly sorry that my reclusiveness must have given you some pain. Also, it devastated me to miss Mollie's wedding and funeral. I could not - I simply could not - be there, and it felt like exile, not from my wretched home but from my true family.

Everything I said in my first letter is still true. I have launched on a new life, using the last of my tutoring money to buy a plane ticket and get settled. I will stay here for now, not in Lucerne but in the vicinity, and I am earning my living by teaching literature in a convent school - Sister Maria Immaculata's old school, imagine! - where the nuns have seen to it that I fit right in. It is challenging work; if I ever have to teach the Inferno I may slip in your story of Francesca.

Speaking of that, I hope you were successful in freeing "Francesca" for her musical career. If so, I believe that the enclosed key may prove to be just the one to unlock a dilemma for you. Please use it with my love and blessing. I will not forget you.

-Anna

There were two keys, actually, strung on a loop of wire and taped to a little neat square of cardboard to keep them from rattling around and poking holes in the envelope. (Oh, and I could see her clean slim fingers cutting and taping that trim package in the lamplight of a convent garret on a rainy Sunday in Lucerne.) Lucerne, *Switzerland*, Jesus... Lucerne, China; Lucerne, Mars. Anna had stiffed me good and taken herself out of reach forever. My heartload of courtly love began to return to the sludge from which it had sprung.

One of the keys I recognized as her copy of the Orpheum key. The second, it took me a day to figure out since she'd not thought to explain, fit a luggage locker at Union Station. In the locker, barely fitting, was my old cello "Anna", still bearing Yoolie's ribbon claiming it was Francesca. Tucked through the strings were two bills of sale, both dated November 25: one from Nancy von Bayern to Anna Rosen in the amount of $1, and the other from Anna Rosen to Oren Dienst for $1.18 and other good and valuable considerations. You name me the stock that'll appreciate eighteen percent in a day.

I looked around at the dozen grudging travelers mooching around the waiting room on Christmas afternoon; I wished everyone a pleasant journey. I stripped off the ribbon and the bills of sale, put the cello naked back in the locker, and slammed the door.

*   *

Wired to the right kind of rock, those keys fit sweetly to my hand, and I looked after them for a long time as they rose together into the sky over the river. At the highest point of their arc they hung motionless in my sight, though making all speed eastward. All the way to Switzerland, for all I cared. Or all the way to Hell, where if Anna Rosen found them while she and Francesca da Rimini were giggling together about boyfriends, that would be fine, with me *and* Paolo. I wiped my hand on my pants.

Behind me, the sun was nearly down, the western sky a seasonal glow of Weller's and holly berries on a dome more spacious than the Orpheum's, but illusory all the same. In the holy hush beneath it my father tossed and fretted in his narrow conservatory, knowing he'd never have the tenors for the Messiah or a kid who could sing Curly worth a damn. A stone's throw from him Mollie Biedermeyer rested, arms crossed, feeling no pain, waiting in infinite patience for the twinkling of an eye to pass.

Beyond the black dot that hung over the great bed of moving water it was dusk in Illinois, long past sunset in Carolina where Jacob Oxendine sat on a brick porch outside Red Springs with a ring on his finger and a hollow place in his chest, and spoke of cutting more wood.

Tears made me lose sight of the rock, but the spinning must have broken the wire's grip on the keys. Falling free to the Mississippi, one of them in its tumbling caught the last of the sun, a golden flash of gone.

II: 1983

12. Intern

The amber second-line light started flashing on my phone. I punched in on the newcomer with a quick "Environmental Protection Agency, Office of International Affairs, this is Oren Dienst, can you hold a minute?" praying it wouldn't be some congressman's secretary.

"What have I been doing? This is Mort Bralow in Water Programs. Call me back on 4083 when you got a minute yourself."

"Gotcha. We're pretty short-handed up here, you know."

"No kidding? Call me back."

OK, that one was cooled, and I scribbled the number while I got back to my lunch date. "Sorry to stack you up like that. Noon at the Willard OK?"

"Get a table out of sight. Don't bring your beeper and don't wear a wire."

"Sure."

I was still pondering that as I picked up the notepad and punched Bralow's line. I knew him by name as a fellow parishioner at All Saints, and I could vaguely conjure a short guy with a fringe of brown hair, playing Joseph in the Christmas pageant. But I had come up through another branch of EPA, and All Saints didn't force on each other the company of individuals in its flock. We arrived, we found anonymous comfort in elaborate and unvarying liturgy, we departed. I glumly eyed the stack of reports I had yet to plow through while the phone at the other end rang its little butt off. I was well into page two of the top one when Bralow picked up the line.

"Oh, yeah, right. What was that about, did I say?"

"Nope, sorry."

"Yeah, just a second here. Three things have happened since I called you . . . oh, yeah. We got a letter from some kid in Alaska wants to come here and work for free, you know, what's that called?"

"An intern?"

"Right, a student, anyhow, gives you as a reference. We kind of like the looks of her, and god knows we could use some off-budget help. You know her?"

Another goddamn student. "Hard to tell. Did she give a name, or is this an anonymous application?"

"Huh? Of course not. Ge - something. Gewissner. Allmut C. Gewissner. Funny name. You know her?"

Yes, of course I did. A.C. Gewissner's birth announcement reached me in late August of 1954, a long time ago indeed: *"Mr. and Mrs. Markus Gewissner take pride in announcing the birth of their daughter Allmut Cushing Gewissner, 9# oz, 21", on July 7, 1954".* It was just in time for me to get a note of congratulations off to Markus and Sophie - particularly Sophie, for carrying to term and safely bearing a whopping baby - before I plunged into fall classes, including thermodynamics with real bullets this time. I offered my best wishes to the new baby and sent along a rattle and a <u>Mad</u> comic, figuring she could graduate from one to the other in either order. I politely inquired after the health of everyone directly involved, and also about the origin of little Allmut's name. Which brought one of Sophie's letters:

Dear Oren:

Thank you for the gifts and the letter about our new baby. "Allmut" is Markus' Grandmother's name, and it means more or less "Ready For Anything" in German, or so says Markus, which fits with his ideas about her being conceived in a Lightning storm, and so forth. Some funny folks here say All Mut, no pedigree, but they don't say it around Markus. I mostly call her Sugar or AC. She is really sweet, but is not very good about letting me sleep at night. I have quit my job to take care of

*her, and Markus is working double Shifts to make up for it, so I
do not see much of him; and just now, between us, that is OK.*

*I have taken the <u>Mad</u> into protective Custody, and
I think I will give it to AC for her twelvth birthday - if we make it
that far.*

> *Take care -*
> *Your friend(s)*
> *Sophie*
> *-oh, well, and Markus, too.*

So aromatic, ungainly Sophie had added a dependent
and a streak of irony, and that was all to the good. Had I been in
a mood for jollity I might have grinned about Reddy Kilowatt
carrying the nickname AC, but that was a fuse that led under and
behind the solid wall of black glass I was keeping between
myself and the events of the previous year.

I met AC herself - and five brothers and sisters - about
sixteen years later, when a letter arrived from Alaska on my last
day as an associate professor of chemical engineering at North
Carolina State. I had taken a break from packing boxes and
grading final exams to pick up mail and leave forwarding
instructions to the brand-new Environmental Protection Agency I
was about to join. This was only about the eighth letter I'd had
from that direction in the intervening years, and half of those had
been birth announcements, including that of the twins Markus Jr.
and Mary Catherine, just about coinciding with my decision to
quit working for a living and get a doctorate. (One of the
exceptions had been an excruciatingly scrawled thank-you from
12-year-old Allmut Cushing ($A_{\odot}C_{\odot}$) Gewissner in the summer
of 1966 when, true to plan, Sophie had relinquished what must
have been a pretty dated and brittle <u>Mad</u>, along with instructions
to thank the donor.)

With the new envelope in my hand, I thought back.
Actually, the last birth announcement had been almost eight
years previous, while I was on the engineering faculty at Ohio
State. Could long-suffering Sophie have had the bad luck to
conceive an afterthought this late? Hell, she was still young
enough, and the little square envelope had just that look. I
entered my office and tore it open while I picked up a ringing

phone; then let it dangle while I scowled at the unbelievable card in my hand. A voice honked faintly from the phone.

"hello?" Aw, hell.

"dr. dienst? hello?" Aw, Jesus, why? I thumped the phone down on the empty desk and slumped back in my chair, my eyes filling with grief I wouldn't have thought was there for this news.

Mrs. Sophie C. Gewissner
Allmut, Anna, Markus, Jr., Mary Catherine,
Karen, and Oren Gewissner
Announce with sorrow the death of their beloved
husband and father Captain Markus Karl Gewissner
Lost and presumed drowned in the shipwreck of the trawler
Boreal Kid
on or about June 15, 1970

Requiescat in Pacem

The card was stiff and formal, but the note with it was torn from a Peter Max tablet and showed what looked like gummy bears dancing over a rainbow made out of fish and butterflies. *"Dear Oren,"* it read in toto, *"Markus went down with his ship in a terrible Storm. The survivors say he was a real hero. The memorial service is next Saturday."* I looked at the postmark and the calendar, and concluded that the Saturday in question was the day after tomorrow. I did not let myself think or plan, I just called Piedmont Airlines. My caller – some kid worried about his final grade, I guessed – would just have to contain himself a little longer.

My recollections of that weekend in Anchorage in 1970 are of a chaos of people: Sophie, who had solidified into a handsome, rugged woman; strangers who were wives of other crew, surviving and lost; other strangers who had evidently been devoted to Markus, or to Sophie, or both; a minister; teachers and counselors from the kids' school, friends of the kids, and the kids themselves. My namesake Oren Gewissner turned out to be a sturdy second-grader who looked at me impudently while we were being introduced, then stuck out his tongue and ran away. Eventually I earned his forgiveness for stealing his name, by inviting him to the Holiday Inn for a swim.

AC Gewissner was long-legged and broad-shouldered like her mother, with her father's chiseled features. She looked as if, in normal times, she might have lived up to her "ready-for-anything" name. She was, of all the children, the most crushed by her father's death, leading me to guess that she had enjoyed a first-born's status as his favorite, possibly going back to the highly Teutonic circumstances of her conception. She was having a tough time putting up with all the solicitude, including that of this unknown guy who had flown clear across the country to add to her grief by knowing her father before she had.

When I asked Sophie, I thought privately, over kitchen-table coffee, if she was all right financially, AC wheeled around the doorway and informed me icily that she, AC, was sixteen, which was old enough to work, and that she not only intended to do so, but had already arranged to convert her summer job to a permanent one at higher pay, so they were going to be just fine, thanks; and stalked out to the yard, where I could see her biting her lip and glaring at the sky while she scuffed through a carpet of spring flowers.

"OK," I said. "Here's what I'd like to do. I'm going to leave a little something to help you get started. If you find you don't need it, send it back. If AC gets upset, it's a loan, but I don't care when it comes due. How's that?"

Sophie looked at me levelly for a moment and said, "Oren, it is killing me to say this. Markus didn't believe in insurance. It's for shoe clerks, he said. We're in for another tough time, and I accept your offer. You are the kindest guy I ever met, except Markus sometimes."

"You said that before, Sophie, but I've got to tell you - I was laughing at you and Markus too, when everybody else was."

She started to smile, and groped for my hand. "Shoot, Oren," she managed at last, "Who wouldn't of?"

AC left in the middle of the memorial service, stomping up the aisle in her hiking boots with her jaw set and a faraway look in her eyes; and I tell you, she looked so much like Markus, and was doing so exactly what Markus would have done, that half the onlookers smiled and the rest burst into tears. She had not reappeared by the time I had to catch my flight back through Seattle and Chicago, so I left her a note saying I'd enjoyed meeting her, that the Markus I knew would be proud of her, and if she ever got to Washington, blah blah. In September I got a check for $47.50 drawn on the account of Allmut C. Gewissner along with a stiff note on paper with a totem pole up one side, thanking me for my kind gesture to the family and apologizing for what she called her rude and egotistical behavior in June.

I knew better than to return the check, so I cashed it, and when another one ($53.00 this time) came a month later I returned that one with a note saying that I'd invested the first $47.50 on a stock tip and made so much on it that the loan was wiped out. For verisimilitude I enclosed a check of my own for $41.73, saying that was her split of the windfall. I don't know that she actually believed that, but I counted on her being too much like Markus to admit I might be kidding. In any case, that was the last I heard of her until Bralow's call.

In the meantime, with Markus still leading the way, I had eased over the peak of my powers and started the long descent through middle age by trading the pampered omniscience of the professoriate for a middle-management job in what quickly became one of the biggest scientific bureaucracies ever assembled, Mr. Nixon's Environmental Protection Agency. It was all new, the elaborate and farcical regulations about conflict of interest, the autocratic corporate style of management, the constant need to watch what one said; in short, it was a demotion from meritocrat to underling, rival, or boss, depending on who you were. In a year or so I began to feel at home with it; long before that, when I turned around to check, the door back to Academe had closed behind me.

I passed the next ten years worrying about toxic wastes and hazardous solids while the hundred-pound lump of sludge I carried away from my fiasco with Yoolie, Arnold, and the Fire Bird dwindled and clarified and thinned until it was no more than a glassy sliver that only bothered me when I took deep breaths. It lodged just where the top of a cello rests, and I suppose playing might have had further solvent effect on it, but that was out of the question when I couldn't bend my elbow past 90°. I carried that little dagger inside me while I paid dues for my complicity in the Molar spill and took on enough responsibility to rise in the Solid Waste Division, then jump to a management slot in the Office of International Activities, where I found my engineering training all kinds of useless in dealing with environmental inactivists in the UN, the OAS, and the US Department of State.

Two "further mishaps," to quote Alfred Saxon (whose retirement party I dropped in on while I was back in St. Louis to bury my mother in 1965, and went entirely unrecognized by the old educator) intervened to put markers on the passing years: namely, I got married in 1971, and a genial actor was elected President of the United Mistakes in 1980. First mishaps first: I think I can do justice to my marriage in a sentence or two.

Well, her name was Cindy, and I met her at a "Washington in the Capitol" 15th reunion, where she regaled me with stories of Quant lab until I recognized her as Cindy Something, that Cindy the lab partner, and she seemed kind of lonesome living in Alexandria and nursing a divorce from a Nixon press aide, and she was still about as cute as she had been; and I was lonesome too, nursing no divorce but an apparently total inability to get interested in women; and when I explained that, she said, Well, at least you won't tell me my eyes have made rosemeat of your heart, and I laughed, maybe a little tightly, and said, Were you that cheerleader, and it was worth a drink, so we had dinner and this and that, culminating a month or two later in a trip to Bermuda, where her kind of cute looks just blossoms around those little mopeds and real Bermuda shorts and pink sand. So one night after a pretty stiff course of Chablis I so far lost my general disinclination as to uphold some standard of masculinity, long enough anyhow to mistake it for love, which led to a quiet ceremony a month or so later, the mutual purchase and occupancy of a condo in a high-rise called "Montecaro" in Silver Spring, a vasectomy, a fair amount of pleasant fun, some disappointments, quite a few disappointments, hurt feelings, counseling, reconciliation, separation, and a divorce in which I kept Montecaro and Cindy kept everything else, the whole childless interlude being done with before the 20th reunion rolled around.

None of it was Cindy's fault. I would say, and hope, that the whole thing was a net plus for both of us, in that we quit while we were ahead. I just wish I'd had better sense. Cindy went straight on to lasting bliss in the arms of a cotton lobbyist who, one time when I ran into him at a defoliants hearing, told me he thought the world of that little girl. I congratulated him, and actually meant it, and asked him to take her my kindest regards. He said he would, and I hope he wasn't kidding.

What? You can wait around for a punch line as long as you want; you won't hear anything glum or sour from me about Cindy. Actually, her gift of daisies when I was in the hospital getting over Arnold Rosen's attack was such a nice gesture that she could have been Lady Macbeth during our short marriage and not wiped out that little deed. For my part, though, that one shot at blissful pairing had been more than enough.

The whole Reagan business proved to be by far the more troublesome mishap. Of course, he brought some competent, principled people into government with him, and if you are one of those, it was nice having you around for a while. But he also brought a lot of crazies and crooks, and our share of these wound up squatting on top of Interior and the EPA like Larry, Moe, and Curly had landed jobs running the Vatican. Well, maybe that's not fair; who would know more about pollution than the guys who make it?

But worst of all, my old double-dating buddy Rick McIntear, now known in Missouri as Mac the Knife, in the interim having slashed and burned his way to the top of Molar Chemical Company, and become a power donor in Republican politics, cashed in, after the 1982 elections, for a spot in the office of the Deputy Administrator of EPA. From there, he set about wringing whatever tribute he could from his fellow industrialists while hamstringing our enforcement practices and manpower to the everlasting advantage of Molar Chemical. His respect for the natural environment, his fellow man, and the truth had, if anything, waned a bit since 1953. I encountered him in person walking down a hall on his first day in the spring of 1983, surrounded by prospective staff and currently employed flacks, out on a first survey to see what might not be nailed down. He greeted me as if no time had passed at all. "Aaron! Buddy! Happy New Year. Saw you on the chart, knew I'd have to look you up. How's your little dancer friend?"

Well, that pretty well set the tone. "Doing fine, I expect," I said. "And your own lovely ... Nancy, wasn't it?"

"I wouldn't know. I left her in a hotel in Reno trying on martinis." He slipped an arm around one of the flacks, a Latin-looking woman maybe half his age. "Like you to meet my administrative assistant, Liana. Let's get together one of these days over some lunch, see if we can work together on some things here."

But before that could happen, I had my lunch at the Willard, and heard much more than I wanted to hear about Molar Chemical's Mexican subsidiary, MexiLar Metals. We'll have to deal with that in due course, so we can save the details. For now, maybe it will be impressive enough to say that the Mexican government was complaining about MexiLar's lax practices in regard to proper and conscientious observation of its environmental regulations, particularly in regard to the disposal of hazardous wastes.

I went straight from that lunch, trying to get my $17 BLT to sit well over the gruesome stuff I had learned about MexiLar, to a follow-up appointment with an orthopedic surgeon I had finally resorted to when my screwed-up left elbow progressed from stiff to sore to agonizing during the course of the last three years. A whole team of guys had gone in there through the miracle of arthroscopy and spent what seemed like most of a day cleaning out chips, grinding off spurs and overgrowths the thing had thrown up to keep itself from bending more than it could stand, and drilling little holes and screwing together what had opted not to heal itself. I had the whole thing on local and demerol, so it passed in a sort of boring haze, while I noted but did not worry about the little whistles and looka-*that*'s I kept hearing behind the curtain on my left.

Now, not forty minutes after I'd checked in with his office manager, I walked into the surgeon's sanctum for a follow-up. He took me over to one of those vertical light boxes they use to look at x-ray negatives, and flipped three of them up under the clips. "I want you to see what we've done for you in some kind of context. This first one is a normal left elbow - actually, it's your own right elbow, put up backwards. That's pretty much what an elbow joint is supposed to look like. The next one, that looks like a train wreck, is your left elbow the way it was last month. I'm damned if I can see how you used the thing at all, or what this bone guy that first set it thought he was doing."

"I don't think he thought it would matter that much. I was under arrest on suspicion of murder at the time."

The guy raised his eyebrows. "Hm. Anyhow, this third one is what it looks like now. If I move the normal one over next to it, you can see that it ain't normal. But it's a lot closer, and in particular, I can't see any reason it shouldn't work pretty well, though if I ever hear of you, oh, doing pushups on it, I won't want to hear about it."

"Not much chance of that."

"Yeah. Let me see you bend it."

I tried. It was still a little sore from the poking around, but it wasn't that. I held my arm out with the palm up, and did an unloaded arm curl. It worked OK, up to a point, and then it just got so stiff and painful that I couldn't bend it any more. That point was about the same old 90°.

"Hmm. OK, let me help a little." And he took my wrist and held my elbow, and just bent the thing right back until my fingers were touching my shoulder. "See? It bends just fine. What's stopping you?"

"Well, I don't know. It just starts hurting as it gets up there toward 90°, and I can't force it any farther."

"Hmm. You got any psychological objections to bending your arm?"

"Of course not. I don't think anybody's had that kind of thing since about 1925. Anyhow, I can bend the other one just fine, see?"

"Well, I'm gonna give you a course of exercises, and see if we can't build up muscle tone and strength in your upper arm; for one thing it hasn't had to do anything like that for - how long was it?"

"Mmm - almost thirty years."

"Jesus. Anyhow, try the stuff in this booklet for two weeks. If you don't get some improvement, enough to encourage you to go on with it, don't bother to come back here, 'cause I wouldn't know what else to say. I'd suggest . . ." He walked over and closed his office door and lowered his voice. "Honest to god, I'd suggest acupuncture. Cripes, if any of the other guys in here heard me say that, they'd die. There's a ton of 'em in the yellow pages, and I don't know one from another. Pick one that sounds good to you and give it a shot."

When I got back to my office, there was a pile of little "While You Were Out" slips on my desk, of which only two bear on the current tale. One was a no-return confirmation from Bralow saying he'd found a slot for AC Gewissner on my recommendation, and she would be arriving in a month. The other was from Rick McIntear's office requesting an immediate conference on a matter of mutual concern. Well, I had been at EPA for over a dozen years, roughly 365 times as long as McIntear, but he outranked me. I called his office and found the pliant Liana on the other end.

"Oh, good," she purred. "Dr. Dienst, Mr. McIntear is free in a half hour, and he really did want to see you as soon as might be possible. Please hold for a moment while I see if that will be convenient for him." I said nothing, since you can't send a rueful reminiscent grin over the phone, and she was back in about three minutes. "Thenk yew for holding, Mr. Dienst. Mr. McIntear will see you at four. Shall I tell him you'll be here?"

"Does he know you even asked me?"

Liana's voice lost the Brit tones she'd been using, and became pleasantly Latina. "Oh, shoot. Escuse me. Please don't tell him."

"I wouldn't dream of it. Please tell Mr. McIntear I begged you to let me see him at 3:30, and you stiffed me until four."

She cleared her throat and laughed coolly.

"Here's the situation we got before us, Aaron. We got some wild hare in the Mexican government that's leaking complaints about US firms desecrating the Mexican landscape

216

with toxic wastes - ha, as if you could desecrate Hell - and it's making some of our guys a little nervous about undue interference, intrusive regulation, that kind of thing. Not that we're likely to have a real public relations problem down there, bunch of greasers anyhow. I'd appreciate it like hell if the International Affairs fellas would get on this through - what, OAS? Tell them not to get their hair in a knot, ask 'em who didn't get greased enough and how much it'll take, that kind of thing. Think you can handle that?"

"Rick, Rick. Doesn't this have a kind of familiar ring to you?"

"How's that?"

"Well, seems to me the last conversation we had was about a tank car that didn't jump the tracks in Webster Groves, and didn't spill anything, and what it did spill was spring water, wasn't it, and nobody died, two of them white."

He snorted. "Those were the simple old days, weren't they? No, I think the very last conversation we had ended with you falling on your ass out in the woods behind Yoolie's place; but even this doesn't remind me all that much of that, and here's why. Back then, you didn't work for me. But there is one kind of nostalgic detail, now that you mention it. Wasn't there something about signing an affidavit, after you knew what you were signing was false?"

"I covered myself on that with the County Attorney's office. And I still don't work for you."

"Technically no, but you and I work for a lady that's a lot better friend of mine than she is of yours. And thank you for reminding me about that little stab in the back with the affidavit. It cost Molar a bundle to grease the County, and don't think we didn't see your face on every bill."

"Moving right along . . ."

"Moving right along is what you're going to be doing, Dienst. We need some help from the International office on this, and I'm pretty sure we can get it."

"How can we help? Oh, I get it, you want me to go up to the Mexican delegate to the OAS and ask him who I should bribe, and for how much, to keep MexiLar safe from undue regulation, and I guess while he's at it, how much for him personally, and in what currency?"

He smirked. "Not bad."

"It doesn't work that way."

"Not in so many words, maybe. I've dealt with those guys, Dienst. People dismiss 'em, say they're just a bunch of greasers, but the guys - "

"True enough. You said that yourself not five minutes ago."

"I was referring to the general public. The guys that run things, they're as sharp and tough as you'd want. They'll keep us in the clear down there, but you have to make it worth their while, just like an American. What I'm asking from you is absolutely standard business and diplomatic practice, and you know it. This isn't some two-bit tank car rolling down a hill in darktown. This is profits and shareholders and jobs; American jobs and American votes." He stood up, coming to attention I guess, but it drew my attention to the desk he was getting ready to pound on, and suddenly I needed to sit down. Resting in a walnut mount by his tacky onyx pen set was an object about which I had heard, and even written, but had never seen: a hunting knife about ten inches long with a staghorn handle carved into the shape of a naked woman. Mollie may in her terror have missed the symbolism; I think it was meant to be Diana, Goddess of the Hunt, if you picture Diana reincarnated as Barbie with horns. The blade looked discolored, but sharp as hell.

McIntear (the Knife) was still orating as the buzz faded from my ears: "...tell the honorable from St. Louis County one of their native sons is sitting in the International Affairs Office at EPA and costing his people jobs and profits? Know how long you'd last then? And not just you, your whole bunch over there and everything they're trying to do. Politics, Dienst. The art of the possible, the home of compromise. I love it, don't you?"

"I'll get back to you on it. How did you get that knife?"

"Do that, and soon. It was Yoolie's, the cops brought it by after that crazy old maid knocked his brains out. Nan or her mother didn't give a crap about it, so I took it. It seems to make a point to people. So to speak." He looked humble. "You know, Aaron, hardly a day goes by I don't say, 'Thanks, Yoolie' for all he gave me, hating my guts every minute. I kinda can't help hoping he can look up from hell and see how far I've gone on his dime. Now get out of here and clean up those greasers."

I turned to go, but when I had my hand on the very nicely polished knob, he had another thought. "Oh, yeah, Aaron, wait a second. Speaking of Yoolie's stuff, and ..." He doubled up with laughter. "<u>And</u> speaking of clean. Jesus. I almost forgot to tell you. When I was packing up after Nan and I split, I ran across a bunch of Yoolie's skin flicks, including some with some familiar names on the cans. So I loaded up Fire Bird and ran it. Jesus, he must've loved it, there were three or four copies of it in that box. I know I sure did. That hose sequence was dynamite, didn't you think, the way it cleaned the paint off her? I bet you knew who it was then, even before the fireman pulled the mask off. God, no wonder you were so hot for that little honey, left Nan and me in the lurch downtown and all. She must've had your nuts in an uproar the whole time."

I turned and smiled at him. "Rick, I can see we're not going to have an easy time of it here. We represent different points of view and completely different goals. I expect it's going to be one scene like this after another until one of us quits. It's encouraging, though, to see that you're the same moronic bastard you always were. It gives me hope."

"It'll be you, Dienst," he hollered. "Get the hell outa here and do what I told you to, or start packing."

As I walked into the outer office, Liana, on her rolling chair, was skidding wide-eyed to a stop with her knees under her desk. A piece of paper teetered and slid off the corner nearest Rick's door. In the elevator, I thought of a great line to toss at her on the way out, the next time we were in that exact situation.

I pulled the DC and Maryland yellow pages out of the phone table with a practiced motion that avoided flexing my left arm - the arm that was not going to flex if it could help it - and started looking for acupuncturists with offices along the Metro Red Line. There was no point in exposing myself to mugging and mayhem by threading my way to most of them; anything in Southeast, most of Northeast, and a lot of Northwest, like

Adams-Morgan or the low numbers north of K, would be inconvenient and risky.

As promised, there were a ton of them. The one that caught my eye was off DuPont Circle, and anyhow, I just liked the name: Donia Ma, O.M.C.D. I figured the initials were just garbage, since no two of the ads had the same set, but the ad was laid out in a pleasing way, with no use of dragons or yin/yang stuff, but with a sense of style. When you can't possibly make an informed choice, make a pleased one, I say. Donia Ma herself answered the phone, which also pleased me; I got more than plenty of phone-upsmanship on the job.

"Yes, I can take another patient. Will you describe your problem to me?"

"You don't need to see me?"

"Of course. But it will be helpful if I can think about it before you come in."

"Well, that makes sense. OK, I have trouble bending my left arm, since I broke the elbow about thirty years ago."

"You have had this condition for thirty years, and you just now turn to acupuncture?"

"There was good reason for it not to bend before, but this spring I had arthroscopic surgery on it, and the surgeon says it should bend, but it won't."

"Ah. Describe the injury, please."

"Describe it?"

"Yes. How did you break it?"

"By falling down stairs."

"Not so much that as by landing at the bottom, if I may presume. Did you try to catch yourself by holding your hand outward from your body?"

"No, I sort of crashed into a stone windowsill."

"Ah. So was it the outside of your elbow that hit the sill?"

"Yes."

"Ah. Any other parts injured at the same time?"

"No. Well, wait, yes. My left shoulder, but it - "

"Aha. And was there any other injury at that time, or within a year of it in either direction?"

"No, I don't . . . Yes. Two broken ribs."

"Merciful heavens. Are you a prize fighter?"

"No, I was just going through a pretty rough time."

"Evidently. And the ribs were broken where?"

"Toward the back on the left."

"And at about the level of the other injuries?"

To answer that I had to look behind the black glass wall, and it was not an immediate, easy question to answer. Donia Ma seemed to perceive this over the phone. "Never mind. I will find them when I see you. That will do for now. I will study upon what you have told me, and I will see you at 11:30 pm next Wednesday, please. Wear a loose-fitting shirt. Thank you."

"Wait. Eleven thirty at night? You're that busy? Maybe you could recommend someone who could fit me in during the day."

"Anyone who would give a daytime appointment to one with injuries all along the meridian of the triple burner would certainly be someone whom I could not recommend. If you cannot come at the proper hour, I cannot help you."

"I see. This is a matter of propitious times of day?"

"Please do not make it sound like superstition. It is a matter of a harmonious time, yes."

"Mmm... Well, you're the doctor."

"Indeed. Next Wednesday evening, then?"

Indeed. I liked her voice, which was West Coast American with only the faintest Oriental overlay; I liked her dry, minimal, precise choice of language, and when I got there, already yawning since I kept a bureaucrat's hours of 7:30 to four, and rose at five to do it, I liked her office. A narrow flight up over a hair stylist on Connecticut Avenue north of Dupont Circle, it was cozily furnished with comfortable furniture, a good-sized fish tank, and neutral grays and tans. Not a lacquer box or fan anywhere, nor anything gold or persimmon. Even the fish were tan and silver. Donia Ma OMCD herself looked as if she might be Irish-Chinese or some such combination. She looked somehow both young and experienced; of that age during which very little aging seems to occur. She might conceivably have been a product of the Korean war. Or she could have come from San Francisco of ancient stock, for all I knew. I never asked her.

Her features were Eurasian, her hair in a jet braid that came to her waist.

She was as stiff and precise in manner as her speech, and wore a grey smock. I suppose she stood about to my shoulder before I sat where she instructed and took off my loose-fitting shirt (why loose-fitting if it's coming off anyway?).

She began by asking me to sit as straight as I could, consonant with relaxation, and stationed herself about ten feet away and facing exactly along the centerline of my body. She stood like that, just looking at me in a defocused way, long enough for me to get a bit restless and thus to feel like a dumb, impatient Westerner. I closed my eyes and listened to Bach.

"That is much better. Good for you. Now please raise your good arm, the right one, and touch your right shoulder." I did so.

"Good. Now the other one."

"The one I can't - "

"Please." OK, she needed to see it not work. It didn't.

"Keep trying. What do you feel when it reaches that point?"

"Pain."

"Is that all?"

"Weakness."

"And?"

I got a little irritated. "Annoyance, frustration, humiliation, anger."

"Yes, good."

"What's good about that?"

"You are not afraid to tell me frankly what you feel. That will be most helpful to us."

"Look, you're not going to shrink me out of this, are you? I've no patience at all with that stuff."

"Of course not. Do I advertise as a psychiatrist? I practice acupuncture. However, there is a great deal more to it than sticking needles into you at any hour of the day like some of the quacks you could have fallen among. You tell me you called me out of the yellow pages. Let me ask you: why did you choose me out of all those who advertise there?"

"You're on the Red Line."

"So are at least six others, not to mention other lines."

"I liked the looks of your ad."

She smiled. "You see?"

"No."

"You will. Would you like me to stick you with needles now?"

"Is that the next harmonious thing to do?"

"No. The next thing to do is for me to continue to examine you carefully, as I have been. We may not get to needles this evening at all. But I promise that you will feel better when you leave. Please give me your left hand."

She took my offered hand and began to massage it, beginning with the ring finger, making little puffs of comfort run up along my arm; and maybe they stopped for a glance at the elbow on the way past. "How was your injury treated, when it first occurred?"

"Well, I had a cast, and a rig that held it straight out from my body for a while, and then just a cast in a regular sling."

"Mm. And the broken ribs, let me see . . yes, here they are, it is as I feared. What was done for these?"

"Well, I gather there's not much you can do, is there? They taped it up pretty tight, and after a while it quit hurting." Donia Ma heard this with the air of one taking the case history of a refugee from a civil war or an earthquake, displaying a professionally appropriate level of regret with economical little head tilts and frowns while she listened. Western medicine is hell. And so it went for almost another hour as she walked all around me, looking behind my ears, asking questions, taking my pulse in about three places on both wrists. How, I asked her, could my pulse be different in one wrist from the that in the other?

"It should not be, but it most certainly is. You can feel it for yourself. Feel here . . . and now on this wrist, in the same place; and now in this place on the left side . . .and now on the right. The same heart sends the blood out, but it suffers very different things on the two sides, does it not?"

At the very end, she set fire to a kind of a punky blob of stuff like incense, but larger, and held it over about a dozen places on my left arm and shoulder, including the elbow (at last). Each time, she said exactly the same thing:

"Now, I am going to place this hot material near your skin. Do not worry, I will not let it burn you. Please tell me when it starts to hurt." And I did, and she would then move it to a new spot, saying "Now, I am going to place this hot material . . ." and so forth. I gathered it was a sort of incantation, and I thought suddenly of Jacob Oxendine's manner of giving Mollie the pain medicine. It made me somehow sad and happy at once.

When she finished with that, having made me wince with a last treatment on the end of my left ring finger, she laid her fingers on my pulse(s) again, gave a little pursing of her mouth that might have conveyed satisfaction, and said, "That is all that we can do for this session. You should begin to feel a bit better soon, but I must tell you that the thirty years of paralysis have caused very profound weakness all along the meridian of the triple burner. Forgive my asking; are you married?"

"No, I am not. I was -" She cut me off with a little grimace.

"Please. I did not mean to pry. I am tired, that was not a good question for this session. However, traditional Chinese medicine is holistic, and that is both good and difficult. A Western surgeon can open up your elbow and set it right in one session, and if he asks you if you are married, or if you once were a musician, or a thousand other questions, he is either being idly social or intrusive, because he will not make any therapeutic use of your answers to those questions. He has done what he can do for you with his knife alone. And I am more than willing to acknowledge that there was great need for a knife in your case; it would have been impossible for me to help your elbow while it was in that shattered condition. Now, however, it is not simply the elbow, it is the whole meridian and through it the whole person. I can not repair your elbow, it is already repaired. Perhaps, though, I can heal what prevents a perfectly serviceable elbow from performing its service."

"You need to fix my whole person to make my elbow work?"

She smiled. "It sounds extravagant, I suppose? But of course, I cannot fix the whole person, only such parts as are susceptible to my art, and are related to the injured elbow. It may be, we shall have to see, but it may be that other problems will be ameliorated by doing so."

Ameliorated.

"Ameliorate away, Donia Ma."

"Thank you."

As I walked down the stairway from Donia Ma's office, it occurred to me to wonder about the time; past one AM. Metro would be long since shut down. I would have to find a taxi back to Silver Spring, and I had wanted to get an early start on a neglected stack of reports, still festering on my desk from last week. I stepped out into the warm night and felt a strange little rush of freedom. I wasn't at all sleepy; why not taxi over to the EPA right now and work till I was sleepy, and doze in my office? If I got enough done I could leave when the transit system turned on again, go home, nap, and change. I looked around for a cab, and found three, all parked and empty. Did they close down too at this hour? I had almost never been downtown this late, and certainly not looking for transportation.

Instead of getting worried, I felt the heady feeling grow. I was outside the lines, and I could do anything I wanted. The rain that began to spatter down Connecticut Avenue only confirmed that. Yes! I could walk to the EPA in the rain and get there soaked and tired at 3 am if I wanted. And that was exactly what I wanted. And I'll tell you something else, I told myself. My arm feels better. I tried bending it, and it stopped at 90° as always. But it certainly hurt less. It felt as if, OK, it was still locked, but maybe it felt the right key sliding in, or was somehow willing to consider unlocking.

Of course, it would be dangerous walking through downtown and all the way to EPA's lonesome exile in Southwest at this hour, and there would be little or no help if I got mugged. My euphoria focused to goofy cunning. Well-off guys got mugged, right? Mean-looking down-and-outers got left alone. This would be an exercise in survival, and I felt up to it. I went back in the stairwell and sat on the bottom stair to think it through. Tools or weapons? A set of keys, my EPA ID card, and a Swiss army knife. I pulled it out and opened the "big" blade;

sharp enough, if any thug should come unsuspecting within 3½ inches of me. I cut a strip of cloth off the tail of my shirt (part of the image anyhow) and wrapped it around the blade. In a pinch, it wouldn't do to be fumbling and picking at the blade, and this was the only way I would figure to leave it open without shredding myself. I scooped up some dirt and dust from the corners of the stairs and smeared them over my wet face and arms. Watch it, muggers. He's scruffy, he's armed, and he's stealthy.

By the time I was ready to go it was almost 1:30. The rain was coming in sheets when I reached Lafayette Square at the foot of Connecticut Avenue. The White House glowed reassuringly; it was Morning in America and the Marines were on watch. I gave the square, which was full of shadows and ambush, a wide berth and crabbed my way around the executive gleam to Pennsylvania Avenue on the far side. The rain slacked off a bit as I started down toward the Capitol, working backward along the triumphal route of newly inaugurated presidents. There had been sporadic traffic on Connecticut, and this persisted, cars that gave a four-headlight glare off the steaming pavement, including plenty of cruising taxis. But this wasn't about getting safely to Silver Spring any more.

As the rain slackened and stopped, stillness grew over the city. I could hear a freight clanking lonesomely over the Conrail line somewhere to the south. The only other sound, and it was almost constant, was the distant cry of sirens. Fire, cops, ambulances, none of it good news. All around me people were dying in the cool of deep night while vagrants slept in doorways. The District of Columbia committing genocide on itself. Sui genericide. I passed the Willard, thinking of a daytime self munching its pricey BLT within.

The door guard glared at me, and when I paused to wipe the rain and sweat out of my eyes he swelled alertly. I shuffled past a cup-rattling beggar dressed as Uncle Sam in stained tailcoat and spats, with my day face on. What he thought he would find of charity at 2 am - if he was capable of thought at all - was beyond me. I walked on, wet clothes flapping against cold sweat, half whispering the piano line to "Nights in the Gardens of Spain," my internal DJ's idea of good sound track. I suppose I should have been glad to escape "Singin' in the Rain." Or "The Rain in Spain," for that matter.

At 4th Street, where I would turn to plunge straight south to the EPA, I sat on the curb to rest while the mist thickened again to drizzle. I had been walking for almost an hour. The exhilaration was gone, but not replaced by regret. I was wet, tired, and dirty and I settled into anesthesia, letting myself get wetter and dirtier, sliding downhill, not worried, not hopeful. Fourth street led away, and as the drizzle gathered itself to become rain again, I followed it, over hills and under bridges. Somewhere between the Mall and the Southeast Freeway, what I had taken to be my shadow walking beside me thickened to become a man, bulky and muscular, in a reversed ball cap and baggy silk jacket, keeping pace stride for stride, watching me out of the corner of very dark eyes. This was the next part of sliding down, I supposed; simple fatigue and discomfort could be had at the Silver Spring Athletic Club.

We plunged under the Southeast Freeway, where vagrants sat apart and tried to keep a grip on their shopping bags. A figure rose, and fell into stride with me and my mugger. He was painfully thin, and wore floppy pants and a ragged maroon sweater, unzipped, with a patch on the shoulder that said "Metrobus Operator - 30 Years," and the name Charles stitched over the pocket. Under the sweater prominent ribs gleamed in the traffic lights. He had an ulcerated sore on one cheek, and he looked overworked and little appreciated. After another block - I could see the end of 4th Street and the EPA gleaming in the distance - he spoke across me to the other:

"Man keep his own counsel."

"Hyeh! That's all he gonna keep; probly the best thing he know to do."

"Believe that's what I'd do, I was in his sorry-ass shoes."

I kept my own counsel.

We walked another half-block, in step like The Spirit of '76, and Silk Jacket spat on the pavement. "Well, look here, we gonna do somethin, le's do it."

Charles snorted. "I spose. That's a easy thing for you to urge, seein you got the easy part."

227

"Easy part? What so easy about it?"

"Sheeit, folks do it all the time, almost never fuck it up."

Silk Jacket slapped his forehead. "Oh, good one. Hardy har."

"I guess I'm not in form tonight." Charles enunciated this with the peevish irony of one reading *"Number Six, Reignleigh Court"* off a facade.

"You certainly are not. I guess this conversation, this whole conversation, has come to a natural ending point."

I stopped, and rain came down hard. We were a half-block from the little park at the end of 4th Street that abuts the EPA. My companions stopped and faced me, lounging side by side, and Charles of the Metro was holding a knife, a real pigsticker a good ten inches long, balanced delicately on his fingertips. The other stood there grinning, the one who had done the ironic voice. I squinted hard at him. If these guys were hip enough to recite lines from a thirty-year-old quarrel, they were too hip to be real. Sure enough, I thought I could see a park light shining through his chest. I started to walk straight at him, but Charles reached out and put his knife against my throat.

"Hold it right there, dumbass, you wanna get cut? We ain't through with you."

I could feel the point digging into my throat, I could feel blood trickling down from it. I stood rigid and looked again at the knifeless one. I could read signs through him, but Charles and his knife were opaque.

"Excuse me," I said. "I need to get to work here. I don't know where you guys came from, or what you're up to, but if this is a mugging, here's my wallet. I'll keep the ID card if that's OK, you don't need that."

"Don't tell me what we need. Gimme it all. Watch, too. What else you got?"

"You want my knife?"

The transparent one spoke up. "Knife? My heavens, Charles, the man was armed. We been messin with a armed man. We lucky to be alive to tell the tale. Le's have it, Whitey."

I pulled out the Swiss army knife and tossed it to him, to see if it would pass through. He caught it and grinned at me. "You tryin something here? OK, Charles, how much he got?"

"I'm countin. Thirty, 35, 36, 37. Thirty-seven bucks. And a Visa card. Boy oh boy. Here, you take the cash."

"An you get the card? You kiddin me? That card's worth thousands, man, you expect me to take 37 lousy bucks?"

"It'll get you where you goin. What you gonna do with a Visa? They don't take no plastic where you going. Here, take the Metro card too. It got - shit, I can't read it."

"Never can read them little suckers."

"Started out with ten fifty on her."

"Metro don't go where I'm goin, neither."

"Naw, but it go to Shady Grove, thass a good half way."

They looked at each other, and the transparent one took a little breath and squared his shoulders. "Listen, you a smart-mouth dickhead, you know that?"

"Kiss my ass, nigger."

"Who you callin nigger, you ugly-ass dick-suckin whore?"

"Tha's good. Hol' him still now." Charles smiled at me. "This might give you a little discomfort." Silk Jacket closed in on me, backing me against a trash basket, while my heart pounded and little useless squeaks of breath came out of my mouth. Charles dropped into a crouch and began making elaborate knife passes out of a gaucho story. Silk Jacket stood with a look of scorn on his face. Come on, dipshit, what's all this kung fu crap? You gonna do him, do - Ahhh! Me? Aww, Jesus, not me! Him! You cut me real bad, awww, shit . . ."

I stood paralyzed and watched him drop to his knees, blood and intestines spilling onto the pavement and splashing onto my shoes. Charles stared down at the dying man, his face a mask of rage and sorrow. The victim fell against my legs, thudding solidly, tackling me to fall over him. A stockyard stench rose from his belly, and I caught myself with a hand that plunged into the slippery mess on the sidewalk. From above me, Charles remarked, "You be feelin better any day now." He sighed like an overworked surgeon. "What makes folks think they got a choice what they get, an' when they get it?"

As I scrambled to get my balance, I vomited and tightened my shoulders against the stab I knew must come. A small wind drenched rain over us, and my feet slipped as I scrambled away from the bloody mess on the sidewalk. But when I looked up, Charles was gone. Fourth Street stretched empty for blocks in both directions. My empty wallet lay on the sidewalk. I looked down at the too solid corpse still emptying into the sea of death at my feet. My Swiss Army knife was still in his hand.

13. Rivers

"The body of Christ, the bread of heaven." "The blood of Christ, the cup of salvation." "The body of Christ,... " "The blood ... "

A crew of priests and seminarians worked their way along the altar rail toward us and I knelt to take what they were giving, dreading it and unable to refuse. The choir broke into "Sacred Head Sore Wounded" first with Bach's harmony and then the organist's, full of spastic progressions and parallel fourths. It fit the text by sounding sore all right, but I didn't hear any quarter-millennium's worth of improvement in it.

"The body of Christ, the bread of heaven." I accepted a rough-torn chunk of bread in folded hands. It smelled of death and putrefaction, and I put it in my mouth. "The blood of Christ, the cup of salvation." I gagged over the blood in the chalice and managed a sip. Next to me, AC Gewissner doubtfully did the same, and we rose to cycle neatly to our former places. The flavors of body and blood lingered in my mouth, on my breath, and I wondered how AC could stand it.

She was dressed in Sunday boots and jeans, here at All Saints with me because she had arrived that week from Alaska and felt she owed a thanksgiving mass, not so much for safe arrival as for confirmation that such a place as Washington, D.C. existed at all, that out of a city with three times more people than the whole state of Alaska - counting timberwolves on each side - her Uncle Oren had stepped forth to greet her.

Pushing 29, AC was recognizably the woman who had been under construction at sixteen, during my visit for Markus's funeral. She was big-boned and rangy, with muscular arms and fine-cut features. Her face and hands were tan and finely wrinkled, and there were already grey threads in her brown ponytail. In fairness, she looked like less like a semidependent nuisance – as interns tended to be – than a tough and competent forest ranger, and that is what she had been for half of the dozen years since I had seen her. Two years ago, it had been made clear to her that if she wanted her opinions about opening Alaska for development and drilling to be listened to, she would need a loftier seat from which to speak, and that this would require finishing the education she had dropped at Markus's death. She had talked to me about Alaska until one o'clock the first morning, her body still on Anchorage time and her eyes wide.

"Those big oil companies, they talk about this benign 'footprint' they're going to leave, as if they were this big gentle giant who's just gonna ca-arefully reach in, see, and just sip up this little bit of oil, and leave this little tippytoe footprint. They go in there, those places'll never be the same. And I'm not that opposed to it, hell, let 'em make their killing. I just want to see people put some kind of thought into it and not make a mess of land the natives had first."

Wanting that, seeing Sophie financially settled and eventually remarried, the younger children raised and in the cases of Anna and Mary Catherine with children of their own, she sent herself to Conifer State College, where they would give her educational credit for her forest-ranger experience and help her work out a degree program in Wilderness Management or some such. Her "contract" included a one-semester internship in Washington seeing how the pros and the pols thought they could manage wilderness at a distance of 3000 miles. She came in doubting anyone here knew wilderness from windmills, but she was going to give it a shot, and she felt need of all the protective blessing she could invoke.

After the Eucharist we hauled ourselves up Wisconsin Avenue in search of something cooked. This was the heyday of the fern bar, and AC thought it was a great idea when we bushwhacked our way into a place called Away From His Desk, up toward Chevy Chase.

"Boy, Uncle Oren, this is just like the rain forest," she said. "They have slug problems in these places?"

"Only in the phones. Look, AC, I guess it's fun to be somebody's uncle, but - "

"But only if it was true? I've thought of you as Slick Uncle Oren ever since you scammed me about the hot stock tip."

"You're not going to dredge that up, are you?"

"No, no, I'd have done the same thing myself. But I owe you. We just need to find the right currency."

"We'll see. Tell me about your internship."

Her eyes widened. "Water," she said, and dipped a chunk of cauliflower in her glass.

"Mm?"

"Water. Life. Maybe desert people feel like I do, but with them it's scarcity. We've got so much water, but you can't have it till it melts. But then! Streams full of fish, meadows full of flowers, muskegs, fog. I love it all, even the ice fogs; more than anything else I love streams, creeks. Running water. Ever since I can remember, it's funny, water has been this huge thing with me. I guess it has to do with the spring coming, how long and dark the winter is, and when the sun comes back, pretty soon the water does too. We had this little creek right in our back yard, and when I was little I played in it all the time, building dams and making little boats for it, just anything that would get me good and wet, as long as it wasn't frozen. I think if Mother'd not been so busy getting pregnant she'd have probably tried to put a stop to it. But then Daddy would've said, Let me live dangerously. Nights, I'd lie in bed and listen to it rush out back, down to the bay. I knew all the rocks and waterfalls in the whole stretch, and I could pick 'em out, each one from all the others by their sound. I could lie under the covers and listen to each one in turn, working my way upstream, remembering what I'd done there that day, or the best thing I'd ever done there. Some of 'em were real quiet, just little slicks with a soft sound that you'd have to listen a long time before you could hear it. But I wouldn't let myself go to sleep until I'd heard each one. When I got about maybe eight or ten, I'd hear voices in the loud ones. I found out I could make them say anything I wanted. If I was mad at one of the little kids, I'd listen to the creek, and pretty soon it'd be saying stuff like, You know, Anna is just a baby, she can be a real brat, can't she, not like AC. AC's by far the best girl in the family, AC's quite grown up now - "

She stared at her glass for a full minute; but it was no stream of consciousness. "Anyhow. Enough - how's that go, David Copperfield crap. What I'm doing here, I'm in the Office for Water Programs and I'm supposed to be helping out with . . . oh, what's that thing that means 'make a rule'?"

"Develop a regulation?"

"Right. Lessee, that's . . .vel-op a reg-u-lation, eight syllables that mean three. That's one thing I'm sure gonna learn, right?"

"Talk more and say less?"

"Yeah, anyhow, our group is supposed to 'develop regulations' for wilderness-area surface water contamination."

"Make rules for crap in wild creeks?"

"Agh! It's starting already."

"Long as you can translate both directions, you'll be OK."

"Oren, you can't imagine the pollution that shows up in these little wild streams. Fly ash, pesticides, heavy metals, aromatics, the whole catalog. It just breaks your heart to have these little cricks chattering away like children, but come to find out they're a bit sick."

I let the quiet grow, and remembered Jacob Oxendine's rivers. "How do you feel about quiet rivers full of leaf tannins?"

"We have 'em. I don't like 'em as well, the Indians have bad stories about them."

"I used to know an Indian from North Carolina, said it's all sand and pine trees in his part, no rocks, so the streams have cut these smooth channels in the sand. They move along through cypresses without making a sound, even at flood times. He says it's the quietest thing you can do, take a boat out on them, coast along on what looks like tea, and not hear anything but your own breathing."

A.C. made a little face and a shrug, and tinkled the ice in her glass. "Sounds creepy, but I guess you'd have to grow up there, or at least be there - as the saying goes."

I grunted. "I grew up on the Mississippi, and it was too big to talk or be quiet. It had another trick, just giving these random splashes and sucks. You had the feeling - well. Just a lot of mud and water all the time, like a big graveyard sliding south." I'd had enough of this line of talk. "How's the apartment coming?"

"If you'll give me a ride home, I'll show you. But it needs a lot of cleanup from the pigs that were there before me. Jesus, Oren, the filth! My god, don't these people <u>ever</u> clean <u>anything</u>?"

"You'd be surprised. How long were they there?"

"I don't know. I got the impression a couple of years, maybe."

"I bet they said the same thing when they moved in. A couple of years in a city is plenty of time for a place to get dirty."

She shuddered. "I better not stay that long, then."

We finished our meals in relative silence. The food was good, and A.C. tucked into it like a ranger. I was still too close to my recent religious experience to have much appetite. Something nasty was at large within me, had been since my session with the acupuncturist Donia Ma. I intended to take it up with her next time; if her art left one subject to small unpleasant miracles and undead metaphors, if that were to be the price of a painlessly functioning body ... well. In the meantime, I would keep a low profile.

AC had rented the ground floor of a row house on B Street, in Capital Hill. She unlocked the street door, apologizing again about the dirt. But in fact it looked pretty clean to me, except for a couple of duffels sitting in the middle of the entrance hall. AC grunted in surprise. "Oh, yeah, I think I have a housemate. The landlord said a gir - a woman in one of his other places is breaking up with a guy and needs a place quick."

"Watch it, you'll have the guy at the door all hours, asking for his Dead tapes and his I Ching set back, and begging you to talk to her for him."

"I don't think so. Story is, he decided he liked another guy better than her, and that guy's moving in."

"Ah. How unpleasant for her."

"I'll say."

*   *

"Ah." Donia Ma looked up briefly. "How unpleasant for you."

"Ah? Strikes you as unpleasant, does it, to be slipping around in guts and vomit, waiting for a knife in the back?"

"Of course. You surely didn't enjoy such a situation?"

"No, I didn't. Just, I guess I'd have groped for a good deal stronger language for it."

Donia Ma only raised her eyebrows and sat back from her crouch over my left wrist, leaving in it the needle she had gently, painlessly worked in.

"Dr. Dienst, my skills and training are not in rhetoric. They are, such as they are, in medicine. Do not think me hard hearted; I am sympathetic to your condition. The unquestionable parts of your experience are that you left here quite late last week, and that over an hour later you found yourself having stumbled over a corpse in southwest Washington. Much of what you relate about the journey between those points is contradictory and difficult to believe. But we need not seek an explanation for what you experienced then nor for the - forgive me - unpleasantly literal perceptions that accompanied your celebration of the Eucharist. Let us suppose - no, let us <u>accept</u>, that two apparently unrelated, possibly hallucinatory men accosted and robbed you, that one was brutally murdered by the other, who then disappeared, leaving behind a real corpse. The important point for you to accept is that the dead man is now dead, and you cannot bring him back to life. That incident, unpleasant as it was, is over. I do not suppose you caused his death, except through the innocent act of providing a nucleus around which it could grow. Does the stone morbidly regret the water that flows over it? It knows that more will come, and more after that. If you had held the knife and done the evisceration, I would say the same. It is in the past. It cannot be undone, and it has no connection to the present or the future. Accept it. Don't consume yourself with regret."

I sat for a moment and looked at the needles that were hanging out of my arm. They certainly did not hurt. I felt only warmnesses - puffs, messages, something - flowing from one to the next, all the way up to the one in my neck. "Then nobody's responsible for anything? What good does it do to 'accept' horror and brutality?"

"What good did you intend to do?"

I opened my mouth, waited for words, and closed it again.

"Yes, you see? If the fury and humiliation that sicken this city were yours to clear away as a gardener prunes away vines or a surgeon useless chips of bone - or as I may with care and good luck disperse the trouble that has affected your arm - in such a case you should of course go about getting rid of them, not in fury yourself but diligently, hopefully, welcoming the difficulty and confident that the work was yours to do. That is not the case."

"Isn't there a saying that all that is necessary for the triumph of evil is for good men to do nothing?"

"Yes, a very moving one, aside from its sexist language. Do you consider yourself a good man?"

"I don't know. I try, I guess, most of the time."

"That is commendable. You try to be good. Have you not found, though, that the hard part, and what is almost always unexamined about your saying, is to know for what one is to be good? A saw is a good tool, but not for every job. You might as well say that the triumph of rust requires only the inaction of good saws."

"Well, that's a bit oversimplified, surely."

"In what way?"

I shrugged. "People aren't saws, or any kind of tool. They're 'good' for many things, they're complex, adaptable, creative - "

"Of course. Nevertheless, each person is fitted for some complex, creative tasks and unfitted for others. The mayor of Washington has the skills to reduce the level of chaos in this city, and if he does not, we will be justified in regarding him as we would a lazy gardener or a careless surgeon. But you do not have those skills. Perhaps, beginning at birth, you might have acquired them, but you did not. Accept that, and ask yourself what skills you did acquire, and for what they are good."

I found myself getting a little impatient. "Goodness, if it were that easy."

"Easy?"

"Have you no idea how hard that question is? Here you sit, in harmony with your skills, speaking out of the calm center and all that. I don't know what doubts or conflicts you may have worked through on the way to becoming what you are, but I cannot believe - I cannot <u>accept</u>, excuse me - that you understand what you're saying when you sit there like something out of <u>Lost Horizon</u> and blithely recommend that I do the same." *Good one, Oren.*

She was silent as she began slowly rotating the needles, one at a time, and pulling them part way out of my arm. "I accept your rebuke, including the colorful and forceful manner in which you expressed it. I see I was being unrealistic and patronizing, which is a very great temptation of traditional Chinese culture when it confronts European guilt structures."

"I accept your, mm, your acceptance of my rebuke. I greatly esteem your thoughtful advice and the fact that you care to give it."

"Oh, for goodness' sake, Dr. Dienst. Thank you for the compliment, but you surely understand that you cannot possibly best a cryptic Eurasian in loftiness of discourse."

"You win. I should remain crude and smell of - what is it? Sour milk?"

She smiled, and twiddled a needle or two before she spoke. "You smell to me of spruce wood, varnish, and rosin. It is quite pleasant, really. When are you going to let me hear you play?"

I looked at her, then at the floor, from old habit maybe. Donia Ma was on the way to becoming a needle in the butt. "Very well, Great and Powerful Ma. I am looking everywhere, but I can't find the little guy behind the curtain. How did you do that?"

"Do what?"

"Divine, somehow, that I once played cello."

"I tricked you, but only gently. Your way of speaking is that of a musician, and so are your pulses. Your gestures are those of a string player. I did not know which instrument until you mentioned it just now. I suppose that someone born to be a judge or a diplomat might mask such a background; but only by betraying his real calling by his impassivity. Fortunately, you are the most transparent of men. I am quite serious, though. I do not think your healing will be complete until you begin to play again."

Transparent, eh? "Well, to turn it around, there's no way I can play until I'm healed. See, you need to bend ..." I made a disbelieving noise, and reached over to grab my wrist and hold it up by my shoulder where for the first time in thirty years it had risen on its own. It hurt, it was weak, it began trembling right away, but the elbow was closed way past 90°. I let it go, and it flopped back into its normal range, but I didn't care. I looked at Donia Ma with respect, and she gave me a cool smile in return.

"*Just so*, if you will forgive the corny phrase. This time it is apt. Congratulations. You are a very long way from healed, but I think we now see that healing is possible. That is very satisfactory. Please obtain a cello and bring it to our next session, which will be, oh, I think Wednesday at the same time. I trust you do not plan to walk across town again this time."

"Once was enough. Though, now that I hear it back from you, I have to wonder when the hallucinations started. I don't suppose that smoky stuff you burned - "

"No. But it was my fault all the same. I asked you a personal question, about marriage, just after treating you. You were in a vulnerable state and the question was evidently traumatic. It badly upset you."

"Well, really, I don't think . . ."

"Permit me this blithe assertion. You will recall that I was taking your pulses at the time, and there can be no more reliable observation. You may have perceived nothing because you have trained yourself not to perceive. One does not, however, train the forces within one so readily. Did you feel light-headed, euphoric, when you decided on that course of action?"

"Oh, well...yes."

She bit her lip. "It is entirely my ill doing, and we are lucky you were not the one stabbed. I cannot excuse myself that wretched carelessness."

"A physician recently advised me to accept what is past because it cannot be undone. I think no harm was done that would not have been done in any case. Don't consume yourself in regret."

"Ah." She grinned, looking almost human. "Physician, heal thyself. The ancient and inscrutable wisdom of the Occident."

I smiled. "Just so."

*   *

The roar of a cocktail party makes it difficult to understand any one person's speech. I could, like A.C. and her waterfalls, have extracted any sense I liked out of the murk of sound. In this case, it sounded like, "The bones of our mothers and fathers burst from the ground."

I turned to the interpreter who had come along on this, but he responded with a shrug and dipped his nacho in a nine-inch pot of guacamole that stood at hand. If the old man were speaking English already, what was there to translate? It was an OAS reception, packed with Anglos and Mexicans with a 50% surcharge of translators, and at least two of any trio was talking all the time.

"Señor," I said. "Your English is very clear, but with the noise in this room it is difficult to understand you. I'd like to suggest that we step out onto the balcony where we can speak more quietly. Perhaps you would also be so kind as to join us, Mr. Torres, and continue your invaluable service in translation if it should be needed."

Torres looked glum at having to leave the guacamole, but I handed him a little foam-plastic plate to bring provisions, and he brightened marginally. Out on the balcony, the hubbub of the reception was replaced by the roar of traffic, but at least the Metrobuses didn't belch competing languages.

"Now, then," I said. "Please excuse my difficulty in understanding you. You were saying that the bones of your mother and father . . ."

Torres swallowed a mouthful of nacho and guacamole and, a bit thickly, provided context. "My esteemed guest is the mayor of Manosduros, a small town south of Nogales."

"A village," interjected the mayor. "There is no reason not to speak plainly."

Torres bowed, ate a nacho, cleared his throat and continued. "For many years, Manosduros has enjoyed a certain prosperity based on very widely dispersed veins of silver and gold in its hills. Those metals were there for the taking, but only to those who knew how to select just those rocks that would yield up a few flakes and threads of gold. It was a perfect village industry; enough to afford a living and a few luxuries for the few hundred people of Manosduros, but too low-grade even at its richest to be tempting to serious prospectors.

"Five years ago a Mexican firm with United States managers, MexiLar Metals, came to Manosduros and offered the people what seemed a very high price indeed for access to the richest lode, a ridge called Montoro, not even to buy it but only to rent, with mineral rights, for five years. Because Montoro was common land, approval required a meeting of the whole village, with a representative of MexiLar present to answer questions. A few villagers were opposed, but when the terms of the offer were explained by the plausible Mexilar man, they were laughed down."

The mayor shrugged. "They offered more than we could earn from mining in twenty years, for only five years' access to Montoro. How could we lose?"

"Ah," said Torres. "But you know, Dr. Dienst, that is a question that often finds an answer. One week after the agreement was signed, a day after the first payment was accepted by the village - with the signature of Señor Paños here - the answer presented itself. Bulldozers and shovels and large trucks drove into Manosduros and out to Montoro."

Paños dropped his arms in resignation. "Japanese trucks, Dr. Dienst, of insane size, with tires as large as a house; shovels that picked up houses and dropped them in the bed of one of those trucks. Bulldozers with blades the size of a boxcar. In six months what had been a mountain with gold ore for generations to come was a hole twenty meters deep and 500 meters on a side, and where there had been a canyon there was a new mountain of crushed rock, no piece of it larger than a walnut. This mountain was fitted with hoses and sprayed day and night with a cyanide solution that is capable, I understand, of extracting the gold from solid rock. You are a chemist, are you not? Is that true?"

"An engineer. Yes, it is. It'd be a slow process, but..." I shrugged. "In time, sure."

"How much time?"

"Well, that would depend on the temperature, and on the size of the rocks. I take it, it stays pretty warm in Manosduros?"

"It is temperate. But not frigid, no."

"Well, I'd guess you'd have half the gold out in maybe a year, and half the rest in another couple of years. It would also depend somewhat on how much cyanide was pumped over it."

"So three quarters of it in three years?"

"Or so, yes."

"Ay!" cried Paños. "Fools that we were! They had five, and in less than that they mined all of our gold, all of it. One more time, Ingeniero, that the northerners have made fools of the simple peasants to the south. And I am the mayor of this village of fools, the chief fool."

Don't blame yourself, I thought. What's past can't be undone. "And the bones?"

Torres sighed. "More misfortune. After they had gotten used to seeing armored trucks leaving the extraction and smelting houses - "

"Even simple Mexican fools could see they were taking away our twenty years' worth of gold every month," grated Paños.

"...Yes. In any case, it all ended quite suddenly. A few weeks ago those few Manosdurans who had been taken on as laborers were given pink slips and a 100-peso 'termination bonus'. There was a great rumbling of the insane trucks and shovels, and in a day the entire operation moved out. When they walked out to Montoro to see what was left, there was nothing."

Nothing, that is, but a mountain of crushed rock looking pale and crumbly, and at the foot of the canyon, closed in by an earthen dam, a huge pond of still water where the cyanide solution still trickled out the bottom of the rock pile. Across the top of the dam was a chain-link fence five feet high, with signs warning of poison within; and the bodies of a few wild fowl who had been unlucky enough to choose it for a landing and nesting site. And so matters remained for several weeks, while the workers spent their bonuses and the village government tried to figure out what to do with their four years' rental fee and their pond full of poison.

The second problem was solved in a natural way when a spring rainstorm - a rare event, but not unheard of - filled the pond above the black plastic liner that MexiLar had used to keep the dam water-tight. Water spilling over the earthen dam eroded a small notch in it, and when this notch grew down to the liner, the plastic bulged outward into the notch and tore open. In three minutes there was a breach in the dam two meters across, and in five the dam collapsed. A wall of cyanide solution six feet high came down the canyon and poured into the Manosduros River.

"A river, Dr. Dienst, that normally runs about six inches deep and ten feet wide, during the wet season. When the wall of poisoned water passed the village, it undercut and flooded the church and the cemetery. The relics beneath the altar were invaded and desecrated, and at the cemetery, coffins and bones were washed out into plain view from the places they had rested - the oldest of them for more than four centuries."

"Washed out, no," spluttered Paños. "It was not simply a flood, Ingeniero, we have seen floods. That water, even the dead were afraid of it. Leg bones stumbled over broken coffins, skulls were grinning with terror. I watched liquid greed, the folly of our village made into poison by our clever friends to the north, pour down upon the honored sleep of our fathers and their fathers before them. And they fled as if Satan himself had come for them."

*   *

Because that OAS reception happened on a Friday night, I had the weekend to muse on Manosduros, and to write out questions for file research about what MexiLar promised the village about cleaning up and sealing off their site when they were done with their high-speed, low-tech rape. OK, no Nancy Drew this time, but I was not going to keep hands off. There would be guarantees and assurances, signed by MexiLar and Molar higher-ups, and if it was explicit and damning enough, it would skewer Rick McIntear good, send him back to St. Louis in public disgrace, embarrass his fellow greed merchants, get reparations for Manosduros, and maybe avenge, a little and very late, those who'd lived and died by Molar's carelessness in 1953. Oh, sure, and pay him back for his glee over Fire Bird. Politics: the art of the personal. Don't you love it, Ricky?

In the meantime it was Saturday, and I had an urgent piece of shopping to do. I was sentenced to bring a cello to my next session with Donia Ma, and that meant finding one. The yellow pages coughed up the names of four violin makers, two of them in the Maryland suburbs, and at ten o'clock on Saturday morning I walked into the larger of those, Gustav Schneider, in College Park.

Though it was a step or two above Pietro Di Salvo's shop in size and stylishness, in fact Schneider's felt almost the same: the same shabby welcome mat, the plentiful array of labeled drawers, and above all the smells of glue and varnish. There was a rack of cellos to the left of the door, but I did not go to them. I expect all six of my pulses and however many there may have been that Donia Ma hadn't told me about yet, were registering jumpy and contradictory data, had she been there to finger them. I walked over to the file cabinets of music, and opened "A - Dvorak" and started thumbing down the row of manila folders. I was amused to see four or five new editions of the Bach unaccompanied suites - the pop fame of Pablo Casals had come and gone with Camelot since I last looked at cello music, but after all these centuries, what was left to edit? - and astounded at the prices on them. You can put up with thirty years worth of inflation when you see it one year at a time; but a ten-fold jump is striking when you see it all at once.

When I got to the Beethoven Sonatas, I pulled out the newest looking edition and turned to the slow movement of the A Major, to see I guess if the editor had put a footnote, "The Meaning of the Universe is to be found in the first eight bars;" but the secret was still safe. Hearing it as I looked at the page was enough, too much, and I walked over to the rack of cellos, suddenly sure that I would find my old one there.

I did not, thank God. It was a line-up of the usual suspects bearing every color of varnish but all with ebony (or fake ebony) fingerboards, to a cello. One had the carved head of an angel in place of the scroll, and I pulled it out for a closer look. That was enough to bring attention from the man behind the counter, a squarish, genial-looking guy with a blue apron and grey, European-cut hair, presumably Schneider himself.

"Something nice in a cello today?"

"Well, let's see what you've got." The angel simpered over an alien device far smaller than I remembered.

"That's a very nice Lorenzo Bordoni, late nineteenth century Siena. I'm selling it for the owner."

"Well, I'd guess it's not for me. I haven't played for thirty years, and I'm - "

"Coming back to it, are you? That's a very nice instrument and a good investment. She wants fifteen for it, but I'm pretty sure she'll take 13 or 14."

"Thousand?"

Schneider smiled thinly. "Fifteen thousand dollars, yes. I take it you've not been following the market for a few years, either."

You tell me the municipal's gonna pay out that kind of money, year in and year out. Nancy von Bayern was trying on some pretty tall martinis if the Testore had appreciated that way.

"Look, - Mr. Schneider is it? - let me be frank with you. I used to be a pretty good player, but I broke my elbow back in 1953. I've had it repaired, and my, uh, physical therapist wants me to start playing again more or less to - well, as therapy. I'm not even going to sit down with this one, it'd be a travesty. In fact, what I came in to ask was, if you'd be willing to let me take one out on trial, with the understanding that the chances are at least even I'll never buy it, or any other."

He looked out at the parking lot (mine was the only car), and then at the cello. "How much better than even?"

"Ninety-ten it won't work. I'm not even sure I want it to."

He nodded and sighed. "I'm tempted to tell you, take this one anyway, next time she calls I can tell her it's out with a prospect. But sure as I do, a real buyer'll come in. OK, tell you what. I'll help you out if you promise that if you do go back to playing, you'll give my shop first consideration for buying one."

"Well. I couldn't go above a couple of thousand, though."

"At that price you can't do better than a Gustav Schneider, no factory-made parts, all carved right here in this shop. When you buy it, I'll throw in a set of Tomastiks on it."

"Dominants?"

"Sure."

"What are they running these days?"

"List $95 for a set, I can supply 'em at $63.50."

I grinned. A clean ten-fold since 1953. "There was a time," I said, "when I considered myself God's gift to new cellos. It's just doctor's orders that brought me in here, and I'd be lucky to get through 'Twinkle Twinkle Little Star.' I appreciate your willingness to contribute to my rehab."

"Hey. Even cripples gotta buy rosin."

*   *

"mGood afternoon. Mr. McIntear wishes me to ask of you what progress you may have made in connection with a matter upon which you and he have previously conversed, involving certain complaints lodged with the Secretaries of State, Commerce, and Trade by the Government of Mexico."

"I see, I guess. Would these complaints involve among others enterprises undertaken in the State of Sonora by MexiLar Metals, a wholly owned subsidiary of Molar Chemical Corporation?"

"I am sorry, sir, Mr. McIntear did not share that level of detail. He merely asked me to jog your memory on the matter, and to obtain a report of your progress."

"Hm. You can tell Mr. McIntear - wait a minute. I guess this isn't Liana, is it?"

"Ms. Mariconas is no longer with this office."

Boy. Liana must have really screwed something up, or else this charmer must look a thousand times better than she sounded. I was sorry to lose what I had thought might be an ally in McIntear's office. "I see. I'm sorry, but my secretary did not pass on your name. You are ...?"

"My name is Diana Tucker-Fitts."

"Please inform Mr. McIntear that I have recently had a full and frank discussion of the Manosduros affair with the Sonoran trade representative, and with a representative of the cognizant governing body, and have come away - "

"Not so fast, please . . . cognizant . . yes?"

"And I have come away quite struck by the level of concern and responsibility exhibited by MexiLar."

"I see. Thank you, Mr. Dienst," she purred. "I'm sure Mr. McIntear will be most gratified by your report."

"No doubt he will. mGood afternoon, Ms. Tucker-Fitts."

"Dr. Dienst? You look kind of funny. Are you off now?"

"Guess not. What's up?"

"There's a Miss Gewitter? Gewindsor? on your other line."

"OK, put her on . . . Hi, AC, how's the water biz?"

"Hi, Oren. It's OK, I guess. You want to have lunch today, and I'll tell you about it? And you can meet Jana."

"Jana? The, uh, the housemate?"

"Uh huh. You're gonna love her. But that's not why I called. Remember the time you told me about that Indian guy, from North Carolina?"

"Jacob?"

"I don't think you mentioned a name. Anyhow, there's a bunch of 'em in town to contribute to the scenic rivers docket, and complain about toxic waste dumping in a river down there, and I got the job of showing them around. I guess you always stick - have the interns do that, right?"

"What else are interns for?"

"Making coffee. Anyhow, I happened to mention you'd known one of them in St. Louis, and one of these guys got sort of interested, and - wait a minute. What was that name?"

"Jacob Oxendine." I heard her repeating it dimly off-mike, and some even more distant voices, and then she was back on.

"He definitely wants to meet you. Can I bring 'em up?"

I looked at the stack of reports. The one that had been on the bottom was near the top, but a dozen more had slipped in below it. "It'll have to be short, or I'm no bet for lunch."

"We're on our way."

They were a crew of solid guys in leisure suits or jeans jackets, most with dark eyes and carefully combed black hair that reminded me of Harvey Napperson's; but a few with Jacob's grey eyes and taffy curls. Though they were certifiably Native Americans, their speech and manner were those of Southern farmers, which is what most of them were. After a round of introductions and pleasantries, one of them got to the point:

"We understand you knew a Lumbee in St. Louis during the 1950's."

"Jacob Oxendine, yes."

"Good. Though St. Louis is a big city, and that's not an uncommon name in our country. Do you know who his folks were?"

"His folks?"

"His kin."

"He didn't talk to me about his family. But some other things I do remember. It's been a while, though. He was extremely kind to me when I needed some help, several times. He was from a town - mm, it had Springs in it. He'd come to St. Louis to work in the small arms plant during World War II. He was a machinist. He looked a bit like you, sir, in the, uh, the green suit. Mr. Locklear, is it? How's Jacob doing?"

Locklear nodded. "That's the fella. Red Springs, but not in it, some ways south, toad the river. He left Robeson County cause he wan't content with a halfway education and a job in carpenterin or farmin. Wanted to be somebody in the world. But he used to say, after he come back home, Comes a time the world gets to movin faster than you want to go, and a wise man will step aside and let it. I kind of picture dyin - this is still Jacob, mind - like I'm standin by the tracks, and this big train is swingin down the line into the next century or somewhere, and I'm just wavin goodbye to the caboose. You're young, you wanna set in front and drive. You get my age you cain't wait to get the hell off and let it go."

I smiled. "Well, you know he has somebody waiting for him by the tracks."

"Yes, and that's what we was wontin to ask about. Jacob took a heart attack last fall cuttin wood, and he died right there with the saw in his hand. I don't believe he expected to go so sudden, and he never left no instructions as to what's to be done in the way of his wife, as we understand, back there in St. Louis. He's buried down by the Lumber River, out of his church there, and he did love to be on the river. But we knew he'd got married, and his folks say he'd ought to be buried with her, or her with him, one. Did you know the lady he married?"

"Oh. Gosh." I thought of Jacob Oxendine last week for the first time in thirty years, and now he was dead in the woods with a saw in his hands, and buried by just the river, probably, that I'd told AC about. "Yes, I did. Mollie Biedermeyer."

"Nice lady, was she?"

"Ye - Excuse me." I blew my nose. "Yes. About the nicest I ever knew."

"Uh huh, well you suppose her folks would have objections if we was to bring Jacob out there and see to burying him with her?"

"You know, I don't think I ever knew where she was from either, or what kind of family she had."

One or two of them allowed themselves just the slightest, most polite of eye rolls at this. Knew her, thought the world of her, got all choked up, and didn't know her folks. See what we got running the country, no wonder it's a mess.

I plunged on. "But I guess I'm in the best position to find out. Thing is, I've been to Mollie's grave, and I don't recall that she had a big enough plot for a second one nearby. I expect he counted on being buried in your country, and maybe bringing Mollie there. Would it make any difference to you?"

"Don't be <u>no</u> difference, on the Last Day."

"Well, no. But between now and then . . ." A thought struck me. "Buried by a river, is he? Does it ever flood?"

They exchanged shrugs. "Backs into the cypress," one of them said. "Woulten' flood that cemetery, you askin that."

I saw Jacob in his window looking across the Mississippi, and Mollie beside me looking up at him. It was three decades of sentiment that gave her a girlish look I hadn't seen at the time.

"I believe Mollie would have been glad to know she'd be with Jacob by the river he loved."

14. Jana

"Oren Dienst, this is my housemate Jana. Jana, meet Oren. He used to be a friend of my folks' and now he's my friend too. Jana's an artist."

"Hi, Jana. Glad to meet you."

We joined a good-sized line looking for seating, and I looked over the housemate. She was, first of all, tiny; well under five feet, and slim for that. If she weighed 95 pounds wet, I'd have eaten the towel. Her face came to a little pointed chin and perched atop a longish neck that tapered up out of a black scoop-necked leotard that in turn disappeared under a bright orange felt skirt. The leotard reappeared below only to disappear for good into little-girl-sized red sneakers. Dominating it all were owl-eyed blue sunglasses and a poof of red hair in a do that must have been modeled after the spider plants that hung in the best salons. The whole effect was a bit like a skyrocket, maybe seen by the crew of an airliner a few thousand feet above. Even in a jaded Washington lunch crowd, heads turned when Jana and AC walked past together.

If her recent romantic fiasco had dampened Jana, there was no sign of it. She banjoed twenty words to AC's five and my one, including a quick bio that covered in five minutes the ten years since she'd left Norman, Oklahoma in the middle of her last year of high school and knocked around hard in the half-world of "serious" art, and ending with who was exhibiting at what gallery - neither artists nor galleries ringing any bells with me - and who wasn't exhibiting at all, whether for lack of inspiration or of means or, more bafflingly, because to do so would be to reify the concept beyond hope of repair.

"Mmm, excuse me," said AC to that, "but if a person says they're an artist but never exhibits, how do you tell?"

"Well, shit fahr, AC. You got it right away, see? It's not exactly rocket science - excuse me, Dr. Dienst - is it? You <u>don't</u> tell, and that's just it. What a drag, going around with these little name tags, 'HELLO, I am *An Artist*, Have a Nice Day'. You're an artist if you say you are, just like Picasso and Rembrandt or anybody else. They didn't get little stickers from the government proclaiming them artists."

"Well, OK, but Picasso and Rembrandt exhibited works - didn't they?" I asked, suddenly doubtful. I certainly wasn't there to notice.

"To their friends, mostly. But lookit Kafka - he instructed his best friend to burn all his manuscripts."

"But Kafka actually - "

"So did Peter Wolf, but in his case the friend obeyed, and that's why you've never heard of him."

Jana pealed agreeable laughter at this tentative offering from AC. "Right own! Now we need to establish the canon of Peter Wolf criticism, starting with the feminist one that he's just another dead white guy being shoved up our tails by the Old Boys."

"Hey, also," I piped in, trying to be helpful, "there's only one empty set, so by publishing it, Wolf has preempted the whole genre for all time. A single writer has exhausted the form, from the tentative beginnings through high flowering, to the decadent period. Has this happened to visual art too?"

"Not my field, I'm afraid," replied Jana, coolly.

"Jana's a performance artist, on natural themes. Our sort of stuff, Oren. She has one called Tectonic Tease, where she takes three hours to take her shirt off."

I looked doubtfully at Jana. "Is the point to do it so slowly that you can't tell it's going on? I mean is that why it's called that?"

"There you go again. The point, the meaning. It just is, that's all. Some jackass asked Beethoven the meaning of one of his sonatas, he set down and played the whole thing again."

"Well, let's hope that doesn't happen with Tectonic Tease. It must be exhausting to go through it once."

Jana looked intense. "It's keeping the cloth from flopping and moving fast that's tricky. Took me months to find the right kind of shirt, I could be in absolute control of every second."

Every second of three hours. Months of practice, for something you could understand just by having somebody describe it. "Do you find that people sit through a whole performance?" I asked, knowing the answer.

"Course not. But they come back ever once in a while to see how far I've got."

AC looked up from her menu. "You better not let anybody make a tape of it, or they'll just put it on fast forward."

"Well, of course, I got a dozen tapes of different performances, and I expect some of my buddies have made copies. Fact I know they do, because the last thing Allen did before we broke up was, he threw a coming-out party and played four of them back to back. So to speak."

I snorted. "Come on. <u>Several</u> videotapes? Isn't the whole idea of your kind of art the concept? Isn't that why your friend who got us into all this doesn't actually exhibit?"

Jana looked haughty. "You want to know why that story about Beethoven has a point? Cause it's so bizarre. Nobody could stand to sit through even two back-to-back performances of a major sonata, let alone a dozen. It'd be unbe<u>lie</u>vably boring. And what that says is, his whole merit consists of simple novelty. Once that wears off, you actually feel restless and nauseated sitting through it. That's art? And after Beethoven you get Liszt, and, Schu*bert*, and Schu*mann*, and Brahms, and by the time that's all over with, hell, no wonder everybody's fed up. You look at my performances - and I don't mind if you do it on fast forward if you're in a big hurry - whatever merit they've got, it isn't based on simple novelty. Only the tiniest, stochastic things will change from time to time, like exactly how the shirt is going to fold and wrinkle, how my hair blows if it's outdoors, the weather, the light. One time in Chicago a pigeon came and landed on my arm. People were breaking up, but I was thrilled. I always put that one last when I run the tapes."

"Jana, I give up. I feel like we're talking cosmology here, and I keep asking questions where the answer is, 'You can't ask that.' What question should I be asking here?"

"You cain't ask that; but the answer is, the avocado with sprouts and a bottle of Saratoga."

We did finally get around to hearing AC on the subject of her water quality project. It was frustrating going for her, since she had strong first-hand experience of the way wilderness streams looked, acted, and tasted in the field, but only a spotty grasp of the chemistry of natural waters and no tolerance at all for the legal and bureaucratic side of EPA. "It's just the damnedest stuff, Oren. How do you <u>stand</u> it? Don't you want to scream and kick somebody?"

You cain't ask that. "Well, I probably got used to it a little bit at a time. When it bothered me at first, I used to think, well at least I'm not grading exams, where I find out how little they've learned, and where it's a death sentence to forget stuff. Now that Vietnam's over, I guess I'm just used to it."

"Well, I can't wait to get back in the field. I mean, I'll do this project, and I'll do as good a job as I can, but when I get off that plane I'm not even going home, I'm going to run all the way out to Morning Creek and stand there with my feet in the water."

"Like that, what's his name, the Greek guy who had to keep touching the Earth? Did your mother ever tell you . . ."
I had a sudden attack of conscience.

"What?"

"Skip it, it's not something I'm free to tell you about."

"Aw, Oren, you can't do that. Come on, now."

Trapped. Jana was looking in a little mirror, checking the orange explosion, tactfully not listening. "Oh, well. Did your mother ever tell you what she was doing when you were conceived?"

"Well, that kind of goes without saying, doesn't it?"

"Sorry. I meant the circumstances."

"Just kidding. You mean the storm, right?"

"You know?"

"Oh, yes. That was the first thing I asked when they gave me the birds and bees. Daddy was real proud of it."

Jana put down her mirror with a sigh. "For shit's sake, I cain't ignore this forever. Give."

So AC gave a version of her own conception only a little less Wagnerian than the one I'd had from Markus almost thirty years before. Jana was delighted. "Shazam!" she cried. "What I'd give to perform <u>that</u> in Lafayette Park. No, wait! On the Capitol dome, with Ms. Freedom. Yes!"

When I got back to the office there was a note taped to my phone:

While you were out <u>Mr. McIntear</u>   *Called*
Please Return Call At <u>X6093</u>
Message: "What the ---- was that supposed to mean?"

I could imagine poor Gloria Mondale, a Virginia Baptist, struggling with the organizational mandate to pass on accurate messages, and finally bringing herself to write the four dashes. I punched his number and got Tucker-Fitts.

"Ah, yes, Mr. Dienst. Mr. McIntear wishes me to give you a personal message in regard to the Mexican incident. Can you drop by this afternoon, please?"

"To get a message from him? Can't you tell me right now?"

"It is written - it is a written message."

"OK, put it in interoffice mail."

"My instructions are to see it personally into your hands."

"I'll be here until five or six."

She was six feet tall, with glacial eyes and a demeanor she must have learned from a governess. She was lean as leather, except for a bosom that surely owed much to Dow Corning. A gold pin in the form of a riding crop rode securely below her left collarbone. Though her face was quite beautiful, reminiscent of Janet Leigh, there wasn't a lot of fun in it, and I could not imagine what had induced Rick McIntear to cash in Liana for this. She strode into my office slapping her thigh with a stiff white envelope which she handed to me with an impatient air. I tossed it into the In basket.

"Mr. McIntear instructed me to wait upon a reply."

"Very well, Ms. Tucker-Fitts," I said carefully. "You are welcome to wait here if you wish; there's a chair. But I expect Mr. McIntear may begin to wonder where you are after a day or two. Perhaps it would be more productive for you to wait at your own desk, where you can get on with other matters."

"You don't take my meaning - "

255

"Yes, I do. Thank you for your personal delivery of Mr. McIntear's message. As you can see from the other papers that preceded it into the basket, it will be some time before I can give it the attention I'm sure it deserves."

She threw up her hands in a remarkably human gesture, and left.

Dienst:
I don't know what you meant by the message you left with my office, or why you're getting yourself involved in that Manosduros business. I gave you clear instructions to chill down the greasers, and I meant it. I will expect an appropriate response from you today.

The stupid bastard actually signed it. I made a photocopy, and picked up the next report in the stack.

*   *

Donia Ma watched as I unpacked the cello and plinked the strings. "Put it aside for now, Dr. Dienst. I do not wish you to risk our progress by beginning too soon. You have not tried to play it yet, have you?"

I had not. I had taken it and the bow out of the case and looked at them, just to be doing something, but nothing had tempted me to go farther. I was skeptical of the whole project, and I had learned not to pick at old sores.

"Please sit down, and we will see where matters stand, and how we may assist them in healing before you try playing."

She picked up my wrist and began making the rounds of my many pulses, and applying gentle massage, and needles, this time combined with the burning moxa she had used the first time. She worked quietly, single-mindedly, her motions were soothingly familiar. Packets of something I can only describe as good news flowed from my fingers to a spot behind my left ear. They seemed to be doing great things on the way up. Had it been a whole being instead of a piece, my elbow might have been sitting up, smiling, and sipping at a bowl of warm broth. I slipped into a trance while it was going on, and when she began to work the needles out I smiled at her with affection.

"Donia, you are a master. That felt wonderful, and I'm sure my elbow is getting stronger and looser."

She smiled. "Thank you, Dr. Dienst. I hope it will continue to feel wonderful. I hope also that you will not take amiss what I now must say to you: I am called Donia Ma, and that is how I think of myself. I know you mean it as a friendly gesture when you use only one of my names, and I take it as such. In fact, I feel friendly toward you, I admire your openness and your stoicism in regard to, mm, to your painful condition. I would take it as an even more friendly gesture if you would unfailingly use both names when you address me by name."

"Very well, Donia Ma."

"You are offended."

Good guess. "I'm embarrassed that I've offended you."

"Please don't be. I am not offended. It is entirely my idiosyncrasy that I am unsettled by needless uncertainty. It assists me in concentrating when I know what to expect, even in such apparently trivial matters as the use of my full name if it is used at all. One of the things I enjoy about dealing with you is that you avoid using hearty vocatives like "young lady" or "my friend" in greeting me. I consider them nothing less than attempts to trivialize and dominate another by imputing an unwelcome definition, and I admire you for avoiding them."

"Thanks. It will take getting used to, and if I slip, it won't be from perversity. I could think of the first name as a sort of honorific, like 'Queen' or 'Captain'. Hmm. 'Donia' Ma. Yes, I think that should work. Said that way, we could think of a 'donia' as a sort of graceful hereditary healer, a status attained by birth and by long and difficult study. In very ancient times, only emperors had donias. The donia occupied a high position at court, and lived in a special apartment with its own herb garden and fountain. It is an honor to be healed by you, Donia Ma."

While I spoke, she reached out and held my left elbow delicately, her fingers probing its simplified architecture. She looked up at me and smiled. "You are kind and humorous, but also a very remarkable person. Of course, there is no such traditional meaning, but you have described with great accuracy a tale I made up for myself when I was very young."

Well, there were three interpretations I could think of for that, none of them particularly exciting: first, that Donia Ma and I were soulmates; second, she was lying, but for her own reasons wanted me to think that we were soulmates; third and most likely, that my tastes in spontaneous invention were those of an adolescent girl. The whole business was just a little heavy and squishy, like a peach an hour past perfect ripeness. On the other hand, or arm, I could not deny the effectiveness of her work.

"Do you think I should try playing a bit now?"

"Let us try. For heaven's sake, though, begin very carefully and simply. It is always best, and in this case it is imperative."

"No danger. You may have improved my elbow, but even with a perfectly sound elbow, I would be thirty years out of practice."

She only smiled politely at this, and I picked up the somewhat raw-looking Gustav Schneider cello and the bow he had thrown in. I pulled the strings into tune standing up, not daring to reach back to the pegs while I was sitting. That's a maneuver that needs strength, coordination, and a tightly bent left elbow.

I sat, and played only the open strings, with my left arm dangling; and then slowly lifted my left hand into position on the strings. I started out high up in the thumb positions, since those involve the least bending of the elbow. I tried a D scale at the octave, the bare minimum. It went all right, in fact amazingly well, considering. As I carefully worked my way down to first position, bending my elbow more and more, the sound grew stronger. The tears started, to my embarrassment, on the E major arpeggios in second position. I left that session with admonitions ringing in my ears not to be brash, not to force, not to risk injury to my elbow ever again, but for heaven's sake not ever again to allow what she called the strong winds that blew within me to be frustrated, lest they again seek false pathways … and so forth.

We made further weekly appointments for a while, and then let them become biweekly, as what she could do for me approached the limits imposed by my age and my job. After

Easter I half-jokingly asked her if she thought she could do for my whole mortal body what she had done for my elbow, and she got very solemn and dark of eye and said things about drastic and rigorous treatments that might or might not work; and generally acted as if I had idly suggested popping the hood on the Ark of the Covenant.

I called up Gustav Schneider and asked him for an exact price on the cello, bow, and case, and sent him a down payment, and then spent quite a few Saturdays at the Public Library browsing and checking out cello music. I began to treat Schneider's really pretty mediocre cello with ceremonious respect, and it began to sound better. I never picked it up unless I had a minimum of a half-hour to give it, with time at the beginning to check the bridge and tune carefully and to calm myself, and at the end to clean the strings and stand it neatly in its corner; a middle-aged guy's got time for that, a kid never seems to. There would be times, even at work, when I would lose myself in the world of four strings that stretched away down the fingerboard like railroad tracks, thinking exclusively of fingerings and phrasings. I thought I had lost that world forever, and my gratitude to Donia Ma was great. I gave whole evenings to Bach and Reger and Hindemith, getting the cello broken in and my fingers toughened up and clever again, and then looked for an orchestra that might welcome a half-decent player with a cello to match.

The Rock Creek Philharmonic fell all over me; they had foolishly contracted to undergird a performance of the Beethoven Ninth by one of the bigger church choirs for Summer Solstice, and they were desperate for experienced string players. We set up an audition, in which I succeeded by the ruse of copying some of the tough cello passages at the library, and swotting hard on them in advance.

While we were in rehearsals for the Beethoven, AC Gewissner took me to a performance of Tectonic Tease by the Capitol reflecting pool. We combined it with a visit to the National Gallery, dropping back every half-hour or so to check Jana's progress and watch her for a while. I admit I was astounded at her certifiable ability to do something without appearing to move. AC brought a Polaroid camera, and we entertained ourselves and a high school class from New Mexico by taking pictures ten minutes apart and verifying that, indeed, slight progress had been made in the interval. About two hours into it, the shirt was definitely coming off, and was at the stage, AC said, that gave Jana the most trouble, with a lot of cloth hanging about that she didn't want to let slip. So of course just at that point the park police sirened up, summoned I think by a lady from the Virginia suburbs who had seemed pretty unsympathetic and offended. A couple of cops got out and started telling Jana to put her clothes on. AC rushed up and distracted them with Jana's permit, and pointed out that Jana was wearing underwear - specifically, a bodysuit - and that there was absolutely nothing indecent involved, that the whole performance was clearly described on the permit, and that the permit was signed by the very park police themselves.

Jana did not react in any way, just kept moving at a pace that would have required Fast Forward to detect, with a glaze of concentration on her face. In the end the cops backed down, but said they were going to write a full report, and that she had better not pull anything like this on park grounds again. Maybe what miffed them was the fact that the bodysuit matched Jana's pale skin color exactly, had inconspicuous edges, and was printed with freckles, a navel, and nipples. You really had to look close to see that it wasn't skin, and they did.

I heard second-hand about a couple of other performances, both built around Jana's remarkable control of her wiry little body, including one called Mass Extinction that was reviewed in both Intermission and the Blade, and one that had something to do with global warming. But it wasn't exactly my idea of art, and I let AC keep me posted.

It was fun watching friendship flourish between AC and Jana. They were so radically different except in the one thing that mattered, seriousness about their work. They called each other Mutt and Jeff, but of course tiny Jana was Mutt. AC was as proud as a big sister about Jana's growing reputation, and Jana in turn became a fairly familiar sight around AC's part of the EPA, and we would occasionally meet at my office to go to lunch when we could get away. Once, she and AC came in just as

Diana Tucker-Fitts was delivering another of Rick McIntear's nagging notes about relations with the Mexicans.

"Who in the almighty was that," asked Jana, after T-F had stalked out, "Julie Andrews' evil twin?"

"That was Diana Tucker-Fitts. She's secretary to - "

But I had to break off to help AC get Jana under control. She was sprawled against a bookcase, screaming with laughter, and it wouldn't have done for that to get back to Rick.

In late May, I got a letter from a Reverend Plummer Chavis of the Lumber River Evangelical Baptist Church informing me that the mortal remains of Mrs. Jacob Oxendine would be laid to rest next to those of her husband the following Sunday afternoon. I thought about it a bit, and looked at road maps, and then called up Rev. Chavis and told him how Mrs. Oxendine had asked me to play at her original funeral, and I had been forced to default on that request, and would he mind if I provided a little music to go with the re-interment?

"Well, what style (*stahl*) a music was you thinkin ta play?"

"Uh, well, Mrs. Oxendine loved classical music - I thought something along that line - "

"Naw, sir, I meant what instrument you'd bring? We don't have but a organ and a little old upright, and that's right hard ta bring out to the yard."

"Oh, I see. I play the cello, that's like a big - "

"I know what a cello is, brother. I don't suppose folks'd mind a bit. Had you thought about what pieces you'd play?"

Careful here. "Well, I can do 'Amazing Grace' pretty good. But Mollie loved classical, and she'd asked for Bach at her funeral."

"That ain't classical, that's bay-roque. Whyn't you play - oh, lessee, here - oh, the Sayrabande from the C Minor Unaccompanied Suite? Be's kinda mournful, but uplifting, don't you find?"

"Um. . .Why not?"

Another look at the map and some calculations gave me the strong feeling it would be a good eight-hour drive each way, and flying with a cello almost always costs two tickets. I mentioned it to AC, and found to my surprise that she was eager to go along, provided we could make a side trip to have a look at the Lumber River.

Well, that was fine, though I knew I would not get AC without Jana, and goodness knew what impact she'd have on a country funeral. But AC promised to make her behave, or at least keep her shirt on. And when we stepped out of the car under a canopy of mossy cypresses in the churchyard of Lumber River Evangelical Baptist, she was wearing a severe black dress against which her poof of red hair looked like a highway flare, and she was prepared to be somber if it killed her.

A hearse and a small crowd of mourners stood nearby; they were ringingly silent after the roar and chatter of our nearly nonstop drive. The cemetery stood on a little bluff over the deepest, darkest, quietest river I had ever seen. AC and Jana made a beeline for the bank and stood looking down at it; I joined them after I unpacked my cello. Bottomless tea glided by, the color pierced in one spot by sun that lit sandflakes in silent turbulence. A mockingbird in one of the cypresses began to offer a selection of what he'd heard in the last month. I set myself up on a folding chair by the river, with my end pin dug into a cypress root. It occurred to me that you might find rare or shy birds by listening to the mockers that had heard their song in the deep woods. A soberly dressed gent came up and introduced himself as Reverend Plummer Chavis.

"Dr. Chavis, I apologize for sounding as if I thought you were ignorant on the phone. You picked exactly the piece - one of them - that Mollie wanted."

He chuckled in a pleasant country way. "Please forgive my little bit of vanity, Brother Dienst. I couldn't deny myself pullin your leg just a little. A long time back, Jacob give me a copy of what Mollie'd wanted before she died, and he said he wanted the same. We had a fella from over't Pembroke State to play it on the organ, and we all liked it right well. But if you'd want to th'ow in Amazin Grace, I'd expect it'd be a comfort to Jacob's folks, which is here."

*　　　*

"Jesus Pete, Oren. I never set through such a sermon in my life. I mean, she's been dead how long?"

"Thirty years."

"Shit fahr. And him six months. What's left to say?"

AC and I, and even Jana after her fashion, were quieted down by the whole experience. AC had new data about quiet rivers, and I was chastened at the sight of Mollie's casket - a little dulled but certainly intact after thirty years - being lowered into place against Jacob's. I wanted to sneak back at night and cut holes in the sides to let them hold hands while they waited. But I didn't dare mention it, or Jana would have seen to it that we did. Over dinner and drinks in the bar of the Wideawake Motel on I-95, we pooled our impressions of the service, of the place where Jacob and Mollie lay, and of the whole region. Jana remained relatively pensive, and I asked her if she'd been gathering material for a new piece.

"It's not quite like that, O," she said. "I never stop gathering material. This was a big piece, maybe, but sometimes they get so big that you can't get it all in, or out, in one stiff chunk, so I might not recognize it on down the line. Little stuff, like that stack of paper on your desk, or Lady Diana Snooker-Shits - well, I've gotten a lot from AC and the EPA. He sure can play the shit out of that cello, though, hey, Jeff?."

"Thanks, I think. It was a good setting."

"It was wonderful," said AC dreamily. "It changed how I think about water. I'm so glad you brought us, Oren." But she wasn't looking at me when she said it. She was gazing softly at Jana, and Jana was gazing right back. And it wasn't too long before they decided to take their nightcaps off to their room, leaving me to sit gazing into mine, feeling old, naive, and lonesome.

The note from Rick McIntear that had been the occasion of Jana's merry introduction to Diana Tucker-Fitts had started me to thinking about Manosduros again. The note about chilling greasers, leaked to the Post, would probably have made a few Republicans blanch and possibly sacrifice Rick; but I thought I could see a better, more thorough, and more straightforward approach. If MexiLar had an agreement with the village of Manosduros, in the best of all worlds signed by Rick, with language about liability and site cleanup after shutdown, I could, in the open and without using press leaks, instigate a federal suit against Molar for violating the terms of an international contract through a wholly-owned subsidiary. And if my chiefs at the EPA - loyal Reaganites to a man and woman - should balk, the 'greaser' note might come in handy as, mm, a lubricant. But I had to get my hands on that contract.

Before we left Washington, I had started with EPA International archives, and turned up a properly labeled, empty folder. The records clerk said nobody had checked out the contents; I bet not, indeed. Calls to Commerce and State were fruitless, and so was one I tried, just for the record, to Molar headquarters in St. Louis. They had it, I was sure, but they were not about to say so, and kept asking who I was, and did I have authority or a subpoena. At that point I got off the line, gave it up, and went to North Carolina to bury Mollie. But Jana's reference to "Ms. Snooker-Shits", done in a sort of attempted imitation of her voice, got me to thinking again, sitting in this lonesome bar while everybody else seemed to be having such a good time. And after a while I, or the bourbon-and-soda, thought rather well of the only new idea I'd had on it in days.

*   *

When I logged on the next Monday, I typed "LISTUSER LIANA." There was a portentous moment of nothingness, and then several lines of information zipped across the screen:

NAME	LOGIN ID	ROOM	PHONE
Liana, Hector	HL91	234	5353
Mariconas, Liana	LM46	B434	6896
Smid, Molliana	MS21	875	4083

The middle one looked right; if so, Liana had not been fired, but transferred to payroll. I gave it a shot. "Liana?"

"Yes?"

"Um, I think you and I met a few months ago. This is Oren Dienst, in the International office."

"Yes?" Not impressed, definitely used to getting this kind of call.

"I hope I'm not bothering you for nothing. Are you the Liana that used to work for Rick McIntear?"

"Yes . . Oh, you the guy called him a dumb bastard?"

"I think moronic was the word I used."

"You guys with the PhD's, you always try fancy language where simple stuff will do. Otherwise, you got him pretty good. Dumb bastard came on to me when he come here to get signed on for pension, tell me I'm too smart and good-looking to be running the pension desk, why don' I come and be his executive assistant. Huh. When I find out what that means, my boyfriend come here and straighten out Mr. Stud McIntear and now I'm back here, except I'm working <u>for</u> the lady that run the pension desk. And Lady Diana you-know-what is sitting up there maintaining a decorous and highly disciplined office and disciplining Richard on the weekends."

I slapped my knee. Starting with "Lady," the Latina accent had dropped away and been replaced by perfect mimicry of Tucker-Fitts. "Liana," I said. "You've had a tough break. I've got something I need to talk over with you. Are you free for lunch?"

"My boy friend gonna be right there."

Over lunch, we worked it out; and right after, she came up to my office to give it a shot:

"mGood ahftanoon. This is Diana Tucker-Fitts, with the Environmental Protection Edgency, in Washington, D.C. I am Mr. Richard McIntear's confidential assistant, and Mr. McIntear has requested that I obtain information from you regarding the contract between MexiLar S.A. and the village of Manosduros, State of Sonora. . . . Of course; my password is *Thanks Yoolie*. . . Thenk you; I will hold."

I made impressed faces; Liana gave me a wink and wrote some words and numbers on a pad, and adopted a waiting air.

"mGood ahftanoon; my name is Diana Tucker-Fitts; the code word is gold-digger; the file number is 81-8047-SON." Another wait; then "And the other copies remain at? . . .Yes; I do so appreciate your assistance. When that file should be returned to you, would you be so good as to give me a call. I beg your pardon? ...My name is Diana Ticker-Futz, and my number - excuse me, Diana Tutter- Diana Ficker- Aw, shit! Madre de Dios!" Slam.

"Aw, Oren, I screwed it up good, din't I? Geez, I'm so sorry . . ." But she was having a tough time not laughing, and so was I; so we did.

"Never mind, Liana. You were doing great. And we learned something, I guess?"

"Yeah, their copy is out of the folder, but there's a copy in the state capital, an' one in Manosduros."

"Well, you did fine. You think you could do a number in Spanish if I need you?"

"Course, but not now. I gotta get back to work, an' get the sno-cones outa my mouth."

"That's fine. Adios y gracias, Senorita FitzTucker."

She laughed, I laughed, she left, and I sat back and ran my hands through my hair.

*   *

"A river of nearly pure yin, Dr. Dienst. A very appropriate place to bury someone. I myself so strongly incline to the yin that it would be a place for me to avoid. It is more healthy for me to visit sandy beaches by the ocean. Did you feel good about your playing?"

"Yes, I did. I was paying an old debt to Mollie, and I had always wondered about Jacob's people and their country. In fact, it was pretty much as I'd pictured it."

"Strongly archetypal scenes never surprise us."

"I guess not. Well, as always, you've made me feel a great deal better. I'm having to work hard on the Ninth, and this week we have three rehearsals and the performance."

"Well, you will be quite busy, then."

"Yes." I grasped the nettle. "Donia Ma," I began, and her expression became neutral. "I hope you will consider coming to our concert, as my guest - as my honored guest. And after that, well, . . ."

"It has become time to conclude your treatment, do you not think?"

"I think it has. I suppose there is only so much you can do with a guy who's a half-century old."

"Without commenting on that, I will say that we have gone as far as acupuncture alone will take us. If you will cast your mind back, you will recall that I was far from certain that we would accomplish all that we have. I would certainly enjoy seeing you play in the context of other players. Would you like a final session on the afternoon of the concert?"

"Yes, I would. But I would feel comfortable about it only if you would do me the honor of dining with me afterwards."

She looked at me consideringly, even worriedly, and she fingered her braid. "Would you be considering this a 'date', a social, male-female encounter?"

"Not if that makes you uncomfortable. Taking the afternoon and evening as a whole, something between that and an appointment."

"An appointment with social overtones."

"Call it that. You are my physician. And besides, I have no idea whether you might have a husband or other person you're attached to. If so, they are included in the invitation."

"There will be no one else."

We were only 90% ready to play the Ninth - it is a bear in every movement, not just the famous choral finale. Luckily, the choir was acceptable and the soloists were excellent, just heart-breaking on the parts where they suddenly emerged out of the din with their melting joyous harmonies. As for the cello and bass solo recitatives, the tenor probably had sympathizers when he broke in on them with the plea, "Oh Friends, not these sounds."

Well, I will not wax ironic. We gave a decent, middling-good performance, and the genius of the composer ("simple novelty", sez Jana!) transcended and transformed us; it was a great experience, even if I was faking a bit on the *prestissimo*, hell-for-leather whirlwind of broken scales at the end. The etudes of my youth were too far in the past to rescue me when I was concentrating on keeping the elbow relaxed and fluid. Afterwards, it was an unfamiliar Donia Ma who found me backstage, eyes shining, her grey smock abandoned for a severely festive dress of some kind of oriental cut. She was patently excited, the first time I had ever seen her so.

"Oh, Dr. Dienst, I cannot begin to tell you of my feelings. I had forgotten why that's supposed to be one of the pinnacles of Western culture, but now I know. But I wonder whether even Beethoven or Schiller could possibly have experienced joy like what I felt to see you in the midst of it, playing freely, hopefully, with all your heart. I was ... most gratified." *Let the dots represent stepping back, releasing my hands, re-establishing a clinical distance.* "Did you experience discomfort in your arm?"

"Not a bit. It only feels a little tired and hungry. Are you ready to eat?"

"I would enjoy a modest meal. What do you suggest?"

"Food. Give me a second to pack up."

At La Basilica, I watched her trying to find a middle ground between clinical and social modes. She was reluctant to abandon the high she'd experienced, so she talked it out in a characteristically dry exposition of the dangers of a physician's hubris when a patient succeeds, or even survives, she modestly laughed, a demanding and risky course of therapy.

"Survives?"

"Oh, there was never any physical danger; but if our sessions had not achieved what they did, would you have tried anything else?"

"Probably not."

"There, you see?"

Through the prosciutto-melone, the pasta, and the fritto misto (all of them shared, since neither of us was calm enough to eat much), I helped things along by talking about her practice and my scientific career, about music and politics and - to the extent discretion allowed - the MexiLar mess.

She reciprocated by describing her distress over having to turn away AIDS sufferers. As far as she could see, it was a disease that was out of reach of the powers of acupuncture, which was saying something for her.

"You've treated patients with AIDS?"

"A year ago in California I attempted therapy with one, advancing only as far as moxa treatments; but it was quite clear from his response - or lack of it - that there was no point in taking his money or raising his hopes. There are situations to which all my training and any amount of thought provide no solution. When such things arise, I step aside."

We fell silent. I began to relax enough to feel the fatigue I had coming after the effortful evening. As I was leaning back and thinking how to check the time, Donia Ma licked her cappuccino spoon and laid it carefully across the edge of her saucer.

"Dr. Dienst, you will recall the untoward consequences of my carelessly asking you, at the very beginning of your treatments, whether you were married. So I hope you will believe me when I say that I have weighed very carefully what I am about to ask."

She took a breath, looked as if she were already regretting something, and then plunged ahead. "You are in fact not married, I believe. Do you have access to a partner for the purpose of intercourse?"

"... for the ... ?"

"My training leads me to believe that a severe injury on the meridian of the triple burner such as you suffered - not to mention the consequent deprivation of all musical activity - must have had a substantial melancholic impact on the flow of sexual energy as well. You do not object to my raising this topic?"

"Um ... Go ahead."

She examined the spoon again. "It well may be that the whole body healing of which you once lightly spoke to me . . . I have given your question a great deal of thought . . . Dr. Dienst, it may be that further healing will require regular sexual activity, preferably with a female partner, and in the context of knowledgeable attention to the entire meridian. If there is such a person ...

"Were you thinking of writing a prescription?"

"Forgive me. I did not mean to be intrusive."

I relented. "It is for you to forgive me. I didn't mean to be - well, let's say I regret having been flippant and defensive. I am neither married nor in any other way have access to regular sexual activity. This has not been a successful feature of my life recently. Of my adult life, in fact. You ask with clinical intent, I suppose." I looked at her eyes carefully, and saw myself mirrored. "Or am I to see your question as clinical, with social overtones?"

She reached over and picked up my left hand, exerting pressures and frictions and so forth, and little warm whatevers rose up my arm and reported to the appropriate meridian, where they had what I must believe was the intended effect.

"Please do not think me merely forward or wanton. You are vigorous and healthy, and you are a man with artistic temperament, learning, and reasoned political views. Above all, you are my patient. I would consider it an appropriate extension of whatever therapeutic success I have had with you, to offer to share intercourse with you."

Share intercourse with. AC would certainly have relished that five-fold multiplication of syllables. Was I being hit on and exploited? Yes, but not without warning. The fact was, Donia Ma's treatments were deeply sensuous experiences, and I had at some point become rather interested in her myself, in a baffled way. "Donia Ma, I hope you understand that I have not had a great deal of success in sustaining loving relationships with women, on those rare occasions when intercourse was shared."

"I am not seeking a sustained or loving relationship. Among other things, that would badly compromise whatever therapy you may wish to continue. I do not seek to become your mistress or your wife. I am suggesting an isolated instance that will be as nearly as we can make it without history and without consequence aside from its possible beneficial effects upon your healing, and therefore upon any future relationship you may wish to establish with another. Can you approach it in that sense?"

"I think so." I knew so. No history, no future; what a physicist would call a stochastic event. My life had been a sequence of stochastic events.

We drove separately to Montecaro; in the elevator, Donia Ma slipped her arm through mine and smiled reassuringly, but remained otherwise aloof. She looked around the condo with cool interest as I put the cello in its corner and threw my coat over a peg. She picked up the geode I kept on the bookcase, and said, "If you need a bit of time to straighten up the bedroom, please go ahead. I do not like to walk in on the intimate furniture of another's life."

In fact, I had - just as a precaution, mind - straightened things up rather nicely during the quick half-hour I'd had between the therapy session and the concert, but had the sense not to say so. "Thank you. Would you like a nightcap?"

She looked mildly startled. "I believe not. I am very relaxed. I will browse your bookshelves."

So I went in and took a little time to hang up my performance clothes and put on a presentable robe. When I reentered the living room she had turned off all the lights but one, and was curled up on the couch with her shoes off, reading a Scientific American by the glow of the desk lamp and playing with her braid. "A very interesting article here on neural transport," she said. "Did you read it?"

"I was saving it. Would you like to reconsider on the nightcap, or in fact on the whole project? Or are you ready to share, uh, some neurology? We might achieve transport right here."

She put down the magazine and smiled; warmly, but no paroxysm. "You will joke, will you not? I wish us both to enjoy a pleasant, therapeutic, and - satisfying experience. To be certain of that, it might be helpful to agree on certain parameters in advance. You already know that I am not seeking a long-term relationship. In particular, I certainly do not wish to become pregnant, and I am fertile just now." She began fishing in her purse. "So - "

"I'm vasectomized."

"Ah. Reversibly?"

"Irreversibly."

"Fine. I prefer having a gentle light on, but not music. It will be both enjoyable and therapeutically convenient for me to be on top from time to time, and I hope you will not be bothered by that. I also enjoy being undressed by my partner, as long as it is done gently and playfully. It would be nice if that were to take some time."

In the light from the desk, I saw that a slight gleam had appeared on her brow. "No part of my body is off limits, but please do not introduce elements of bestiality or sadism. Let's see . . . you will find that I am already, what with the joy and excitement of this evening and all this talking about it, not to mention your own evident readiness to begin, somewhat advanced in readiness myself. So - "

Oh, for heaven's sake. I stopt her mouth, as they used to say, with kisses.

An hour later, I lay with my left arm over Donia Ma's hip, catching my breath, half-asleep. I was ready to reconsider some of my old notions about the emotional lives of fiddles, having been played by an expert myself. I was exhausted in body, mind, and sense, including the sense that every possibility had been explored. "Knowledgeable attention to the entire meridian," indeed. In the confusion of half-sleep, with "*Seid umschlungen, Millionen*" echoing in my head, I believed that I would belong to her as long as she wanted me, and then I would pass on for centuries through a succession of players. When grey light penetrated from the east, she was gone. In the living room, the Scientific American was returned to its place, and there was no indentation in the couch pillows.

*   *

"The body of Christ, the bread of heaven. . ." I knelt and received it in crossed hands. It smelled of yeast and harvest. I placed it in my mouth, and it tasted of wheat.

"The blood of Christ . . ." I bowed over the chalice, it filled my vision, the tang of grapes and alcohol rose from it. I sipped and the strong wine mixed with the bread in my mouth. The seminarian decorously wiped the spot where my lips had been, and I rose to return to my place. The choir sang of grazing sheep and faithful shepherds, mercifully free of dissonance or other improvements. I knelt among strangers, glad of the unvarying gift of the sacrament, the comforts of religion; the pretend, but very sufficient, miracle of the Eucharist.

15. Projects

Even high "middle age" (a term that assumes I would live to be 100) is no protection against acting crazy if it's only the motive that is crazy, and the actions themselves perfectly reasonable. At twenty, the roar of hormones and the clatter of incompetence will always drown out the sweet voice of reason. At fifty, the noise is less; if anything, the deafening hush of the tomb is tuning in from afar. So you'd think the promptings of fantasy would have to pipe down in deference to grave matters just over the horizon. All that means is that they can speak calmly and expect to be heard. And what they were saying during the summer of 1983, while I re-learned to play the cello and shared occasional intercourse with Donia Ma and came to terms with the idea that I would leave no trace of myself in this world, was that it would be neat, fun, satisfying to see if I could find and repurchase the cello "Francesca," having loosed her upon the world thirty years before.

A crazy project, you'd think, to find one cello out of the hordes of every description sawing way out there. Well, it wasn't as hopeless as all that. Cellos are bought and sold all the time, usually through a relatively small number of dealers, and dealers keep records. If Francesca had passed through the hands of a dealer in the thirty years since I left her outside that apartment in Chicago, I would have a chance of tracking down her present owner and making a very attractive offer for a cello that had cost its first real owner (Yoolie von Bayern didn't count) nothing. Apply whatever inflationary factor you like to that, and you're still at a pretty affordable price to a buyer whose bank accounts were unburdened by dependents.

Thus spake the inner voice one Sunday afternoon at Montecaro when I was working on a piece for the Rock Creek Symphony. Oh, all right, it was an orchestral suite from Porgy and Bess, summer-pops stuff and a pretty far jump from the Pinnacle of Western Culture. But no pushover to play well, just the same. The cellos have a swingy melodic line *("I got no lock on the door, that's no way to be..")* with a ton of sharps, in the middle of the "I Got Plenty of Nothin" section. You have to do it in high positions on the G and C strings, and I was getting plenty of nothin out of the rookie cello I had doubtfully picked out from Gustav Schneider. It sounded like a cello being played over a telephone.

"A good cello would have handled this just fine," said the calm and reasonable inner voice. *"You'd sound like a real player. Wouldn't it be neat to get Francesca back after all these years?"* It was a striking thought, but so unexpected that bringing up the name "Francesca" was a process in which I was already hearing the first syllable before I remembered what the next two were. The name peeled open like a long-closed book. I lost my place in the music and sat there thinking about it.

A hard look at the idea turned up two things: first, it would be easy and cheap to give it a try, since it would involve nothing more than asking Gustav Schneider to access the dealers' grapevine on my behalf, and if I really wanted to be thorough about it, running a classified in <u>Strings</u> and maybe <u>The Strad</u>, trade journals that catered to American and European instrument markets. And second, I recognized who had sent this plausible, intriguing idea onstage: it was the backstage Yahoos of ambition, those impractical jokers who would never give up on the idea that I should have been a concert cellist, never mind that it was forty years too late to start down that road.

Not that the rekindling of professional ambition was mentioned consciously. The fools within us are too canny for that. They just sent, while I was struggling to make music on the Gustav Schneider cello, a sudden, eidetic, multimedia, four-sense image of how that Gershwin passage would sound and feel with Francesca in my lap and a hushed Lincoln Center audience before me. And if ambitions that were still thinkable back when I did hold Francesca arose with the fantasy, well, they guessed that was my problem.

Ah, the Backstage Yahoos, those incorrigible mutts! What they'd been up to during this long dry spell, I couldn't guess. But hell, Republicans and Democrats spend decades out of power without changing a bit, so I suppose they had spent the time 'way backstage, playing Monopoly and making rude jokes about my scientific career, never growing up, and maybe one day in desperation finding a way to make my elbow hurt so badly I would have to get it repaired. They couldn't have figured on Donia Ma, of course, but I bet they couldn't believe their luck when she walked onstage talking about energies and triple burners and the purposes of stochastic intercourse. Well, I could sift the fun out of their notions and leave the rest to advancing age. It occurred to me that I could probably look forward to another quarter-century of playing if I took care of myself. Did I want to spend that struggling with an inferior instrument? I stashed my nameless surrogate in its corner and sat down to compose a classified for the trade journals:

FRANCESCA: I will pay above market for a cello bearing the following label: "Francesca/Petrus Salvatoris me fecit/ in Urbis S. Ludovici/ Anno DOMINI 1953"
O. Dienst, Montecaro, 11555 Georgia Ave. Silver Spring, MD 20202

When I talked to Schneider about it the next day, he was grumpy and reluctant at first - maybe he sensed in my eagerness a reflection on his own products; but I reminded him I'd never promised to make his cello a lifelong instrument, but had given it a good breaking-in, which would mean that he could turn it around at a good profit, and furthermore stood to make a pretty easy commission if he were the one to track down Francesca before my ads appeared. When I put it that way, and when I divulged that I had made Francesca's varnish and been her first player, either the profit motive or the sheer romance of it swept him away. But most of the summer went by and the classified ads came out, without the least result. Around the end of July I got a call from Schneider asking if I was still interested in that cello, and did it have to be Francesca.

"The answer is yes. Why?"

"Well, a little auction house in Boston has a dark cello like the one you described, but the fingerboard's fake rosewood, and the name's 'Anna'. The description and the rest of the label, year and all are the same, so I wondered it you'd remembered it right. I put a hold on it; the owner's asking five, but the appraiser doubts the attribution, and you could probably get it for three, three and a half."

Boston, huh? See how these things work? My good old cello, for which my folks had shelled out a very hard-earned $125 in 1950, and who had to have been pulled out of the Union Station luggage locker by a cleanup crew, tossed on a cart with orphaned luggage and dead pets and sold at salvage, was now rubbing ribs with gentry at a Boston dealer and carrying a price in the thousands. I almost told Schneider the appraiser was right, I had pasted that label in her myself; but I had no reason to scuttle her pretenses.

"No, I've seen that cello, I used to work in Di Salvo's shop. He put labels like that in instruments he was proud of. But it's 'Francesca' I'm after."

"Well, you and somebody else. A couple of guys told me they had inquiries for this Francesca cello a while back. One of 'em thinks it sold at Sotheby's a year or two ago, but the other one swears not."

I gritted my teeth. "Is there any way to check?"

"Sure, I've got the Sotheby catalogs, but if he remembered the date or the auction house or the cello wrong - even if it <u>was</u> an auction - it'd be a wild goose chase. Be patient, Dr. Dienst. How's that little beauty of mine coming along?"

"OK. Fine. You'll have a winner on your hands in a century or two, but that's longer than I can wait. Gotta go, I've got a call on my other line. Keep on it."

"You bet, Hotshot."

"Office of International Affairs, this is Oren Dienst."

"This is Diana Tucker-Fitts. I thought you might wish to know that Mr. McIntear is on his way to your office, and he has the Deputy Administrator with him."

"That's very kind of you. However, no warning is necessary, I hear them in the anteroom now."

" ... 'Because,' says the judge, 'according to the plaintiff's testimony, you're the lessor of two weevils.' "

A pause, then hearty McIntear laughter. "A hoot, chief. I gotta remember that one, next time I talk to a Rotary. Lesser of two equal ..."

In they came, grins fading. My phone rang, I picked it up, and was informed by my secretary that Mr. McIntear and the Deputy Administrator were here to see me. Thanks, Gloria. "They're right in front of me, Mrs. Mondale. Hold my calls for a while, will you? Thanks."

"You're welcome, I'm sure." Music swelled - Stormy Weather, I think - and she clicked off.

"Aaron, I don't know if you've met the Deputy Administrator, Ferd Bakker. Ferd, this is Aaron Dienst."

"Oren. How do you do."

"As you were, Dienst."

"Thank you." *Uh-oh.*

"Dienst, I've had the opportunity lately to review your performance evaluations for the past several years. You're doing a good, solid job with us."

Thanks for that "us," you parvenu. You've been here how long? But since my performance reviews could in no way be the subject of this visit, I just looked at him expectantly. No amount of groveling would deflect what was coming.

"Yes, a good, solid job." He ran a hand around his jaw, and found it about as he expected. "All the tougher, then, when I get reports of unprofessional behavior."

"Reports, sir?" I asked, looking at Rick. Might as well make him look as much like a tattle-tale as possible.

"That's right. Mmm, Rick here has the particulars. Rick?"

Rick looked disgusted. "OK. My office manager in St. Louis called last month and said somebody imitating my secretary called, using confidential code words, and tried to get proprietary information about a mining operation we - our Mexican partners established in Sonora. So I finally got the phone logs, and that call came from this office. What's the policy on obtaining proprietary information by fraud?"

Bakker grunted. "It's a serious matter. What do you say to that, Dienst? Was it you? Nobody on your staff would attempt fraud, surely?"

I leaned back and looked at the ceiling for a bit. "You fellas have been here how long? Ricky, a few months; plus, sir? Two years or so?"

"Not sure what you're getting at, Dienst."

"Just thinking back. I got here on July first, 1970. That was a stinking hot day.. I came up here straight from National and tossed my bags in a corner, and I put in an eight-hour day, starting at four in the afternoon. By then it was too late to get in to my apartment, so I slept in the office and put in another ten hours before I ever even unpacked. I believed that much in what this agency does. I was in Emergency Response then, but a few years ago I moved over here to International Affairs. I've become one of those guys your gang are calling entrenched bureaucrats. I wonder if you know what it takes to become one … I'm certainly going to answer your question, sir, just bear with me if you will. Well, I'll tell you what it takes. You either have to work your ass off, or cover it with bullet-proof armor."

"Could we skip this? Your ass is way out of line on this one, and you and whoever you got to imitate Tucker-Fitts are going to - "

"Honest to God, Ricky, you don't change, do you? I guess I already remarked that, though, back when you first came here. What I was going to say, sir, is, I did both. I guess that says I'm armored, and if you did get through the armor you wouldn't find anything to put in a sling, 'cause I'd worked it off, cleaning up after folks like Ricky, here, first in the US and then trying to cooperate with OAS folks. That MexiLar mess is exactly in my department, so you couldn't keep me off it without firing me. But speaking of ballistics and armor and stuff, I'd like to invite you, sir, to glance through this, if you would." I handed Bakker a copy of Rick's "chill the greasers" memo. "This is sort of a yardstick, if you like, of the level of stupidity we're dealing with here."

He glanced through it, grunted again, and walked over to the window to review the traffic patterns on M Street.

"What I'm getting at here, Mr. Bakker, is the way a guy like Ricky comes in here and thinks there's no dues to pay, no history, no consequences. I'd be - "

"Consequences is what we're talking about here, Dienst. Let me cut through the bullshit and ask you flat out. Were you responsible for that call to Molar Chemical?"

"Of course."

"Who else?"

"Who else what?"

"Don't try to stall me. Who did the impersonation?"

Tough one. I dropped my chin to add a bit more treble resonance, and did my best. "Mr. Richard McIntear has requested that I obtain information for his - "

"And you think this silly little note from Rick is going to cover your ass in the face of that?"

Rick broke in. "Wait a minute. Where'd you get the code words?"

"It is silly, isn't it? I guess I'm betting you, or Ricky, won't want it to leak out, yes. Look here, it's got two names and an initial." I turned to Rick and looked him straight in the eye. "Any fool who knows how you got where you are would know what you'd pick for a code word with Molar, Rick. Don't make me tired. Now, let's talk about likely targets for a leak, shall we? What, the press, Congress, the OAS, the Republican National Committee, boy, the Democratic National Committee, the Mexican ambassador, the Sierra Club. That's what, seven, and of course the press alone means at least three major media, namely newspapers, newsmagazines, and TV. That about accounts for the nine envelopes my lawyer's holding, but if you have any other suggestions, I'd be glad to add them. I'll even tell you the code words I've set up with him, in case anything happens to me: 'Mail them'."

Ferd Bakker snorted and headed for the door, and Rick took his place at the window. "You know, Dienst, you haven't changed a whole lot either. All you can think of to do when you get in trouble is to find a cop, or tell teacher somebody's being mean. That's the way you handled that spill back in '53, and this is no different. I guess it's gonna work for you again, but I gotta say, it doesn't fill me with respect. Why don't you stand up on your own two feet and fight?"

Good question. I turned around with a shrug. "What spill, Rick?"

Rick threw up his hands. "Ah, go screw yourself, Dienst. Sir, I apologize for exposing you to this jerk. I won't press this matter any further."

"Good idea. Dienst, I don't care if your luggage is still sitting down in Emergency Response, it'll be handy if you ever involve yourself in this Manosduros incident again. You're out of that loop, is that understood?"

"I understand what you're saying, yes. I think the best I can say to that is, if I do anything else on it, it will be because I feel strongly enough about it to lose my job over it. I appreciate the clarity of your position, though. Maybe you'd be best off to can me right now."

"Mmm...No, I guess I still value McIntear's butt enough to keep it covered for now. But this kind of thing won't work twice, you know."

I sat down, a bit suddenly for complete dignity. "I wouldn't expect so. I think Rick's right, surprised as I am to hear myself say it. If I get into this again, it'll be in the open. And I guess you'd be involved only if Rick forgets his own advice and runs to you again for backup, wouldn't you think?"

"God, I hope so. You guys are gonna drive me nuts, sticking out your tongues at each other. Come on, McIntear."

"Payroll, this is Liana."

"This is Oren Dienst. Two things. I hope you didn't tell anybody about our little phone prank last month."

"You think I'm nuts?"

"Guess not. It's just, there's a little heat, nothing I can't handle, and you're not involved and never were. The second thing is, can you make a phone call to Mexico for me? A straight deal this time, no tricks. But it can't be from anywhere here, so I guess it'd have to be from my home phone. Are you free tonight?"

"Boy, is that a lame one. I thought I heard 'em all."

"Bring your boy friend. He's welcome. I'm not trying to pull anything, Liana. At least, not where you're concerned."

"I don' know. He's outa town a week on a mail run to El Salvador."

Hell. I couldn't wait around that long, they'd have the whole thing tucked out of sight for good. "How about if my, uh, niece, works here at EPA, comes along?"

"She got a phone, I don' have to go to your place?"

"OK, sure, we could do that. When?"

"Have to be Monday, I gotta work on my baby sister's first communion. I could do it Monday, though."

Best I could do. "Let me call AC and set it up. I'll get back to you."

It was fine with AC, it was OK with Liana. I quit thinking about it so I wouldn't get nervous.

*   *

§§

STOCHASTICALLY OCCASIONALLY YOURS
A sacrament of one act

Scene 1

> *Opening: An empty interior. After 5 seconds that seems much longer, a telephone rings, but no one comes onstage. Instead, after the fourth ring we hear clicks and beeps and a recorded voice.*

Voice of Oren Dienst; *muffled, as if speaking over a bad telephone:* Hello. This is Oren Dienst. Please leave your message at the tone, giving date and time, and I'll get back to you as soon as I can.. . .*(beep)*.

Voice of Donia Ma; *also telephonic, but clearer than the answering machine*: Dr. Dienst, this is Donia Ma. It is 5 pm on Friday. I'm afraid I will have to cancel our therapy session for tomorrow, since another patient is having an emergency. However, I would consider it a pleasure to reciprocate your dinner invitation of last week. Would you be free to join me for dinner this Sunday? I would suggest that Evensong service at the

Cathedral would serve very well as a preliminary. Please call me to confirm. I do apologize most sin-*beep.*

Enter, immediately following, Donia Ma and Oren Dienst.
Dienst: What were those little things called?
Donia Ma: Collectively, dim sum.
Dienst: Sounds like Ronald Reagan doing the budget. Would you like a nightcap?
Donia Ma *(Mildly surprised)*: I believe not. I am very relaxed. I will browse your bookshelves. If you need a bit of time to straighten up the bedroom, please go ahead. I do not like to walk in on the intimate furniture of another's life.
Dienst: Well, as a matter of fact, I -
Donia Ma *(Picks up Scientific American)*: A very interesting article here on neural transport. Did you read it?
Dienst *(Bemused)*: No, I'm still saving it. I guess this is where you say -
Donia Ma: I wish us both to enjoy a pleasant, therapeutic, and - satisfying experience. To be certain of that, it might be helpful to agree on certain parameters in advance. You already know that I am not seeking a long-term relationship.
Dienst: Of course. Didn't we -
Donia Ma: In particular, I do not wish to become pregnant. I am fertile just now, *(Begins fishing in her purse)* so -
Dienst: Well, I'm still vasectomized.
Donia Ma: Ah. Revers -
Dienst: Irreversibly. Still. That's the thing about irrev -
Donia Ma: Fine.*(During the following speech, Dienst at first looks at her in some disbelief, but then wanders over to the bedroom door and stands with arms folded, watching her with a smile.)* I enjoy having a gentle light on, but not music. It will be enjoyable for me to be on top from time to time, and I hope you will not be bothered by that. I also enjoy being undressed by my partner, as long as it is done gently and playfully. It would be nice if that were to take some time. No part of my body is off limits, but please do not introduce elements of bestiality or sadism. *(Her voice has become a little husky, and a light gleam has appeared on her brow.)* Let's see . . . you will find that I am already, what with the joy and excitement of this evening -

283

Dienst: Of Evensong?

Donia Ma: - and all this talking about it, not to mention your own evident readiness to begin, somewhat advanced in readiness myself.

So - *(There is a moment of silent inaction, during which Donia Ma looks at Dienst expectantly.)* So -

Dienst: I get it. Now?

Donia Ma: Please.

Dienst: *(Stops her mouth with kisses, etc.)*

-Curtain-

Scene 2: The same, word for word.
—————   -Curtain-

Scene 3: An interior. Dienst and Donia Ma are found lying together in a bed. Dienst's arm is over her hips.

Donia Ma: I believe that the value of an act, whether in a therapeutic or an erotic calculus, lies in the act itself and not in its peripherals; its setting, its history, its consequences. If it is good, it will be good again. If bad, well, it is over and done with, and cannot be undone, so we need not consume ourselves in regret. You do not regret our lovemaking, do you?

Dienst *(Sleepily)*: Of course not. You say that history is irrelevant to the act, but I enjoyed the second time more than the first, and this time more yet. So there's -*(yawns deeply)* - there's some historical process at work, surely?

Donia Ma: Only for a time. During the first occasion you were unacquainted with my needs and desires, and during the second you were still not aware of my preference for minimal variation. This has been the best so far because that initial period of learning is over, never to be repeated. From now on, it can be exactly as if you had come to me from the first, knowing what you now know.

Dienst: From now . . . On?

Donia Ma: You do not wish to make share intercourse with me again?

Dienst: Of course I do. But anyone enjoys novelty.

Donia Ma: Oh, but there is novelty. There are a thousand small details that will vary randomly, stochastically, from one time to the next. The time of night, the color of my clothing, exactly how you will arrange my braid, whether it is raining or windy outside, the various sounds of traffic, your delightful little deviations from the exact things you said the first time. Your peaks of response are narrow, but they are very high. That is the kind of minimal variation that I can appreciate, when the larger structure of the experience is fixed.

Dienst: But -

Donia Ma: Hush. It is time you were asleep now.

-Curtain-

§§

*   *

On Monday, August first, AC and I stopped in to the payroll office to pick up Liana for the call to Mexico. I finally figured out, sitting there in the afterglow of my productive meeting with Rick and Ferd Bakker, that it was dumb to mess around at second hand on the Manosduros incident. It was not out of the question that - as Rick would have surely put it - the whole thing had been blown out of proportion, that maybe a headstone or two had been undercut, the cyanide had been destroyed by time and oxygen, or even by Mexilar before they left. Or, once one started down this skeptical trail, that they were still there working away, or had never been there. Well, no, they'd been there, and there had been some kind of "incident," I knew that much from reliable Rick. But it was imperative to visit the site myself, and while there get a first-hand look at the agreement they'd signed, and bring away a copy if possible. Molar was going to enough trouble to hide it that I was sure it would be good reading.

I introduced AC and Liana, whose eyes widened a bit at the towering cut of AC's jib. "Lessee, she's your niece, that right?"

AC cocked an eyebrow at me, and I had to say, "Well, sort of an honorary niece, yes."

Liana shrugged. "Thought that went out with velvet drapes. Please to meet you, AC."

"OK, guys, let's go, so we can get Liana on her way before the family suspects anything. You have an umbrella, Liana? Looks like rain out there."

"Really? Hell. Jus' got my hair done. Well, we shou'n't be out much, I think?"

"Just to the parking lot, and then wherever we can park at AC's, I guess. How's parking where you are, AC?"

"We have one spot that comes with the apartment, and Jana's supposed to be out in Fairfax doing Mass Extinction at a mall opening, so we can use it. Oh, and listen. If she gets back in time, she's got a new piece she wants to show you. You too, Liana, if you want to stay."

I looked at my watch. "She's not going to take off her shirt, is she? I've got a big meeting at 7:30 tomorrow . . ."

"No, no. it's called Read Only Memory. She says it's for you, and Mollie and the Lumbees, and a lot of other stuff from the North Carolina trip."

So up 4th street to the Mall, I watched clouds massing over the Volvo neighborhoods of Northwest and getting ready to descend over the city, while AC and Liana got acquainted, which involved figuring out what friends they might have in common, and which males at EPA were the worst oglers and gropers. As we passed the Capitol, the first fine drops began to hit the windshield, and AC said, "That's the light stuff blown out in front of the storm. We're gonna get a real soaker, I bet. Left here, then right, Oren."

We worked our way past St. Mark's church, and into a neighborhood of old-looking, pastel-painted town houses. "Nice neighborhood," Liana and I said, more or less together.

"Thanks. Left at the light, Oren, and it's half way up the block. What is this call supposed to be about, anyhow?"

I started what I hoped would be a quick executive summary of the problems I'd had getting a look at the MexiLar - Manosduros agreement. AC had known about the "incident" since our trip to North Carolina, and half-way through the continuation of that she interrupted: "It's that house up there on the left . . .shoot, Jana's home; we'll have to park somewhere, and that's tough. Mmm, the door's open. Maybe she's just on her way out. Stop a second, Oren, see if she comes out."

So we hovered in the street with hailstones making a racket on the car. Liana looked green and wide-eyed, and AC started to fret as the hallway door swung to and fro a couple of times. "What the heck's she doing, leaving that door open?"

"Maybe she didn't. Don't you have other tenants?"

"Yeah - "

"Guy pulling out up there, Oren, lucky us."

I checked the mirrors and bolted up the street to hover behind a fat RV that was easing its way out of a tight space. AC frowned and fidgeted, and finally said, "I don't like that open door, Oren. I'm gonna make a run for it." And she was dashing across the street, barely missed by a blinded motorcyclist trying to make speed through the rain, jumping the river in the far gutter and skidding into a sprint over wet leaves.

"Dios, she look like a halfback," remarked Liana. "She oughta change her name. What the AC stands for, anyhow?"

"Allmut Cushing."

Liana shrugged at that, and the RV finally cleared the parking space. "She some girl, OK. You know her from before?"

"I knew her mom and dad when we were students in the '50's."

"The '50's? You go back to then?"

"You want to wait for the rain to die down, or shall we run for it?"

Liana looked at her watch. "Gonna get wet anyhow, an' I gotta get home. Le's go."

So we did, gasping at the force of the rain and the sting of hailstones, wincing at the blam of close thunder. Liana slipped on some leaves and bounced hard against an iron fence, so I held her hand as we dashed down the block. From inside the house, I expect our arrival sounded breathless, lighthearted, horribly inappropriate. As we tumbled in the entrance laughing and whew-ing, AC's voice came from an open door, choked with anger.

"Oren! Don't let Liana in here."

16. Something to Deal With

At first, you couldn't see that the whole thing had fazed Jana at all. When we picked her up at Georgetown Hospital the next morning, she was sitting brightly in a wheelchair at the hospital door, and she thanked me brightly, warmly, for "going to all this trouble for nothing." And she chattered all the way home about art, and the Fairfax mall opening, and how sorry she was she hadn't got to do Read Only Memory for me, and again (and again) what a shame it was I'd taken this trip, not to mention last evening, for nothing.

What AC had found in their apartment was a rape in progress: Jana, the victim, nearly invisible under the bulk of a thug named – we later learned – Paul Hartley McCauley, who went by the street name of "Dead," and who'd invaded three homes and raped five women in the Capitol Hill area that month. AC's entrance alarmed the guy, and in a flash he threw at AC the knife he'd had at Jana's throat. AC told me later that she still had no idea how she'd dodged the thing. Apparently without thinking, AC pulled a service revolver from her purse and shot McCauley, who died bloodily, still atop Jana. Who continued to apologize for what a bother she was being.

About halfway home I caught AC's eye in the mirror, and it was bright with tears. When we pulled up in front of the apartment (scrubbed again from top to bottom by AC between midnight and 6:30 am, when I had to go and get cleaned up for my meeting) Jana started to get out, and found she couldn't walk, so AC and I made an arm cradle and carried her in. It was like carrying a canary. Jana continued perky and talkative, never mentioning the events of the night before, nor referring to her injuries except by omission ("AC, could you brang me the ashtray?"). I told AC I would check in on them after work, and would call her supervisor and see if I could get her a sick day. She looked if anything mildly surprised at the notion that there would be any question of her going to work for the foreseeable future.

At the end of the day, I walked in on a scene out of Tennessee Williams. Jana had apparently neither slept nor paused for breath all day. She was hoarse and disheveled and in pain, and she'd begun to pick restlessly at her clothes; AC had helped her change six or eight times. The sedatives the hospital sent, which should have steamrollered her negligible body mass, seemed to metabolize away before AC could take the glass back to the kitchen. AC herself was not much better off, glazed and creaking with the strain of staying calm and cheerful for Jana when she had her own bloody nightmares to deal with on top of fury about the rape and fear about its aftermath.

I took one look and ordered AC out for a walk around the block. Jana looked as if she really didn't want AC to leave, especially to leave her with me. I told Jana I would stay outside too, if that was what she wanted.

"No, no - " Then she saw the point. "I'm being a pain in the ass, aren't I? Something to deal with. Shit! I'd sooner be dead. I reckon everybody in Washington knows what ... knows about - "

"Jana, I don't guess more than a dozen people know anything, and most of those are cops and doctors. Would it help you to talk about it?"

"What's to talk? You were there. You saw the whole fuckin thing. Ha! Good description. What, you want to hear more about it? You need to know how it felt?"

"No - of course not. I want you to be healed, and sometimes talking is a start on that."

"Not to any guy, I'm not talking, I don't care whose uncle you're not. Agh! This is killing me, you've stayed so cool about us. But you look, I've seen you doing it, and that's where it starts. You do it pretty slick, OK, but I know -"

"Wait a second, Jana. Let's not get into stuff like that, or the next thing I'll be arguing with you, and trying to win. Would you consider talking to another woman?"

"She ever been raped? The stupid bitch called up from Rape Crisis hadn't. She got the wrong file or something, thought I'd been persuaded in a GW frat house by some sweat-face Ed major. I told her, Get fucked at knife point, I'll call you."

"I don't know. But she's very perceptive, and she understands a lot about people, and sickness, and - "

"I ain't sick. That fucker in the mask, he's the sick one. Where is he, anyhow? Did they get him?"

"He's dead, Jana. AC shot him."

"Oh, yeah. Shit fire, poor AC. Jesus, what a mess."

She put her face into her hands, and in her pajamas, with her straggly hair darkened to auburn by sweat and woe, she looked more like a teenager with the flu than the darling of the "Style" section.

She drew a shuddering breath. "I'll be OK, Oren. Shit, half the women in the world get raped, and they carry on. It's *material*, wouldn't you guess?"

"Can I use your phone?"

*   *

"Dr. Dienst, I share my impressions with you only because I trust you not ever, ever to speak of them to anyone, including those two women. And because there is no one else I can speak to about it; and I am more worried about your niece than about Jana."

"She's not my niece, but no matter. What makes you worry about her?"

"She speaks of you quite firmly - and fondly - as her uncle. She is abundantly, badly traumatized by what has happened. She is quite other-worldly, very much a lover of the Earth, if not of its population. Jana, on the other hand, small as she is, and brutal as her experience was, and as painful and humiliating her injuries, is tougher. I do not believe - I am not confident of this, but I do not believe the situation was new to her. Though she has lived no longer than AC, she has lived more adventurously among people. She is slight and spectacular in appearance, and she travels in a world that is cavalier about invading and denying personhood. Without in any way making light of her having been raped, I believe she will recover sooner than AC will recover from the double burden of having seen the rape and then bloodily killed the man who did it. Did she tell you ... he was not only raping Jana, he was bragging about it, and about getting around to AC when he was finished with Jana. To sum up, Dr. Dienst, enormous harm has been done, and very great harm may yet flow from this incident. I talked to them as earnestly as I could about the need to isolate that horrible experience, to prevent its infecting the past and future of both women."

"I remember the lecture clearly."

"Yes. Unfortunately for them, of course, no part of their experience was hallucinatory. And in this case, I speak not only metaphorically. That man, according to Jana, had lesions on his body. She reported this to the emergency room personnel, and they gave her antibiotics against ordinary venereal diseases. I certainly hope we are facing nothing worse than that."

"Oh, Christ. You mean AIDS?"

"Dr. Dienst, I don't know. I didn't see the man or his disease. But it was not at all difficult to see that Jana and your niece . . .well, I assume you were surely aware that they had established a physical relationship?"

I sighed, rumpled my hair, drummed my fingers. Of course I was. "Well, but..."

"Who knows, at this point? I certainly don't."

Me either. "Did you talk to them about that?"

"I did not consider it my place. I know and trust you, and I believe that you also know and trust me. That trust does not subsist between either of those women and me." She sighed, and gave me a look full of yin. "And really, Dr. Dienst, it is quite late and I should be going home."

"I am very much in your debt for going to see them. I know you helped them. Would you like a nightcap before you go?"

She took my hand and began the little tuning-up pressures and frictions. "I believe not. I am very relaxed. I will browse your bookshelves."

Yes, I'm afraid so. Amid the death and wreckage, Donia Ma and I went off to bed. Say, or think, what you will; the whole mess was way too much for me, and we were ready for something pleasant, strenuous, and without history or consequences. Why not? In the morning, it would be exactly as if she had never been there, anyhow.

The next day, AC came into my office with a street map. "Oren, where's Columbia Road?"

"It's up in Adams-Morgan. Why?"

She looked evasive. "Oh, there's something I want to go to."

"Sit down a second, I'll show you. But I need to finish the paragraph before I forget what I meant."

She sat down - her knees buckled, more accurately - and when I looked up from the keyboard where I was redrafting what I wanted Liana to ask the mayor of Manosduros, she had put her head back and gone to sleep. Maybe it was the first sleep she'd had in the 60 hours since we walked in on Jana and Paul Hartley McCauley.

What she wanted to know about Columbia Road was, that was where McCauley's funeral was being held. And as much as I argued and wrangled, I couldn't talk her out of it. She went, and she met Mrs. McCauley, Paul Hartley's mother. The consequences of that would emerge some days later, and I'll leave them to then.

16. Curtain

My second-line light flashed as I was in the middle of lining up Liana Mariconas for another try at phoning Manosduros. It was not being easy; a decent interval had passed since our first try had ended in blood, but not enough, I judged, for me to ask AC for a return date to make the call. Saying, in effect, Well, glad that's over, and about that phone call...

So I was trying to persuade a skittery Liana to come to my place for the call, and she was finding every reason not to. By the time we had worked out that she and her back-in-circulation boy friend would come out together, make the call, and go on from there to a movie that was only showing in Silver Spring and Georgetown ("We don' go to no Georgetown, Oren, nothin there but tacky boutiques an' panhandlers, you know?") the little yellow light had given up and gone brown.

For a change, though, Gloria Mondale had picked it up; a few seconds after I finished with Liana, the phone rang, and "Let's Fall in Love" came through, followed by news that a Mr. Gus Snyder had called, that I could reach him until five, and that I had the number.

"Did he say what it was about?"

"No, sir. Good news and bad news, he said. About a girl? Francisca?"

"Francesca!"

"Yes, perhaps that was - "

"Thanks." I looked at my watch: five minutes to five. Sure, I had Gustav Schneider's number, right on my dresser at home. I took the phone off the hook as prophylaxis against incoming calls, and snatched the Maryland yellow pages off the shelf. And there, after flipping through a very long section devoted to Video this and that, I found the four Violinmaker entries huddled at the bottom of a column, among them G. Schneider, Dealer and Luthier. Two minutes to five. I punched the 12 digits it took to call from a Federal office to a shop ten miles away in Maryland, and got Schneider on the eighth ring.

"Man, you just barely got me. If I hadn't been looking for a call on that Lorenzo Bordoni, I'd have never come back. OK, well, shoot."

"Well, I think you called me. About that cello?"

"You don't mean the Bordoni?"

"No, the one you were looking for, for me."

"Right, right. Good news and bad news."

"You found it, and the owner won't sell."

"Close. I found it, and the owner just sold it."

"Damn. Do you think they'd change their mind, either the seller or the buyer?"

"I strongly doubt it. You remember I told you somebody else might be looking for that same cello? I think the new owner's that guy."

"Do you know who it is?"

"Some Italian, I think."

"Geez, they don't have enough cellos in Italy?"

"Got me. Maybe they liked the name. Wasn't the maker Italian?"

"Hyphen American. Damn, that's discouraging, though. Do you know the guy's name?"

"No."

I drummed my fingers and looked out the window. The backstage Yahoos were jumping up and down and beating their chests and puffing out their cheeks with fury. "Well, what about the seller? Is it a done deal?"

"As far as I know, it is. But you could ask her."

"And she is . . .?"

"Lessee. Got it here somewheres. Yeah. A Mrs. Merton Meyerson. Lives in Chicago. Impression I get, she's a widow and it was the hubby's. Took it to a dealer there when he passed on, who sold it for her in a flash, since he'd been contacted by this Italian."

"Hmm. Wasn't he contacted by you, too?"

"Sure. I expect the Italian sounded more urgent, or sweetened the guy, or just called him first. Hate to disappoint you, but I did my best."

"Of course you did." *No you didn't, you crook, you want to sell us one of your miserable boxes,* the Yahoos hollered. "Thanks a lot, Mr. Schneider. I really appreciate your efforts."

"Enough to take another look at the Bordoni?"

"Well, I might drop by and give it a shot on Saturday, if you still have it by then."

"I might. There's a possible buyer, but she's trying to get the owner down to ten, and I know it won't work. I still think twelve'd drive it off the lot for you, though."

"I'll think about it. I'd have to try it out in a couple of rehearsals, though."

"Understood. No problem."

"OK. I'll give it a try. Look, you don't have that lady's address and phone, do you?"

Schneider sighed, as who could blame him? He knew he'd see me on Saturday only if the route to Francesca were truly a dead end. "Yeah, yeah. Mrs. Merton Meyerson, 4710 Lincoln Avenue, Chicago."

He gave me the phone number, too, and before I left, I tried it. No answer, no answering machine. I had to smile, though. Francesca had stayed right in Chicago where I'd left her; Maybe this Meyerson was the very guy who'd come out and said "Hello?" and distracted me enough to break my elbow. It was like getting a message from a historical figure. Well, in a way. AC Gewissner came in as I was loading up my briefcase with Manosduros-related papers and notes, preparatory to trying again to get a copy of the MexiLar agreement. For a few days she had seemed just marginally less depressed than she had been before Dead McCauley's funeral, but it was only shades of grey.

"Hi, AC. How's it going?"

"OK."

"Really?"

"Why not?"

"No reason, I guess, or anyhow none that I couldn't guess at."

She walked to the window, the same that had served as a thought-marshalling point for so many before her. "I'm fine. It's just, a lot of bad things have happened, and I can't seem to get them to stop."

"What else is going on?"

"Oh...nothing you can help with, Oren. Honest. I'm not trying to be mysterious or difficult - God knows! I don't know why I came in here."

I tried not to look at my watch. I was meeting Liana in five minutes in the parking lot. "Would it help if I just listened?"

"Maybe. Some time. I can see you're busy now . . ."

I squared all my stuff into a stack and put it in an envelope. "Tell you what, AC. I have to meet Liana in five minutes, and I don't dare be late, or I'll never get her on board again. Walk down to the parking lot with me, and we'll get started. And I want a definite date for a really long talk this weekend. Would that help?"

"Oren, you're not my uncle. You don't - "

"You forget, I was there too, and I like Jana too. Could we team up on this? Come on, let's get down there."

She didn't say yes; she came into the elevator with me, and when the door closed she just started. "It's just being so, I don't know. So hard, with Jana. She doesn't want any reference to the whole rape business, but if I talk about anything else for any length of time, she tells me to stop being 'tactful.' I know it hit her really hard - Jesus, how could it not? It about kills me to remember it, so how's she going to feel? I just can't see why she's turned against me. She wasn't that way at first."

"Mm. Remember, it's humiliating that we came in and saw her like that."

"Well, of course, Oren. I've done everything I could think of to get her over that. After a week of TLC, I tried - one time - to kid about it, just us girls, you know. Jesus, big mistake, she never lets me forget it. I've tried just seriously telling her how I feel, I've tried talking about other things. Nothing works."

I leaned against the fender of my car. The heat of the parking lot had felt good at first, since the Reaganites - with the Environmental Protection Agency in the lead - had cranked the air conditioning back to full blast to show what a sanctimonious fool Jimmy Carter had been with his conservation decrees. After a few minutes in the murky glare, though, I was starting to sweat.

"How about you, AC?"

"What about me?"

"Well, aren't you upset too?"

"About Jana? What have we been talking about? I love her, Oren. A year ago I'd never believe I could say such a thing, not to some friend of my parents."

"Or your uncle, either? I meant about shooting that kid."

She stood there and looked at the traffic, and then shook her head. "I don't know. I went to his funeral up in Columbia Heights, and met his mother. Even she says he was a lost cause. He knew it himself, Jesus, he bragged about being dead already, why he took that street name. But I sure wish it hadn't been me. I was aiming for his arm, you know that? I was just trying to make him drop the knife. Well, he dropped it all right – damn near killed me with it. But I killed him. I don't care if all the cops and prosecutors in Washington stood up and cheered and sent me home, I don't think I'll ever get over that."

The child of Markus and Sophie. "Have you been able to get out in the woods since you've been here?"

"When would I do that? . . .Sorry. No, I haven't. No time, no car, and I've been OK hanging out with Jana, and doing her kinds of things. Bars and galleries."

"What if we gave Jana a rest for a day and went out to the Blue Ridge or somewhere. Saturday, say. Can you get through a day if you know you've got a break coming the next day?"

"I don't know. Winnebagos? Candy wrappers and condoms on the trail?"

"Not if you get into the forest on the west side. That's a lot less populated, but sure, it's not Alaska by a long shot."

"Oh . . . OK, Oren. Let's do it. You doing this to be nice?"

"No. Well, nice to both of us. I've got some favorite places I haven't seen for months, and I need a break too. Would you be my excuse?"

She shrugged, and we stood in silence while I worried about her, and wondered whether to start worrying about Liana. On that front, at least, I was shortly relieved.

"Hi, Oren, we late? Let me introduce my boy friend, Hervé. Hervé, this is Oren Dienst, and his niece - I think - AC."

"How you been, sir? AC? You the lady plug that guy, was raping your roommate? Good goin'."

I'll say.

*   *

"Don't worry, Oren. These little towns, they still keep old-time schedules. Take the middle of the day off, then work late. He'll be there. Prob'ly talking to some guy, lettin the phone ring. We the kind of people get impatient, he don't want to deal with us. If not, we'll wait." A muffled voice came over the line, and Liana made a face and hung up. "Phone company get impatient now. What's the deal, you can't let it ring forever no more?" She shrugged and dialed again. "Don' cost you nothing, maybe drive him crazy enough to pick it up, he hear it stop and start again."

In the end it took three full cycles of dialing and hanging up until a bark came from the other end just after the start of the fourth. Liana greeted him like a Chicana Girl Scout - with just a hint of something even nicer underneath - who would really like to get to know Señor Paños once this boring business was over with.

I have no idea what she really said, but I had provided a variety of scripts into which she could branch as necessary, first to wade through whatever layers of non-Anglophone bureaucracy there might be between us and Paños' direct line (there were none) and then to start with a simple friendly anonymous quest for information, falling back through a series of increasingly deceitful covers about journalistic and then Federal inquiries, each riskier and less verifiable than the last.

As it turned out, Señor Paños was still so worried and outraged that he was more than happy to discuss the details of what MexiLar had promised with any caller whatsoever, or at least one as sweet-voiced as Liana. She wrote out on a legal pad - this truly gifted linguist - a running series of notes in abbreviated but readable English that, as far as I could see, didn't lag or slow down the real-time conversation at all.

And yes, as a matter of fact, MexiLar had promised the moon in the way of cleanup, that having been one of the points on which the few skeptics in Manosduros had managed to influence the final agreement. MexiLar would guarantee a safe, non-toxic, and shipshape site, with full restoration of the original scenic appearance within one year. They had posted a bond for cleanup, all of $5,000, which must have been worth a brief smile to the accountant in St. Louis who wrote it off the debit side of this multimillion- dollar coup. I held up my hand in a time-out gesture, and Liana pinned Señor Paños to the phone with a brief burst of friendly verbiage.

"This is good stuff, Liana. Can he send us a copy?"

She asked. "No way. He is holding on to the only copy they have for dear life, and wouldn' consider sending it even to the distinguished Señor Ingeniere Dienst, whom he remembers with much affection."

"Well, I meant a photocopy, not the original."

More talk. "The nearest copy machine is in Nogales, a hundred kilometers away. How important is this, to send him and two constables there to make a copy?"

"I guess there's no point even asking about a fax?"

"I truly doubt it, Oren." She spoke briefly, smiled, and turned back. "He had the opportunity to watch one in action during his recent visit to Washington, D.C., and has put funds for one in the next budget. However … "

"Never mind. I really need to go there myself. Tell him if he would be willing to let me see the document and take me on a tour of the site, I will be pleased to bring a portable copier and leave it in Manosduros as a token of my personal thanks."

Liana pulled a "big man" face, and relayed this news to the Mayor. "He says fine, and he will await your pleasure; and please to bring me along. Don't even think about asking, and I don't think he believed the part about the copier."

"Pentagon surplus, one year old, still in the carton, and mine to dispose of as I see fit for the betterment of International Environmental Cooperation. If I decide to get scrupulous and reimburse for it because this is my personal project, it'll still cost me less than the plane ticket. Get a good address, and tell him I'll send word as soon as I know when I'll be there. Tell him it'll be within the next couple of weeks, and meantime, lock that agreement away and don't give it to anybody."

"No danger there, I think." She signed off with florid and lingering politeness while I went to find Hervé, who had refused a beer and settled down with a Scientific American.

"Great article here on neural transport, Dr. Dienst. You read it?"

"No. I've heard it well spoken of."

*   *

On Friday over lunch hour, I got Mrs. Merton Meyerson of Chicago to pick up her phone, and got two pieces of news, one of them a good deal better than the other. The maybe-good news was that there had been some kind of hitch in the electronic transfer of funds from the Banco Degli Artigiani in Milan; she had already given the Chicago dealer permission to ship Francesca, so now both the cello and the money to pay for it were in Italy, a situation that did not please Mrs. Meyerson much.

"Would you consider canceling the deal over it?" I asked, without much hope. "Whatever they paid, I'll be glad to match it, plus 10%, and reimburse you for the cost to ship it back."

"Well," she said vaguely, "that's very attractive of course, but I don't know . . ."

No point in coming across here as a crazed opportunist. "I know you wouldn't want to go back on your word on a done deal. But if it really falls through, my offer still stands."

"I will ask the dealer," she said. "But I honestly doubt that this will prove to be more than a temporary hitch. In case it doesn't, please leave me a number where I can reach you."

I did, and got the second piece of news. "I'm afraid," Mrs. Meyerson apologized, "that I'm quite poor at catching names, and I really didn't catch yours. If you wouldn't mind spelling it?"

I didn't mind, but the silence that followed was far too long to result from the slowest penmanship.

"Hello?"

"Mr. Dienst, I don't quite know what to say. Are you Oren Walter Dienst?"

My father used to take me on what seemed like very long walks, and when we got back he'd swing me up into Mother's lap and say, "Walker's his middle name, momma."

"Walker. But - "

"Well, I guess I know why you're so anxious to get your hands on that particular cello. But you're too late, I'm afraid. I've already sent it to St. Louis."

"I beg your pardon? You sent it to St. Louis? I thought the buyer was an Italian?"

"Yes, of course. I was referring to your paper."

"What paper?"

"Come, Mr. Dienst. You are not fooling me, and I frankly resent this whole charade. You are no more a cellist than I am, and you are wasting my time. I sent your confession, which we found in the case when I took it to be sold, to St. Louis, to Molar Chemical, where I assume they will know what to do with it. Good-"

I managed to gasp "Wait!" before my knees buckled. I sat on the floor by the phone table. "You mean that thing was still in the music pocket? Good grief, and you sent it to Molar? I will be damned. Honest, Mrs. Meyerson, I'd forgotten all about that. It's ancient history." I hoped. Rick McIntear would have a time with it because, unlike the recantation I'd filed with the County Attorney, this version implicated me directly in at least a temporary fraud. "Hello? Are you still there?"

"I am. You claim you were calling only about the cello when there was a damning document with it that is signed by you, a chemist of some kind? Why should I believe that?"

"Well, I'm not sure I would either; but please believe me, that referred to a closed incident, and I participated in it under duress. In fact, that whole mess is something I'd rather forget about."

"I bet. All right, Mr. Cello-player. You have a cello now?"

I reached over and got Schneider's cello out of its corner and plunked the strings into the phone. "Hear it?"

"Yes. Oh, my. You really play?"

"Yes. Not professionally, but . . . well, I play."

"Let's hear something. Right now."

301

"Gladly. Bach OK?"

"Prelude from the G major Unaccompanied Suite."

"Stand by."

I tuned up and played it as well as I could with shaking fingers. When I finished, I picked up the phone gingerly. "Mrs. Meyerson?"

I heard a nose being blown. "Oh, my. Mr. Dienst. You're not too bad, but when Merton played that, I used to just melt. It's half the reason I married the guy, rest his soul. Well. You may not be the crook I thought you were, but I think I'm going to say this. You want that cello so much, you come to Chicago and put a check in my hands, let me look at you. Are you willing to drop everything and come here? Wednesday, say?"

"I guess I could arrange that. Sure."

"All right. Make your reservations, but call me Tuesday night. If the Italians still haven't paid me by then, and if you can put a check in my hands for - oh, half of it, say - I'll cancel on the Italians. You'll still have to arrange to get it over to America, though. I don't think they're gonna send it out of whatever goodness of their hearts."

"Probably not. And how much would half of it be?"

There was another longish silence. Here was a woman who did not believe in using fillers while she thought about something.

"Mr. Dienst, I have to confess. Anything I charge would be an abomination. We got it for free. The dealer said I ought to get $8,000 for it. Can you imagine? I told him I didn't need a penny over five, and that's what the Italian fella is supposed to pay. Would that be too much for you?"

"No, it wouldn't, and what's more, I'll stand by my first offer of a 10% bonus. That'd be, well, $5500. How's that?"

"Too much. $5250, not a penny more."

"You're a tough bargainer, Mrs. Meyerson. Tell you what. If we can agree on this, I'll tell you who left it on your doorstep."

"There you messed up, smart guy. It wasn't ours, it was Wolf's, that Merton played quartets with. It was you, anyhow, had to be. What did you do that for?"

"Long story, Mrs. Meyerson. Stay tuned."

The momentum of euphoria. I know it was the relief of having something - anything - not go completely wrong that made me call Donia Ma and propose that she drop everything and come to Chicago with me, just for a lark. The notion trampled all over our unspoken, unspeakable role assignments, but I plead stupidity. This particular piece began very shortly before daybreak on Saturday morning with a very realistic dream of dancing with Donia Ma, a thing we had never once come close to doing, the band playing *South of the Border*, Donia Ma fitting herself up close to me and whispering in my ear, "Yes, Oren. Let's do it," which I knew meant, Let's run away for a honeymoon in Manosduros. Up to then, our interludes of therapeutic sex had followed a pretty regular rhythm, always prefaced by the same script. I began weaving in variations and puns to see if I could make her break character, without much luck. But knowing her particular needs and preferences did let me play a more active role during what she called the "technical phase" - meaning, for you younger folks, the actual screwing, as distinct from the setting-up of the occasion, the verbal foreplay, and the talk-down to sleep afterwards. I suppose the slight self-assertion went to my head a bit.

Anyhow, setting up the occasion was always a mild challenge. One of the rules I learned early on was that I was not to have expectations, even to the penciling-in point, of sex every Sunday or every other Sunday - though that became pretty much the schedule - since that would not only demean our relationship to a mere weekend affair, but it would imply a history, planning, a routine; and none of these had been true the first time, or would be properly stochastic. There always had to be, like then, some other ostensible purpose to our meeting, like attending a play or sharing a meal, after which I was supposed to invite her to the condo for a nightcap, which invitation she would always receive with mild surprise; a pleasant, unexpected, maybe a little eccentric notion. Never, never did we 'share intercourse' at her place, though she never told me why. It was just one of her rules.

Once, awkwardly enough, we were actually in her office finishing a rare acupuncture session when something in her eye informed me that she was in a sharing mood. I never had to be convinced; I began my lines ("Would you like a nightcap?") and was startled to hear her accept, but allow that she stocked no nightcap materials, and did I still have that very pleasant plum brandy she had once enjoyed. So, nothing for it but to bundle into the car, the little film of moisture already bedewing her brow, and hightail it for Silver Spring, tripping over each other to get to the elevator, stepping on each other's lines to get through the dialogue. Disrobing that time had little of the dilatory playfulness she so enjoyed.

Well.

Something has let me get a little waspish here, and Donia Ma, taken as a whole and recognizing the enormous good she did me, certainly does not deserve it. I have written it, it belongs to the past, I cannot unwrite it. Blame it entirely on the closer, which went up, as they say, at 7:30 am on Saturday, August 20, 1983, the day after my conversation with Mrs. Meyerson.

§§

Scene: An interior. There is a neatly made bed, a book shelf, a liquor cabinet. No actors are present on stage; we hear only their voices, lightly distorted as before by telephone fidelity.

Donia Ma *(Anxiously)*: I beg your pardon? You wish me to travel with you to Chicago? For what purpose?

Dienst: Well, I thought it might be fun to get away together, you know. Have a little sort of a honeymoon, I guess.

Donia Ma: What an extraordinary notion. We are not newlyweds.

Dienst: *(Nettled; apologetic)*: Oh, right. Silly me.

Donia Ma: Dr. Dienst, let me correct, if I may, what appears to be a natural and understandable misapprehension. I will begin with an apology. It is evident that our recent regular sharing of intercourse has led you to become fond of me, and the fact is that, for my part, -

Dienst *(Waspish)*: Yes, perhaps I have. I guess that happy little song you sang to me as we were drifting off last time was what misled me about your own -

Donia Ma: You were not misled. I have become very fond of ... our regular meetings. But don't you see, Dr. Dienst, I can do you no further good if I become emotionally involved. What kind of physician is it who sings pleasant little love songs to her patient?

Dienst: A happy one, I'd have said.

Donia Ma *(Warmly, rewarding the correct answer)*: Exactly! Happy; not alert, judicious, diligent, all the things a good physician should be. I was in danger of becoming a bad physician to you, and I would rather - *(sighs; but when she speaks again, the warmth has become judicious diligence)* I would rather we had no relationship at all, than that of a trusting patient to a bad physician.

Dienst: And you can't imagine anything but a physician-patient relationship?

Donia Ma: That is the relationship that has been the basis of our success. I believe it would be a mistake to imagine that we could be as successful in other roles.

Dienst: "Success"?

Donia Ma: Yes. We have succeeded in freeing your musical and your sexual functions to a substantial degree, wouldn't you say?

Dienst: Madam, were't freer or more substantial I'd needs spend on tailors what fiddlemakers get.

Donia Ma *(Laughs)*: Very amusing, Dr. Dienst. You really can be quite funny.

Dienst: Never such a hoot as when I've dropped character. I apologize for misinterpreting our relationship.

Donia Ma: Dr. Dienst, it is for me to apologize. I hear the hurt in your voice, and it just illustrates how thoroughly I have neglected my own proper role. "First, do no harm," another excellent rule of Western medicine, and I have broken it. And furthermore, I have been aware of my carelessness since I caught myself singing that little love song when I was with another patient. I am grateful to you that you precipitated this conversation; I was at a loss how to do so myself. There are, after all, situations to which all my training and any amount of thought provide no solution. When such situations arise, -

Dienst: I know. You step aside. Is that it?

Donia Ma: I would not have put it that way.

Dienst: But you did.

A pause.

Donia Ma: I see. You are being funny again.

Dienst: Not intentionally. But then, they never are.

Donia Ma: Funny and inscrutable. I have an uncle like that.

Dienst: I must meet him some time.

Donia Ma: I would just as soon you did not.

(Another considerable pause.)

Donia Ma: I believe I hear the bell downstairs. If there was nothing further ...?

Dienst: I don't think there will be. Thank you for your many successful therapies. Goodbye, Donia.

Donia: Goodbye ... Oren.

- Curtain -

§§§

17. Sacrament

AC and I had a quiet drive out past the Blue Ridge to the western mountains, seeking relief from our real lives. AC looked out the passenger window and I out the windshield for a while, and then after a rest stop we exchanged views, without saying much. I had walked in at nine that morning on a tight-lipped scene full of Kleenex and suitcases. Jana was leaving for California to reclaim her center, and was vague about how long that might take. I was willing to bet it wouldn't happen before AC went back to Alaska, and if I hadn't been so freshly put in her position by Donia Ma, I would have been hearty and avuncular with AC about how this was for the best, how AC could hardly expect Jana to move to Alaska, while AC couldn't expect to be happy and productive forever on the fringes of Jana's world. And so forth. I saved it. AC knew all that, she was no teenager but a boomer with grey hairs, and she was hurting. And besides, I was hurting too. At Strasburg, we stopped at a little convenience store to buy cold drinks to go with the lunches we'd glumly thrown into AC's pack, and I palmed in a flat bottle of dark rum. It looked like being a long day.

At the trailhead, I showed AC the map. Knowing her genetics, I didn't expect her to dally around waiting for a middle-aged bureaucrat to puff up the trail with her. "There's a good lunch spot at the top of the second ridge, right here. You'll know it when you get to it, it has these white sandstone slabs rising almost straight up out of the valley, so you can see out over the Shenandoah for a long ways. Do you want to wait for me there, or shall we split up the lunch now?"

"I'll be there. What, about two?"

"OK. Take it easy, AC." She gave me a funny smile; she was out of sight before I had the map folded.

I walked, I tried to be happy that I was in the woods again. For a while, back in the '70's when I was feeling good about the EPA and my role in it, I came out to these woods fairly often, maybe a dozen times a year in all seasons. I got to know the ridges and the geology pretty well. In the past couple of years, I don't think I'd been out here more than twice. But in fact today I was having trouble seeing the trees for the forest of depression.

I felt, first of all, rejected by Donia Ma, but behind that selfish and mean-spirited, and then stupid. And yet another layer down, horny; it had been almost two weeks since my last un-date with Donia Ma, and this weekend we would have been, by our don't-mention-it protocol, due for a reprise. I had planned to spring the Chicago trip during the overture, before the nightcap line, but I let myself be carried away by the thrill of nearly catching up with Francesca, and I jumped the gun. *And did you feel light-headed and euphoric when you set out on that course of action, Dr. Dienst?*

No, I felt lucky, and heavy of loin.

I got to the sandstone slabs, wringing with sweat, a bit before two, and leaned against them in the heavy sunlight. I saw no sign of AC. I was certain I had not passed her on the trail. Not that I had been all that alert or judicious during my funk-ful walk, but I knew AC well enough to know that she'd never let me get ahead of her. I leaned against the sandstone parapet and looked out over the woods below. A hot, stiff wind was blowing off the valley against the cliff face, and hawks circled in the updraft, planning supper. The quartzite rose in a sheer unbroken face to the ridgetop where I stood, the last three feet of it, no more than six inches thick, forming the parapet I was leaning on. Idly, I picked up an acorn and rolled it down the slab of rock. It plunged and bounced farther and farther out from the wall until it dwindled from view, a long drop below me. The motion interested a hawk for a few seconds, and it made a pass at the bouncing dot, but when it saw what it was chasing, gave a contemptuous flip of wing and zoomed along parallel to the cliff and about fifty feet below me, rising straight up when the clear sandstone ended in a line of cedars clinging to a joint in the rock. And that is what led my eye to AC.

She was squatting on the top of the parapet at the far end a hundred yards away, balanced on the balls of her feet and leaning outward against the hot wind. I gave a gasp of fear - even at this distance I could see her swaying in and out with the rise and fall of the wind. All it would take for her to tumble down the rock face like an acorn would be the least misjudgment, a sudden drop in the wind, even simple fatigue. I had no idea how long she had been there, waiting to see if she would live or die.

"Oh, Jesus," I whispered, and I stepped cautiously away from the parapet. I ran down the trail toward AC, trying to be quiet. When I got to her, her eyes were closed, tears streaming. I could see quivers of fatigue running up her legs from the calf muscles that were holding her balanced, but I certainly didn't wait to see more or think of tactics. I grabbed her jacket and pulled her back on top of me.

She gave a squawk of surprise, and we both fell onto the trail, where a piece of sandstone cracked into my butt so hard I saw stars. AC jumped up and glared at me for a second, but then she began to breathe hard, a kind of 'huh, huh' that never resolved itself between laughter and crying. She staggered over and sat down beside me, hyperventilating and pounding the earth, until she managed to say, "Oh, Oren, my God! I thought it was Dead McCauley."

"AC, what in the world were you doing up there like that?" As if I didn't know. She didn't answer for a while, too busy with gut-ripping exhalations of anger and sorrow. After a time she calmed down, and I could see when the ranger stepped in and took charge. She looked at the sky with red eyes drying fast, an AC gesture familiar from years back.

"I don't know. I was waiting for you, and leaning against that rock wall, and the next thing I knew I was up on it. I don't remember doing it, and I was scared as hell for a second, and then I thought, well, I must really want to jump, or I wouldn't be up here. I just stayed there listening and thinking about things. After a while I found I could lean on the wind, and that was comfortable, and I thought, well, if I'm supposed to jump, the wind will stop, and it'll all be over with. So I kept on thinking and getting kind of tired waiting, and then there you were. Are you OK?"

"Well, my butt hurts, and I'm hungry. How about you?"

"Same, except for my butt." She drew a breath, and put on her armor again. "It would have been grass, though, if you'd been any longer. See? Wind's stopped."

We ate lunch there, leaning on the rock slabs and looking over the valley. I let AC point out various interesting sights, and showed her the notch in the far ridge, maybe two miles away, where this trail crossed it and plunged down past prime camping sites on the way to the North Fork of the Shenandoah. "Maybe some time - "

"Yeah, I know. I found a really good one, by a waterfall."

"Wait a minute. You've been to the other side of that ridge, and back, while I was coming up here?"

"Sure. When I used to hike with the family in Alaska, I was always the first one to get to the campsite. Of course, it was never this hot. I was a little tired, I admit."

I looked at her in awe. "Holy shit. You left Markus and Sophie Gewissner in the dust? You know what they used to call them when they were students?"

"All kinds of stuff, I expect. Mom was usually slowed down with babies, or being pregnant, but it used to gall Daddy some, all right." She turned to me. "Oren, would you be willing to camp out here tonight? I really don't want to go back to Washington tonight and find - well, whatever I'd find. I'll face it tomorrow when I have to, but I'll tell you, when I was up on that rock, every time I thought about walking into that apartment I'd lean out a little bit."

"Well, we'd have to go back down for food, and we don't have a tent or anything . . ."

"Well, we can save some lunch and eat light. I don't mean stay for a week. Just overnight. I've got a plastic tarp and line we can put up for shelter if we need it."

I tried to remember what I had left behind to do this weekend, other than brood about Donia Ma. "All right, AC. Let's do it."

"OK, fine. I'll go on ahead and grab a spot. You know the one by the waterfall?"

"Yes. A great one. By all means, go get it. Though, come to think of it, I haven't seen a lot of people."

"One bunch, you must have met them, with the purple and teal outfits?"

"And the radio. Let's hope there's no more like that up there."

"I bet not. I bet we'll be lucky. I feel real lucky now. But I won't leave it to luck. See you there."

"OK. And - AC? No more thrills?"

She patted my cheek. "Only the thrill of arrival. Arrivederch'."

Arrivederch', for surely. How long would it take Jana to crystallize into a blade inside AC?

By the time I got my bruised butt to the campsite, the sun was setting over the far ridge, and the waterfall was playing deep continuo to a chorus of cicadas bitching and jeering about the heat. AC had a fire going, either out of Alaskan habit or just for something to do. Her tarp was rigged between four trees, and she had collected enough moss and leaves to make what were recognizable attempts at soft spots under it.

"I figure if we put our outer clothes over that and sleep in our underwear, it'll be fairly comfortable, and goodness knows we won't get cold. I was worried about bugs, but I've got a little repellent, and they don't seem too bad, even by the water."

"Late frosts. We've had a low-bug year."

"Huh. That doesn't seem to bother 'em in Alaska, but I guess it's different bugs."

I slumped against a tree and said, dreading the answer, "OK, how much lunch do we have left?"

"OK. Three, four, five fig bars. An apple, that's for liquids and toothbrushing. I mean I guess we couldn't drink this, right?"

"Not unless you fancy three days of diarrhea."

"Hmph. Anyhow, half a braunschweiger sandwich, and half a cheese sandwich. Which sandwich do you want?"

"I don't care. Either way, we'll be ready for breakfast when it happens."

"Oh, pooh. The Indians used to go out in the woods and fast for days, so they'd have visions."

"Well, I have to be back at work on Monday, so I brought a vision short-cut." I held up the little flask of rum.

"Now you're talkin'. Great for cuts and bruises, too."

I looked at her carefully. "AC, are you all right now? Really?"

"I don't know." She held out her hand for the flask. "Let's have a swig, I'll have a diagnostic vision."

We passed the dusk by making a wordless project out of the fire, and finally just sat against trees and watched it burn itself down while we accounted for maybe half of the little flask of rum, leaving us in pretty deep gloom all around. Eventually we split the apple and crawled under the tarp - not exactly replete, but not hungry any more. AC watched my wincing business of getting out of my jeans and settling against the moss, and clucked.

"Let's have a look at that butt."

"Well, uh, I'm sure it'll be fine."

"Oren, don't be a prude. Roll over." And in the last of the firelight she yanked down my underwear and clucked again. Next thing I knew she was rubbing rum into the bloody place, which certainly bore out Socrates' refutation of the Hedonists, that there are plenty of things in this world that are pleasant and painful at the same time.

"This is gonna get sticky," she remarked as she pulled up my shorts and gave them a smack. "Gin or vodka would've been better."

"I'll think of that, next time," I gritted. "Thanks, AC. I'm about zonked, so unless you want to talk, or tell jokes or ghost stories - " I bit my lip. AC said nothing, but I had plenty to say to myself. Goddamn smart mouth.

I lay there and listened to the waterfall and pretty soon found it knew the script. Would you like a nightcap? Thank you, replied the chaos, I am quite relaxed. I will browse your shelves. I'm vasectomized. I enjoy being undressed . . .

Rick McIntear and Ferd Bakker drove me out onto the bridge where Montoro had been so I could see for myself the enormous, bottomless hole they had made. The sound track was silent Bach, and look here, Donia Ma stepping naked from Rick's back seat, and she was going to show me something new - at last - involving midair sex. "It will be just as if we were on the softest bed you can imagine, Dr. Dienst. You will enjoy it, I promise."

Nobody pushed, but naked and coupled we fell, faster and faster. "Terminal velocity, Dr. Dienst. Union Station coming up." I looked over her shoulder and saw the Mississippi rushing toward us, little splashes and swirls shining. I clutched at Donia Ma and trapped her skull in my left elbow and began to pound on it, on her smug, impenetrable brain, with a stony fist, and with joy I felt her crunch like a limestone fossil and I was trying to scream

when I woke with faint moonlight in my eyes to hear AC crying softly beside me.

I listened while my pulse slowed, and decided she was sleeping. I thought about the pros and cons of dormant and conscious sorrow, and finally reached over and touched her. She sighed and ground her teeth. "Yes."

"There," I said. "Don't cry. Things will get better, AC."

She took another deep breath, and held it for a long time. When she breathed out at last, it was a shaky laugh. "Oren? Is it you?"

"Yes. I'm here."

"Oh. I just had the most amazing dream. Betty McCauley – Dead McCauley's mother? - was here, down by the creek where you were sitting, and she looked right at me. She looked so hard, it scared me, and then she asked me, Was it you? And I said, Yes, I just had to save Jana, I didn't mean to kill him. And she shook her head, and looked at me as if I was her daughter - you know? - as if I'd done something that was both good and bad, and she said, *If it wasn't you it'd be another one.* She understood. I think she forgave me. I'm not really awake, you know, but maybe I can forgive Jana. She can't help what she's doing. I understand that. It's OK. I still love her, I love her more than ever, but I'm not mad and hurt any more. Maybe I will be when I wake up. This is great, Oren. You should try it."

I tried it. I took my time and started small. I thought about Ferd Bakker and forgave him for my nightmare. I forgave

Gloria Mondale her lite music. "All right. I forgive Donia Ma." It was no big epiphany.

"You forgive Donia Ma for what?"

"Oh, it's a long story."

"We have all night."

"Isn't it almost morning?"

"Certainly not. I don't think it can be much past midnight."

I didn't believe that, but I had no basis for any other belief. I looked at the moon with my half-century astigmatic eyes and I let the usual interesting array of streaks and halos play around it while I began at the beginning and talked about Donia Ma and me. I didn't leave out anything. AC dozed off twice, once waking herself with a solid snore, and in between made little listening grunts and uh-huh's. I think maybe I dozed off myself for part of it. By the time I reached the end, somewhere in the whole story I had - without ever wanting to, and still hurt and mad as hell at her - "forgiven" Donia Ma, and found it meant letting go. "What it is, I guess is, I'm mad at myself for mistaking fondness and therapy for love. Or devotion, or whatever would let you drop everything and run off to Chicago for no reason but to be with somebody. Silly me. God, it's hot."

"It is, it really is..." AC's voice trailed off to blend with the night bugs and the waterfall, and I leaned on an elbow to look at her. The moon had long since slid into the foliage on the far ridge, and by the few straggly photons left I could barely pick out the black globe of her head and the muscular curves half-covered by her tee shirt. She was lying on her side, legs sprawled and her upper arm raised behind her head in an attitude that thrust one breast toward the faint starlight. Running the pre-copulatory lines with the waterfall had done Pavlovian work on my autonomic nervous system (triple burner, if that makes more sense to you) and I found to my fury I was getting restless and aroused. Hold it, Oren. Think of a cow. The stupidity of getting turned on by a virtual niece half my age and pining for another woman was of no moment to the old triple burner, blazing away as if it were Donia Ma beside me rubbing the knuckle of my ring finger. I closed my eyes and gingerly rolled onto my side, facing away from AC, trying to keep my sweaty shirt between me and the moss beneath me. *She's not really your niece, you know,* said the waterfall. *She wouldn't mind at all if you just rubbed her neck a little bit. She'd like it. Fifty's not that old, for a guy. We bet if you just rubbed her neck, she'd wiggle her butt back into your lap like Donia Ma. Wouldn't that feel great?*

"Oren?" whispered AC. "Are you asleep?"

"No." Trying not to sound guilty or furious.

"You know what the waterfall's saying to me now?"

"Uh. What?"

"It sounds like Mama telling me to get out of these sweaty clothes and get bathed. How about a dip? I'm just broiling."

"A dip? Skinny?"

"Well, darn it, I left my suit back home. Yes. Does that bother you?"

"I guess not."

"Liar. Am I giving you a hard time?"

"Slightly."

"I'm sorry. Go to sleep. I promise not to drip on you when I come back."

She stood up, and a second later her t-shirt plopped down by the edge of the tarp, sending out a little puff of woman sweat. There is no smell like it. A faint, swaying form groped its way toward the voices of the waterfall, and I lay there feeling hot, dirty, and mad. When splashing sounds rose above the steady chatter of the fall, that was just too much. I rose in my turn and stripped, pulling briefs away from a taffy-like patch of rum and blood, and felt my way down to the water.

"AC?"

I heard her voice over the racket of the water. "Oren! Get your aging body in here. It's cool and nice."

I followed the sound, and when I was knee deep I saw a hand reaching out of blackness. I grasped it and let her pull me into the center of the pool, with the waterfall clamoring beside us and sending jillions of cool little bubbles rising along our bodies. At the base of the falls, the flow had worn out a pool, chest-deep and as black as a cave under the shelter of the cliff and the trees beside it. Looking back to the shore, I saw a faint shimmer of starlight, but none of it penetrated to where we were. We were alone and invisible.

"This is swell, AC," I projected over the noise. "Think you could sleep here?"

"What?"

"I said," I shouted, "Let's sleep here."

"Last one awake has to promise to pull the other one out."

I smiled a silent and invisible smile, and sang a deep note I was confident would be lost in the roar. I hunkered down until the water was under my chin and felt the coolness seeping through the sore muscles and baffled inner workings of my body. The bottom of the pool was lined with smooth, fist-sized rocks, and I picked one up.

"Oren." AC groped across my chest until she found my arm, and pulled me close, face to face so to speak. I still could not see her, but I certainly could feel her. She wrapped her arms around my waist, and said something in a quiet voice, placing her mouth close enough to my ear that I could feel the little rum-and-apple balloons of her words. Alarm and affection wrestled over what little space was left below my heart. I twisted to minimize frontal contact. "AC, I'm not sure this is such a good idea."

"Don't be scared, Oren. I need to talk without shouting. I need someone I trust to come very close and tell me what they see."

"All right. I just want you to realize that things might happen over which I may not have full control."

"Meaning?"

"Well, for Pete's sake ..." Ah, Jesus. "Meaning that when a slippery naked beautiful woman wraps her arms around a guy's waist, he's going to respond, I don't care who she is, unless he's in a coma. And maybe then. I just don't want you to think I'm getting any ... well, ideas."

A dry laugh. "Oren, in the last month I've fallen in love with another woman, I've killed a guy, and I've just missed killing myself over it. With all due respect, that sort of puts that stuff in a larger perspective. I won't get upset if you don't. For that matter, I'm not some hard-rock lesbian, and you're not really my uncle. I'd be honored to go to bed with you any time, though

I guess it'd be like going to bed with a cross between my father and Carl Sagan."

I had to laugh. "Well, that solved that problem. How many times can you do it in one night, Dr. Sagan?"

"Billions and billions," she howled. When we had subsided a bit, I wrapped my arms around her in turn, dropping the rock behind her. "AC, thank you for the vote of confidence. That feels better than actually getting worked over by Donia Ma. Do you want me to tell you what I see - not now, it's like the inside of a cow, but what I've seen all year?"

"Yes."

"I see a strong, handsome woman with a good brain and the right attitude. I see nothing amiss or awful or wrong."

"But . .?" She was actually bracing herself.

"But nothing. That's it. If MTV did integrity and compassion videos, you'd be a millionaire."

She was silent, and then I felt her invisibly crying again. "I'm sorry," she said. "I'm sorry. Jana called me a murderous bitch last night, and it really stuck. I thought, OK, she got that absolutely dead on."

I drew a breath through my teeth and put a soothing hand on the side of her head, feeling warm tears on her cheek. "Jana's not going to do anything but hurt other people until she gets over what happened to her. I think you've got to let her go, AC."

She buried her face in my shoulder and I rubbed her neck, indeed, feeling only strength.

"Oren, will you baptize me?"

"Huh? Why?"

"I don't know. Mama and Daddy never did. I feel horrible and sad and bloody. Can't Protestants baptize each other?"

I considered. Wasn't there something about the priesthood of all believers? What did that encompass? "Well, if not, I guess I'll just have to take the responsibility. I think if it's an emergency and there's no ordained minister nearby . . ."

"It is, and I sure hope there isn't."

"OK, then. Here goes. I think there might be some preliminary stuff about acknowledging Jesus as your Lord and Savior. Is that want you want?"

"Not exactly, but then I'm not sure what I want. I want to feel clean all the way through."

"Well, I'll try. AC, do you feel as if there are things you need to confess, to get off your, uh, your conscience?"

"Yes."

"What are they?"

"Well, for one thing, I don't feel very good about having sex with Mutt." She sighed. "With Jana."

"Why not?"

"It's indecent and unnatural."

"Who thinks that?"

"Well, everybody."

"Not everybody. Did you do your best to make Jana feel loved and protected, and did you praise and admire and support her artistic career?"

"Yes, I did."

"Did having sex with her feel consistent with how you felt about her in other ways?"

"Yes. I think so."

"Did she enjoy the sex, and did she initiate it as often as you, and did you ever cajole or force her?"

"Yes, to the first two, sure, she initiated the whole thing. And no to the last."

"Then I don't see anything indecent about it. But just in case, I absolve you. What else?"

"Well, no ... oh, Jesus, Oren. I murdered that boy, I really did. I didn't just kill him, I hated him, and I was hating him when I shot him. I said I was aiming for his arm, but that's bullshit. There wasn't time to aim at anything, but you notice I got him three times dead center. I was either trying to kill him, or I was awful lucky."

"He was raping Jana, and bragging about it, right in front of you."

"I could have saved her without killing him."

"How?"

"Well, by ... I don't know. By waiting until the cops came."

"And let Jana go on being raped, humiliated, in pain, with us there, while we waited for the distant wail of sirens?"

"OK, OK. But the fact is, I killed him on purpose. No matter how rotten he was, he was alive, and life is good, even for rotten bastard rapists."

Well, she was right about that. "You saved other women from suffering what Jana did. There's a woman walking around D.C. right now, and life is good for her because Dead McCauley was too dead to rape her this week."

"That's probably right. But maybe he'd have reformed. No chance of that now. I murdered him."

"All right, you did. Are you sorry?"

"Yes!"

"Do you acknowledge yourself a murderer in the sight of God, and beyond any hope of redemption, except by grace?"

She buried her head tighter in my neck. "I guess."

"Do you, or not?"

"Yes, yes. I do. I killed a boy, and that makes me a killer. A murderer."

"That's a very serious matter."

"I know. Jesus, of course it is."

"What are you going to do about it?"

"Do?" She was crying again now, softly, bitterly.

"Yes. You can't bring Dead back. What can you do?"

"I don't see anything I can do."

I stroked her head. "Don't forget Dead. Always remember him. Maybe you'll have a chance to adopt a homeless baby, or have a baby of your own if you want to. When you do that, do it remembering Dead McCauley. You are such a thoroughly good woman that I know you'll find ways to add to the goodness of life instead of taking it away, and you'll do it many times over. What name do you want to be baptized by?"

" ... I have a choice?"

"Apparently so. The priest always says that. Well, sure. You could always change your name legally, anyhow. What say?"

"Boy, the times I got called 'omelet' when kids found out what A. C. stands for. No, I guess Allmut Cushing. What else could I be?"

"Indeed. This is a long way from holy water, but ..." I found the top of her head, and picked up a handful of water and pressed it there. "Allmut Cushing Gewissner, I baptize you in the name of the Father, the Son, and the Holy Ghost; I declare you absolved of the matters you have confessed, and Ready For Anything. Here we go."

I lowered us, legs tangling, into the fizzing, pitch-black water, and we floated free from our mooring on the stony bottom. Turbulence pitched us over and delivered us under the plunge of the falls, and I lost track of up and down until my nose scraped the bottom. We rose to stand directly in the battering. It was a chaos of breath, slaty water, and pounding blood. I felt AC pulling at me, and the water receded; and then we were on the bank, with AC a rising ghost next to me shouting for joy under the stars.

I had long since dried, sitting naked against a tree on my sweatshirt in the humid darkness, AC opposite me against a rock. We had dozed more or less in synchrony and talked about nothing much and whatever in particular until a deck of cloud began to extinguish even the starlight. What had been a moving blur with darker pockets of shadow became only a voice out of deep blackness. Maybe my own reciprocal disappearance was what released her to talk ever more frankly about Jana, what Jana liked and hated and needed, and about the cost of that to AC, what she had learned from Jana and had taught her. She was ambivalent about whether Dead McCauley's rape of Jana had been the detonator of their relationship, or a hindrance to the self-destruction that was waiting in the indefinite near future. AC was too sturdy to sign on for a permanent bout of Jana, and in fact Jana had been perfectly frank that she expected this liaison, like all previous, to crumble.

"She's not made to live with for long, Oren. She's a complete egomaniac, I hated her by the time she got raped, and I still love her."

"So you think you'd have broken it off without that happening?"

"Maybe sooner. The rape screwed it all up, we both saw I couldn't kick her out in that shape. And that drove her crazy, the brat."

I wondered whether to reciprocate AC's frankness by talking about Cindy Something, and going through the Love Decades without loving anyone. While I was making up my mind not to, AC began singing.

It was some kind of alien song that appeared slowly out of the waterfall and used it as accompaniment, becoming invisible as it passed in turn behind the bellow of the plunge pool, the alto splashing of the surface, and the random tones that burst like bells through white noise. It went on, sometimes falling silent without stopping, returning again above the sound of the water. It was sad, alive, baffled, the most perfect song I could never have conceived existed. I'll tell you what it was, this naked song: it was music incarnate. When I heard only the waterfall for a long time, I got up and crawled toward where the song had been, finding AC by putting my hand down on her foot. That gave me a fix on where most of her must be, and addressed the darkness there.

"AC, that was ... I'm just ..."

"It's a Tlingit poem about a girl whose lover goes off to sea and leaves her pregnant and lonely, she's sure he's drowned, and she sings this lullabye to the baby inside. She says her water is made of tears and rain, and the baby knows what its father knows, drowning in salt. It's pretty sad, all right, but not completely sad, since the girl figures she'll throw herself in the sea too, as soon as she's sure about the guy not coming back, and then they'll all be babies together in the mother ocean's belly. I haven't even let myself think about it since Daddy - since his funeral."

It was a little hard to talk. "Is the music Tlingit?"

"No, that was just me, I sort of let the waterfall lead me through it."

I thought about that. "Real music by real people."

I felt her hand on my face, the fingers cool and firm. "I didn't mean to upset you. Why are you sad?"

"I'm not sad. I'm crying about the song."

"Baloney, Oren. Don't bullshit me, please. You're sad about something, you have some sad thing going on under the … well, under the surface guy. That was the first thing I saw about you, when I first met you. That's why I was so rude when Daddy died, I didn't think anybody had any right to be sad but me, and maybe mother. You've been more cheerful this summer, up to now. That was Donia, huh?"

"Donia Ma," I corrected her, absently. "I guess, coming and going. All men are sad."

"Huh. They manage to hide it pretty well, most of them. Look over there. I think I'm starting to see the waterfall."

There was no way to know what she meant by "over there," but by just staring wide-eyed into the blackness, I did begin to think there was some kind of a wavering pale shape more or less in the direction of the rushing sound, though it was not exactly where I'd thought it was. The sky still looked black, but the trees overhead were blacker still, so it looked as though this lifelong night might be reaching an end. The thought of daylight felt like sunset. A bird broke the monotony of the waterfall, and then another, and AC and I sat together and listened to them, and pointed out emerging shapes, finding the pool covered by fog that hid the far bank and trailed off into the canopy of trees, a crowd of reluctant ghosts leaving a party. At some point we rediscovered that we were naked, and AC ambled over to the tarp and picked up our clammy underwear, shaking dirt and bugs out of it and holding it at arm's length. My rum-and-blood patch had hardened to a reddish puck overnight.

"This'll be fun. What say we go naked all day?"

"Great, except the purple and teal gang might be a little shocked. I think I'll see how little of that muck I can get away with, though."

In the end I lent AC my shirt, and we packed out everything but the bare essentials. Hiking back to the car, she sauntered along a few feet ahead of me or a few feet behind, scratching bites, looking at things along the trail, in no great hurry. When I finally remarked on this, she shook her head.

"I always wanted to get there first. I know this won't last, but just for now, I feel like I'm there."

I slept half way back to Washington and drove the other half, thinking about murderous dreams while AC slept. Donia Ma never did tell me what other things the triple burner was supposed to keep hot, but it seemed to have a life of its own. And please don't ever ask what I meant by picking up that rock by the waterfall. AC woke up with a little hiss of dread when we hit Washington traffic, and I stayed with her when she walked into her apartment. Which was a good thing; the place was a mess, empty hangers and papers and crumpled posters all over the floor, and a rat's nest in the bathroom. Jana was gone, except in spoor.

"If you'll lend me some clothes and go out for some breakfast, I'll tackle the top layer of this. What say?"

She gave a wide-armed, wet-eyed shrug of disbelief, and disappeared into a hall closet. "Promise you won't laugh?"

"No."

"OK. Shithead had some crazy stuff she used to dress me up in."

I had my choice of a lobbyist's suit by Gucci, camo shorts and tank top for an Israeli commando, hockey pads, a priest's robes from the Inquisition, and a Washington Bullets uniform. "Damn, she took the Jiffy-Lube outfit."

"I guess the commando gear would be about right for what we're into here. If we get really hungry, I can see what I can raise with the other stuff. Dare I ask what I'm missing from the other side?"

"I won't tell you all of it, but my favorite was the duck suit."

"Double cream and sugar with double coffee, orange juice, and an almond Danish. A big almond Danish. Hit the track."

"Yessir."

I found some trash bags in the kitchen and started stuffing things in them, not being terribly careful about sorting it after the first half hour, so I almost trashed the videotape Jana had left stuck in the dish drainer, with a note attached:

The Cello Francesca, *or* Balderdash

Death Dyke: Give this to bOrin' if you think of it. Look at it yourself if you feel like puking some day. You were a better class of bitch than almost any I ever got bored to death by.
- Jana

It was "Read Only Memory." I burned the note and flushed the ashes down the toilet, and wandered over to the VCR. What the hell. I played it, and it was OK. It started with the title on a CRT, and that started to crawl and blend, and the next thing you knew it was Jana, dressed in tea-colored silk rags. The sound track was a single mockingbird, but Jana was clearly and silently dancing the C minor Sarabande, using only her arms. I got about that far when AC came in with breakfast, so we rewound it and ate Danish and slurped liquids while we watched Jana. By the time it was over, she had referred, movingly, to Mollie and Jacob, to the cypresses, to Bach and the Reverend Plummer Chavis, and to the sunlit tumbling of sand in the river; and every moment she was also the river itself moving silently under the mockingbird's song.

There was a little appendix called Entirelymental Perception Agency, featuring Ronald Reagan moderating an argument between my teetering stack of paperwork and Diana Tucker-Fitts (all parts played by Jana of course), that left us laughing with enough momentum to make it through Jana snarling directly to the camera:

"AC and Oren, I know you're laughing now, so fuck you both very much for everything, and goodbye."

The screen turned to hissing snow, and AC's grin faded hard. She hit the remote, and a sweating preacher boomed into view, calling down the blessings of the almighty while a 900 number crawled across his pulpit. "Shit fahr, O," AC twanged, "*I* cain't tell no difference between her and that clown. C'mon, let's get the rest of this trash in the trash."

When we had worked together through the early afternoon getting all traces of Jana purged from the apartment - administering its third top-to-bottom scrubbing of the year, endangering the floorboards - AC hit me in the belly with the

Sunday paper and shoved me in the direction of a futon that was unrolled on a leafy little sunporch in the back.

I think I lasted about three minutes over the dappled editorials, humid breeze through the vines turning pages whenever it wanted, before I conked out solidly. I escaped the nothingness to find myself still asleep on the futon with AC kneeling over me in a flaming silk baby-doll nightie that came about to her belly button, and a real District of Columbia fireman's helmet.

"Had a 911 call at this address, sir, tenant came home and smelled burning paper. Tenant says she's very glad you caught it and *thank* you very much. Just wanted to check if it's under control."

"No, it really isn't, officer." I started to float off the futon to explain about the dangerous triple burner, probably a fire code violation, but AC hunkered next to me, anchoring me with a knee while she unbuttoned the commando shorts. "Stay close to the floor, sir; air's better down here." She lowered herself over me and cradled my head against the silk. "See? Isn't that much better now?"

18. Road

Mrs. Merton Meyerson was a solid, sizable woman, a former middle school principal in a lime-green pantsuit. She welcomed me into the cluttered apartment she had shared for over forty years with the late Merton, a professor of Renaissance literature at Northwestern.

"It seems impossible it's over," she greeted me at the door. "Look out for the boxes. It's taking me another lifetime just to work through Merton's things, though nothing's being as hard as this cello. But all his music, all his European doodads we picked up on trips. Not to be a bad hostess, take that stuff off the green chair, you want coffee? I'm living on coffee, cigarettes. All his books, ayee, the books! My friend Dora said to me, Get a guy to come, he'll do all the packing and take 'em away, for that any price at all is a fair price. So I did, and you know what happens, first book the guy picks up a ten-dollar bill falls out, and the next one a poem I wrote Merton the day before we got married in 1942. I said to him, go, I'll call when I've opened every single one of these damned things. It's not the money, God knows, forty years of TIAA I've got more money than I ever dreamed of; but what if I sent away something else like that poem, something Merton wanted me to see when I was going through his things after he was gone? And you know what since then? Two recipes, a ticket Munich to Dachau, three dollars, and a Dear Abby, in three rooms full of books. Cream and sugar? The whole time, what I started to say, every book I'm thinking, I remember this book, it was only a couple years ago Merton found it, I remember he read me this piece out of it last week, made no sense to me. He's gonna come through that door and want to know what I think I'm doing here. But the book says on the inside, Paris, 1948, and I said goodbye to Merton three months ago at Forest Grove. How does that happen, I ask you?"

I smiled. "A little bit at a time, I think. Did he - did your husband play the cello here, in this room?"

"That's another thing. I'm in the kitchen and the fan on the stove's running, or water running, something frying, all that noise, I hear Merton plain as day, Bach, Bruch, same little mistakes, going over it. But I shut everything off, the music's gone too. That's half the reason I don't cook any more. People say old people don't eat right, I'll tell you why. It's too easy to hear what you were used to hearing from the kitchen, right up to footsteps. No, thank you. A Slimfast and a cup of coffee'll do me till I clear the decks around here. So, still nothing from Italy. You ready to give me a down payment?"

I pulled out my checkbook. "Yes, I am. I can't believe this either, I'm actually buying Francesca. I mean - I hope you'll hold that check until we're sure this Italian won't come through with the whole thing at the last second."

She gave me a considering look. "No, actually, I'm going to cash it. Even Slimfast costs something. I guarantee you'll either have your cello or the money back, as far as I'm concerned."

"You're saying you'll refund it if he insists on keeping it and paying you?"

"Certainly. I look like the kind of person would sell the same thing to two people?"

"Of course not. It's just a long jump from paying you for half of it, and actually getting that guy to give it up. Who is he, and where do I find him, anyhow?"

She held up a hand, poured herself more coffee, and lit a cigarette. "Not so fast. You haven't kept part of the bargain. I need to know why it's got to be that exact cello, if it wasn't that business I found in the pocket; and you said you'd tell me who left it on Leon Wolf's doorstep, which was obviously you. Why?"

"Mrs. Meyerson, I can't give you just a short, simple answer to either of those."

"Have more coffee. You think I'm booked so solid I can't hear a long story?"

Even pared to the essentials, it took me a half hour to get Francesca the Cello onto Leon Wolf's welcome mat, and another to reconstruct why, at this late date, I was pursuing her again. Mrs. Meyerson had a principal's ear for elision and gloss, and she challenged it every time. I kept Fire Bird out of it, but almost nothing about my two relationships to Molar Chemical or my reconstruction as a cellist at Donia Ma's hands escaped, and a careless reference to how "we" had witnessed Mollie Biedermeyer's re-interment in North Carolina almost dragged AC, Jana, and Paul Hartley McCauley stumbling through the smoke and the piles of books and the steaming coffee.

At the end, Mrs. Meyerson only stubbed out her ninth cigarette and smiled a savoring smile. "Crazy kids. I got to wish you all the luck in the world, Mr. Dienst. The cello's sold. Here."

She tossed my check on the table between us, where it started to soak up coffee while I stared at it. "But - you won't sell it? What'd I say?"

"Did I say that? I said it's sold, it's paid for. I never heard such a string of dumb fool kid stunts in my life, and believe me I've heard 'em. Don't look so hurt, a broken arm and two sad love stories isn't enough to pay? Keep the check, keep the bill of sale, I'm way ahead. I had thirty years of good music out of your foolishness. The guy you want is named Beneventi, and he lives in some place called Dorf - oh, Felsburg, I think."

"That's in Italy?"

"Evidently. I got a little thank-you note from him when the cello got there, and it had Italian postmark and stamps on it. Probably close to Austria or Switzerland somewhere."

"Can I see the note?"

"Sure, absolutely." She waved expansively at the broken landscape of books and boxes. "All we got to do is remember which book I stuck it in."

In the end, two cups of coffee and a full bladder later, Mrs. Meyerson pounced on a copy of Life that had been on an end table beside us the whole time, and a card fluttered out. "There. I knew I hadn't put it far away, it only came a week ago."

She handed it to me, and it didn't add much to what I already knew. "Greetings from Schloss Felsenburg," it said in spiky European handwriting, "where the lovely violoncello «Francesca» arrived safely today. We warmly thank you."

It was signed by F. R. Beneventi. The front of the card was a hypercolored picture of a smallish castle, picturesque enough as glimpsed through flowering branches against a mountainous background. Printed against the glaring blue sky was "Dorf Felsenburg, Schloss / Castelroccia, Castello."

"Geez. This guy lives here? What, he's a duke or something?" Flaring torches, poisoned cups. I was supposed to snatch Francesca out of the reluctant hands of some Italian noble, who probably had ways to see that my disappearance was discreet and permanent. Maybe I could get AC as bodyguard.

"I have no idea. He could be the gardener, for all I know. What I do know is, he takes things and doesn't pay, which doesn't surprise me all that much, if you know what I mean. I'll do what I can for you by wiring him to cancel, and instruct him to turn the cello over to you. Don't take any foolishness, is my advice."

Yes. I would wear a green pantsuit.

On Thursday morning, I went straight from the Chicago-to-National redeye to my office, and by midday I had lined up an itinerary that would nicely eat up the money I hadn't spent on Francesca. I did finally persuade Mrs. Meyerson to take a token amount that would allow me to present a bill of sale to F. R. Beneventi and such customs agents as I would surely encounter in the course of a Washington - Dorf Felsenburg – Manosduros - Washington round trip. The whopping expense of buying tickets at the last minute was compounded (confounded, I almost wrote) by the airlines' insistence that I book a seat for Francesca on the last three legs of the flight. ("Of course, Mr. Dienst, you are welcome to bring your instrument as checked baggage if you wish, but you may not bring it as carry-on. And our liability for loss or damage would be limited to a very modest per-pound rate.") I shuddered, gritted my teeth, and agreed to a second reservation, traveler's name Francesca Cello Dienst. As a little surprise bonus, the airline threw a 10% surcharge on Francesca's seat because it was the last one open.

I braved the Mexican phone lines and got hold of Señor Paños, and made an appointment for the following Tuesday during late business hours to have a look at the MexiLar -

Manosduros agreement and tour the disaster area. *Film,* I wrote on my notepad, though I was more likely to forget the camera in the flurry of getting things together between work and my flight. The rest of the day I chewed down through the stack of unopened mail, unread reports, and undone jobs on my desk, and made sure AC could drive out to Dulles with me and bring my car back to town. I avoided returning calls, including one from Diana Tucker-Fitts and, at 5 o'clock, one directly from McIntear. I told Gloria to keep him on the line, and let him listen to "Yesterday" and "Time on my Hands" before he slammed off.

"He's not a very pleasant person, Dr. Dienst," she reproved me. "I hope you will not ask me to do that again." I apologized and sent her home to deserved tranquility. And as I was clicking the latches on my own briefcase, the outer door opened and Rick McIntear was with me in person.

"Hold it right there, Dienst. I don't know where you think you're going, but you're going to give me some information, and I mean now. Have you been poking around in the Manosduros business again?"

"What makes you think that?"

"The agreement's disappeared."

I frowned. "From where?"

"From the mayor's office in Manosduros, as if you didn't know."

I laughed. "What, you mean you sent somebody there to make it disappear, and he found out it was already missing? They put it somewhere safe, I expect. Can't say I blame 'em, can you?"

"I want it back."

I tossed my hands. "Rick, you want so damn much. Why don't you give up on this one? Christ, you're in no danger from it."

"Not that I need personal counseling from you, Dr. Snotnose, but you have no idea what you're talking about. If that thing blows wrong, it could cost me this appointment."

"Aren't you the guy I heard complaining to the press about the big salary cut you took to serve the nation under the Gipper? Could it be you're realizing other benefits?"

"So what? Everybody knows that's why you come here."

"Well, everybody but the professional staff and the interns who actually do the work. Don't you have enough money?"

He gave a snort that did double duty as commentary on that, and preface to his next observation: "I hear you got an intern working pretty hard for you, Dienst. My sources tell me you took off into the hills with her last weekend. What was that, water quality stuff, or international affairs?"

"Aw, for shit's sake, you silly dork. Not that I owe you any explanations, but I've known her since ..." I shrugged. I really didn't owe him an explanation, so why get into it? He wouldn't make much of an effort to understand the midnight baptism or the 911 call. "Are you spending good money having a bunch of private eyes follow me around? What the hell do you expect to gain from that?"

"No, the IG's office is doing it for free. My folks in St. Louis tell me they came by this childish statement you lisped out back in 1953 about how you signed off on a document you knew to be fraudulent. Now, I admit the statute of limitations on perjury is pretty well expired on that, but it got them interested, and that and your campout ought to be enough to neutralize any stink you think you can make about Manosduros. So I'm telling you right now, back off, or else."

"Oh, no. Oh, my goodness. Or you'll go public with a thirty-year-old confession by a minor that he acquiesced in a forgery you perpetrated in the first place, because your father-in-law threatened to reveal all about his pornographic movies? God, I can't wait. Publish and be damned, I think is the formula."

Rick stepped in close and grabbed my jacket. "You stupid fucker!" he screamed. "You'll fuck up everything, won't you? Won't you?"

And he shoved me back against the desk, where my left elbow crunched down on the phone with an impact that may have been painful enough for the phone, but from my side felt like I'd dipped it in molten lava. I honestly saw, not stars, but floating black dots, and one of them said, *Oh, Dr. Dienst, I warned you to be vigilant against further injury to that area.*

I screamed with pain and fury and shoved Rick away with my feet, and for the next, oh, ... Thirty seconds? Ten minutes? we shoved and punched and grappled and kicked, nobody getting any particular advantage and without the least display of style or experience from either contestant; nothing but desperation on Rick's side and clear, bottomless hatred on mine. Books, reports, and office gadgets hit the floor with every lunge and grapple, until we were slipping around on layers of paper that made it harder to land punches or avoid them. And I have to say, it felt great, even when I turned my ankle on a fallen stapler and hit Rick in the ear instead of the eye I had in my sights. I mean, you couldn't do this all the time, not more than once in a career, near the end. But this was that once for me.

And then AC Gewissner was standing open-mouthed in the doorway and fishing in her backpack, and I punched Rick in the nose - at last, Jesus, what an epiphany! - and shouted, "AC, no! Don't sh-oof" because Rick's counterpunch got me in the solar plexus, and I was on my knees on the rug waiting for what Rick would do next, hearing clicks as AC cocked her pistol, and then a yelp from Rick. When I got a breath, Rick was handcuffed to the radiator and dripping nose blood on my carpet, and AC was standing over him, pinning her hair back in place.

"Handcuffs?"

"Ranger issue," she shrugged. "You didn't think I was going to - "

"No, no, sorry. Jesus, what a mess. Rick, can't you stop that?"

"Fuck you."

I put some newspaper under him a let him drip while I stood up to assess the damage. Good God, my arm. I bent it slowly, carefully, and it seemed to work, in a sulky kind of way. AC looked at the wreckage and raised her eyebrows at me.

"AC, I don't believe you've met Mr. Rick McIntear, an old colleague going back to when I knew your parents in St. Louis; and come to think of it, acquainted with your Dad, who beat the crap out of him for insulting your mother one afternoon. Mr. McIntear is Ms. Tucker-Fitts' boss, and he has managed to convince the Inspector General's office that you and I have something going on the side."

She eyed Rick coldly. "Mr. McIntear, I can't say I'm pleased to meet you. It would hardly be fair to slap your face now, and it would get blood all over Oren's office. But I'll expect satisfaction for the insults at a time of your choosing in the next five days."

"Five days?" I asked. (Satisfaction?)

"I got my reservation for Anchorage while you were gone, and I called Mom. She sends her love to you. She says Anna has a new baby girl, and it's been a warm summer, so all the rivers are high. God, I can't wait."

"I think I'm going to puke," said Rick, and he didn't mean it only as commentary. Up it came, all over his pants and the newspapers. He had the bare grace to look embarrassed.

A smell of half-digested seafood filled the office, and AC rolled her eyes. "I think when I get home I'm going to have another baptism and get Washington out of my nose."

I thought of AC in some freezing pool. "Take a friend," I said, regretting it wouldn't be me.

"I already know who it's going to be."

And I left it at that. We closed the door on Rick McIntear and his mess, and on the way out I flipped on Gloria's radio to more or less cover his shouts until the cleaning crew came on. It would be an uncomfortable evening for him, but I absolutely had to have some clear time to get cleaned up and get out to Dulles. *"Take the A Train,"* scrubbed of interesting harmonies, followed us to the elevator.

At the airport, I told AC not to park. At the terminal, I came around to the driver's window and kissed her firmly. "I owe you a big one, AC. ...For the rescue, I mean." I started to say more, and actually found the sense not to. "Please give my love to Sophie and the other kids if they're around. Specially little Oren."

"Little Oren is a deckhand on a salmon trawler, and you're nuts about owing me anything. Think back. We're <u>way</u> even."

"We're way ahead. Thank you for everything."

"You too, Oren. Good - "

A cop blew a deafening blast and started advancing on us, waving at AC to move. "You lovebirds wanna get somethin goin, do it in Long-Term," he advised. "Move it out, Honey."

AC threw back her head and laughed, and drove off. ".. in Italy" came back from the stream of traffic, but it might have been somebody else entirely.

*   *

Munich is the airport of choice for the far north of Italy, and as my silver Airbus cleared the coastline over Delaware and I settled in for my second night in a row on an airplane, I was still panting and grinning in spirit from my scuffle with Rick McIntear, half planning to mourn AC's departure from my life when I got around to it. If anyone had asked me if I were proud of myself, or satisfied with the damage, or any other sarcastic, responsible question, I might have come to earth sooner, as I knew I must. But I postponed it by not thinking about Rick handcuffed, fuming, plotting vengeance to the tune of "Up a Lazy River," or of AC; or even of Donia Ma. But there was something else that I could think about, now that I had a little distance: there was no need for me to accept some self-invented aging bachelor persona. Donia Ma, give her her due, really had cured me of the hangups and frustrations that had plagued my adult life, and AC - bless her for what it cost to put on the firefighter outfit over a sore heart - had certified general viability. OK, too late to fix the Cindy fiasco, unrealistic to think of finding another AC, even if she'd been inclined that way. But Washington was crammed with pleasant single and divorced women in their forties who wouldn't mind keeping company with a fiftyish guy with good assets and a cello with a romantic history, whose birth he'd witnessed, and who now played rather well; and whom it would be fun to know.

"Fun to know," for heaven's sake. That's the state I was in. It is depressing, the rush a good fistfight lends. Maybe I could put a personal in CityPaper: *DWM, rec'tly refurb'd, new mgt, ISO...* The horror. But I could think of three women right in the Rock Creek Symphony who would be worth investigating. Hmm, including a handsome and knowing percussionist named Kate Swain who had shown overt signs of ISO herself during a post-concert bar hop while I was still under Donia Ma's care. The point was, life was far from over, in fact in that way it was starting anew, and as soon as I was back in Washington I was going to let it. Maybe Kate Swain, maybe a series of women, maybe a May - Well, a July-September marriage. I could even contemplate fathering children, who would rescue something more of myself from death than a share in the birth of a cello. Lamaze classes, peewee soccer, maybe even as final proof of immortality a grandchild before I shuffled. I spent an hour or so elaborating this perfectly reasonable dream over a couple of splits of Lufthansa champagne. The old Backstage Yahoos, whose fingerprints were all over this Francesca project, had interpreted the events of the week as a definitive mandate. They were strutting and grinning like Republicans, buying houses in McLean, requisitioning limos, reading the Plum Book, while the voices of sanity, the voices of mentors and role models, glumly settled into understaffed offices in dim corners of my personality; places like The Maturity Foundation and The Institute For Realistic Options. Are you better off now, crowed the Yahoos, than you were thirty years ago? You see what comes of thirty years of unchecked common sense? Yoo B'long to Us.

They had a straightforward agenda and a very simple strategy: get my sexual energies mixed up with the re-acquisition of Francesca, and let that drive the next step: once Francesca was back between my knees where she belonged, I was to quit messing around with engineering and politics and get cracking on my concert career. Never mind that I was fifty years old; Backstage Yahoos, by their very nature, are immortal and timeless, and consider their host to be permanently eighteen.

Chagrin arrived with the bleary dawn over County Cork, hours before I was ready. I clutched my head. I was at a crazy altitude, sighing down over the Channel, or Belgium somewhere, on an errand that had set me back staggering sums, to a very uncertain destination; behind me an office, like my EPA career, a gory shambles, my buckler against the forewarned and surely hostile F. R. Beneventi an unlikely $5000.00 bill of sale for Francesca written on the back of an acknowledgement-of-condolences card left over from Merton Meyerson's funeral, and marked Paid In Full on behalf of the Estate of Dr. Merton

Meyerson, which itself of course had no documentation of ownership of Francesca in the first place. What on earth had possessed me? I rubbed my face with the hot towel and stared out the window. Far to the southeast a few mountain peaks showed against the sunrise glare. Alps, no doubt, harboring on their southern flank the noble Beneventi in his fortress. "What the hell," someone remarked a few rows away, his voice muffled by the mounting pressure in my ears. "What the bloody hell."

In Munich I taxied to the train station and inquired about schedules to Dorf Felsenburg. After some back-and-forthing with a semi-helpful agent, we decided that what I really wanted was Bolzano, south of Innsbruck over the Brenner Pass, there to rent a car or take a bus to the nearby village of Dorf Felsenburg. In the afternoon, had a bit of a wait in Innsbruck, so I called Gloria Mondale to see how long I had to live at the EPA.

"Oh, Dr. Dienst, I am *so* glad you called. There are security men all over your office. We had a break-in last night."

"Oh? Is anything missing?"

"I think not. We only came in a few minutes ago. Your nice diefenbachia was tipped over, there's dirt all *over* the rug by the radiator. We think it was some kind of environmental hooligans, that picked an office at random. The lock was broken, there's blood thrown all over your files, and a silly slogan spray-painted on the wall."

"A what?"

"Some kind of slogan. 'Alexandria City Drug Cabal, Ready For Anything.' What that's supposed to mean, I'm sure I don't know. We have no drugs in Alexandria."

AC-DC, Ready for Anything, Allmut. I tried to keep the smile out of my voice. "Do you think I should come back to Washington?"

"Certainly not. Security is taking care of it, and they're not telling us anything or listening to anything we say, anyhow, though it was I who found the knife. You enjoy your trip, and by the time you're back it should be all cleaned up."

"The knife?"

"Something these dreadful hippies left on your desk. A great big knife with a handle in the shape of - well, a lady."

"Good grief...all right. Are there any messages?"

"I don't think so. Yes, that Miss Fitts called from Mr. McIntear's office. You're to please call him upon your return." Her imitation was not as expert as Liana's, but it wasn't bad. A moment of silence was averted by "My Funny Valentine." I thanked Gloria and went off to catch the train.

From Innsbruck, the railroad makes its first serious assault on the Alps, climbing amid massive walls of rock and spectacular bridges. I watched it all streaming north past my window and thought about AC. How long had it taken her to get back to my office, release Rick and get him settled somehow - acquiring Yoolie's knife in the process, good God, had he had that with him during our fight? - and then converting the wreckage of my office into an ecofreak breakin? I couldn't begin to guess. The whole thing was humbling. Was she fitted by birth and training to clear the weeds from other people's gardens? Or just a good woman who recognized no barrier between need and remedy? I envied whoever it was she had in mind to baptize. It would have to be done in sunshine this time, though. Too cold in Alaska for midnight skinny-dipping, surely. Not a lot of people around, anyhow. Spray, laughter, a rainbow. Maybe she would not forget me.

I dozed from that point to the Italian border check at Brenner. After that I stood by the open doorway of the last car and let myself be carried backwards through towering rock that bore little mark of the millennia of human traffic that had crawled to and fro beneath it. About all that marked the fact that I was now in Italy was the change from German to bilingual signs ("Bressanone/Brixen") on the stations that receded behind us.

In "Bolzano/Bozen" I emerged into a hustling, smoggy downtown, full of what-the-hell energy for my errand, and looked around for a car rental agency, a bus station, or a source of information. In the end, I approached a taxi driver and - once we had settled on a mix of German and English as our clearest channel - learned that the last bus to Dorf Felsenburg had left an hour ago.

"But, sir, there is no reason to rent an auto, depending upon your plans. Dorf Felsenburg is no great distance, you can almost see it from here, and parking there is quite a problem. I would be glad to drive you."

"Well, if it's in sight, maybe I should just walk. Would you be kind enough to point the direction?"

"Certainly, sir. You can see the church just there, about halfway up." Sure enough, a spire emerged from the side of a mountain to catch the afternoon sun, at what looked like nosebleed heights over Bolzano to the south. I laughed. "How much?"

By the time we reached Dorf Felsenburg, nudging with polished fenders through masses of lederhosen the driver said encased some of the two or three thousand tourists who stayed there any week of the high season, the sunlight had taken on a distinctly late-afternoon tint, and there was a crispness of altitude and lengthening shadow to it.

"And your specific destination, sir?"

Hmm. I almost said the castle, Schloss Felsenburg, but something - cowardice - restrained me. "Well, I think the principal hotels or pensions would be best."

He looked doubtful. "You have no reservation? It is the very peak of the tourist season."

"This was a very impulsive trip. You can drop me where you think it's most likely, and I will take it from there."

"That would be the Hotel am Kirche. It's the biggest, and there are any number of guest-houses within a block or two."

"So be it."

The concierge at the Hotel am Kirche looked stunned that I would be trying to get a room on a walk-in basis. "Heavens, sir. We have been booked for six months. Not only is it the height of the tourist season, but the music festival opens tomorrow. Is that why you have come?"

"No, it's personal business. Perhaps I would be better off to go back to Bolzano for the night."

"I can make some inquiries for you, sir. Some other hotel or guest house might have had a cancellation."

"If it wouldn't be too much bother . . ."

"Not at all." She retreated into a sun-drenched room that overlooked the valley to the west, and made six very fast phone calls, four in German and two in Italian, before returning.

"As I feared, sir. Even the hotels that cater to" - here the tiniest quiver - "*Italians* have waiting lists. You would do best to stay in Bozen and return in the morning. I am certain you will find something there. In fact ... if the Sir would trust me to recommend a hotel?"

"Absolutely. You have been most helpful."

"The Hotel am Bahnhof. It is close to the station and very pleasant. I will ring them to see if they have room."

"Very kind."

She did, and they did. "Your name, sir?"

"Dienst." She looked pleased, and maybe for the first time in my life I didn't have to spell it. Maybe it was the lack of silent letters.

"They will hold a room for you until 9 tonight. sir. You can return on the aerial tram, it is a pleasant experience if you are not, ehm, what? Giddy?"

"Only with fatigue. Thank you so much, you have been very kind. Where do I find the tramway?" She directed me, and I walked out into the cool sunshine. It made me think of AC again, so it was a moment before the music registered through the traffic and the murmur of strolling tourists.

Baroque, as crisp as the air, cleanly played and swirling on the light breeze that was touring the square before me. I wandered toward it, but by the time I got it located in a good-sized church across from the hotel, the final chords had sounded. The door was open, and I could hear the usual bossy voice rising above the snapping-shut of cases and the clank of folding chairs with final announcements and reminders. It was such a familiar, comfortable sound, though the words themselves were in some kind of impenetrable dialect, that I was encouraged to peek in.

Sure enough, a small orchestra seemed to be in the process of breaking up. There were two cellists, a man and a woman, and I was sure that I had stumbled across F. R. Beneventi himself. I approached, and was heartened to see that he looked meek enough. On the other hand, his cello was a reddish, bunged-up affair with an ebony fingerboard and bore no resemblance to Francesca. I stopped awkwardly five feet from him, sure I was mistaken, but he had seen me coming. "Signor?"

Oh, well. "Mmm. Signor Beneventi?"

340

The guy looked pleased that I wasn't after him. "Ecco, signore," he beamed, and pointed to a good-sized, determined-looking guy who was making short work of covering and locking the harpsichord.

"Thank you," I hesitated. "I think it's a cellist named Beneventi."

He turned and bowed toward his colleague, now standing at her open case draping a silk cloth over her cello and tucking the bow and music in their respective pockets; vulnerable, gawky, a bookish tomboy grown up, her corduroy jumper draping the graceful slight paunch of early pregnancy. She glanced over her shoulder and said, "I am Francesca Beneventi. I will be with you in a moment. And the signor would be ...?"

The signor would be damned. No sinister duke but a pleasant mother-to-be with no poison cups that I could see. Of course the stiletto would be strapped to her thigh. "Please don't let me hurry you," I said, craning to see the cello. "I'm afraid you will not be glad to see me. I am Oren Dienst."

She smiled coolly nevertheless, latched the case and turned, extending her hand; but instead of stopping at handshake level, it rose to her open mouth in the classic oh-my-god position, and the face behind it acquired the color of a vanilla malt. When her eyes closed, I had time to think, Good God, the baby, but not do anything about it before she crumpled - fairly gracefully, really - onto the chair behind her and lowered her head to her wool-clad knees.

She sat swaying for a moment that allowed me to kneel and steady her before a hooraw burst forth. In no time there was a knot of people pressing around us, yelling what was probably Tirolean for *Stand Back, Give Her Air.*

A couple of them did stagger back then, to be replaced by the Signor Beneventi who had been busy at the harpsichord. He knelt by Francesca, speaking soothingly in Italian, and displaced my hand with a solid and possessive arm around her shoulders. When she didn't answer he glared at me, asking probably some legitimate question.

"Non parlo Italiano, signor," I assayed. "Is English OK? I am Oren Dienst, from the United States. Your - wife, is it? -

seems to have been taken poorly just as we were meeting each other."

"Ah. The American who thinks to buy my wife's cello."

"Yes."

"I'm sorry you have had a long trip for nothing. There was a simple mixup about the funds, but the payment was wired to Chicago yesterday."

"Well, I'm sorry too, but Mrs. Meyerson accepted my check, and I have a receipted bill of sale with me. I think you will find that she will not accept your payment."

He turned to his wife with a shrug. "These things are never as simple as anyone believes, that's what I think. What is it, cara? Are you all right?"

Francesca raised her head, smiling dizzily, fuzzy dark eyebrows still prominent against a clever, small-chinned face. "I am ashamed of myself, to be so delicate. Mr. Dienst, you very much resemble my father, who is dead. You gave me a shock for a moment."

"I do apologize."

"How could you know?"

"Well, yes." *Glad that's over; about that cello. Damn your eyes for being female, and pregnant, and being named Francesca; this is going to be sticky.* "See here, would the two of you be free to join me for a restorative drink, or dinner? Under the circumstances, I surely owe you that much, and we can discuss the situation in regard to the cello."

The male Beneventi looked superior. "During the tourist season, no restaurant is worth the wait. Perhaps in a few months. For tonight, you will be our guest, Dr. Dienst. Though there is nothing much to discuss."

Something told me I'd regret taking them up; but the Yahoos, who had been watching all this from their power seat somewhere in my belly, countered with hard-headed advice not to let Francesca out of my sight. I hesitated, but what the hell did I have to lose? *Your dignity, your bill of sale, Francesca, your life,* answered the inner counselor readily enough; but the Yahoos shouted him down. *Stay with that cello!* they shrieked. *Be charming!*

"Very well," I said, smiling firmly, sincerely, unbudgeably. "What there is to discuss is my receipted bill of sale and Mrs. Meyers' cabled instructions to you to turn the cello over to me. As long as you understand that I will not change my mind on this, why, yes, I would be glad to join you for dinner."

In their car, stuffed in the back with my suitcase, the cello, and what appeared to be a tank of propane, I mulled over the situation. The feeling of getting in over my head was strong, and was certainly abetted by the fact that the Beneventis kept up a rapid, affectionate banter in Italian, of which one word in fifty made sense to me. It was nice to see that them so devoted, since it humanized them; on the other hand, it made them less vulnerable targets of my unfriendly takeover. Our way led us through orchards that were shadowed with the drawing on of evening, tiny trees heavy with apples and pears. Francesca Beneventi, apparently deciding that she would have to play the role of social lubricant, turned to me and filled me in on the uses she had for a cello.

Ludovico was a professor of keyboard at the local university, and she herself played on a semiprofessional basis and taught privately. As they had both turned 29 this summer, they had decided, half-reluctantly, that it was time to begin their family, even if it meant a temporary disruption to Francesca's musical career. But their source of income and real profession was farming, which they did on the unpromising and craggy lands around the castle. "These are our orchards, Dr. Dienst. Are they not handsome?"

"Very handsome. You live in Schloss Felsenburg, is that it?"

"More or less. It is mostly a ruin; Ludovico bought it by paying its overdue taxes, and we have made some rooms habitable for ourselves and for my mother and grandfather. And of course for the baby. We have no electricity, and the telephone is solemnly promised to arrive before the baby. It will be a long job to bring it back to what it was in the Thirteenth Century."

"Fourteenth," grunted Ludovico. "Il Trecento is the 14th Century in English."

She kissed him wetly on the ear, he smirked, and I stared at her. The setting sun was in my eyes, and it was otherwise getting pretty dim, but damn, there was something absolutely, strongly familiar about her. Impossible to say where the familiarity lay, though; it was as much a matter of gestures and body management as it was of face.

"Excuse me; have you ever performed in the United States?"

"Me? No, regrettably, I have never been there. Maybe some day."

Well, OK. Maybe it was some variant of deja vu. Even the combination of face and gesture when she said "Me?" seemed an expected gestalt. A dream figure, maybe, but if she were supposed to be some fated *anima*, my unconscious was up to its usual incompetence; choosing a woman born twenty years too late, married, devoted, and pregnant. I gave it up as the road wound us up a small hill, topped by what appeared to be a half-demolished cathedral, with windows set in here and there. We turned in to a courtyard filled with bales of hay, fruit baskets, and firewood split and neatly stacked, of a length that spoke of good-sized and non-recreational fires within. A dalmatian barked and squirmed irresponsibly as we got out.

"Alex! Down! Shut up! This is our ruined castle, Dr. Dienst. Let me take your bag. Francesca, maybe you would let your mother know that our guest is here."

Off went Francesca up a curving stairway in the interior wall of the courtyard, the beneficiary as she climbed of a kiss and a pat on the butt from Ludovico, who seemed to have been softened by her moist treatment of him in the car. Off went Ludovico after he asked me if I wouldn't mind waiting for a moment out here while he went to see whether, as he put it, my room was fit to occupy. "I would rather you did not need to climb over sawhorses, Dr. Dienst. We are just done with plastering it, and you will have the honor of occupying a piece of newly domesticated territory, which will be the nursery."

"Oh, please," I said, "I have a room reserved in Bolzano tonight. Really, I appreciate the thought, but - "

"Nonsense. Did they book you into that wretched Bahnhof Hotel? They always do that to innocent tourists. It will be dark soon, the tramway will shut down, and you would spend a lonely night in a Teutonic fleabag - and for what? To deprive us of the pleasure of a guest who will inhabit our latest triumph over the decay of this pile of rocks."

I appreciate florid baloney as much as the next guy, so I gave an accepting kind of shrug that was half an apology to better judgement. On the other hand, a night at the Bahnhof Hotel? "Fine, then." *David Balfour gropes around a deathtrap ruin by stormlight.* But in fact the whole scene here was remarkably free of menace. Somewhere water burbled peacably as I wandered over to the western edge of the courtyard, which ended in a parapet overlooking miles of fertile-looking valleys. I shared the sunset with another, a very old man bundled against the chill in rugs and a scarf on a chaise, motionless and feeble looking, with his back to the courtyard. This would be the grampa, I supposed, set out in sunshine to doze away the afternoon. He didn't look as if he'd remember to come in at nightfall, so I made a note to tell Francesca in case he turned up missing, where I'd seen him. Alex the dalmatian finished urinating in all corners and gave him a sniff, checking vital signs probably, and came over looking for cheap affection. I occupied a chunk of parapet discreetly removed from the old man, and rubbed Alex's ears while I admired the view and wondered what to do now.

Here was this thoroughly likable young couple living a dream life of music and farming and castle-building, who had found Francesca-the-cello first and had honorably paid for her, and furthermore had possession and were at home in a country notorious for its Byzantine financial legalisms, its capricious officials, its corruptible judiciary, and its home-court clannishness. Why wouldn't the easy gesture of giving up Francesca also be the gracious and right one? I who believed in the souls of cellos, couldn't I see that this would be a far more promising setting for Francesca than life as the occasional hobbyhorse of an aging amateur?

No way, shrieked the Yahoos, jumping up and down. *It's our cello, we were there at the birth, we paid for it fair and square, and we're going to have it. What kind of bleeding-heart claptrap is this?* I clenched my teeth and turned angrily from the parapet, and bumped square into Francesca, turning the corner at the foot of the steps. She staggered back a bit, and looked shocked again.

"Good heavens, Mrs. Beneventi, you must think I'm out to do you in. I do apologize."

She gave me a puzzled smile. "Out to do me in? That is a - an idiom of English, is it? Mama was to have returned from Venice today, and I thought we would find her here. She has been delayed, apparently. I thought you would like to see a picture of my father."

It was a framed pencil sketch, *Francesca* in a schoolgirl hand at the bottom, of a fortyish-looking guy with a mustache, standing at the rail of a ship, water and mountains in the background. He was looking straight at the artist, smiling fondly, with a perhaps exaggerated twinkle in his eye. He did look a bit familiar, and I guessed it came of his resemblance to what I shaved every morning. Preserve me from ever growing a mustache, though. "He looks very nice, and he certainly does resemble me. Were you on a cruise with him?"

"Oh, no. He died when I was quite young. He was on a cruise ship on Lago Maggiore with Mama, and they had a photo taken. I drew that years later when I was angry at her, which is why she is not in it. I aged him a bit to bring him up to date, and I dumped her overboard. It is a pleasant kind of power, isn't it, to change reality to suit oneself?"

"My own father died when I was a boy. I wish I'd had the talent - "

"Oh, here comes Mama now, good. I must go and help her. Here is the photo that came from, you can get a more realistic look at them." She and her fetal passenger spun off in the direction of a taxi that was slowly disgorging an elderly woman in the courtyard in a yelping tangle of shopping bags, an aluminum crutch, and Alex.

She was dressed in quintessentially Mediterranean black, with a black scarf against the afternoon chill. I didn't want to stand and gawk at her, a stranger interloping her castle, so I turned away and feigned interest in the photograph Francesca had thrust at me. I had about time for a glance, a thunderstruck double-take, and a grey feeling that I was about to follow Francesca in a graceful swoon when I got a solid whack on the head from behind and fell to the paving stones, whether from that or from the photograph I couldn't have said. I was too busy struggling to my feet and grappling with the suddenly vitalized codger from the chaise who was whaling away at me with both hands and issuing little fluty grunts in what seemed to be pretty much German, though it could have been anything.

Francesca noticed what was going on and sprinted back across the courtyard, yelling "Opa! Stop! What are you doing? Oh, please, Mr. Dienst, don't be alarmed. He doesn't know what he's doing, I'm afraid."

Oh, yes he did. When I finally got a grip on his cane, after a few whacks on places that Rick McIntear had made tender, he shriveled back into feeble senility, one side of his face sagging and neither eye fully sane. But in case he needed another reminder, he could always check the photo. There are no mountains in the background, since the dusky glint of water in the background is not Lago Maggiore but the Mississippi River. The young couple smiles dizzily, holding hands, their elbows propped on a pipe railing next to a life preserver. The woman is slim, nearly as tall as her companion, one foot raised to the lower rail, her body a graceful integral. It is easy to see that she is pleased as punch at the bulge she made in the boy's trousers. He looks like someone swatted him with a sledgehammer. She must have had to keep that picture away from Papa for years.

"Mama," pronounced the well-brought-up Francesca Rosen Beneventi, "I would like to introduce Mr. Oren Dienst. He is here about my cello. Mr. Dienst, may I introduce my mother, Mrs. Anna Rosen."

19. Francesca

I opened my mouth with no words in mind, but she got in first anyway. "How do you do, Mr. Dienst. I am sorry that you have made this long journey for no purpose. *Whatsoever*."

"Anna." This was a dumb joke; I tried to keep my voice affable, but all on its own, it modulated from feeble through pettish to indignant, touching nothing pleasant along the way, finally Peter Lorre snarling, "The pleasure must be largely mine, Mrs. Rosen. May I ask how it's going with you? How it's *been* going? How the - "

"Francesca," she broke in. "I'm sure it's time for Opa's supper and bed. I am quite tired from my trip, do you think you could be such an angel as to see him through it, you and Ludovico? I will entertain Mr. Dienst for a *short* while." Francesca looked a little baffled, but she seemed to know better than to object. Off they went, Anna taking a hand in getting Arnold Rosen aimed at the kitchen before turning to deal with me, giving me a chance (wasted) to think.

She had aged hard, my ardent dancer. The tiny lines that so charmed me in 1953 had settled into deep scoring, and had been joined by many others. The midnight hair was iron now and cropped boyishly, ridiculously short; her lips were thinner, the killer eyes had retreated and become watchful. Her body was still slim, but twisted in some subtle way that had made the crutch a long-time companion. She looked tired, and not just from a trip to Venice.

"Anna," I began with a game smile, "you look - "

"Shall we skip the pleasantries? You look middle-aged, and I'm sure I look older than that. What are we to do about this? Why the hell are you here in the first place? Well, I know the answer to that. How did you find that stupid cello I was fool enough to tell Francesca about?"

"Where would you like me to begin?"

She lifted a dismissive hand. "Really, I don't care if you begin at all. Ending and leaving will do."

"Well, let's start with the obvious stuff. I had dealers looking for the cello, I expect you did too. We were both successful. You got there first, but in fact the former owner - "

"Yes, well, I will leave that to you and Francesca to settle."

Hey. Why all the prickly crap? Didn't we even get one *Oh, my God, it's you*? Well, come to think of it, she had Mrs. Meyerson's cable giving my name, and had done any omigodding days ago. But not even one for-old-times embrace? I mean, what was the whole first half of this about? On the other hand, why was I feeling something far closer to fury than to joy?

"OK. Let's go on to the harder stuff. What are we to do about what? Francesca? Am I her father, is that what's - ?"

"No, you are not. I absolutely do *not* wish to discuss it."

"I suppose you wouldn't, and I will respect that, but it won't be five minutes before she takes another look at those pictures and decides I am. And I think it may be too late to wish not to discuss it, unless we mean thirty years too late. She has already innocently informed me that she turned 29 last month, in other words, conceived in the fall of 1953. Well, all right. You may well not wish to discuss who else might be her father, but I've got to hand it to you if you were actually screwing some other guy; it was certainly all I could do to find time for - "

"Shut *up*, Oren."

"She explained."

"I owe you no explanation."

"Quite right."

I stalked to the parapet at the end of the courtyard and looked at a cold western sky, the twin of the whiskey sunset that had overseen my ditching her keys in the river. In that instant I was back on the levee listening to the muddy suck and splash of the Mississippi; I was astounded at the godawful fury I felt, twisting the little transparent blade under my heart until I could hardly breathe. A thousand accusations welled up, and I sorted through to see which would be most hurtful, showing how much I'd learned from Donia Ma about managing the past.

"OK, I get it. I actually understand, it makes so much sense of everything. That's the way you could break away from Papa, isn't it? That's the one thing that would get you kicked out and on your own for good. The Blessed Zone and its uses, and who was I to know if you were giving me good data? Or how many of us there were? Did the other ones, the other twerps, did they know about me? Never mind, you did it, good going, God, you've got guts, and there certainly weren't any sperm banks you could go to back then. But I must say it hurts like hell that you didn't even give me a chance to be more than that to what might have been my own child. In fact, I don't even begin to understand it. Oh, wait, unless you never really saw me as anything but a way out. That'd make sense too, God, I must have been perfect for your stud pool; young, stupid, too horny to stand up straight. I mean, look at us in that picture."

"I beg your pardon? You have the vile, cynical effrontery to pretend I exploited you to become pregnant on purpose? How respectful, what a tender gloss on the emotions of young lovers, and God, how devastatingly realistic. Let me see, I don't suppose you have actually experienced pregnancy and childbirth yourself, have you, in your distinguished scientific career?"

"Good one. Course, neither had you, when you started on it. Look, Anna, you say 'the emotions of young lovers' as if they were characters in a story. I don't know how it was for you, though I once thought I did. But let's just be devastatingly realistic for a second here. One minute we're the hottest thing that ever hit the Orpheum, I was a basket case over you, and the next you disappear, like that, pow, no warning, no communication, no forwarding address. You thought I wouldn't notice, is that it, *Gee, wasn't there this woman that loved me?* You were pregnant, we know that now, and you were obviously through with me; what else can I - "

"Oh, all right! Right, right, *right*! You win, Oren. That was it, I was desperate, fool that I was. Well, I see I cannot hide it from you any longer. Unfortunately, one of my other lovers drew the long straw, so to speak. You may be Francesca's guest, I suppose we must go through with that, but you are *not* her father. Please offer my regrets, I will not be joining you for dinner. I think yet another thirty years, and pray God far less, ought to see me past the possibility of further reunions in this world. Kindly do not seek one before then." She began hobbling toward a door through which I could see Arnold Rosen seated with a bib around his neck, drinking a glass of wine with both hands.

"Don't worry, God damn it. And as for dinner, I can't bear the thought I might disrupt your pleasant ménage any further. You may convey my apologies to Francesca yourself. If I hurry, the Bahnhof Hotel will honor my reservation, and I intend to hurry. Tell Francesca I'll be back in the morning for the cello, and don't think I won't. Goodbye, Anna."

She didn't answer, except to slam the door.

Rage carried me down the road from the castle to the village of Dorf Felsenburg and found me a taxi; fury saw me through check-in at the dismal Bahnhof Hotel in Bolzano and to a room where, for the first time, I realized I had left my suitcase at the castle with Ludovico. Angry selective consciousness, choosing what to see and think about and what (absolutely) not, carried me to the bar downstairs, where crankiness got two cold, crisp martinis placed before me and engulfed. After that it was the martinis' job to sit me at a table, order a meal, and keep changing the subject whenever Schloss Felsenburg or any of its denizens tried to butt in.

And they did a damn good job, I must say. At a loss at first, they drew my attention to a Wiener schnitzel before me and the imposing liter of beer that came with it almost without asking; the dim, probably dirty, paneled décor, the Forst Lager and Jägermeister logos, the huge, ornate beer taps, the tables full of horse-faced Bozeners grinding away in impenetrable Tirolean dialect, the soft-eyed Italianates who had stumbled into this nest of lost empire but were too stubborn to leave. *Bars,* remarked the martinis, *Great places the world over. How about that Kate Swain?*

I thought of Kate Swain in the Georgetown bar where - oh, only once or twice, but not accidentally - she leaned across me in her black, scoop-neck concert dress to get a napkin or some goldfish, let her knee barely brush mine while she told me how her ex never wanted her to be a musician, had no sense of rhythm - certainly not the rhythms of a percussionist - or of the joy of regular practice and performance. Kate Swain was clean, sensuous, and rounded; she worked out regularly at a Bethesda health club and looked it, matronly fullness disciplined by tight abdominals and wonderful posture. She was smart and funny and carefree, except that she cared deeply about music. We had been friendly, I had been pleasant, or a bit more, for a rehearsal or two and then preoccupied with Donia Ma. I hoped she had not given up on me, would be open still to an exploratory approach when I got back to Washington.

Two stiff martinis, a liter of beer, and two grappas to the good, I dawdled over coffee and lined up other prospects to place beside Kate Swain, but I had to admit I couldn't come up with any that didn't, as they say, pale. What it was, she seemed uncomplicated. Available maybe to other men, maybe lots of them, I would have to see; but certainly available to me. Great. Condoms, though, Jesus. Any more, you really didn't leave home without 'em. I sat in a bubble of silence and ran lines with her, and I never once veered into the Donia Ma script or into what I should have had the presence of mind to scream at Anna Rosen.

I looked up to find that the silence was real, compounded of the collective absence of all other customers and the chill patience of a waiter and a bus boy lined up aft of the bar waiting for me to look at my watch. After midnight. I rose competently and focused at the assembled staff, making the finger-rubbing sign of one ready to pay up at last.

As I climbed the stairs to my room, not at all sleepy but racked with fatigue, a last neuron fired: Com - what was that? A piece for percussion and cello, couldn't I do that, *commission*, that's it. Ring Kate Swain's doorbell in a straw hat, carrying instead of candy and flowers the new piece bearing a nuanced dedication, perform it with her? I could, I could. She would be...

My bed had been turned down, a little paper-shaded lamp burned beside it. I sat down to untie my shoes. Despair poured from the black corners of the room until I drowned. I would have been overjoyed to see how quickly I fell asleep, if I'd been conscious of it. I had expected to stare into the darkness for hours, too tired, too depressed to escape. In fact, except for some passages that consisted only of accelerations, then an interior, I passed the night without thought and woke to the terror of a bedside telephone.

Christ, I sat bolt upright in pitch blackness, heart ripping through half my life expectancy with every bang; naked, stifling hot. The phone screamed again, and I groped for it, figuring out it was not the alarm clock I hadn't brought, or a fire bell.

"What! Jesus."

"Herr Dienst?"

"Yes. What in hell time is it?"

"It is nearly six o'clock, sir. There is a lady here to see you."

"Oh, for - all right. Christ... Is the restaurant open for breakfast?"

"Of course, sir."

Of course. "Bring her a cup of coffee, or whatever she wants, and tell her I will join her there shortly."

Showering and re-dressing in the clothes I had traveled in, I tried to find words, a history that would overwhelm her. The effort was made stupendous by my jetlagged hangover, and pointless by the fact that I did not know which of the two ladies I knew here awaited me, or what they wanted. I guess I would have bet it would be Francesca, here to argue about the cello; but it was Anna. She was still dressed in black, stirring aimlessly at a cup of coffee in a far corner of the buffet. She looked younger than I remembered.

"Has it been another thirty years already? You don't look a day older, I swear."

"Thank you. You look like someone who has left his spare clothes behind. Again."

"Coffee, please. You remember that, do you? What else?"

"I would like to know how much of what you said to me yesterday you believe."

Out the window: a baggage cart, three variously defaced enamel placards reading Bozen/Bolzano leaning against a stone pillar; in my head, consciousness that it was midnight in Washington; and very little else. "Some. Half, maybe, but don't ask me which half. I half-believe all of it. You say I'm not Francesca's father, and you ought to know. It's hard to believe you had other lovers, but I don't believe in unlimited parthenogenesis, either. You'll forgive a certain moodiness, even this late."

"I have a request: This is being very difficult for me. Please don't go out of your way to make it more so, will you?"

"All right, Anna. Thank you. What brings you?"

"I wanted ... Well. You were right. Francesca confronted me immediately with questions about you, about the photograph. I think she overheard us wrangling in the courtyard, and she would not be deflected. She is not your child, but I did use you, your personality, your talents, your endearing if glaring flaws, and that photograph, to manufacture a father for her in place of the real one. I told her he was a cellist named Aaron, he was killed in a climbing accident soon after she was born. I know she will make it her condition for allowing you to take away that cello, that you tell her everything about us. I am here to beg you not to do so."

"Why did you do that? Who was the real father?"

"You ... please, you don't want to know. It has nothing to do with what I'm asking of you."

"I don't get it."

"I'm not asking you to. I just cannot bear the thought of Francesca prying and questioning into the past until she convinces herself of some stupid mistake, for example thinking that - "

"I meant, I can't understand how you think you can sit there and ask me to help you perpetrate a hoax about Francesca's father, and tell me I don't want to know who it was, when for Christ's sake it's the one thing I would care about this whole mess, if I cared about any of it."

"And do you?"

"Do I care who else was screwing the - " Anna looked at the waiter bringing my coffee, and I lowered my voice. "Screwing the love of my life when I thought I was the love of her life?"

"Care, screwing, love, jealousy, pain. Thank *God* it's over with. No one has, as you so respectfully put it, screwed me since Francesca's conception. Honestly, does it matter now who that was?"

I pushed back from the table. "What a goddamn stupid question. I tried to think of some more respectful way to put that, but honest, it's beyond the effort. I've got to hand it to anybody who could think anything else."

She looked at her hands while we paid attention to our breathing. "I can't afford for you to be hostile. If you won't cooperate on any other terms, I'll tell you; on the condition that you never reveal it to anyone. Ever."

Her face was full of shame and horror; those were the lines cut deepest. I tried to relent, waving an arm. "Anna, for heaven's sake, all right, forget I asked. It's over with, it's history." But it wasn't. I tried sounding understanding: "Look, was it Rick McIntear?"

"Don't, Oren. I said I'd tell you. It was... God. This is impossible." She lowered her head almost to the table, and when she spoke again, and I could barely hear her say, "It was Julius von Bayern."

I laughed, probably sounding like I'd been shot. "Anna, for the love of God. <u>Yoolie</u>?"

"I told you, you didn't want to know."

"I certainly didn't want to know that. But I guess it makes sense. He was sophisticated, he had a ton of money, he certainly had every reason to hate me. Hell, I knew you made those movies for him, didn't I? Stupid me. Hey, remember that Oren the boxer pup, the comical way he used to hump the knees of his betters?"

Anna held her head. "Oh, for God's sake. You see why I didn't want to tell you? You *always* get it wrong. Why can't you give me one tiny break?"

"Let's see. Guess I'm just my usual doofy self, here. What break can I possibly come up with? It's yours."

"You can imagine I would make love to Yoolie von Bayern voluntarily? You can really think that?"

" ... Gee, Anna, I've lost track of what I can imagine any more. Are we talking rape here?"

"Good, Oren. Yes. The second time, certainly."

"The 'second' time. Leaving aside for a moment, then, the question of the first time, how many? How many *total?* I'll *kill* that fucking ..." Shock paralyzed me. I stared at her hands.

She stared at my face, and then out the window.

"Oh, Jesus, Anna. You ... *you?*" Funny. It didn't feel at all like shocking news. It felt like when, in a dream, one turns at last to confront the faceless pursuer. She reached out and touched my head where she'd once slapped it hard before I could move. Her fingers were still smooth, graceful, long free of splinters. She looked tired.

Just tired. "Thank you," she sighed. "It's taken care of."

I am as reluctant to report this as I was to hear it. The first time was two days before I arrived there to steal Francesca, as Anna lay weeping in the von Bayern's guest bed, an easy target when Yoolie came in and began gently to apply salve to the welts Arnold had put across her back. He had to be a little forceful before the end, but she was already defeated, and she didn't put up much of a struggle. Hearing Anna describe it all those years later, it was rape, all right. I listened and seethed, and bent one of the Hotel am Bahnhof's coffee spoons into a W. Afterwards, Yoolie was boyish, repentant, swore never to let her seduce him like that again, at the same time assuring her it had been a beautiful experience for him, he bitterly regretted, while fully accepting, that he could never be for her what he so much wished, blah blah.

She said, "I half believed him. I wasn't capable of thinking or getting away from there. I couldn't think of anywhere I could go. Everything had gone to hell, all the way completely to hell, and it was my fault. The next morning I was sure I was pregnant. I could feel it all over my body... I should have killed myself then. I avoided Yoolie, I tried to have Nancy with me all the time. I told him never to do that again, and he just smiled. A few days later, he got me again."

The second rape was much rougher, an involuntary remake of the last part of Fire Bird out in the barn the afternoon after my night visit, while Nancy and her mother were off spending and I walked the streets of Chicago with Francesca under my arm. He needed help from the gardener to subdue and hold Anna, and he skipped the boyish-repentance part at the end, walking off with instructions to the gardener to let her go whenever he wanted. There was almost a third when Anna fled to the Orpheum hoping for help from Jacob and Mollie. Yoolie was there to inspect the repair work in progress and saw Anna before she saw him. When he tried to trap her in the dressing room, she screamed for help, but Jacob was away on his errand and Mollie could only watch while Anna fled, found the rough two-by-four, and turned to surprise Yoolie with it. He probably never knew she was left-handed, or that she had such quick hands with a bat.

When Yoolie was dead, Mollie called Anna to the balcony, comforted her and walked her through every detail of the attack, made her bring the bloody two-by-four up the ladder and help Mollie grip it hard enough to get splinters. She got Anna to see that it would do Mollie no harm to be identified as Yoolie's victim and executioner, and acquiesced in turn to Anna's stipulation that I was to be kept out of the whole thing, where I had told her I wanted to be. They figured out a role for Jacob, who'd been sent on his long errand when Yoolie spotted Anna entering the Orpheum, that relegated him to pretty much the same innocent dupehood as mine.

In the hours they spent cooking it up - sorry, in the hours it took them to "devise a credible and workable scenario" that would withstand any probing or innocent blundering the cops or Jacob and I could throw at it, they became very close. The three of them (I include fetal Francesca) became Universal Woman: self-sacrificing, doomed, manipulative, innocent, nurturing, pregnant, vulnerable, lying, lethal, every good thing She can become, to right the universe after brutal unconscious male rapine.

Well, I do not grudge them that bond. It pleased me that women I'd loved should love each other. They'd certainly earned it; it gave completion and closure to the whole headlong affair; and I consider the thirty years of pain I shared with Jacob Oxendine and the healing ceremony by which the Lumbees and I reunited him with Mollie more than adequate restitution. The thought of Yoolie von Bayern spending those thirty years frying in hell didn't bother me much either. With any luck, he and Dead McCauley might spend the next thirty eating each other's bowels, waiting for Rick McIntear and Jana to join them.

The Cello Francesca, *or* Balderdash

The next morning, in any case, Anna found Sister Maria Immaculata and gave her enough of the story to get a letter of introduction to Magdalena Haus in Lucerne, the stigmata of unwed pregnancy being at least as bad as those of manslaughter. The ticket to Lucerne cost almost all she had earned tutoring Spanish.

She reported all this in a dry, remote voice as if we were running a seminar in deviant behavior. It was too much for me, though. "God, Anna, why didn't you call me? Why didn't you try to get in touch?"

"Ask a twenty-year-old to take on Julius von Bayern or the homicide squad for me?"

I picked up her hand. "I'd have dropped everything any time you asked."

She withdrew it. "You may speak generously. And no doubt you mean it now. But it would have looked different then." What she meant was, I'd *said* different, when I told her I was through with her until she grew up and escaped Arnold's stifling tyranny.

We were silent for a long time, sitting in the Bahnhof buffet and looking back at our salad days. Anna began to speak again; about loneliness, humiliation, and despair at Magdalena Haus, about one failure of nerve when she wrote to me, concealing her location and her situation; and a second when, on a summer day in the eighth month of her pregnancy she not so much stumbled, nor exactly threw herself, but in a kind of resigned hybrid, let herself fall down a flight of stone steps at the convent. She recovered consciousness to find herself in labor, with a broken arm and a cracked pelvis. Francesca was saved and so was Anna, but the aluminum crutch entered her life then for good.

I can't say I sat digesting all this, it was indigestible. But after as much of a pause as seemed possible, I said, "I may be sorry I asked, but I'm glad you told me. Is this why you've been so hostile?"

"I beg your pardon. I don't recall being hostile."

"All right. You want me to say what to Francesca?"

"I want her to know that we were friends, which I think is true, but not that we were lovers. If you can't participate in the harmless fiction I offered her in place of the truth about her father, at least do not destroy what she has grown up with. You and I were close friends, lovers of books and music; and that's all."

"All right. I certainly owe you something, and - "

"You owe me nothing."

"Anna, allow me. I was your lover for all that time, and then I - "

"Three weeks."

"What?"

"Three weeks. That's what our great love affair amounted to."

"Oh, nonsense. Depending on when you start counting, but it was certainly all that fall."

"We first made love on October tenth, and the last time was November second."

"You kept track of that all this time?"

"No!" she snapped, then shrugged. "I kept track of it for a few years."

Whatever that meant. "Intensity counts. I loved you for a long time before we made love, and for a long time afterward. I'm not sure I don't still." I regretted the words and the rueful tone before I'd finished; I tried not to notice how quickly her face turned away. "I did everything I could think of to get back in touch with you, but the fact was, I didn't manage the main thing. You went off and had your baby, and I had promised to stay with you if you got pregnant."

"Not that way."

"I didn't specify, did I?"

"It's water under the bridge."

The Chain of Rocks. "Not if Francesca's upset. She seems like a perfectly fine kid. Look, if you're not going to tell her the truth about it anyhow, what would be wrong with her thinking I'm her father?"

"She is a perfectly fine woman. I made a weak, stupid mistake in naming her Francesca, and then in helping her find that cello with her name in it, and I would not have done that if I'd thought it would lead you here. I will not abet more fantasy that can only lead to more pain. 'What a goddamn stupid question,' Oren."

"Yeah, touché, but what pain? All sorts of people have grown up happily without knowing their real fathers. Adopted kids, for example, or the results of extramarital affairs..."

"I won't have it. The children you invoke grew up with *some* father, but this would force us permanently into a false position in respect to her, and to each other; and what possible reason could I have had for concealing your existence all these years, telling her you were dead?"

Easy does it, Oren. Stupid question indeed. The plan involved acquiring a cello, not a daughter, and so did the Kate Swain option, if Kate Swain was not just some Yahoo red herring. "I can't think of an answer to that."

"Nor I. Will you help me as I'm asking you?"

What kind of guy would snatch the cello of his dreams from his own daughter anyhow? All I dreamed for the future required that Francesca Beneventi neither be my daughter, nor even think particularly well of me. I reached for the check. "All right."

*   *

By midmorning I was sitting in clean clothes at a picnic table in the Felsenburg kitchen garden with coffee, buns and butter, listening to voices in the burble of the spring as it plunged into a watering trough, looking over the Adige Valley snaking its way toward the southern haze and smog through the sunny tag-end of the Alps. It was a different view from the westerly prospect I'd been admiring when this whole mess fell on me, and pretty in its own way.

I could claim I was getting used to the idea of Anna Rosen, not as a long-ago, mysteriously absent girl who had once been my lover, but as a living, middle-aged (oh, we could both live to be 100) mother, a near grandmother, the product of cruelty and neglect (including mine) visited upon the nymph I had thought I loved, and so forth. What I was really doing was vetting the situation according to the bureaucrat's six-point checklist: what were the (1) dangers, (2) obligations, and (3)

opportunities in it for (a) me, and (b) my work unit and
protegées, which I guess would be Francesca the cello, and the
Yahoos.

Parts 1a and 1b were easy to answer. Any Yahoo could
come up with a bulky and emphatic white paper against getting
involved in any of this except as raider, taking the Francesca that
was rightfully mine and getting the hell out; which would answer
3a and 3b as well. It was 2a: what were my obligations? that was
the problem, since Yahoos have no obligations. OK, I had
written to Anna, I had appealed to her in person for some kind of
reconciliation after Arnold's raid; had I ever really loved her?

A three-week affair, bOrin, sang Jana from the burbling
water; I could see her a thousand feet over the scenic valley,
throwing a key into the Mississippi with infinite slowness. *A sad
case of hyperactive gonads humping around a semiconscious oaf
in love with sex.*

Shut up, Jana. I certainly loved her. Ought I think of
loving her again or anew, this woman for whom sex was, thank
God, long over with? Now that we'd weathered the worst of our
re-encounter, a happy if sexless ending, sunset years with the
childhood sweetheart etc. appeared a possible outcome. But I'd
forgotten Anna Rosen, and that's the truth. I had kept her shut
behind the Wall, and I hadn't let her name pass my lips or cross
my mind for almost thirty years, and I'd never have recognized
her at Felsenburg if I hadn't been primed by Francesca's pictures.
She'd survived those years fine, or well enough, without me,
including bearing and raising Yoolie von Bayern's little girl to
whom I figured only as a deceased fake father. Far too much
water had passed under all our bridges for a reunion to mean
anything.

Lord; instead of following up the Manosduros business
and returning to Washington in triumph with evidence and
affidavits in one hand for a kill-or-be-killed with Rick McIntear;
and with Francesca Cello in the other, for a shot at Kate Swain? I
don't know whose gift to women I thought I was, if anyone's. But
a tart-tongued, crop-haired, peri-menopausal matriarch could be
nobody's gift to Oren Dienst, or what's a Hell for?

To close out the menu for thought, the Backstage
Yahoos, who didn't give a damn what passions were getting

sawn to tatters out front, were holding a rally to keep up a hard line on the cello. *You've spent a ton of money on her already,* they argued. *You walked through almost thirty years with a paralyzed arm for her sake. You're holding a very expensive plane ticket from Munich to Mexico to Washington in the name of Francesca Cello Dienst. Francesca Beneventi has everything she needs, and you have, well, exactly what? A mortally wounded career, no family, a crater in your life, so what if it came from friendly fire, and a third-rate cello by Gustav Schneider, honest, it makes us puke to listen to the thing. You deserve that cello, and you're going to have it.* They were using the floating-leaf passage from the Bohemian Nocturnes as the soundtrack, the clever bastards, and I could feel its resonances in my belly. Smetana, smoke, coffeehouses; a trip to Prague with Kate Swain.

I was sitting there with all of this in a Morris dance in my head, staring into the sunny haze, when Francesca Beneventi entered my vision carrying a basket of green walnuts and a trowel.

"Would you like some more coffee?"

"No, thank you, Francesca."

She looked out over the valley for a time. "It never used to get so hazy when we first came," she said, absently. She turned and faced me, a long hand draped over her belly. "You are not my father."

"No, I am not. Regrettably."

"But you are so like him. Did you know him?"

This was a contingency Anna hadn't discussed; it was my turn to examine the smog. Jana was still out there, hipshot, waiting to see what I would say.

And after hesitating for more than a split second, there was only one thing I could say, and be believed. "Yes. Yes, I did know him."

She lit up. "Really? You knew my Papa? Oh, my god, could you *please* tell me about him?"

Hell. "Sit down." Trying to say it gently. "OK. I'll tell you a bit about your father. He was charming and wealthy. But he was not a very good man, Francesca. He devastated your mother's life, and when I got in his way, he came close to ruining mine as well. He ... well. He died soon after you were conceived, and I have to say that nobody was consumed by regret over it. Not even …" I stopped.

Francesca began to bounce the trowel on the stone wall, moodily, pinka-ping. "Go on."

"That's all."

She looked crushed for a moment, and then seemed to reconsider. "Oh, really. You tell me these bad things, but you give no details. I think you are not - Look, Mr. Dienst. For a long time, for years, I've known no one could be as wonderful and talented as the father she invented for me. It was you in that picture, Mama admits that now. Was there an Aaron?"

"None that I knew."

"Was there a cellist?"

"I suppose that was me."

"Why does she tell me nothing about my real father, only things that turn out to be you? Do you have a sister who played the flute?"

"Not a sister. There was a woman who was very kind to your mother and me."

"To Mama and you? In what way?"

Oops. I shook my head. "I shouldn't have said anything. It's not something that I ... she was just a very kind person."

The trowel clanged against the stones. "Gesu Maria! This is infuriating. You and mother sit like schoolmasters and decide what you will or will not tell about <u>my</u> life. Don't you think I should be allowed some knowledge of my own father?"

"Yes, I do, but you must see there are things about which I would not know, or about which it must be up to your mother to decide what to tell you. I can speak to her about it, and urge her to be frank with you. But some things are not mine to tell or not tell."

"Very pretty. I think you secretly loved Mama, and you are still jealous of my Papa." She picked up one of the walnuts, a green ball that fit nicely to her hand, and looked down the mountain toward the barn, gritting her jaw. "That goddamn hawk is after our chickens again."

And she hummed the walnut after a raptor that was soaring in circles over the barn. It sang out over the barnyard, coming close enough to give the hawk a minor scare; it gave one or two contemptuous flaps and headed downwind. The walnut, with a lot of hop on it, sailed impressively out over the valley. Jana, of whom no one could have said that speed on the basepaths was her principal talent, was out by a mile. Francesca turned to me with a wincing shrug.

"I shouldn't do that when I have to perform this evening. Well, look. If you and mother think you're fooling anybody with that Platonic friendship business ... The minute I told her you were coming about the cello, it was plain as day you and she had a history that involved more than books and boats. I can understand her embarrassment in regard to myself, after some of the speeches she's given me. But it is beyond me why you collaborate with her, she so clearly jilted you for my real Papa. I regret interupting your ... your reverie, if that's what it was."

Jilted. She turned toward the kitchen; gawky, dignified. I was unmanned. "Francesca, you make me regret very much that you are not my daughter. You're right, I wish you were, but I can't change the facts. I'll talk to Anna; I have to warn you that you may wish I hadn't."

It took a lot of talking to convince Anna that my coming had retired the Aaron myth, and some version of the truth was needed now. She was furious that I had told Francesca as much as I had, but we worked out a mutually agreeable father to replace Yoolie, and a somewhat amicable parting for us. After lunch, we reconvened in the dappled garden, Francesca and I on one side of the picnic table, Anna and Ludovico on the other; Arnold puttering vaguely in the background. Anna did the talking, appealing to me for details like Mollie's last name and the exact circumstances of the Molar spill, laying out our affair in enough detail for anyone to see how completely engulfed in each other we were, speaking as clinically as if describing the pitiable symptoms of sick and deviant half-wits. I kept quiet even when I thought she was being a little hard on us. When she finished with Arnold's attack at the Orpheum, I intervened.

"You left out my mean little speech to you, Anna. Maybe I should give Francesca at least the gist of it."

" '*Jesus Christ almighty*'," she said without emphasis. "'*I absolutely give up. Goodbye, Anna. You're wonderful, but you're way too much for me to manage alone. Come and find me if you decide to grow up and leave this maniac.'* Of course Oren had just been knocked unconscious by Opa. Trying to protect me."

We sat long enough for Opa, maybe triggered by the words, to mutter and wave his cane at us from where he sat on a bench by the kitchen. Trudging through the thing again, I felt wretched. Sorrowful, guilty, still mad. Oh yes, and covetous about Francesca-the-cello. Ludovico came to the rescue by stretching and observing that maybe these things were best taken in small doses, and he, for one, had some practicing he absolutely had to do.

"You sound to me like a perfectly decent young couple. Pity you didn't get together in the end. Dr. Dienst, as you know, the Dorf Felsenburg festival opens today, and Francesca and I both have solo appearances this evening, which I hope you have time to attend, and to remain with us for the weekend. What would you say to just a bit of chamber music? Francesca is anxious to hear you play. Do you feel up to it?"

I looked at Francesca. She looked anything but anxious to let me near her cello, but otherwise pretty calm, given the weighty stuff we'd been discussing. She seemed more or less satisfied at the story so far, though she did raise her eyebrows at Anna during the Fire Bird part, to my (much delayed) satisfaction. It was a relief to stop. We'd been getting near the nub of it, the heavy sludge territory on both sides.

"If Francesca would allow me to use, uh, her new cello?"

Francesca gave me a neutral look, behind which Yoolie von Bayern bristled. "Of course."

I found the complete Beethoven sonatas in the familiar Peters edition among Francesca's music, a perfect beginning of a whole new life. "The A Major sonata OK?" I asked. Ludovico shrugged, having I guess played it and dozens more with Francesca, and sat at the keyboard, rippling practiced fingers over some of the runs in the last movement. Francesca brought the cello out of their bedroom. There, at last, was the one cello for me. I took a moment to look her over. There were a few nicks, enough to speak of thirty years of regular use, and someone had added a wolf suppressor. The form and colors, the high arch of the belly, were more graceful than I'd remembered. The varnish had lost the uniformity that stamps a brand-new instrument, and had begun to take on the patterns of age. On the upper bout, where the player's sleeve brushes, it had thinned and lightened. In another thirty years it would be bald, and the first of many over-coats would have to be applied. I wanted it to be my sleeve that did that. I would give Francesca her new varnish on my eightieth birthday.

Ludovico was a fine player, and Beethoven wrote the great Opus 69 sonata as an equal partnership of two strong voices. My opening solo was gracefully matched by Ludovico, who gave it a breathless quality, as if the piano itself knew what lay ahead for it, and felt its pulses jump in anticipation. As for me, unless you are a string player and preferably a cellist, I can't begin to describe the sensation of playing Francesca again. The silken sound was the same, but much more freely available than when she was new. She had blossomed under Meyerson's playing, she responded gladly and generously to whatever I asked. There were plenty of times I was glad I knew the part well enough that I didn't have to read notes through the blur in my eyes. The opening allegro and the Scherzo went well enough, I felt, and we arrived at the end of the Scherzo having established an alliance that allowed us a deliciously *rubato* resolution that left it suspended for a split second, then gently put it down. I exchanged smiles with Ludovico. Then, oh yes, Adagio Cantabile, the Meaning of Everything.

Ludovico's solo introduction of the one theme of this pregnant movement - a single 2/4 bar - transcended the pettiness, sang an aria for a Mozart heroine declaring love for the tenor. I entered on tiptoe, no vibrato, the merest chilly breath of sound on the high f sharp; Ludovico glanced at me and understood, and gave his playing a matte finish that blended perfectly with mine. In the sixth bar, both instruments crescendo and become warmer in tone, and we did it in step, inserting a tiny crack of silence between the top of that crescendo and the sudden quietness of the seventh bar. And it is in the eighth bar that the cello must leave its airy perch and take up the theme, warming to it in the brief space - everything in this movement is so compressed - of three sixteenth notes on b that take less than two seconds to play. During that two seconds I looked up and found Anna's eyes locked on mine. I picked up the pretty, domestic theme.

When we finished the finale, a little breathlessly, I embraced Ludovico - there was nothing else to do - and returned the cello to Francesca with a reluctant flourish, then followed her down the hall as she went to put it away.

"Oren, that Cantabile was really quite amazing. I think I will always play it that way."

"Thank you, I think. I'm very much looking forward to hearing you this evening. But for now, I think a walk and a nap would be very good for me. Can we postpone any more talk about your father?"

"It's obviously painful to Mama." She shrugged and looked down at her little paunch. "I can't see why, but I suppose there may be things I'm better off not knowing about my own blood. Let's postpone it for a while. Maybe some day ..."

"Maybe. I think you're being generous and wise not to insist, for now. If Anna is feeling anything like what I am about all this, she certainly doesn't need more stress on top of it."

She entered the room she shared with Ludovico, and I paused by the door. Looking at me in mild surprise from the mantle was the little limestone fossil I'd saved from pulverizing on the dock at Molar Chemical. I went over and picked it up. "You know, I gave this to your mother thirty years ago, back when - well, when . . ."

Francesca looked at me squarely. "Well, that accounts for how a mythical mountain-climber could have left me a perfectly real rock. Weren't you and mother as fond of each other as Ludovico and I are, or any other loving people?"

I tried to foresee traps. "We certainly were. The way you expressed your fondness for Ludovico in the car yesterday was what made me believe I had known you before. Anna and I were like that, even to her particular emphasis on ears."

She laughed, a little raggedly. "But if you were so attached to each other, why on earth . . ."

"I thought we agreed not to open this subject again."

She sat on the bed and combed her fingers through her hair. "Papa."

"Yes. But really, Francesca."

She rose and threw out her hands, and started to open her case; then turned, sudden grief in her eyes, gripping the cello Yoolie had snatched from me. "*You* killed him! Oh, my god, I see, you killed *my Papa,* and fled to a life of guilt and shame, because he - "

"Francesca, stop this, I'm begging you. I'll tell you one thing, because I can't bear for you to think that. No, I absolutely did not kill your father. But wild horses - "

She relaxed with a shaky, scornful laugh. "Mother always says that. How wild horses wouldn't induce her to - whatever. When I was little, it frightened me that a horse with claws and a long, snaky neck was going to take her away from me. One of you got it from the other, but I suppose you won't tell me which?"

"Sure. I got it from her, on an occasion you are welcome to hear about some time, if you absolutely promise not to think I killed your father. For now, if I understand the agenda, you go on stage in four hours. Don't you have some dressing and warming-up to do?"

"All right. I may not ask you any more about Papa, but you can't very well beg me not to think about it." She gave me a reluctant smile. "Thank you for telling me about mother's tactics in regard to ears."

"Heavens. Don't, whatever you do, tell her I let that out."

"No. But I don't promise not to tell Ludovico."

Ludovico, I thought, caught on to things quickly, and I wouldn't be surprised if he'd broken up our session at the picnic table because he had asked himself the same questions Francesca asked me, and had drawn his own conclusions. When I finally found the nursery, I collapsed on the cot and listened to the distant voice of Donia Ma in the spring; and had to be shaken by Ludovico to get ready for the concert.

Dorf Felsenburg has a medium-sized concert hall with carvings around the proscenium that wove themes of Christianity, hunting, and death in that peculiar mix so loved by Tiroleans. It was stuffed and buzzing with substantial personages, mostly locals and Bozeners who'd bought their seats a year ago, with a scattering of tourists guaranteed to be wealthy in view of what it took to patronize scalpers. I sat beside Anna, who had put aside her black for what I guess was her special-occasion outfit, a black skirt with an integral grey top with about forty buttons up the front and down the sleeves. The lights dimmed, the audience quieted except for a few tourists, quickly whistled into silence.

The Felsenburg Festival was an exhaustive affair designed to wade through the history of music from early times to the present, more or less in order. Tonight's Session I.A.3 would clean up a little unfinished business in the later Baroque and make a first pass at the 18th Century. The aim, I gathered, was to be able to say at the end of the two weeks, By God, we heard something from every decade of the last forty. A long program began with a decent, crisp chamber orchestra - those I had heard practicing in St. Martin's Church - playing the overture to *The Abduction From The Seraglio*. They had no conductor, but seconded the concertmaster with admirable precision and flexibility. Francesca looked regrettably at home with Francesca, take it in either order. Ludovico followed with Couperin, pieces from the "Folies Francaises", done lushly and wittily. A few times he glanced up from the keyboard to wink at us, but kept a stony forward face as he went through the "Benevolent Old Cuckolds" section.

Then there was a break while the harpsichord was carried off and players reshuffled on the stage. Francesca came front and center, from which position she would conduct and perform the great Haydn C Major cello concerto. The moment she sat down, she became as graceful as the cello, her awkwardness a memory. When the others were seated and tuned, she raised her left hand, waited until she sensed total attention, and started the orchestra behind her on its introduction with a precise gesture that involved all of three fingers. She sketched along with the bass line, laying out a few bars before the solo entrance as if to gather her powers.

And what an entrance. A thundering C major chord, the first any cellist learns, and she rose an inch from her seat with it. The C Major Concerto is a "masculine" piece, rational and forthright, and this slender, pregnant girl gave it a steely performance that took full advantage of the flexibility of the tight group behind her. Their attention to the shrugs and twiddles and head-flips by which she conducted them when she wasn't playing, and to the clear, singing sound the two Francescas produced when she was, made them not so much partners in a performance as part of a single instrument. The opening Allegro was majestic. The slow movement was heart-breaking; I have never heard anything like it.

The finale is marked *Allegro Molto*, and Haydn isn't kidding. It is a bit of a thing among cellists not to dawdle or stumble over its gymnastics, but Francesca took this to another level of velocity, of clarity, of dead-on rhythms, of not just accurate pitch, but pitch that exactly fit, and advanced, the harmonic structure of the writing; and with a wonderfully controlled flexibility of tempo and loudness that set every passage in a fresh and surprising context. Francesca (the cello), as she never had under my hands, sang as the angels sang at the Creation. Halfway through it I found myself breathless, gripping Anna's hand in delight, stunned by the starbursts of sound, the birdsong, the fireworks, and above all by the all-conquering joy of absolute mastery. Haydn himself could not have imagined his work more perfectly realized.

At the end, after a final revelry of scales, there is a quick three measures of orchestral underscoring, conducted by Francesca with modest finger-snaps and a grin of triumph that made her look all of 12 years old. Only the first half of it penetrated the applause. I leapt to my feet, and turned to lift Anna to hers. We were awash in a cataract of noise, of *brava's* and cheering, both the hometowners and the tourists weeping and yelling themselves hoarse, and I'll tell you, I cheered as loud as any. And when I found I could not hear myself for the noise, I said in a conversational tone, "Anna, I did really love you then." Just to see if it was true.

By midnight or so, we here home, gathered around the kitchen table. Francesca was in the ozone layer, and the rest of us, even Alex and Arnold, were keeping her there with praise and toasts and enthusiastic yelps. The Yahoos were utterly silent, having I guess gotten through their heads the difference between a talented amateur with limited staying power and a hard-working, sublimely gifted professional.

They looked the other way when I said as much to Francesca. She stood up and gave me a beaming hug, and the only thing that spoiled the moment was the cute little bulge in her tummy that nudged against the blade under my ribs: Yoolie von Bayern's seed, lined up to inherit Francesca. No, I thought. You're a great player, but I need her more than you do.

20. Balderdash

Sportsman's Park was no more, torn down years ago for the slick new stadium on the waterfront. The Browns were gone too, but someone had found them and brought them back, rebuilt the Park for one day. A good day it had been for Francesca Beneventi too, going three for four, making a couple of fine plays in center. It was all down to this, now, Francesca with her back to the wall in deep center, Kate Swain rounding third and pounding for home in a thunder of percussion, and only an angelic, a celestial throw had a chance in hell of getting her.

Francesca pulled a green walnut out of her glove and let it fly. In my vision, from the centerfield bleachers, it soared heavenward, climbing like a saint. At the top of its arch, a dot hung motionless in my view, and I was there with it, looking down at endless waters, starting to fall.

I sat up and found matches, squinted against the glare, and made out 3:30 on my watch. That certainly figured; it was a 3:30 kind of notion. But as I got up and put on a robe and, lacking slippers, my running shoes, coming more and more awake, it refused to assume the sheepish colors of a dream idea. I eased into the pitchy corridor, needing space, wondering about getting outside without stumbling into a pile of clattering lumber or a sheer drop-off. I stuck to the now familiar way back into the kitchen past Anna's room. Her door was ajar, with dim light emerging. Maybe I wouldn't have to pace until dawn.

I knocked gently on the frame and a little snore answered, a model of the one that newly pregnant Anna had sent into Yoolie von Bayern's conservatory thirty years ago. But it wasn't clear whose it was; when I put my head in I found Anna and Francesca curled together in the glow of a kerosene lamp. They were still in concert clothes, a book fallen from Francesca's hand, her head on Anna's shoulder. Nothing could have spoken more plainly of the childhood I hadn't shared. I knelt as quietly as I could for a look.

Here indeed was Anna; or at least what Anna had become in thirty years. Next to her, a long-limbed, clever-faced blend of Yoolie and the Anna I remembered. I sat back on my heels and defocused my eyes, trying to refute the null hypothesis. Well, it would be a struggle either way, and that's all I could bring myself to believe.

I eased through the kitchen and into the garden. At the corner of the hulk behind me there was moonlight, and I walked carefully toward it. A gate let me through into the courtyard that overlooked the western valley. Arnold's chaise lay empty in a pool of silver, and I lowered myself into it to pursue the idea that had brought me awake. I got no further with it. Too many variables, not enough equations. Thank god the Yahoos were sleeping somewhere. I didn't want them in on this. A stranger's face filled the moonlit valley, sleeping next to another stranger and then so was I.

I woke to a gleam of moonlight on aluminum, and Anna was standing at the wall. With waking came the realization that ambiguity was all I had. I wasn't ready to face Anna with it, but I couldn't skulk here behind her either.

"Anna."

She gave a little start and turned, her face now in shadow. "I didn't see you here."

"I didn't mean to scare you. Would you sit down for a minute?"

"I suppose. All right."

"Come here. Sit down." I slipped off the chaise to make room for her, took a breath, and opened the can of worms. "I'd like to hear the evidence that I'm not Francesca's father."

"Oh, for heaven's sake, Oren. Women know these things. Besides, you always wore a condom. And I started feeling pregnant right after Yoolie ..."

"Wait. I don't deny that women know things. But are they always right about the things they know? I'm sure Yoolie didn't bother with birth control, the miserable bastard. But what about our very last time, when Arnold found us? Do you remember whether I wore one then?"

Silence. In moonlight, everyone is pale, so I can't say that Anna was more than that. But she sounded pale. "Of course not. I can hardly stand to think about it. Please don't make me."

"All right. But I'll tell you, I've been trying to remember back then, sorting it out from all the other times, trying to get past Arnold breaking in and beating the hell out of us. It isn't easy, but I'll tell you the truth. No matter what little glimpses I can get of that, I can't picture myself putting down my cello and calmly unwrapping a condom and putting it on. The whole thing was just way too emotional. I'll bet you anything we were unprotected. And if so ... well," I shrugged. "I got there before Yoolie did."

Anna let out a long breath and folded over until her head touched her knees. "How tenderly you put it."

"I know. I need to work harder on tenderness when I put things. But it's true."

"Truth. It makes me feel like some, some . . . I don't know. It isn't flattering. It makes me feel like a doe in heat, you and Yoolie butting your heads over me."

"That's not so far wrong. I don't know about the doe part."

She got up with an impatient gesture and hobbled over to the parapet. "You're telling me over half my life has been based on a lie. How can I thank you?"

"A mistake. Well, a possible, certainly an understandable mistake."

"Shit. That's intolerable. It makes me into a lifelong fool, it puts my entire life since 1953 under the heading of 'understandable mistake.' "

"You sound like you'd rather she was Yoolie's child than mine."

"Peh. I don't think 'rather' plays much of a role during rutting season. Do you?"

"Damn it, Anna, I'd be on thin ice trying to guess the answer to that. Could we try and face up to this, for Christ's sake? I thought we were talking about the difference between a baby conceived during a reconciliation by, well, loving parents, and the very same baby conceived by rape."

Win, by all means. Have you thought what this would mean for the Kate Swain project? I went over and stood beside Anna, and we looked on the empty streets of Bolzano a thousand feet below. Anna put a thumb and finger over her eyes and began to shudder.

OK, here's the pop quiz: you're out in the moonlight with a woman. You don't want to get involved with her again, and she certainly feels the same about you. It's pushing 4 am. You've just said something that really upset her. Suggest three intelligent, humane courses of action, discuss advantages and disadvantages; select one and describe the likely outcome. I tried a comradely arm around her shoulder, but she shrugged it off. "All those years of shit for nothing. I can't face that. I can't stand the idea it was all a dumb mistake. Please don't make me think that."

"Why for nothing? I don't think that's what I'm asking. I'm asking you to consider there's a chance her father's not Yoolie von Bayern for god's sake. In any case, she's certainly your daughter, you raised her to be the fine, great person she is. You wouldn't lose that either way."

"Oh, thank you. What makes you think you're her father, any more than Yoolie?"

"I don't, necessarily. She's a fine cellist with a terrific arm on her. But the most I can claim is ambiguity. She looks more like you than either Yoolie or me."

Silence, then more tears. "She spent hours throwing rocks in the lake when she was ten, there must be a whole reef of them down there. You want me to believe that's your genes? That I've crippled myself for life because of a stupid mistake? Excuse me; a stupid *understandable* mistake, fool that I am. It's a horror, and it's all my fault, silly little slut who couldn't even keep straight which - "

"Anna! Stop! Do you think I want this to be true? It's certainly going to fuck up - excuse me. You did what you had to, every step of the way, with no help from anyone, least of all Francesca's father, whoever. You're a goddamn hero. Just ask Francesca."

"Fools often are."

I had no answer. Far below us a single car moved south, a bright blur dragging red sparks toward Verona on an unguessable errand. Anna took my arm and drew herself up straighter beside me with a little shudder.

"Suppose I could convince myself that what you say could be true. Suppose I forgive you, and you forgive me, and on and on; that doesn't change anything. You can't just laugh off thirty years of pain like that. They still happened, they're still there."

I was so tired I was on autospeak. "You bet they are, in the past. We did these things, and we can't undo them, they've been a knife in my belly for thirty years. Not that I would dream of comparing that to what you've gone through, *of course*. I'm not asking for forgiveness, and I'm sure as shit not laughing, but we might as well not consume ourselves with regret. We can live our lives without letting the past infect our living now."

She shook her head and stood at the wall looking over the silver land. "It's a heartless doctrine, and not one I'd have thought could come from you, you were always so ardent and conscious. I fell in love when you got so ardent, you spilled malt on your chin. But I guess there's a certain comfort in this. I promise to think about it. Right now I'm cold and in shock, and my nose is running."

Without thinking, I picked her up. "I might as ... please let me carry you in."

"...All right. Wait, my crutch."

I turned back, arms full of Anna, and looked at the aluminum stick. "Look, I'll have to come back for it, OK? Let me get you in, and I'll get it."

"All right." I carried her through moonlight toward the gate to the kitchen garden, but she said, "No, there's a French door to my room straight ahead, see the lamp?"

"I suppose that's pleasant."

"I love it. I come out here all hours, and nobody . . ." She yawned deeply and almost let her head fall onto my shoulder. "Nobody's the wiser. Oh, God, how can I sleep? That will do, thank you, Oren."

Francesca had disappeared, back to her own turf, I guess, and I put Anna on her bed, still in her concert dress with its hundred buttons. "Is that comfortable to sleep in? Do you want me to bring you a nightie or anything?"

"It's right here. Don't forget my crutch."

"Three seconds." Oh, maybe it was five or ten times that, but no more, and I was back with the crutch. The lamp was out, only a devotional candle burning under a crucifix at the head of the bed. Anna was a ghostly blur in a pale woolly nightgown. She always was a fast undresser, and I told her so. "God, you're fast, Anna. I couldn't have been out there - "

"Well, fast girls have more fun, don't they?"

"You want this by the bed?"

"It hangs on that peg, see it?"

I hung the crutch on a peg under the crucifix. It looked made for the purpose, peg and crucifix from a single cedar knot, worn and discolored from years of use. Anna lay back, and I covered her. Disarmed by fatigue, I couldn't help thinking of other times, and maybe she couldn't either. Her hand came from under the blanket and touched my cheek, gropingly. "I'll think about what you said, Oren. But I'm not sure it changes anything." I touched her hand, and she pulled it away as if it were infected.

How much thinking she managed, and how much progress she achieved with it, I couldn't say. For my part, I crawled into the nursery cot intending to lie on my back and stare into the darkness until I saw a way to get the hell out of here with my cello. What I saw was the sheet, with a drool spot gleaming darkly in a shaft of sunlight; I don't think I even got turned over in the intervening hours. I stumbled down the hall and managed a shower, that is, a self-wetting with a hand-held spray that also managed to douse quite a bit of the walls and floor before I called it quits and myself clean. In the kitchen, Ludovico sat alone, drinking coffee and going over a stack of what looked like invoices. When I appeared, he shook his head and shuffled them into a pile.

"You try, understand, to believe half of what these workmen promise you about schedule and materials, and twice what they say about costs. But they know that, so everything comes in three times too costly and one fourth as fast. I didn't see that nursery plasterer for so long, I think it was his grandson who finally finished the job, and they threw in funeral costs for the old man. Well, did you sleep well?"

"Once I started I did all right."

"Francesca was of course quite keyed up as well. She was very pleased by the performance; and by your kind praise as well, Dr. Dienst."

"Please call me Oren. Are we the only ones up?"

"Opa is in the garden. I suppose I understand now why he attacked you when you first arrived." Sly smile. "Dr. Dienst, you know, Francesca is already very fond of that cello. You play very well, of course, but - "

"Yes, well. It's painful to think about depriving her of it. She plays it like an angel. But that cello means far more to me than it possibly could to her. I watched it being built, I made the varnish, I was its very first player, thirty years ago. It represents something that never happened; in a few years I may feel differently, but I will not change my mind on it now. I like both of you very much, and if I could accommodate you on this I would; but I must suggest that you look for another cello."

Ludovico sat with pursed lips and watched Alex saunter in the open door and have a half-hearted pass at his food. He wandered over and nuzzled Ludovico's hand, belching and farting.

"I understand. I told Francesca I would try. She will make other plans, though there's not much hope of our being able to afford one that good for such a low price. Good Lord, Alex, what a display. God, you stink. What have you been into?" Alex wiped his muzzle on Ludovico's pants by way of explanation, and Ludovico wrinkled his nose. "Have you brought something home again?" He rose and walked out into the courtyard, and I stared out the window waiting for inspiration about the nice little surprise I had dragged onto Anna's doorstep.

Anna herself walked in before inspiration. She had on a black wool wrapper over the pale nightie I had last seen her in. She looked like the Queen of the Sleepless Night, and fatigue lines were in the ascendant.

"Good morning, Oren."

"Good morning, Anna. Did you sleep, finally?"

"Not really." She gave me a cool face. "I would like to apologize for allowing you to carry me in there last night. That was an irresponsible and upsetting thing for me to do, and it just compounded the irresponsible way I've behaved in creating this situation."

"Oh, for Pete's sake, don't worry. I was far from seduced. It was pleasant and expedient, that's all."

This didn't seem to strike the right note with Anna. "I regret it. I spent a great deal of time as nearly on my knees as I am capable of."

"And?"

" 'And'?"

I yawned. "Did your vigil produce a sign?"

"I hope you are not making light of the confusion and shock you have brought me by coming here and by propounding this extremely upsetting notion about Francesca's parentage."

I put a hand on the table. "Anna. The last thing I mean to cause you is confusion and rage. Shock. I truly believe the question of Francesca's parentage, fatherage, whatever, is, well, open. If it weren't for my own stake in this, you'd be welcome to think what you like about Yoolie. I thought you'd be glad."

"You thought I would be glad to have a hideous wound, that almost killed me the first time, reopened in the name of - what? Restorative surgery? Therapy?"

She picked up the crutch. Her face settled into deep lines of effort as she crossed the room and went out into the garden. She progressed slowly from one bush to the next, examining trees that must have been old friends, pinching buds and suckers, tending, pruning. When she reached the parapet, she turned and faced me. "All right, Oren, let's get right to it, you were always in favor of that. When had you planned to leave?"

"I hold a reservation out of Munich for tomorrow morning. To catch that flight, I will have to leave Bolzano tonight. I fly into Hermosillo, Mexico, Tuesday morning. I must get this and the question of that cello settled before I leave."

"Well. That crowds us a little, but it doesn't really change anything. Enticing Francesca to buy that stupid cello was unlucky for both of us, in the end, and typical of the way I've ruined things at every turn; but I can't, as you say, go back and undo it now. I think you must either take that flight - in which case, goodbye and Godspeed - or remain here in Dorf Felsenburg as Francesca's father. I am prepared to live with either choice you make. I will not countenance your coming and going like some absentee sugar daddy."

"Great. Good god, what's that amount to? What you mean is, you're prepared to endure either choice."

"Good guess. It would certainly be a relief for you to go; it would also cause me ... a good deal of pain. But substantially that has happened before, and here we are. If you stay, I will endure having the real Oren Dienst, with all your half-conscious egoistic cruelty, your goddamn half-talents and your - I don't know, your sharp tongue, your laundry, your anger, all the ways you've changed, or never were the Oren I loved. I'd have to be reminded constantly of the fact that I've wasted my life, my only life, over an 'understandable mistake.' Though I suppose, honestly, I could endure all that well enough if I knew you were here for good."

"Thank you for the attractive and flattering offer. Don't put it to me like that, black and white, go or stay. If I didn't think there were unresolved issues here, I'd be gone in a flash. But you can't deny me the chance to - I don't know, sort of ease into this."

"Can't I? I'll tell you one thing, if 'ease in' means for you to drop over here like Lieutenant Pinkerton every so often and put Francesca and me through this, and then leave again, well, no thank you. Absolutely not. Once through that is being plenty."

Hmm. Maybe that was what I had in mind, and damn her eyes for the Pinkerton crack. "No, I meant by that, uh, two things, I guess. Look, this has been a shock to me too, Anna. I'm still reeling. Two days ago you were gone forever as far as I knew, and welcome to it. And the other thing is, stay here and what? Putter around the garden? Help Ludovico with the chores?" Something, the momentum of logic, an absolute imperative that she not win an argument this important, led me beyond where I meant to go: "Look, you say I should drop everything and live here, or drop dead. I'm going to Mexico on EPA business, and it would be bad, truly, for me not to go. Well, you're welcome to come along with me. What about that?"

Want to live a happy life? Don't ask women to go to Mexico with you. The last time I saw the expression that Anna shot me was when I suggested to Markus Gewissner that he and Sophie were maybe getting a little carried away with each other.

"I beg your pardon? You want me to go to Mexico with you? What are you thinking of?"

Well, I thought it might be fun to get away together, you know. Have a little sort of honeymoon, I guess. What an extraordinary notion. We are not newlyweds, blah blah.

"Well, Christ, Anna, not permanently. A vacation for you, maybe, a chance for us to figure out what kind of future would be best for us. To give us a - "

"To give you a chance to decide between the lady and the tiger, is that it?"

Between Anna Rosen in the hand and Kate Swain in the bush? "Think of it as you like, but consider it a friendly, neutral offer. I expect it would be fun."

" 'Fun'. What kind of fun? You don't imagine I - "

"Ever have fun? Well, if you don't, I'm amazed you could think I'd want to vegetate here as Anna's long lost maybe-impregnator. What kind of a life is that? In a year you wouldn't know me from Arnold. I've got a job, responsibilities, all kinds of stuff up in the air. This Mexican trip is part of that. I can't - "

"Of course. Well, goodbye, then." Her mouth tightened. "And is this what we mean when we say 'drop everything any time you ask'?"

"Ow. Tarnation. That's not fair."

"Why not?"

"Well, because, see, for god's sake, it's one thing to drop everything thirty years ago to be with a young girl who's just had a horrible experience and finds herself pregnant and alone with the blood of a wealthy rapist on her hands, and - "

"And quite another to drop your big Washington career and whoever might be waiting for you in - Acapulco, was it? - Just to hang around a stuffy ruin with a murderous old crone? No, I guess I'd better not interfere with your life, had I?"

"Anna! Christ Almighty! There's nobody - *I* invited *you* - You're the one that - I don't even know where to start on such a load of horse - "

"Fine. *Don't* start. As for going to Mexico, wild horseshit couldn't - "

She stopped abruptly, and the damnedest thing happened. She looked up at me with a spark of laughter behind the sorrow and fury, and for just an instant the lines, the twisted body, the grey hair, all the sad costume of thirty years were a transparent overlay, crone makeup for "Our Town," and Jesus, *there was Anna Rosen*; Anna the magical, the infinitely desirable, the only love of my life. And something came whizzing over the horizon out of a dressing room in the long-demolished Orpheum Theater and pierced right through a lovesick twenty-year-old. And there, for that same instant, was Oren Dienst.

Oh, what a goddamn stupid disaster this was turning into. I looked for Kate Swain, but the bar was empty except for a brace of whores glumly sizing up a middle-aged guy with thinning hair and a martini, squinting at the CityPaper personals. I turned back with a shudder.

"Start with the easy stuff. Nobody thinks it's murder for a girl to kill a snake that's bitten her. Crone, that's the nuns talking, they got you into these black dresses and crucifixes and I don't know what, because you were this fallen woman, and it didn't make any difference that Yoolie tripped you and beat you while you were down, you were fallen. And in spite of your wonderful goddamn - " I tossed a hand. "Qualities, you bought that, you let them decide who you are and you went right to the top of your age range and grew as old as you could as fast as you could, and the end of that road is, you're creeping, I'm sorry, cringing around under a shawl with eyes downcast - "

"Stop it! I don't know what the hell you're talking about, and neither do you. You're getting clichés out of Zorba the Greek or somewhere, God knows - "

"The point is, you're not even 55 years old yet - "

"I'll be 55 before - "

"I know when you'll *be* 55, you think I can't add 24 and 30? We're violating Rule One and there's a big penalty for that, but I'll give you another 15 years starting from the hard on you're giving me right now, and then maybe we can talk 'crone' and I'll be a geezer by then, and if we were together, maybe we could still hobble down to the park, and crow and geeze until they called the carabinieri. And in the second place, it's not Acapulco, it's Hermosillo. Wait, it's not even Hermosillo, which I guess might have some slight charm, it's Manosduros for God's sake, a binky little mining town that got ... that lost whatever virginity it might once have had at the hands of - get this - our old double date Rick McIntear. If I don't show up there on Tuesday, Rick will figure out a way to get away with huge crimes, with ruining the lives and desecrating the ancestral bones of a town full of hard-handed, salt-of-the-earth miners... You don't want that, do you?"

Anna's eyes widened, and she looked young for two seconds, then middle-aged and furious again. And while that was going on, Francesca stuck her head out the door, jingling keys. When she saw me, she lifted her chin. "Good morning, Or- Dr. Dienst. Ludovico told me about the cello. I didn't know it meant so much to you, and I think you should take it. Mama, is there anything you need in the Dorf?"

"No, I think - "

"Yes, Francesca. First, thank you very much for being so understanding. You're very kind. There is something your mother needs. Is there a phone?"

"Yes, at the Bar Centrale."

"Please call Lufthansa and whoever else and ask them if they've got an open seat on any flight - "

"Oren, I forbid - "

" - to Mexico in the next two, no, three days. If they do, book it. I'll pay for it and the call, I'll give you a card."

"Oren, stop this. I have not said yes to that stupid idea. Francesca, never mind - "

"Just find out, Francesca. We can always cancel the booking if we decide to."

"If *I* decide to, and I will."

"OK, OK, fine. Thank you very much, Francesca. Wait just a second."

I went back to the nursery for my wallet, and by the time I was back with it, Anna was gone and Ludovico on stage in her stead, nuzzling egregiously at Francesca. I gave her the credit card, saying I wanted to carry her Mama off to Mexico, and she departed with what seemed a genuine smile; I turned to Ludovico, running a hand over my face.

"That is a fine young woman. I certainly wish - "

"Never mind, please. I found the source of Alex's stink. I have a little job, and I could use some help. Would you be willing?"

He led me into the courtyard. Alex was prancing, grinning crazily, by the pipe that brought spring water down from the mountains into the watering trough. The water had nothing to say, posing prettily in the sunlight: cold, clear, fizzing. But it smelled rank, like something dogs think is fun. "Pew. What is it?"

"Something fallen in the spring and drowned, no doubt. It's covered, but not air-tight. The neighbors have herds up there in the summer, and animals wander away and come to grief one way or another. I'd better go up and see what it is. Want to come?"

Yes, I did. I could think of no better use for the late morning than to leave Felsenburg and Anna Rosen behind for a good while and do something gruesome and mindless, somewhere high. "Let's go."

Ludovico shut Alex in the kitchen and picked up a rake and a brush hook from the woodshed in the courtyard, and we started to hike up the slope behind the castle, following a rocky double track past vineyards, climbing where no tractor could have driven. Ludovico swung along easily; I tried not to puff too loudly. I could have lived here, I thought, struggling with crops and weather and unreliable workmen, letting the hardness of the mountain seep into my legs and my chest as the air and sunlight were already doing.

We passed a high orchard clinging to a relatively level meadow, dwarf trees so heavily loaded with pears that they seemed in labor. The track started up a little valley, down which plastic pipe brought tainted water to Felsenburg. At this altitude it was cool in spite of the season and the blazing sun, and a few warblers added notes to the little stream that burbled down one side of the valley. Ludovico knelt by it, and got up with a shrug.

"This smells perfectly fine, though I wouldn't advise drinking it. Giardia, it'll give you a bad two or three days."

"That's too bad; it seems so remote and unspoiled here."

"Nowhere is unspoiled, Oren. There are houses and animals above us yet."

The valley began to narrow and steepen, and near the point where the walls converged, a cistern crouched, capped with slabs of stone.

"The spring rises inside there. It was fortified by the old people, but that's barely ruins any more; it was destroyed in 1310 by the Pope's armies. If you look, you'll see traces of the old walls yet. Let's see what's gotten into it."

One of the stone slabs was of a size to be pushed aside by four hands, and we did, letting sunlight into a dripping pool of dark water, and letting a puff of doubtful air out.

"Uch! I'm glad we haven't been drinking that. And yet, I see nothing wrong. You can see to the bottom, and there's nothing. The trouble may be farther up, I suppose."

We heaved the slab back over the cistern and began to wander up the short stretch of meadow, peering into the woods and rocks above. I found a line of building stones in the tall grass by tripping over them and going to my knees in a skim of very smelly water.

"Ludovico!"

We stood with hands on hips, peering into the mass of brush out of which the water oozed. Ludovico, eying the slope back to the spring, opined that this trickle - a new feature since a rainy July - might easily be the source of the pollution. "This is rocky soil, and it really doesn't filter out very much once the water gets below the roots. Can you see anything up there?"

"Not really. It's pretty dark under the briars. I don't suppose you have a flashlight with you?"

"How's this?"

By reflecting sunlight off the blade of the brush hook, he managed to send an erratic glow into the thorns. "There! Back to the left, see it?"

It was a tuft of wool, blowing feebly on a briar at the edge of the thicket; and behind that, something that looked dead, at best.

"A lamb, I think, from one of the neighbors' flocks. Well, let's get in there and get it out." He began to hack, and I gingerly to pull, at the mass of briars and vines. The smell got richer as we got closer to the source. We launched legions of flies, and before long we were both gagging.

"You know, Oren, we should probably make a bonfire and clean up this thicket. There's kerosene and matches in the woodshed where I got the tools, if you wouldn't mind?"

I didn't. I started off in a loose downhill jog, the way we had come.

At the lower end of the high orchard a stone wall crossed the path, and from its top I could see Schloss Felsenburg lying in the sun below. Arnold Rosen crept into view, headed for his chaise. He looked about an inch tall, much transformed from the bully of Anna's youth and the seven-foot horror who loomed as I lay over her, ribs breaking, sperm afoot and light-hearted in search of its fortune. I hopped down from the wall, and felt the ribs and a good many other bones as I loped down the path on Ludovico's errand.

By the time I got back to the meadow, Ludovico had exposed a pathetic scene: the front three quarters of a lamb far gone in decay, black bones and empty eyes, with fragments scattered; and close behind it, the bloated corpse of a good-sized dog alive with maggots. The stench was amazing.

I gagged politely. "That'll spoil your lunch, won't it?"

"That and the melodrama."

"Mm. Rather than a Christian burial, how about cremation?"

"Yes, and we'll have to dig a trench to divert this water past the spring in any case. I think it should clear itself up in a week or so."

We fell to pulling out the remains not only of the lamb but of the dog that had killed it and then fallen victim to its own choke-chain, looped over a thorny cane of briar.

"The wages of sin, Oren. This is Attila; excuse the pun, but a bone of contention between his owner and most of the farmers on this mountain."

Attila belonged to a hotelkeeper in Dorf Felsenburg, and he was a real favorite of the tourists who stayed there. He knew how to shake hands with newly arrived guests, and he let little children ride on his back; but at night he would raid the flocks. Everyone knew it except the hotelkeeper, who wouldn't admit it even when a lamb's hoof was found in Attila's pen. Something the butcher threw there, he claimed. When Attila disappeared some weeks ago, only the hotelier and his guests mourned.

It took a long time to finish it, hacking the brush away and pulling the corpses out with the rake and finally by hand when they kept falling to pieces. Attila was not as far gone in postmortem transformation as the lamb, but he was the source of most of the smell. He appeared to have eaten some of the lamb's hindquarters, which probably kept him alive some days longer.

In the course of that, and digging the diversion trench, and building a fire big enough to take in its stride our pathetic, stinking offerings, we gradually stripped to save our clothing from destruction, and then realized that we were in no condition to put it on again, and had no resources for getting clean. It didn't bother us all that much, sitting on the ancient stones and poking at the fire while the muck dried on our bellies.

"All we need," I said, "is a shaman to tell stories of the old times."

"I thought you and Anna did that pretty well yesterday."

"It's a different story when it's your own. Anna's very upset this morning."

He raised a polite eyebrow. "It's an old one to her, surely?"

"Not the latest version. I think there's a pretty good chance that I am Francesca's father; not this Aaron, who never existed; and not ... mm, not the guy Anna thought it was, either. And if I am, it changes a lot of things she's built her life around."

"You do surprise me. I would not have thought Anna the kind of person about whom such questions could possibly arise."

"No, of course she's not." I laid out the whole thing for him, starting where we'd left off the day before. He nodded for a while, then lit a cigarette and squinted through the smoke at the valley. When I finished, he flipped it onto the ashes of the luckless animals.

"In regard to the cello, then - "

"Yes, yes. If I'm Francesca's father - I say, if - then I'm in the position of coming out of nowhere and celebrating meeting my own child by depriving her of something she values. From that angle, I'd rather she were a Florentine duke with a dagger on his hip. Instead, she's a sweet, entirely admirable young woman and a fine cellist, so I'm in a bad position in any case. We have no way of knowing the truth about her father, or how she'd feel about it if we did. We could think of some kind of loan, or sharing arrangement..." The Backstage Yahoos, who'd been out of touch and quiet since the concert, spun from watching maggots roast and set up a howl. I felt a stab of rebellion. "But I just can't do it, I can't let it go, waste this trip."

Ludovico said nothing, so I kept talking to prevent silence. "I could give Francesca the cello, just like I could have found Anna back then, been a father to her baby, whoever the real father is, or was. She told me to take a hike, and disappeared. I have a few years left to finish putting myself back together, and a cello - that cello - is a big part of it. It won't be that long before I can't play any cello, and Francesca will be welcome to it then. That's the best I can do. I don't apologize for this, Ludovico."

He shrugged. "No doubt she would be pleased by such an arrangement. In regard to finding Anna, this might happen in some long-ago tale of star-crossed lovers. Real people weigh probabilities and consequences."

"The more you say, the worse I feel. Maybe real people want to be star-crossed lovers. I didn't weigh anything, I signed up for Engineering Physics."

"Meh. I'd have done the same, though maybe not engineering, I could never stand that stuff."

"Want to know something? I never cared much for it myself. Think this fire's safe to leave here?"

"Let's have the brush hook, and I'll clear a little space around it, but the ground's so wet that it's certainly going nowhere. Will it bother you to leave your clothes off until we can use the hose in the garden?"

"Should it?"

We descended to the castle in downhill strides with our clothes on a pole between us; naked, reeking, sunburned. Anna took one look and handed Ludovico a bucket and sponge, and disappeared. Arnold, thank God, was asleep on the terrace, and

Francesca still on her errand. Only Alex had the presence of mind and common sense to bark at us. A half hour later, when I was again my civilized self, comb tracks worthy of Harvey Napperson, I sought out Anna and found her on the west terrace with a book. She looked up with a smug, neutral air when I appeared. Francesca was back, looking dashed.

"No luck on the airlines, I'm afraid, Oren. Francesca says she tried seven major airlines plus Virgin Atlantic, whatever that might be. Not the one for me, I suppose, but in any case, neither are any of the others. I'm staying."

Francesca handed my card back with a crestfallen air. "Papa, I begged them, I tried everything. Every airline has heard every story."

"Oh, well, then … I stared at her. "Papa?"

She looked severe. "Ludovico told me what you said to him up on the mountain. Honestly, I don't care what anybody says. I grew up with your picture as the only Papa I ever had. Now here you are. I'm just going to call you that from now on. That is, if you'd allow it?"

"Allow it? Holy shit, Francesca, I - "

Anna snorted. "Never so interested in anything in my life, isn't that how it goes? The older you get, the more you repeat yourself. I'm sure it's a sign of - "

"Shut up, you infuriating crone. Francesca, you understand there is still every chance your real father was a cruel, arrogant bastard who raped your mother twice when she was young and helpless, younger than you are now."

Francesca looked taken aback. "I don't believe it for a minute, but even if that were the literal truth, I can still choose you for my Papa. I don't know who this other guy was, and I don't want to. Oh, but Mama, how awful; can't he be punished some way?"

"I think he's being - "

"Stop it, Oren. *La Commedia é finita.*" Anna drew Francesca against her side. "You made it all right a hundred times before you were a year old, and you've been nothing but one joy after another since then. We won't worry about that old man any more. He's long dead." She looked at me with something a little like regret, if you imagine triumphant regret.

The Cello Francesca, *or* Balderdash

"Anyway, speaking of long dead, it looks like you'll have to rescue your ancestral bones without me. You could benefit quite well, it seems to me, from some time by yourself to decide what you really want."

"Oh, fine. Thank you for that helpful - "

"Ancestral bones?" Francesca cut us off smoothly.

"Imagine," I said to my daughter. (My *daughter*, Jesus! Just the silent letters made a joyful whisper, a wind dressed in Yahoo motley, capering and giggling somewhere backstage.)

"Imagine it's 1570. A conquistador, Pancho, uh, Villa-Lobos. He's not one of the big ones anyone's heard of, but plenty fearsome and rich enough to bring to his household from Spain to Mexico with him: his glamorous wife Barbara and their four-year-old daughter Madelena, the apple of everyone's eye; and he brings an Italian priest, Padre Ricardo, and a major-domo."

Anna got up with a sniff and started for the kitchen; Francesca reached out and stopped her, folded an arm around her waist and sat her on the wall.

"They live in a huge house on the Pacific coast of Mexico, where little Madelena grows up pampered and happy, her food and shelter more than provided for by her rich, fierce father and her soul, simple as it is, in the care of Padre Ricardo. Villa-Lobos goes off every morning to seek the city of El Dorado, and though he never finds it, he does run across plenty of gold on his way, since this country is pretty well sprinkled with mines. Every so often he brings home a big bag of it and has it made into baubles for Barbara and marbles for Madelena. And, uh, reliquaries for Ricardo. Barbara, who never figured out that being glamorous is nice, but not a life's work, spends most of her time checking out the effect of each new bauble, or combination of old baubles, on her beauty.

"Madelena helps with this sometimes, and spends the rest of the time singing and learning to play various instruments, since she is very musical. The major-domo oversees a household staff of despised Aztec slaves who work there for as long as they can before they contract some trivial European disease, colds or lumbago, and die of it.

"After a dozen years of this, here's the situation: Don Pancho and Barbara have become fat and dull, spending all their time eating, and playing with gold crucifixes; Madelena has grown into a beautiful young alto who can make even the church music of the 16th Century sound like Mozart. Not one of the original Aztec slaves is still above ground. And Padre Ricardo has so far forgotten his vows as to fall in love with Madelena, and we're not talking some comical cleric's crush here, no, but a creepy concupiscence so cruel it makes Madelena sick to see it."

I blinked. Apparently, some narrative demon had taken over the controls. I sat on the wall and stared at the crumbling facade of Francesca's fairy castle.

"One Sunday dinner, after she's escaped from another of Ricardo's stupid double-entendre confessionals, her hand passing the wine to Barbara trembles, and a few drops spill. The major-domo's fingers snap and an Aztec boy named Xltlpec, who came to the house one afternoon over a year ago to pick up his recently deceased aunt's umbrella and was never allowed to leave, rushes forward with linen to mop it up. His eyes meet Madelena's and there is magic. As he leaves to scrub the kitchen they glance again, and before you know it there are messages, trysts, passion, and finally, inevitably, parenthood, all in the space of three weeks. The forbidden love escapes for a time the sluggish attention of Pancho and Barbara Villa-Lobos, but not the evil priest, whose desire for Madelena becomes so inflamed, so twisted that she falls really ill - at sixteen, and now pregnant! - with what we would now diagnose as acute anemia. Ricardo's vicious lust is actually stealing her red blood cells one by one, and then a hundred at a time, and day by day, week by week she becomes pale and tired from the double burden of the child and the clerical vampire who cannot bear to see her happy in the arms of a heathen Aztec. And when Madelena's condition begins to show, he convinces the gullible parents that she has been impregnated by the Holy Ghost, and now belongs to the Church; and naturally must be left strictly in his, Ricardo's care, in preparation for a miracle to come.

"As her pregnancy and her illness race toward crises, Madelena must spend most of her time in bed. Xltlpec brings her only joy along with the meals at which she picks. Don Pancho – a marginally practical man who never really bought the Holy Ghost riff, is frantic, and asks her what will make her well and happy; in an extremity of weakness, she reveals her love for Xltlpec and begs her father to let her marry him, hoping divine blessing will defeat Ricardo's blasphemous lust. Villa-Lobos takes the question to the priest, who of course forbids it. Xltlpec is more than willing to convert to Christianity, if that's what it will take to save Madelena, but Don Pancho lets himself be persuaded by Ricardo that to countenance marriage to even a converted heathen of another race would short-circuit the Second Coming and assure his own excommunication and eternal damnation. Xltlpec is banished from house and country, and given to understand that to return is to incur certain, protracted, and humiliating death. Pancho and Barbara take Madelena to a seaside convent to be prayed over by nuns and Padre Ricardo, but of course it does no good. All of her but her belly slowly shrivels, so she looks like a pregnant granny doll.

"Xltlpec, of course, fights his way through incredible odds to find Madelena and penetrate the convent, carrying her away in the middle of Sunday mass while Pancho and Barbara kneel at their fruitless orisons. The lovers set out to sea in a canoe, seeking an Aztec healing goddess who inhabits the sunset, a statue-who-is-not-a-statue, who moves so slowly that one must speed time itself to see her move, who presses into the soul of the sufferer words like magic needles of unspeakable sharpness that can pass harmless through bones and vital organs to skewer the devils of sickness.

"For three days and nights they paddle westward over a sea as flat and ominous as a mirror while Madelena weakly, and Xltlpec tiredly, sing songs of love and of supplication to the healing goddess, and lullabyes to the child who sleeps within Madelena. At nightfall on the third day, Xltlpec must stop paddling at last and sleep, which he does in Madelena's pallid embrace, while the flat sea acquires a gentle, then a serious swell that lifts and lowers their canoe to a rhythm slower than Madelena's breathing.

"Before dawn comes a storm bigger than anyone in all of the Aztec empire can even remember hearing their grandfather brag about. An enormous tidal wave sweeps the coast of Mexico. Madelena's family and the evil Ricardo are killed outright when the treasury walls collapse and immure them in mountains of gold. Madelena and Xltlpec are found a hundred miles inland in the little village of Manosduros, still in their canoe, which has been propelled up the broad Manosduros River by the storm surge and deposited on the lower reaches of Montoro, just above the new church. Xltlpec is unconscious, wasted to a blistered skeleton by his heroic effort; Madelena, alas, is dead, on her face an expression of fear but also great joy. Through her heart is a needle so fine that it is not found until her body is prepared for burial.

"And buried she is, in the churchyard where the canoe came to its own final rest. Xltlpec, being heathen, is not allowed to visit her grave until he converts to Christianity. He is baptized by the bumbling old priest at Manosduros, though he insists on repeating each response of the catechism in his own language after giving the approved answer in Spanish. He then spends every day at Madelena's grave, never eating, singing to her, listening, sometimes sounding like he's talking to a baby. Some Manosdurans swear to the old priest they hear other voices, barely louder than the wind, but not the wind."

I looked up in time to see Anna roll her eyes; Francesca stood by the chaise, Arnold's blanket dangling from one hand and the other on her belly. She was smiling, but tears were cascading down her cheeks. Arnold looked other-wordly, as always. I plunged ahead.

"Xltlpec, who has been ill with ordinary European sniffles, dies. After he is buried with his family, the graveyard quiets down. And it stays quiet for almost four centuries, until in our times, just this year in fact, evil MexiLar Metals comes along, digging and ripping, and a flood of stinking poison unearths the bones of Xltlpec and Madelena, along with many others, including some so tiny and fragile that they are seen by no one but the despairing skulls of their parents." (Here a small gasp of dismay from Francesca. I decided to lighten things a bit.)

"A commission of forensic scholars is sent by the provincial government to restore sorting-out and dignity to the scattered bones, but MexiLar is desperate to conceal the evidence of their crime. They descend on Manosduros with enormous bulldozers and a dumpster big enough to engulf Schloss Felsenburg, and begin scraping and dumping. A flimsy injunction stops them for a few days, but they are poised to begin again next Thursday, four days from now and four centuries to the day from Xltlpec's burial. Now, I can see to it that the might and prestige of the respected United States Environmental Protection Agency is brought to bear on behalf of the pathetic remains, but I must be there before the injunction expires.

"And I'll tell you something else," the demon's momentum made me say. "I can't do this alone. I need an interpreter, someone really good at Spanish who can spend mornings helping me track down documents and interview witnesses, and a lot of afternoons in the sidewalk cantinas, sweating and licking the salt from her tequila, listening to unemployed truck drivers and expatriate fools grumbling about the heat and the impossibility of ever leaving Manosduros while she sifts their idle bitching for clues to MexiLar's nefarious ..."

I trailed off at last, but it was too late. Francesca turned ardent eyes to Anna, and grabbed her arm. "Mama, you must go and help Oren, you must. You would be perfect."

Anna blistered me with a look, and I backed up: "Oh, really, Francesca, I don't see how that can happen now; and it was just a story I thought you might like. It was only - "

Francesca's eyes lit, and she started to jump up and down. "Wait! *Wait.* Was that ... was it ...oh, what *is* that silly word? Banner ... biller ..." She snapped her fingers a couple of times, and then her face cleared. "Was that *balderdash?*"

I shrugged and nodded, and sighed. "Yes; regrettably. Particularly the last -"

"Ha *ha!*" Francesca raised her arms to the sun, her face shining. *"No one could spout balderdash like your Papa,"* she caroled. You told me that, Mama, and now I see it's true. He *is* my Papa, and he is our baby's Opa." She turned to me. "Will you promise to do that for the baby?"

"Of course, though, it's not something I have much control over. And as for your coming with me, Anna, I really don't see how that would be possible, or at *all* wise. You surely have, well, ... "

Francesca turned to Anna with protective hands over the paunch, my maybe grandchild. "Lufthansa can be bribed. Mama, if you don't do everything you can to save that baby's bones from the dumpster, I will never speak to you again as long as I live. Or - oh, no. Was it <u>all</u> just balderdash? No dumpster, no bones?"

"No, they're real enough."

"And Madelena?"

Anna held up a hand. "Never mind, Francesca. Luckily, there is not a chance in hell of my going. Do you think I would go to Munich and try to bribe some Nazi into letting me on an airplane when I don't even want to go?" She made a dismissive gesture. "And besides, it's just so - there are just so many things up in the air that we haven't - " She raised her hands, fingers spread to indicate all the things that we hadn't. "Well, I bet this will end it right here. There would be no sex."

I blushed, and looked at Francesca, who was luckily bending over Arnold in response to some peevish request. Ludovico knelt quickly, searching Alex for ticks, biting his lip.

"For heaven's sake, Anna."

"Not in front of the children? Will you excuse us for a moment, Francesca?"

"Hm? All right. But you might as well know I'm not going to change my mind about this, mother. You're going, if I have to go to Munich and stuff you on that airplane."

Anna sighed. "She was never like this before she got pregnant."

"Takes after her mother, then, does she?"

"Ha ha. Well?"

"Well, what?"

"You heard me."

"Anna do you know how long it took me to put myself back together on that?"

"Excuse me. If you have managed to do that, you're well ahead of me. You are more than welcome to enjoy whatever residual prowess may remain to you. I just meant, no sex with me."

"I'd feel like a fool and a cad with anyone else."

"It's not my place to deny your feelings."

"Anna, this is most unfair. Can't we agree to disagree for now?"

"Oh, yes, and wait till some hot afternoon in Manosduros, and you've had two or three salty tequilas and so have I, and I'm taking a bath while you're down in the bar with Yves Montand, watching some hooker scrub the floor with her blouse hanging down, and you come up to me while I'm hot and languid in the tub, wisps of hair sticking to my sweaty brow, and you offer to wash my back for me, but it turns out that's just for starts, it all comes back, it's just wonderful, old times, yes, but ... "

"You too?"

"Yes, but then what? I will not have it. My life's work has been to get over you. Don't make me do it all again."

"I thought it was getting over Yoolie."

"Well, I made that 'understandable mistake,' didn't I? From a certain point of view, it was; from another, all he caused me was two or three very bad moments, and a daughter I suppose we may now agree was never his to begin with."

"And I - "

"You almost killed me and Francesca, Oren. When I let myself fall down those steps at Magdalena Haus, it was because I wanted you so badly that I believed that I could *will* you to show up at the last instant to save me."

Words of unspeakable sharpness. Thing is, I didn't feel that much healing going on where they penetrated. I looked out over the valley for a long time, with nothing to say and nothing to think. At last I felt Anna's fingertips on my arm; comforting, ambivalent.

"There. It's over with, and there's no reason to consume yourself with regret. I'm not sorry I said that, but now that I have, I don't have it to say any more. Maybe I'm a little sorry I can't go with you to Mexico, though I think not. When you get back to Washington, why don't you sit down and write to me, with a plain, responsible plan for our parenting Francesca, that doesn't involve Mexico or male-bonding campfires or conversational erections; maybe you could plan to visit when the baby ..."

She probably kept talking at me, but I didn't hear any more, and anyhow, I could have written it all down beforehand. The thing was, I suddenly saw how easy it would be for her to come to Mexico. I had to admit, it wouldn't give me everything I wanted; but what makes folks think they got a choice what they get, an' when they get it?

The truth was, compared to Francesca Beneventi I was no more a real cellist than Yoolie von Bayern, and my reasons for wanting the cello barely better than his. The truth also was that I wanted no thing of wood and wire half so much as I wanted Anna Rosen, in spite of the equal truth that I wanted no such thing under any circumstances.

Aw, to hell with it. I pulled out my wallet and found Mrs. Meyerson's bill of sale. I borrowed Ludovico's pen, and Arnold's head for a desk:

"Sold to Francesca Rosen Beneventi for one lira and other good and valuable considerations."

Think of that, the dope got a lira for it back in 1983.

I signed it and gave it to Francesca, and pulled out the folder of airline tickets to Mexico and Washington. I found the ones for which I now had no use, and sat down on the parapet next to Anna.

"Of course, it wouldn't be strictly honest. You'd have to pose as a cello named Francesca Dienst. But it's paid for. Now, how about it?"

"Papa!" Francesca came running, gawkety-skip, laughing with joy, and gave the double-duty acknowledgement-of-condolences and bill of sale to Anna, then settled on my lap like a jubilant stork. When her paunch squeezed against my diaphragm is when I found that the little transparent blade I had carried there for thirty years was gone at last.

Anna looked down at the card, and at the ticket; then past them down the hillside rich with dust and August where vineyards, Ludovico and Francesca's and the next farm's, marched away down the roads of Bolzano. There were tears, and then her gaze moved west toward Mexico and the sun, while rhythmic irrigation sprays beat ripening time over orchards warm with haze, and farmers swing down roads for home. At the far reach of the valley the mountains rise, and with them her vision, climbing foothills, vineyards, vistas drowned in distance; forests, peaks, naked air and piles of cloud: castles, cumuli, blue pierced by blaze of sun glancing and dazzling the flakes of light in her eyes. No, her head shakes, no, and her crutch grates against the stone. But her hand rises to her throat unbidden; buttons, unbuttons the topmost of the hundred buttons. Behind the fingers - graceful, clean, hesitant - I see her throat's pulse flying.

Epilogue. 2013

We walk the stony track from the Martinskirche back to the castle in cold sunshine. I, Father Pius, Ludovico and Francesca; pregnant Orianna and her husband walking ahead. The ashes rest where they will rest now for that eternal twinkling of an eye until they are raised incorruptible. How Anna razzed the idea that a corpse, and the ground-up bonemeal of one at that, might some day be raised as good as new! But the twinkling was accomplished ahead of schedule, deep in the light-flecked mystery of her eyes. On our best days – which included her last day – it greeted me from within the lines and loving of her face. On days when her body ached and, yes, when she claimed still to regret the impulse that brought the cello Francesca, and thus goddamn Oren, back into her life, it was not to be found.

We had days that stirred that pulse at the base of her throat, like the day that Francesca gave birth to her first baby and named her Orianna after the troublesome pair of us. And when the MexiLar agreement proved indeed to be pilfered from Señor Paños' files, Anna brought me workmen in Manosduros who were happy to depose on the nonexistent environmental protocols of Mexilar Metals, translating for me, sharing my fury and determination to see the thing through to indictments, plea bargains, and sentencing that put Rick McIntear into Lewisburg – OK, not for life as I might have wished and he certainly deserved, but by God for 18 months that astonished him and ended his political career.

We had days that included careful, gentle lovemaking that evoked echoes. We had days of bitter quarreling about matters large and small, and we had the joy of seeing that even gall and wormwood together was so much better than being apart, that it amounted to bliss.

Seeking to free Anna from the crutch, we sought out Donia Ma, but found her DuPont Circle studio converted to a tax advisor's office. No advice there on where Donia Ma might have gone; nor on acupuncture either. An alternative in Silver Spring, a balding guy with stubby fingers, had some of the same moves and advice, and none of the mystique. Anna got some relief, but not the miracle I know she'd have found with Donia Ma. Well, you can't swim twice in the same river.

Over the course of the thirty years we shared, well into her eighties, Anna slowly shed the crone disguise she wore on the day I discovered her, while stubbornly damning the vital longevity that appeared to have condemned her to another thirty years of life, to love and its troubles. Because in fact, for a good few years, it was as if she aged backwards, until she met her proper age – whatever that was. Even on her last day on this earth, her eyes did not lose the golden flakes, the amusement, the readiness to shed tears of joy or sorrow. But time above ground is a temporary thing, always falling toward dissolution as the moon eternally falls toward Earth. As I once urged time forward to the day of the Taum Sauk hike, I look now for the day when I will make the trip for good and all to the Martinskirche. From her hospital bed, brushing aside the wires and tubes, Anna reached up at great cost to herself and invited me, with a touch on my shoulder, to join her there. I suppose we shall see about rising incorruptible; just now, a good long rest seems like the thing for us both.

The Cello Francesca, *or* Balderdash